"Sagger!" yelled the "dune buggy's" antitank TOW operator. "Eleven o'clock low!"

It was coming at them like a curdling, spinning glob of gray spit through the mustard-colored air, and Aussie began his evasive driving, willing his nerves to hold till the last possible moment before going into a turn that he hoped would be too sharp for the Sagger. But Brentwood, in the co-driver's seat, got lucky—a bullet or two from the long burst of his .50 machine gun hit the Sagger. There was an explosion like molten egg yolk, a stream of blackish white smoke, and the whistling of shrapnel; one piece hit the vehicle's front bumper. Aussie felt his left thigh get wet and feared that one of the jerry cans of gas had been hit. But the cans were all right.

"Oh Christ!" It was Brentwood. "Stop!" David downshifted and braked, and an even denser cloud of dust enveloped them from behind as the vehicle shuddered and slowed to a halt. Brentwood was looking back. The TOW operator still clung to the shoulder-height roll bar, but his head was gone; the shrapnel had decapitated him, leaving his torso a fountain of warm, spurting blood.

They only had time to unbuckle him and lay him on the sand before setting off again down the corridor—four miles to go and only God knew what lay ahead. Aussie was struck again by the sheer bloody confusion of war. At this moment neither he nor, he suspected, any of the other fast attack vehicles, Bradleys, or MIs knew whether they were winning or not.

Also by Ian Slater:

FIRESPILL
SEA GOLD
AIR GLOW RED
ORWELL: THE ROAD TO AIRSTRIP ONE
STORM
DEEP CHILL
FORBIDDEN ZONE*
WW III*
WW III: RAGE OF BATTLE*
WW III: WORLD IN FLAMES*
WW III: ARCTIC FRONT*
WW III: WARSHOT*

*Published by Fawcett Books

WW III:
ASIAN FRONT

Ian Slater

FAWCETT GOLD MEDAL • NEW YORK

A Fawcett Gold Medal Book
Published by Ballantine Books
Copyright © 1993 by Bunyip Enterprises, Inc.

All rights reserved under International and Pan-American Copyright Conventions. Published in the United States of America by Ballantine Books, a division of Random House, Inc., New York, and simultaneously in Canada by Random House of Canada Limited, Toronto.

Library of Congress Catalog Card Number: 93-90190

ISBN 0-449-14854-8

Manufactured in the United States of America

First Edition: August 1993

For Marian, Serena, and Blair

I would like to thank Professor Clodus Strassburg, who is a colleague and friend of mine who is willing in being . . . helping . . .

ACKNOWLEDGMENTS

I would like to thank Professor Charles Slonecker, who is a colleague and friend of mine at the University of British Columbia. Most of all I am indebted to my wife, Marian, whose patience, typing, and editorial skills continue to give me invaluable support in my work.

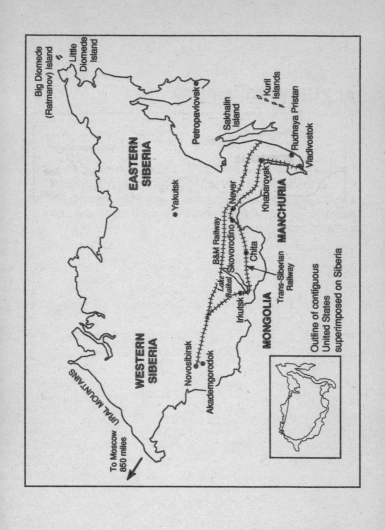

Big Diomede (Ratmanov) Island

Little Diomede Island

EASTERN SIBERIA

Petropavlovsk

Sakhalin Island

Kuril Islands

Rudnaya Pristan

Vladivostok

Yakutsk

Khabarovsk

MANCHURIA

Never

Skovorodino

B&M Railway

Chita

Lake Baikal

Irkutsk

Trans-Siberian Railway

MONGOLIA

WESTERN SIBERIA

Novosibirsk

Akademgorodok

URAL MOUNTAINS

To Moscow 850 miles

Outline of contiguous United States superimposed on Siberia

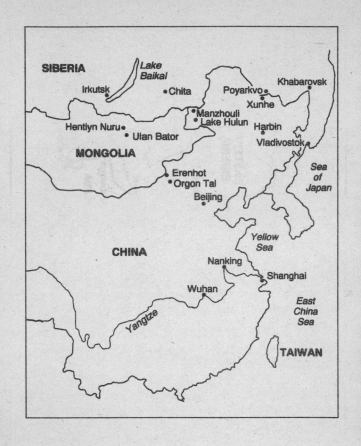

CHAPTER ONE

Khabarovsk, Siberia

"ROCK AND ROLL!" David Brentwood yelled, and everything opened up, from the rip of the P90's 5.7mm bursts to the steady "bomp, bomp, bomp" of grenade launchers, joined by the long, guttural roar of M-60s pouring out a deadly stream of two hundred rpm 7.62 mm fire. The acrid stench of cordite was all about the British and American commandoes, the thumps and rattle of 5.6mm rounds hitting their targets lost beneath the crash of supporting heavy 107mm mortar fire.

Next to Brentwood, Aussie Lewis, glancing at his P90's plastic mag, could see that he had about ten rounds left for the Belgian-made machine gun, the empties' casings spewing down beneath the gun, catching a beam of sunlight that was penetrating the Siberian pines. It was only for a second, but a member of the red team saw it, fired, and Aussie Lewis heard the two tones of a near miss. He rolled quickly, but not fast enough to escape the high monotone or "smoke alarm," as they called the noise from the Miles—the Multiple Integrated Laser Engagement System.

"Shit!" Aussie said as he took out the key from his rifle transmitter, disengaging the weapon, then put the key in his helmet and chest control unit, ending the tone. He saw the grader scratch him from the sheet. It meant that for Aussie,

a veteran of General Freeman's Second Army's crack British/
American Special Air Services/Delta commando team or
SAS/D, as it was known by its elite members, was out of the
war game and had lost a bet with his fellow commandoes:
"Choir" Williams, who hailed from Wales, and his two
American buddies, Captain David Brentwood and Private
First Class Salvini. Aussie had bet these other three members
of Brentwood's SAS/D troop that he'd be the last to be taken
out. And to rub it in, Brentwood, Choir Williams, and Sal-
vini were already demanding their money.

"Bloody scavengers," Aussie retorted. "That's what you
are. Suppose if we get in a real punch-up again and I got hit
you bastards'd probably take my friggin' watch."

"Let's see you smile, boyo," Choir Williams instructed.

"What?"

"Can't you smile?"

Aussie flashed a quick grin as if he was at the dentist's.
"Satisfied?"

"Ah—" Williams said, feigning disappointment to Brentwood and Salvini. "Just as I figured. 'E hasn't got any gold
fillings, lads. His watch'll have to do."

"What a fucking trio," Aussie said. "You blokes
oughta . . ."

"Shut up, Lewis!" the grader ordered. "You want to get
the rest of your squad taken out?"

"No, sir," Aussie answered, muttering under his breath,
"What the hell would he know about it? That bloke hasn't
seen a shot fired in anger."

"Let's hope it stays that way, boyo," Choir Williams said.

"It has to," Lewis said.

"How's that?" Salvini put in.

"Because I'm just getting to know Olga," Aussie replied.
"You know, the one with the big—"

"Yes," said David Brentwood, who, although married,
was always shocked by Aussie's vivid descriptions of female

anatomy. "We know. She's a member of the Khabarovsk Polar Bear Club. Swims in the nude."

"Yeah," Salvini added. "Well, you can have her, buddy. Any piece that swims naked in freezing water isn't playin' with a full deck."

"Well I don't intend playing fucking cards with her, Sal."

"Okay, you four," the grader decreed. "You're all out!"

"That's all right," Aussie Lewis said. "This racket's frazzled my nerves anyway. After firing all these blanks I need a drink."

Normally the grader would have had more to say, and normally the British-American SAS/D team wouldn't have acted so cavalierly, but, as members of the U.S.-led U.N. forces under General Douglas Freeman, they were veterans of the daring raid on Pyongyang in Korea, fierce fighting on and around Ratmanov Island in the Bering Strait, and Lake Baikal in Siberia, and had earned a certain cachet.

Even the most gentlemanly among them, the twenty-five-year-old Medal of Honor winner David Brentwood, was known as one of the toughest of the tough. SAS/Delta training broke anyone else. Besides, everyone, including the graders, was in a fairly good mood these days. Spring had sprung; Aussie Lewis had found Olga, an accommodating if large blond Siberian "bird," as he called her; and pretty soon it seemed that David Brentwood, Salvini, and Choir Williams would be on home leave, David back to his wife, Georgina, in the States, Choir Williams to his beloved Wales, and Salvini to his haunts in Brooklyn. This time, everyone was saying, the cease-fire between Siberia, China, and the U.N. force would hold. That is, everyone except General Douglas Freeman.

CHAPTER TWO

FURTHER WEST OF Khabarovsk, along the Amur River hump in the town of Poyarkovo on the Siberian side of the DMZ, an American soldier was meeting a Chinese "good-time" girl who, caught on the American-patrolled north bank of the Amur when the DMZ went into effect, was making the best of it. Neither she nor the American spoke the other's language, but they understood each other perfectly. He was handing over dollars, and she was about to give him sex with an almond-eyed smile. She smelled of lavender and was dressed in a thigh-split *qi pao* of radiant Ming blue silk, embroidered with tiny golden birds, only a tantalizing glimpse of firm, tan thigh visible. She disappeared behind the fine bamboo screen. The soldier heard the soft purr of a zipper, then saw the *qi pao* being draped carefully over the bamboo divider. The GI closed his eyes and swallowed hard. Oh, man!

He'd been too long in the U.S.-patrolled U.N. demilitarized zone between China and the breakaway United Siberian Republic—both of which the U.S. had had to fight as part of the U.N.'s wish to "stabilize" the area. He was bored with the routine of patrolling "the trace," the DMZ, to see whether there had been violations by either Siberian or Chinese troops as a prelude to possible land grabs along the long-disputed Chinese-Siberian border. Marked by fertile valleys, the still-frozen Amur, or Black Dragon, as it was called by the Chinese, wound itself through mountain gorges and an endless taiga of pine, beech, and fir, separating Manchuria from the old Soviet empire.

Patrolling the border was a dangerous as well as a dreary duty, because before the present cease-fire had come into effect, China and the new Siberian republic had already made an alliance of convenience, albeit a shaky one, against the Americans. It was a cold and lonely duty, too, despite the advent of spring along the Amur, no matter how beautiful the taiga or how busty the Siberian women. In any case, the soldier preferred the Chinese girls. If some of those Siberian women sat on your face you'd be pulp. But on a soldier's pay he would never have been able to afford Spring Flower, as she called herself. The soldier, like many others, had been given the money personally by General Freeman, even though it was known he abhorred whores as being little better than politicians.

Freeman, often referred to as ''George'' for his striking resemblance to the actor George C. Scott, was a legend in his own time, the greatest American general since Patton and Schwarzkopf, and he was walking down the line, doling out money, his own, to his soldiers, telling them to go to the Chinese brothels along the DMZ and not to worry about bringing back change. ''You fellas have a good time now!'' the general said. ''And remember, boys, safe sex—so draw your rubbers from the quartermaster.''

As Churchill had believed that the armistice following the 1914–18 war with Germany was nothing more than a temporary cease-fire, that Germany sooner or later would start another war, Freeman had no faith in the present cease-fire between China and Siberia on one side and the United States on the other. And this ''brothel subsidy,'' as he called it, was his latest effective, if eccentric, tactic: ''A preemptive strike,'' as he explained to his aide, Colonel Dick Norton.

''Washington's not going to like it, General.''

''Washington isn't going to know about it, Dick.''

Dick Norton shook his head worriedly. "Sir, it's only a matter of time before the press gets onto it. They love stuff like this. There'd be hell to pay. And as for the women's lobby!" Norton rolled his eyes heavenward. "Paying dog-faces to get laid . . ."

"Dick, you worry too much. I know that's your job, but I've told you before, by the time I get this business about 'being recalled for consultation' in Washington over with we could be at war again with these jokers. Chinese, Siberians, or both. I don't trust Novosibirsk any more than I do Beijing. This is the second cease-fire we've had, and I tell you it's no better than any of the seventy-five the Yugoslavs had. God-damn it! You'd think Washington could see that. We were sent over here to keep this upstart United Siberian Republic from annexing more territory, and what happened? The Chinese made a land grab into Siberia first and we ended up with a war on two fronts. And *now*, just when we turn the tide on the bastards and look like we're kicking their ass across the Black Dragon River, back into China where they belong, and the Siberians back beyond Lake Baikal where they belong, Beijing and Novosibirsk ask for a cease-fire, and of course those fairies in Washington give it to them."

"The public doesn't want the war to go on, General."

"Dick," the general began exasperatedly, "like the man in the transmission commercial used to say: 'Pay me now or pay me later.' We should have kicked ass all the way to Beijing—teach 'em a lesson like we taught that Siberian Ye-sov son of a bitch. He messed with Second Army and got a bloody nose."

"We got one, too, General, before we stopped them," Norton reminded him—the almost complete destruction of the American III Corps, its blood and equipment streaked across the frozen twenty-mile escape route across Lake Bai-kal, was evidence of that.

"Yes, because the goddamned chinks attacked us when

we were preoccupied with the Siberians so we ended up with a two-front war.''

"General, you shouldn't use that word—'chinks.' You're being recalled now because of what Washington calls your 'intemperate remarks' about those two Spets.'' Norton was referring to two Spetsnaz—Siberian Special Operations, in this case women commandos—who'd tried to assassinate Freeman at his Khabarovsk HQ.

"Intemperate remarks!" Freeman thundered. "Bitches tried to kill me! In my own quarters, goddamn it!''

"I know, General, but after you shot them and said it was a case of 'equal opportunity' employment—well, the feminists—''

"Said in the heat of the moment, Dick.''

"*I* know that, General, but the feminists back home went absolutely—''

"Ape!'' Freeman cut in gleefully. "Listen, Norton, those crazies from the femisphere are free to go ape and I'm free to say what I think because a lot of good men died for freedom all the way from Normandy to here. That's a fact. And I'm not about to be cowed by a bunch of skirts.''

"I know, General, but it's a new world.''

"Yes.'' Freeman sighed. "And by God, I don't like it. More dangerous now than the cold war.''

"Not much we can do about it, sir.''

"I'll tell you what *you* can do about it. While I'm back in Washington getting my ass reamed out for offending the femisphere, you can help keep Second Army razor sharp so that if any more chinks cross the Amur into Siberia we can push 'em back.''

"Yes, sir, we'll try.''

"I know. Have every confidence in my staff.'' The general reached for his coat. His tone dropped. "You make that appointment for me with that Taiwanese admiral—Kuang?''

"Yes, sir. He'll see you in Tokyo. Strictly unofficial. Civilian dress.''

"You order the meal I wanted? No damned sushi. American beef."

"Yes, sir," Norton assured him. "Prime rib, range fed, just like you said."

"None of that steroid-fed crap."

"No, sir. I promise." Norton paused. "You think he'll go for the dessert you've got in mind?" The dessert, the general had told Norton, would be China—if Beijing ever moved across the Amur again.

Their public announcements aside, Freeman was convinced that the top leadership of the old KMT—Kuomintang—party in Taiwan, once commanded by Chiang Kai-shek or, as Harry Truman called him, "Cash my Check," had never wavered in its determination to go back home. Taiwan had infinite patience and, with one of the most powerful armies and navies in Asia, fully intended to return to China and oust the leadership in Beijing if the opportunity ever presented itself, an opportunity their agents had constantly been working for along the coast of the East China Sea since 1949.

Freeman was also aware of something else—something he didn't believe the "fairies" back in Washington understood—that in China there were many Chinas, that one of the great illusions of the twentieth century was seeing China as a cohesive whole—a monolithic structure too big to topple. Since Tiananmen Square especially, internal dissent had grown, not vanished. It had merely gone underground. It had been part of that underground that had enabled the Americans to gain information with which they had been able to blow up the Nanking Bridge across the Yangtze and so sever the long logistical supply line from southern to northern China. Even so, for the moment Beijing still ruled with an iron fist, and the hundreds of individual Chinas had not yet been galvanized into a decisive bloc. But Freeman was convinced they were there—waiting.

"General, I hate to sound like a harpy, but that's something else you're going to have to watch. I mean if the press ever discovers you're talking to the Taiwanese, every tabloid in the country'll bury you alive." In particular, the general knew his aide meant the La Roche tabloid chain—owned by the multibillion-dollar newspaper/industrial magnate now arrested under the U.S. Emergency Powers Act (to combat internal sabotage during the war) for having traded with the enemy. Specifically, La Roche and his front Asian companies, from Singapore to Hong Kong, had been providing Communist China with the weapons and ammunition used against fellow Americans in the slaughter of the American III Corps on Lake Baikal.

"To hell with La Roche—that weasel'll be behind bars after a grand jury gets through with him."

"Even so, General, he still runs the newspapers, and he'll use his editors to whip up opinion any way he wants. You'll have to watch what you say when you're back home."

"I say what's on my mind, Dick. I won't waffle."

Dick Norton didn't believe him. Freeman was a to-your-face man all right, but he could be as selective or as evasive as the next commander in what he said if he wanted to be—witness his mysteriously terse order for "wolf dung and only wolf dung" to be collected and frozen at headquarters. Not even Norton knew what the hell it was about. The only thing the general would say was that he wanted it on standby—"Just throw it outside on the permafrost, that'll keep it frozen"—and that if there was a war with China it could save thousands of American lives.

"Well, have a good trip, sir. Hope to see you back soon."

"Don't worry, Dick," Freeman said, slapping his aide on the back. "I'll straighten everything out. 'Sides, it's spring now in Washington. Puts the Pentagon fairies in a good mood."

"Fairies" were anyone who disagreed with him.

The fairies *were* in a good mood, but as Aussie Lewis would have said, there was a plot on—one supported by the unwitting consensus of editorial writers throughout the country—to strip Freeman of his command and keep him home, this time for good. It was widely acknowledged that he was a marvelous war general but a loose cannon in the peace. Better to send him back to Fort Ord in California, let him retire at his desk where he wouldn't talk about "chinks" and "equal opportunity" when he killed Spets. At least he'd be out of the public eye.

How Washington had got wind of his intended meeting with Admiral Kuang, Freeman didn't know, but upon landing at Narita Airport in Tokyo, Freeman was met by U.S. embassy officials who were to accompany him to the meeting with Kuang. It was all very polite, but Freeman's meeting with the Taiwanese admiral was effectively sabotaged, little more than pleasantries being exchanged. Freeman was furious, knowing he could do nothing but sip tea and drink to Taiwanese-U.S. friendship before taking his flight out to San Francisco via Hawaii.

When Spring Flower emerged from behind the screen, her nakedness had taken the GI's breath away, her breasts far more prominent than the tight dress had allowed. After being without a woman for months in the cold Siberian winter, it was almost too much, and he told himself if he didn't calm down he'd just be wasting the fifty bucks. To concentrate, to divert himself from her beauty for a moment, he rather ponderously counted out the fifty dollars, converting them to yuan in his head, thinking, God, she's beautiful.

"You must take it off," she told him in slow and deliberate English.

"What?" He looked up at her.

"You must take it off," she repeated, pointing to the .45 strapped in its canvas holster and the clip ammo in the canvas pockets about the belt.

"Oh—" he said. "Yeah—sure. I thought you meant—" He pointed to what he meant, and, hand before her mouth, her eyes averted shyly, she gave the most delightful giggle, and obviously thought it not at all surprising that a private would be carrying a sidearm.

"Come," she said, extending her hand.

"Not too quickly, I hope," he said.

"Sorry—I do not under—"

"It's okay."

"I have surprise for you," she said softly, her tongue wetting her dark, cherry-red lips as she extended her hand demurely and led him into the next room, which was redolent with sandalwood incense and illuminated by a pale golden flickering lantern. Seated in the nest of silk-lace-bordered pillows was another girl, her legs drawn coquettishly, her nakedness partially hidden by the pillows. The soldier's mouth went dry, and in a cracked voice he said, "I can't pay another fifty for—"

"No bother," Spring Blossom said. "She wishes to learn. Do you mind?"

He could barely speak. "Oh, man. No, I don't mind."

CHAPTER THREE

Monterey, California

"DAMN IT! HE'S done it again," Freeman said, his general's stars catching the light as he pointed the TV's remote control and zapped CBN.

"Done what again, Douglas?" Marjorie Duchene, his sister-in-law, asked from the kitchen.

"That CBN clown calling APCs *tanks*."

"What's an APC?" Marjorie asked.

"Please don't bait me, Dory—Marjorie." He'd used his deceased wife's name, for, though he'd loved her, she'd had the same habit of teasing him.

"I'm not baiting you, Douglas dear. I've no idea what an APC is—some truck or other I suppose."

"Armored personnel carrier," Freeman grumped. "Goddamn education in this country's going to hell in a handbasket."

"Please don't swear, Douglas. I know it's rough and ready in the army, but now you're home."

"You mean put out to pasture. Those congressional sons of—those 'gentlemen' in Washington recalled me from Siberia for 'consultation.' Haven't called me in for a week, but I know when I go there they're going to give me a 'special' assignment. What they mean is they don't want me in command of Second Army."

"Well, the war *is* over, Douglas."

"War's never over, Marjorie—just interrupted now and then by peace. Good God, in over five thousand years of history we haven't had three hundred years of peace. You realize that?"

"You should go for a walk," Marjorie said. "The tide's out. Rock pools'll be beautiful."

"You know what happens in rock pools," Freeman said, invoking an image that had never ceased to arrest him. "One creature's fighting the other for food and space. To the death."

"Oh, Douglas, that's a forlorn way of looking at the world."

"It can be a forlorn world, Marjorie," Freeman responded. "Second Army lost the best part of four thousand men to Yesov's hordes on Lake Baikal. And that's not counting the casualties inflicted by the Chinese when they attacked us from the south. So what happens when I counterattack, make up some lost territory, and start taking prisoners? Beijing and Novosibirsk sing in unison for a cease-fire, and those—those 'fairies' back in Washington gave it to them.''

''We want peace, Douglas,'' Marjorie said.

''Hell—we all want peace. Problem is, how to *secure* it. You don't think those 'comrades' in Beijing would roll up their blankets do you? This is a breathing space for them. Time to build up their forces again for another northward push. And what if they attack again? We've got a supply line stretched over four thousand miles of ocean between here and Siberia. Manchuria's their backyard. They're going to want to grab as much territory along the Amur River valleys as they can. Siberians and Chinese have been fighting over it for more than a hundred years. Only reason they formed an alliance against us was to try and push our Allied force into the sea. Then without any U.N. overwatch they could carve one another up.''

''Then why didn't we just let them do it?'' Marjorie said ingenuously.

''Because if we let them at it, once they'd exhausted their conventional forces we'd be in an ICBM war, and pretty soon everyone else around them, from Kazakhstan to Southeast Asia, would have to choose sides. We'd have a world war that you couldn't put out, Marjorie. Hell—that's why the U.N. sent us over there. To keep the peace. But I'm telling you, this cease-fire isn't keeping the peace—it's just time out for Cheng and Yesov to rearm, resupply. Meanwhile their 'diplomats' are yakking away with our diplomats. Well, you know what Will Rogers said about diplomacy.''

''No, I don't,'' Marjorie said.

''Diplomacy's saying 'Nice doggie' till you can find a rock. That's what they're doing, Marjorie—getting the rocks ready for their slingshots.''

''Oh, I'm sure Washington knows what it's doing.''

"Marjorie, the last time Washington knew what it was doing was when it declared war on Saddam Insane."

"Go for a walk, Douglas. It'll do you good."

He did, and it didn't. All he could think of was Norton's call that morning about the air-conditioning units.

In Hong Kong, La Roche Industries had received a fax— an order from General Cheng in Beijing, C in C of the People's Liberation Army, two and a half million strong. The order was for everything from American-made Gore-Tex sleeping bags to five thousand air-conditioning units of the kind used by heavy-haul refrigerator trucks. Though Hong Kong was now firmly in PLA hands, it was still used by Beijing, as in the days when the colony had been British, as a capitalist outpost for trade with the West. Chinese-born agents loyal to Britain were still at large in the former British colony, and along with everything else they heard they passed the information about the La Roche order to the American Second Army's headquarters at Khabarovsk via the Harbin-Manchurian underground Democracy Movement. From Khabarovsk, Colonel Dick Norton had called Freeman, careful to bill it as a personal and not an official call.

"These air-conditioning units," Freeman asked. "They portable?"

"Didn't say, General."

"Find out, Dick. Call me back. Ten-to-one they're portable."

"Yes, sir."

As Freeman had sat impatiently reading the lives of Sherman and Grant, Norton rang back. "You're right. They're portable, sir. How did you—"

"Thank you, Dick." When he put down the receiver, Freeman began to pace back and forth in the lounge room, talking to himself.

"What's that, Douglas?" Marjorie called from the kitchen.

Suddenly Freeman had stopped. Now in late March, the spring thaw was in full swing along the Siberian-Chinese-

Manchurian border. "Why on earth—summer! That little turd is going to launch a summer offensive!"

"Where?" Marjorie said, rushing in. "What? You saw a little tern? Where?"

"What—ah, no. I—"

"Oh dear. They're such beautiful birds."

Striding along the beach, Freeman was buffeted by a chilly wind, and unusually wracked by doubt. Was he overreacting? No, that damn Cheng was up to something. It aggravated Freeman so much he felt his skin itch here and there and had to shift the 9mm Sig Sauer Parabellum he always carried further along his waistband so that he could scratch the offending part.

The sea crashed in wildly along the ribbon of sand that was Monterey's beach. He couldn't help but hear the sounds of Second Army's III Corps floundering in the crashing waters of Lake Baikal, Yesov's heavy artillery chopping up the ice, cutting off III Corps's retreat, and the Siberians' Spets and OMON commandos butchering the retreating Americans, the ice floes smeared with Americans' blood. For a while he thought he was alone on the beach, mistaking the lone figure further up for a piece of rock. He or she seemed to be waiting for him. But as he went past the man who was too far up on the dunes for his features to be clear, the man turned and walked away. As the general headed back to the house, his general's thoughts were back along the Amur.

Now he was convinced more than ever that it was a summer offensive. Cheng doesn't want to make the same mistake the Arabs did against the Israelis, he thought. Half the Arab tank crews were prostrate with heat exhaustion. Got to over a hundred and twenty degrees inside those T-72s. Hell, it was so bad Sadat thought the Israeli's MOSSAD had issued the Israeli pilots some new kind of debilitating gas bombs. Wasn't gas, it was the goddamn heat. It would be easy to mount the air-conditioning units on the rear of the T-59s and

T-72s, right near the extra gas drum. He'd equally want his lead tanks cool for a long-reaching preemptive strike. July or August! There could only be one place: the Gobi Desert, bypassing the Manchurian mountain chain on his, Cheng's, right flank, driving into the heart of the American-controlled DMZ along the Amur.

Next question—the big question—was, would the Mongolian Communists come in on the Chinese side? To find out, he began formulating what he would call "preventive medicine," and he did not mean his advice to his soldiers to practice safe sex.

CHAPTER FOUR

THE TWO PLA guards snapped to attention, the red flag fluttering stiffly in the breeze as Captain Lee, aide to General Cheng, chief of the two-and-a-half-million People's Liberation Army, arrived at the Xinhuamen—the Gate of New China—the southern entrance to the Zhongnanhai compound off Changan Avenue. Here a short distance west of the Forbidden City, the party's top officials resided and had offices behind a high wall and around two lakes. Lee had been raised on the discipline of the Tao, his mind resolved never to show his emotions to anyone, and certainly not to his enemy. But this morning he knew he could not contain himself. Besides, General Cheng was no enemy. Lee told the general they'd pulled it off.

"Are you sure?" Cheng inquired impassively.

"Yes, Comrade General. Almost as soon as we placed the order for the air-conditioning units one of the British spies in Hong Kong sent a message north to Khabarovsk via the Manchurian route."

"The Harbin Democracy Movement cell?" Cheng proffered.

"Yes, General."

Cheng's fingers carefully squeezed the end of his Camel cigarette to a point and pushed it with a twist into the end of his Persian blue cloisonné cigarette holder. "And Freeman has received the information personally?"

"Yes, General—a phone call from his Khabarovsk headquarters."

"Are you confident of this?"

"We've had two men watching his house—one equipped with a multidirectional aerial. The transmitter is inside his sister-in-law's house. He will no doubt think we will attack in the summer."

"Good. Freeman has no doubt alerted the Pentagon to this, and his Second Army will be so advised. And then to prevent him from second-guessing us any further, we will kill him."

"But General," Lee began, clearly perplexed, "you said our embassy in Washington has it that he is to be relieved of command of Second Army. Sent back to Fort Ord. He won't be any danger to us there."

Cheng turned to the window overlooking the two lakes, sugary-looking ice still clinging to the banks. "You've not fought against Freeman?"

"No, sir."

"He is formidable. Did you know he keeps a copy of our Chinese general Sun Tzu's *The Art of War* next to his Bible? He well understands Sun Tzu's maxim that 'all war is deception.' "

"Yes, General, but—"

"He may discern my trap if he is given time to think about it. We will not give him that time."

"So long as our agents are discreet," Lee suggested. "When the Siberian Spets tried to—"

"When the Siberian women tried to kill him he was not on his home ground. He was in Khabarovsk. More alert. In California there is a large Chinese population—it would just seem like another citizen approaching him."

"When will it be done?"

Cheng inhaled, and then seconds later smoke came out in voluminous clouds of bluish gray that rose and spilled down off the ancient roof, Cheng's silence his answer. Cheng had risen fast through the party's ranks to head the PLA not only because he was a brilliant strategist but also because he was able to keep secrets, never tempted to tell subordinates more than they needed to know about any operation.

CHAPTER FIVE

IN WASHINGTON, WHERE great faith had been put in the cease-fire, the buds on the Japanese cherry trees—the trees a gift of the Japanese government long ago—were seized on by the media as symbols of promise and reconciliation between two other disputants, Japan and the U.S., after the mutually draining trade wars of the 1980s and 1990s.

It wasn't clear whether the symbolic importance of cherry blossoms prompted the president and/or his advisers to turn their thoughts to what more Japan might give the United

States to make up for the bruised relationships of the trade war and the American and Allied disgust with Japan's checkbook participation, or rather *nonparticipation*, in the Gulf War with Iraq.

In any event, Harry Schuman, national security adviser, saw how Japan might make a conciliatory move. He pointed out how, in order to bolster the idea of building up a multinational peacekeeping force along the Siberian-Manchurian border like the force they'd sent to fight Saddam Insane, the Japanese should be invited to contribute not just yen to offset the huge American contribution but men as well. It was true that under Article 99 of the Japanese constitution, the JDF—Japanese Defense Force—in order to allay old and persistent fears in Asia of a resurgent Japanese militarism—was permitted to send only a maximum of two thousand military personnel at any one time. Furthermore, the two thousand could only carry arms for self-defense. Nevertheless, it was felt in Washington that the presence of an active Japanese contingent would be a welcome addition in bolstering the multinational aspect of the peacekeeping force. In the same way as the smaller Arab nations were asked to be part of the U.S.-led Allied force in Kuwait in order to show Saddam that it wasn't simply the U.S. desire that he vacate Kuwait, it was felt that a contingent from an Asian power, Japan—albeit a tiny contingent—would sustain the idea of a multinational force and so would help deter Novosibirsk and Beijing from any further aggression.

The president liked the idea and put it to the Japanese prime minister, who put it to the Diet, and after "lively" debate the motion was passed, a precedent having already been set by the Japanese Diet sending a peacekeeping contingent to Thailand in October 1992. And so—for only the second time since World War II—Japanese forces were deployed overseas.

It was a colossal blunder, and when Freeman heard the news flash from CBN he was shaving and almost cut himself.

He still used a cutthroat razor, believing a man must have a weapon at hand even in his toilet kit. He walked to the bathroom door and stood glowering through the hallway at the CBN reporter. "Well—now it's official," Freeman rumbled. "Washington's a lunatic asylum!"

"Asylum?" It was Marjorie.

"Good God!" Freeman proclaimed, standing in his khaki trousers, suspenders down at his sides, razor being used as a pointer. "Don't they know—don't they realize that the one thing the Chinese'll never stand for is Japanese on Chinese soil? Chinese'll buy Japanese Hondas, but this is a different ball game. By God, the Chinese *hate* the Japanese."

"Isn't it time for your morning run?"

"Japanese occupied Manchuria for thirteen years—even changed its name to Manchukuo. Then there was the Rape of Nanking—butchering people right, left, and center—and then—" The razor flew out at the screen to illustrate the point for Marjorie. "—Japanese had a biological and chemical warfare unit—used Chinese and some of our boys as guinea pigs. Injected them anthrax and all kinds of diseases as well as gassing them. Chinese have a long memory. By God—"

"I wish you wouldn't use that language, Douglas," came Marjorie's unruffled tone from the kitchen. "Aren't you going for your run soon?"

"Marjorie, Beijing'll see this as a provocation."

"What—you jogging? I shouldn't think so, Douglas."

But even Freeman had underestimated the ferocity of the Chinese reaction. To Beijing it was clearly a test by the West to see what China would do when faced with the fact that the Japanese had been invited by the *Americans* and had accepted. It was proof positive to General Cheng and other members of the Central Committee that Japan, with U.S. backing, was testing the waters, returning to its old obsession, Manchuria—to its old dream of possessing untold oil and mineral wealth that would make Japan independent of other countries for raw materials and make her an even greater industrial powerhouse than she was already.

In the golden light of the brothel, the air redolent with incense and the smell of rice cooking downstairs, Spring Blossom had prepared her surprise well. No sooner had she led him into the other room than Summer Flower, even more beautiful than Spring Blossom, dressed in nothing but a scarlet V-kini, took him by the hand. After they had undressed him and he lay naked except for his dog tags, Summer Flower knelt before him on the floor mattress, her legs straddling his chest, her hands behind his head, swaying gently back and forth over him one second, offering her pendulous breasts to suck, the next moment all but sitting on his face while Spring Blossom moistened her lips and went down on him. He was in such ecstasy he neither saw nor heard the Chinese youth who came in and took the .45's holster and belt.

Arriving in his chauffeur-driven Red Flag at the Great Hall of the People, which bordered Tiananmen Square, for the meeting with the all-powerful Central Committee under Chairman Nie, Cheng received further news of the Japanese intervention and his second shock of the day. Chairman Nie, a painfully cautious man who knew how to play both sides against the middle and who normally questioned the other members until they were numb with fatigue, now quickly concurred with Cheng and the rest of the committee that the Japanese had obviously thrown in their hand in order to qualify for the lucrative kind of capitalist contract feeding frenzy that followed the Gulf War. Then Nie did something that for the premier was extremely difficult—he surprised General Cheng by demonstrating a cunning that even the strategist Cheng had to admire.

For Nie, a politician, the political reality always subsumed the narrower military perspective, yet he now clearly approved of unhesitating military action, explaining, with the smoothing, consensus-seeking gestures of his hands, that while of course it was regrettable that the People's Liberation Army would find it necessary to fight, from an internal political perspective a *xiao guz muo zan dou*—a skirmish—or two on the northern borders of their grossly overpopulated country would have a salutary result. For quite apart from rebuffing the Japanese, it would have the time-proven effect of diverting domestic dissatisfaction away from Beijing's widely unpopular anti-inflationary policies and its ruthless hunt for dissident elements.

Cheng agreed it was axiomatic that internal dissent would be far less tolerated by the masses whose attention would of necessity shift to that of concern for a foreign devil at China's gates along the ancient northern wall of Genghis Khan. Besides, Cheng knew an external enemy in any country had the effect of burying, or at least subsuming, internal squabbles within the party as well as on the street. Such a move of course would also consolidate Nie's power.

Cheng's attack, with the Central Committee's unanimous backing, was set for dawn, April 25.

Cheng said nothing about the plan he had set in motion against Freeman. For Nie and the others, Freeman, for the most part, was an open book—a career soldier of fifty-five who bore an uncanny resemblance to an American actor and whose strategies and tactical brilliance had earned him four stars and the grudging respect of even enemy commanders. His reputation had grown rapidly since his daring attack on Pyongyang earlier in the war and his brilliant defense against the Siberian Aist—giant hovercraft—offensive on Lake Baikal. On the lake he had what little artillery he had brought with him on the airdrop fired into the ice around his paratroopers' positions at the lake's end. This bombardment had created a jagged sea of auto-size bergs that the Aists could not negotiate. The result had been known as "Freeman's Basra," a telescoping pile of wreckage that looked like the

destruction meted out to the retreating Iraqis along the highway from Kuwait.

CHAPTER SIX

IF FREEMAN'S VICTORIES were an open book, he had
a few secrets he shared with no one. One of them was that,
fit as he was, he detested having to keep it up. Jogging
and physical exercise made you too damn hot and sweaty—
unless, of course, you were in combat. Then you were so
busy, so fearful, at times—usually after—so exhilarated you
didn't notice. But he had to force himself to run at least four
miles a day to stay in shape, and go easy on the buttered
popcorn. Monterey's beach was perfect, the sand making it
more exhausting, making him feel doubly heroic, and at the
end he could walk into the ocean. That, as Marjorie said
every time, would "cool you off right enough."

For the past three days, Freeman hadn't seen the figure on
the dunes, and this morning the general was particularly relaxed, going over the old battles in his mind as he jogged
along the water-firmed beach.

He remembered the armored battle in the Yakutsk region
of Siberia where it had plunged to minus sixty degrees, at
which temperature metal became brittle and the waxes in the
hydraulic lines of the Siberian tanks, but not the American
Abrams M1A1, separated out, the oil's constituent waxes
then clogging the tanks' arteries in the same way as lumps
of cholesterol clog the bloodstream. The T-72s and some

T-80s had suddenly become sitting ducks, whereas the American tanks burst through the snow berms at forty miles per hour like exploding icing sugar, picking the Siberians off. It was one of the most beautiful things Freeman had ever seen, and he was thinking of it now as suddenly he saw the lone figure on the dunes once again.

Freeman's world was a Hobbesian one: one in which only the sword, or the threat of it by the sovereign—whether the sovereign was one or many—guaranteed peace and tranquility, and so it was the most natural thing in the world for him to pat the bulge beneath the waistband of his jogging trousers to make sure that the Sig Sauer was snug and ready. His wife had been fatally wounded by a Siberian Spetsnaz—a special-forces sleeper who, along with so many others, had been inserted during the heyday of the love-in between Gorby and the *New York Times* and who, when activated to take out Freeman earlier in the war, had surprised his wife in the house instead, Freeman having been delayed on the flight from Washington. The intruder fatally wounded her, and she died a few hours later in the Monterey Peninsula Hospital.

Freeman could tell by the way the man—Chinese, in a jogging suit—was standing on the dune, staring out to sea, not bothering to turn in the general's direction, that he was waiting for him again. Or was he one of California's legion of ecofreaks—kill all the people but save the whales! And was the stranger the same man as a few days ago?

"Morning," Freeman said, not altering his pace, merely nodding as he passed. The man nodded back.

Son of a bitch looks suspicious, Freeman thought, and immediately thought after that maybe he wasn't. He looked lithe, wiry, and unusually tall. But somehow, maybe because of the smart matching jogging outfit and the Nike pumps—very modern—in some indefinable way Freeman didn't place him as a party member. But then they'd hardly send someone in a baggy Mao suit with "party" written all over him.

Two hundred yards further on Freeman stopped and began

some leg stretches. Love a duck—the Chinese jogger was doing t'ai chi, moving with that graceful deliberation that for once made westerners stare at the Chinese rather than the other way around.

Now ahead, a hundred yards further on up the beach, he saw another figure, and off to his left another appeared atop the dunes.

"Bad news, Dick!" Freeman was speaking as if Colonel Dick Norton were by his side. "One in front of me, one behind, and one on the left flank." The sea was to his right. Boxed in.

"All right, you bastards," Freeman muttered beneath the crash of the sea. "You're going to have to come and get me." Up on the highway he could hear the hum of tires and saw a Winnebago go by—then a bus and a motorbike, but they might as well have been on Mars.

"Well, Dick, I told you to build up the U.N. line—get things ready in case of a punch-up—and over here I've fouled up, my friend." He was doing a few push-ups, during which he could see all of them at one glance. He stopped the push-ups. Foolish to get his heartbeat up too much—could make his aim a little shaky. Still, he wasn't fool enough to think he could get three of them. Two, maybe, but not three. He looked up and saw that T'ai Chi was now moving toward him, hands in his pockets. "Well, Dick, last time I saw a jogger with his hands in his pockets, son of a bitch was playing with himself. Don't like it. You hear that, Sig? Time I played a little pocket billiards myself." He knelt down, as if going into another exercise routine, which immediately reduced his target size. He felt under the jogging suit for the grip—had it, and turned the gun barrel out, still under the cloth, pushing off the safety. He figured T'ai Chi would be within good range in about sixty, seventy seconds, and began the count.

CHAPTER SEVEN

FIVE THOUSAND MILES away it had been a slow morning along the U.N. line. Everything was quiet, and only the four-man SAS/Delta troop of David Brentwood, Salvini, Choir Williams, and Aussie Lewis were unhurriedly busy, checking all their equipment from the transparent mags for the Belgian P-90 to the pencil flares and hand-held, cigarette-pack-size GPSs—geosynchronous positioning systems—they all carried. Jenghiz, the Mongolian interpreter-guide they had assigned them, was fluent not only in the Khalkha Mongol dialect that was used by three-quarters of the population but also the dialects of the Durbet Mongols who lived in and about the mountainous region north of the tableland between Siberia and China that the rest of the world called Mongolia. Jenghiz also spoke the tongue of the Darigangra inhabitants of eastern Mongolia, and that of the Kazakhs, Turvins, and Khotans that made up less than 10 percent of the sparsely populated country the size of Texas.

With Jenghiz they would be going in over the wall, not the Great Wall of China but the big rampart of Genghis Khan in northeast Mongolia, near the Mongolian-Chinese border, and over the two-mile-high Hentiyn Nuruu Mountains south of the Siberian-Mongolian border and eighty miles northeast of the Mongolian capital of Ulan Bator. It was a high country that, unlike the steppes and the Gobi Desert south and east of it, was one of fast-running rivers, deep gorges, and wild, windswept mountains, outcrops of larch and spruce hanging grimly onto rock faces, battered by the winds that alternately came out of Siberia to the north and Chinese Inner Mongolia to the south.

If they were caught, Jenghiz was to destroy Freeman's sealed message. The cover story given them by Colonel Dick Norton would be that while patrolling the U.N. DMZ, the Pave Low M-53J chopper had lost its NOE—nap of the earth—radar, and in one of the many dust storms that plagued Mongolia they had lost their way, straying into Mongolian airspace, the Mongolian interpreter as lost for recognizable landmarks as they were. It had happened before, both in the almost featureless expanse of the Gobi Desert to the southeast and to those pilots trying to negotiate their way around the Hentiyn Nuruu.

But Aussie Lewis reckoned the Mongolians wouldn't buy it. They certainly didn't buy any incursions on their territory by the Chinese from Inner Mongolia, whom they hated.

"This is different," David Brentwood assured Aussie. "We'll be wearing U.N. identification—armbands, et cetera."

"Yeah, until we reach the insertion point," Salvini said. "But what if they come across us while we're changing into our Mongolian garb? You know what they do to spies." He paused. "You know what we do to spies."

"We're not at war with them, boyo," Choir Williams said. "It'd be mighty embarrassing, that's all."

Aussie chimed in, "Maybe, Choir, but Sal's got a point. We could be embarrassed for twenty-five years' hard fucking yakka in some friggin' coal mine!"

"Hey!" David Brentwood said, checking over the clothes they'd slip into in order to travel down through the mountains to Ulan Bator on Dick Norton's, that is, Freeman's, "preventive medicine" mission. David's tone was older than his twenty-five years. He was cutting short the worry talk. "No one twisted your arms, you know. You guys volunteered.

Norton told me that was the general's first directive for this mission. You know the conditions. We get caught, we get caught. Uncle Sam can't do anything. You want to cry about it, don't go!''

It was about the worst insult you could deliver to the elite commandos of Special Air Service or Delta Force. These were men who had gone deep into enemy country from the coast only a few weeks before the cease-fire to help a stranded SEAL detachment near Nanking. These men had been together on Ratmanov Island—had gone down into the labyrinth of tunnels to ''sweep'' out the Spetsnaz.

''We're not complaining,'' Aussie said. ''Just looking at it square in the face, Davey. I think Freeman's doin' the right thing. It's just—''

''Aw, why don't you admit it, Aussie?'' Salvini said, his Brooklyn accent at its height. ''You don' wanna leave little Olga!''

''*Big* Olga!'' Choir added.

Aussie slipped an elastic band around two 9mm mags. ''Don't be so fucking rude!''

''Don't take any pictures of her,'' David said easily, smiling to break the tension now his point had been made. ''Remember, no personal effects.''

''All right if I bring my dick along?'' Aussie countered.

David Brentwood, essentially a shy individual, shook his head at the Australian's unrelenting vulgarity.

''Just keep it in your trousers, boyo,'' Choir Williams advised. ''It might get shot off otherwise.''

Salvini thought this was very funny.

''Oh you're a riot,'' Aussie told them. ''A regular fucking riot. If anybody's going to be missing their member it's the first Mongolian who pokes his nose—'' Aussie stopped and winked at Jenghiz, the interpreter-guide. ''No offense, Ghiz.''

''No off fence,'' Jenghiz said, his good-humored smile of pearl-white teeth framed by a drooping black mustache. It made him look somewhat sinister despite the fine, bright teeth, and Aussie suspected that he grew it more to bug the Han Chinese who for the most part couldn't grow one and who in general regarded facial hair as the sign of barbarians—except when one was old.

"Listen up!" Aussie said. "Ten-to-one I'll be the first to spot a Mongolian. Choir? Sal? What do you say?"

Choir Williams, who'd lost and made money from the Australian's obsession with gambling before, was careful to set the ground rules. "How will we know for sure?"

"Well," Aussie said, "it's not very difficult. If the fucker starts shooting—"

Choir and Salvini bet ten-to-one they'd spot the first Mongolian after the drop—after they started making their way down from the mountains toward Ulan Bator, where they hoped they would be able to make contact with the pro-Siberian but anti-Chinese government. Since Gorbachev's *perestroika* and *glasnost* the Mongolians, though only with a population of just over two million, had started to go their own way and, despite the presence of Siberian garrisons, were determined to make their country their own as far as they could. There were bound to be Russian patrols, but Brentwood's team was to avoid all combat if at all possible and make its way to Ulan Bator with a message that Freeman had once jocularly called, "Let's make a deal."

"By the way," Aussie said, "anyone hear about that poor bastard Smythe?" He was referring to one of the SEAL members who'd been captured by the Chinese, General Cheng refusing to give the American back in a prisoner exchange because the Chinese were maintaining that as Smythe was out of uniform when captured and therefore a "spy," he was not to be accredited normal POW treatment.

The fact that Smythe was hardly a spy, decked out as he'd been in SEAL rebreather and wet suit, was of no account to the Chinese, and the fact that Smythe—a man in his early thirties with a wife and two young children back in Maine—

hadn't been shot was not due to any compassion on the Chinese part but because Cheng wanted to "question" him in greater detail about the SEALs. In short, they wanted to torture him.

"Last I heard," David Brentwood told Aussie, "was that intelligence reports from the Democracy Movement underground said that they'd moved him from Nanking to Beijing. More interrogation probably."

"Poor bugger," Aussie said. "And that Jewish sheila—the one who was—you know—the one who was smuggled out of Harbin north to us."

"What sheila?" Salvini pressed.

"The Jewish bird who told our side Cheng was moving masses of troops across the Nanking Bridge—on their way north."

"Oh," Sal said. "Her. Yeah, I remember. Someone told me she got back to the JAO." He meant the Jewish Autonomous Region or Oblast wedged between Manchuria and Siberia, of which it had ostensibly been a part.

"Or what used to be the JAO before we got here," Sal added. "She's still around. Why?"

"Heard she's some looker," Aussie said. "Enormous—"

"Yes, okay," David said, "we know. Enormous eyes." They all laughed, even Jenghiz, who didn't always understand their English. They said in the SAS/Delta Force that if Aussie wasn't in a firefight he was in bed.

Two minutes later they were told the Pave Low was ready, its big noise-suppressed rotors impatiently chopping the air.

"Still bloody loud," Aussie commented.

"Like your ties!" Salvini joshed.

With that, they were all aboard, and once the rear ramp closed, swallowing them up, the Pave Low's big bulbous nose—the chopper's fuselage flanked by two scallop-shaped fuel tanks—lifted, the rear rotor higher, the chopper's downpush kicking up hard crystalline snow that chafed the faces of its ground crew, who did not know whether they'd see the Pave Low again.

CHAPTER EIGHT

THE MAN WHO'D been assiduously practicing his t'ai chi was now no more than twenty feet away. "General Freeman?"

"Yes," Freeman answered, now squatting on his haunches, arms akimbo, doing breathing exercises. "Who are you?"

"Colonel Wei. Republic of China." His English was impeccable. "I am with the consulate in New York. Admiral Lin Kuang was sorry you were unable to discuss ideas with him and has sent—"

"Identification!" Freeman demanded, standing up, now indicating the Chinese behind him near the water and the other one on his flank up on the dunes. "Those your people?" Freeman added, his tone curtly businesslike.

"No," the man calling himself Wei said. "We might have a problem in that regard, which is why I—"

"Why did you wait?" Freeman said, accepting the consulate identification card and driver's license with residency address and the home address in Taiwan. "Why didn't you approach me back there?" He indicated the dunes further behind him up the beach.

"I did not know—I still do not know, General, who these other two men are. I thought they might try to stop me."

"Or me," Freeman said, handing him back the identification. "What do you want to see me about?" The general's eyes were still on the other two men, one a hundred yards to his right down the beach and the other about the same distance up from him atop the dunes, the brownish green dune grass stubble blowing stiffly in the wind.

"The admiral wanted you to know that if he can be of any assistance he will gladly give it."

Freeman grunted, his tone somewhere between gratitude and frustration. He appreciated the admiral's gesture, but it was just that, a gesture. Too vague a promise. Besides, Freeman was no longer C in C Second Army, and he told Colonel Wei this. He had effectively been relieved of his command. Didn't Taipei read the papers? The La Roche tabloids had been screaming FREEMAN FIRED! for a week. Besides, ID was so easily forged in an age where they were using Xerox color copiers to pass on forged banknotes. "Why the hell didn't you call me at the house?" Freeman demanded, still suspicious. "Instead of this cloak and—"

"Your house is being watched, General. Your phone lines are tapped."

"By whom?"

"We do not know."

"We?"

"At the consulate," the man said, hesitating. "I can give you other contacts to verify my credentials if you—"

"It's all right," Freeman said. "What's Admiral Kuang say—specifically?"

"Only that if you should need his assistance he will do whatever he can."

"You don't seem to understand. I've lost command of Second Army. Furthermore, I'm merely an instrument of national policy. I can't do what the United States government doesn't want me to do."

"We understand, General, but you may yet be returned to command."

"Huh—that'd be a miracle," Freeman commented, looking again at the two other men. Then he knew who they must be. "Goddamn it! They're bodyguards," he said, smiling at Wei. "For once the fairies've done something right."

Still, Freeman wondered, would bodyguards be assigned after you were no longer a threat to the enemy? Well, hell, ex-presidents had bodyguards for life. Was it too much conceit that after his victories he would have earned the wrath of vindictive losers—that they might send someone after him?

"We feel," Wei continued, choosing his words as carefully as a chef selecting his tomatoes for the day, working around it. "We feel that things are in a state of flux in the disputed area between Siberia and Manchuria and that—"

"The world's in a state of flux, Colonel," Freeman interrupted. "It's her natural condition."

"Perhaps, but the signs are more propitious than I think you realize, General. For yourself."

"Even if you're correct—again, what can I do?"

"Should the occasion arise, you would send the word 'mercury' to our consulate. This would activate certain procedures with Admiral Kuang."

"Don't dance with me, Colonel. Does 'mercury' mean you'd intervene militarily?"

"This is possible."

Colonel Wei flew into Freeman, knocking him to the harder sand by the water's edge, blood and bone from his shattered cheek spurting over the general's chest, turning the white foamy sea pink.

"Jesus—" Freeman began. Wei's eyes were frozen in shock, the shot having killed him the instant the depleted uranium bullet had exploded in his brain, creating a hole the size of a fist in the back of his head. Another bullet thudded into him, and Freeman felt a warm sensation flooding over his stomach. Now the general had the Sig Sauer out and, pushing Wei off him, but snuggling in close to the body, took careful aim. The Sig Sauer bucked twice, and the man by the water seemed to hesitate, trembling, looking as if he were shot, but he kept coming.

The man from the dunes had disappeared only to reappear moments later, his head barely visible through the windshield of a four-wheel-drive Jeep Renegade coming straight at Freeman, who fired again to his left. The man by the water crumpled at the sea's edge, the waves issuing over his body, their forward motion rolling cumbersomely toward the beach, the undertow sucking at him, and wet sand pouring over his legs back into the sea.

The four-wheel-drive was now hurtling down from the dunes a hundred feet away when Freeman fired one, two, three, four, five at the windshield. One of the shots found the target, the four-wheel-drive flipping onto its side, careening for a bit on the beach, making the drier sand squeak like the sound of piglets, its wheels still spinning at the sky. Freeman knew he had only a few shots left and ran toward the vehicle from the off side. The man was dead, and Freeman couldn't see where he'd been hit until he realized he hadn't been hit at all. The windshield was a milky spider's web; little glass had flown out. Instead, what must have happened was that as soon as the windshield had been hit, turning opaque, the man had instantly stuck his head out far left to see where to steer when the vehicle flipped, digging deep into the dry sand, his head taking the impact full on and now lolling like a rag doll's.

No one had heard any shots against the noise of the surf, but someone passing up on the highway had seen the overturned Renegade and the body at the surf's edge. When the police arrived they couldn't find any ID on the two men.

"You have any idea who they were, General?" asked a blonde whose figure couldn't be disguised despite the state trooper uniform.

"No," the general answered. "I'd only be speculating."

"Go ahead, General," she encouraged him.

"Guo An Bu—Chinese Intelligence Service—External Affairs."

"Why would they be after you, General?"

"Don't know," Freeman said, "unless they think I'm another Subutai." The general was staring out at the sea, not in the near distance but as if somehow he could see all the way to China. "Subutai," he explained, "served Genghis Khan. Marched all the way from China to the Hungarian plain. At one stage his armies covered four hundred miles, took several cities, and fought two great battles, conquering Poland and all of Silesia—in less than thirty days." He paused, oblivious to the policewoman's stare. "Before that, he'd taken Russia. And before that, Genghis Khan had taken all China. By God, what an army!"

"General—"

"What—oh. Sorry, officer. No, what I mean was there's a good chance it was politically motivated, but I don't want that to get into the press."

"Politically motivated, sir?"

"Yes, that's what I think. Chinese don't want me in the picture, which makes me believe that Wei—that joker over there—was right. Maybe the cease-fire over there isn't worth the paper it's written on."

"You mean the Chinese were trying to assassinate you, General?"

"Either that," Freeman said, "or"—flashing a smile—"someone in Washington!"

Everyone laughed. It happened now and then at a homicide—the tension had to snap. But as the ROC colonel was carried away, Freeman's jaw clenched. No matter what army—when a soldier went down like that, having risked all, knowing the odds, it never failed to move him. At that moment he felt as if Wei were a son in a way that transcended time and borders. Hearing the roll of the sea, he felt that he had been with Subutai, that destiny had thrown Wei upon him to protect him—that God had used the ROC colonel as

a shield and that therefore Freeman's time had not come.
Yet.

CHAPTER NINE

SERGEANT FIRST CLASS Minoru Sato was fifty-two years
of age, one year away from mandatory retirement in the Japanese Defense Force. The company to which he was attached
was part of the Second Asahikawa Division, one of the JDF's
northern army's four divisions. Under the constitution, the
JDF did not get to take either the type-61 or -74 tank or the
FH 70. Also denied them were the 155mm howitzer and
the self-propelled 106mm recoilless rifle. By stretching the
definition of what constituted "small arms," the two-
thousand-man JDF unit was permitted to take LAW antitank
launchers and antipersonnel mines, as these came under the
heading of self-defense. But for the JDF's purposes the re-
strictions were not seen as any impediment to what was
thought would be basically a U.N.-sanctioned observer team
on a ten-by-five-mile strip of the U.N.'s DMZ. In any event
U.S. armor and artillery were in effect "on call" should they
be needed in some unforeseen circumstance. And at least the
two battalions that made up the JDF force were equipped
with top-of-the-line type-89 5.56mm rifles.

With a thoroughness for which the Japanese were known
in their industrial policy, the JDF battalion organized itself
promptly into a classic perimeter defense, with the JDF commander true to his U.N. mission playing no favorites—both

the western and eastern sectors of the perimeter that fronted American garrisons no less manned than the southern side of the five-by-ten-mile sector where JDF troops looked across the Amur River into Manchuria.

The Japanese were determined to look and to be as professional as possible—after all, this was only the second time Japanese troops had been abroad since World War II over sixty years ago, and the nation would be watching, expecting them to meet the highest standards. Japanese pride was not about to be embarrassed by any attack—even by Chinese bandits who in this sparsely populated region of Manchuria could come down from the high country across the river and conceivably launch a raid across the river on the Siberian villages. In fact Beijing had warned the U.N. central command before the Japanese Defense Force had even been despatched that it, Beijing, could not be responsible for the actions of Chinese border brigands. The admission constituted something of a loss of face for Beijing, apparently conceding that part of the People's Republic was not completely under Communist control. But Beijing's caution about brigands was seen by Washington as a genuine effort to forestall any possible misunderstanding should a local warlord and his followers forge over the river and cause the PLA to be blamed for violating the cease-fire.

Freeman, on the other hand, dismissed Cheng's plea as "Beijing bullshit!" claiming that it was a "goddamned facade, a ready-made excuse for the PLA to hit and run wherever they like and then blame it on some bandit."

"Why would they bother?" he was asked by Washington.

"Because it's a hidden message to us that says, 'You boys want a U.N. line, fine—but be prepared to lose men in "border raids" over the next twenty years.' Same as Korea. There are still people in the U.S. who don't know we lose men every year in 'incidents' on that damn Thirty-eighth parallel. This 'bandit' cover is Beijing's way of reminding us that we're stuck here to garrison the U.N. line *and* to pay for it—

a trace ten times longer than the Korean DMZ—for the next twenty years.''

"Douglas," they said in Washington, "is just looking for a fight. Get him out of here. Fast."

And now he was sitting with Marjorie on the eve of April the twenty-fourth, watching the JDF set up camp on the U.N. line. At one point he could do nothing more than shake his head in disgust and disbelief. CBN was already interviewing members of the Japanese contingent.

"Beautiful," Freeman said, his voice dripping with sarcasm. "Look at the background for this interview—you could plot their sections, strong points, and battle positions to the nearest yard. CBN's giving us an aerial shot now—Jesus! Why don't they just send the plans to Beijing and be done with it?''

"Well," Marjorie said—she'd long given up on Douglas's blasphemy—"I'm sure it will all work out for the best, Douglas." She was an "all-for-the-best" lady—she could have turned the battle for Hue into an "all-for-the-best" event. She was getting on his nerves, and he was trying to think of a way of telling her that from now on he had decided to stay up at Fort Ord. He figured his duty to his dead wife, to give Marjorie a chance to "look after you," had long been fulfilled. Though he was watching an earlier taped newscast of the JDF near Poyarkovo, it was already dawn there and a phone call from a sympathetic colleague at the Pentagon informed him that Poyarkovo was as of this moment under heavy attack—U.S. fire-support teams being rushed from both the western and eastern sectors of the rectangle to try to help the JDF hold. The forward slope nearest the Amur, or Black Dragon, as the Chinese called it, was already under heavy 81mm mortar assault.

By the time the Americans got there it was too late for the JDF to regroup and retake the forward slope they'd lost. Now they had to fall back along a five-point reverse slope defense behind a crest on the northern side of the river, the forward half of the five-by-ten-mile area already lost to waves of what were being called "Chinese irregulars."

The Japanese were in shock. While they had quickly placed LAW antitank teams and machine gun nests on either flank, producing a withering fire, a tank ditch as the TRP—target reference point—the Chinese, none of whom were dressed in army garb, were *running through* the mine fields. As one man fell, another used him as a stepping stone just as the Russians had done at Stalingrad. And Chinese were already using bamboo ladders to cross the eight-foot-wide by five-foot-deep antitank ditch only yards below the crest. But where had so many Chinese come from, taking the JDF by complete surprise?

That question was about to be answered by a reconnaissance flight immediately ordered by Colonel Dick Norton.

A Stealth F-117B fighter was at Sapporo Airfield in northern Japan, but a hairline fracture had been found in its RAM (radar-absorbing material) contoured intake grid. The concern was that the fracture, under the enormous stresses imposed on the aircraft, might suddenly become something much larger, possibly radiating out to the wing. In any event this was the reason that the carrier USS *Salt Lake City* in the East China Sea was contacted and ordered to launch immediately a photo reconnaissance of the Poyarkovo area.

Though by now the F-4 Phantom, the wondrous fighter of an earlier age, was all but extinct, relegated to a secondary role as a quick photo recon aircraft, it was at this moment exactly the right plane in the right place and so was given the mission to find out just how much ChiCom activity was going on along the sector of the U.N. line now under attack and how many troops were massing on the southern bank of the Amur, in Manchuria. Was this a local warlord action or merely a tactical probe for something much larger?

As the carrier steamed into a saffron China dawn, twin ribbons of steam rose and broke ghostlike from its angled deck catapults, and the deck director, a yellow dot against the wide gray expanse of sea and sky, watched as the F-4's deck crew swung into action. Suddenly the plane had the most important mission aboard, a return to its old glory, the Phantom's twin nose wheels rising slightly as they passed up over the shuttle, the catapult bridle looped over the shuttle and onto the two wing forgings.

The bridle's slack was taken up, the cable now looking like a huge black rubber band stretched beneath the nose strut, which now rose to full flight attitude, and the wings. On deck the bitterly cold wind whistled about the plane's canopy, kerosene fumes mixing with the salt air of the sea, the pilot watching the deck director raise his hands, turning them as if he were securing twin-valve wheels aboard a submarine. It was the signal to go to full afterburner thrust. The howl of the notoriously smoky J79 engine became a banshee scream, the fighter straining full against the bridle.

The yellow-jacketed deck officer dropped to one knee, right arm extended sideways, pointing seaward out over the deck. His action was immediately followed by the Phantom, as the plane, its pilot slammed back hard against the Martin-Baker ejector seat, was hurled aloft in 2.4 seconds in less than a two-hundred-foot run. The Phantom banked sharply to the left and headed toward the blurred squiggle of gray that was the Manchurian coast.

General William Beatty, the man with whom Washington had replaced Douglas Freeman as C in C Second Army, had surprised the joint chiefs in Washington with the speed with which he'd dispatched his troops to help the Japanese Defense Force plug the gap at Poyarkovo, even though he was not in time to help much. As the Chinese withdrew, they left behind them a savaged and demoralized JDF, Master Sergeant Sato and others killed at the river's edge.

In fact, more Chinese—over two hundred—lay dead than Japanese and Americans, but the shock effect of the Chi-

Coms' attack had been total. American observers were quick to note how many of the Japanese had been either decapitated or had limbs hacked off despite, it was believed, having been dead already as a result of the fusillade of small-arms fire from the waves of Chinese infantry. Most of the Chinese dead had fallen victim to the JDF's mine field; the Chinese, in an eerie action reminiscent of the kind of fanatical Japanese defense that Americans had come to expect in World War II, had used the bodies of their dead and dying comrades as stepping stones in a crazy path of human flesh to cross the mine field.

General Beatty immediately ordered the American First Battalion of II Corps to pursue the Chinese irregulars or whoever they were across the Amur to destroy them and/or teach them the lesson that this was one U.N. peacekeeping force that wouldn't sit still and tolerate such violations of the DMZ.

By 1400 hours the American First and Second Battalions had crossed the slow-thawing ice of the Amur River and were engaging rearguard elements of the fleeing Chinese force on the river's southern—that is, Chinese—bank, the Americans of II Corps already taking dozens of prisoners but struck by the speed of the Chinese withdrawal. Beatty wisely ordered pontoon bridges at the ready should a sudden thaw in the unpredictable spring weather weaken the ice and so temporarily cut off the U.S. supply line. He then ordered two more battalions across the river. It was the high point of his career and his downfall. It wasn't that he had exceeded his mandate in ordering the battalions across the border—in this Washington and Tokyo, pushed by outraged public opinion in both countries over the number of Japanese and American soldiers killed, fully supported Beatty's action.

Freeman had called the Pentagon the moment he had heard news reports of Beatty's counterattack. But his warning, having to go through normal channels, was treated merely as an advisory which, while it stunned those in Washington who never thought they'd hear Freeman back away from a fight, arrived too late to have any effect. By now more U.S. and Japanese troops had been committed, and General William Beatty was within hours of earning the epithet of "Batty Beatty." Freeman had seen immediately—from the rapidity of the hit-and-run Chinese attack—that this was a typical ChiCom guerrilla tactic. More than that, it was a classic maneuver right out of the pages of Sun Tzu's *The Art of War* about trapping your enemy by withdrawing or, as Freeman called it, a "sucker play." Subutai had used the same tactic at the Battle of Sajo River in 1241, withdrawing across the river, dummying the Hungarians after him, before suddenly turning in a massive broad-stroke movement, snapping shut the trap. And this is precisely what Cheng's troops did as they wheeled about in the hills around Xunhe, a village three miles south of the river. Their numbers were swollen to ten times their original four thousand by troops from the Harbin-based Twenty-three Army Corps, who had been rushed forward on a forced march the night before from supposedly "destroyed" barracks sixty-five miles west of the river on the single lane road along the Xun River valley.

Beatty realized his mistake, but too late, for by then the two Chinese pincers of the breaststroke had closed on the southern bank—three Guard companies, 520 men in all, having the express task of mortar bombing the fog-shrouded ice and pontoons, hence not only destroying any natural bridge for an American retreat but smashing their supply line.

Meanwhile Chinese T-59s, up-gunned T-55s, were now moving up the road from the deserted barracks to Xunhe village and toward the bridge—the American First Battalion taking the brunt of the armored attack while Second Battalion quickly made an abatis, sappers from Second Battalion blowing trees at a height of five to six feet from their base, felling them at approximately a forty-five-degree angle, creating a formidable obstacle course of fallen but not completely severed trees along the road, delaying the tanks for two hours. This saved some Americans from death, if not capture, but the bulk of the American force remained cut off from retreat.

The Chinese were so close to them that even if Beatty called in TACAIR strikes, the fog would deny the pilots any reliable identification of friend or foe. The final blood-boiling humiliation for the Americans was the glimpse of a lone, low-flying Phantom fighter, which might have at least made an attempt to rake the old ChiCom barracks with its 20mm cannon, but which made only one low pass in a gap in the fog and then turned eastward, presumably hightailing it for the coast.

Within minutes of the Phantom slamming down on the deck at 150 miles per hour, its tail grabbing the three-wire arrestor cable, its video shown aboard *Salt Lake City* revealed sullen-looking hills in a stark monochrome, covered for the most part with fog, and hills further south devoid of fog but covered with what seemed like thousands of insects, zoom shots showing, however, that they were Chinese regulars advancing along an estimated fifty-mile front against the Poyarkovo section of the U.N.-Manchurian line.

One of the more brazen acts of lying, even by Communist standards, occurred the following day in the U.N., when General Cheng's emissaries tried to explain away the Xunhe "incident" by claiming that the presence of PLA troops was in response to concerns over banditry in the area. Bandits, it was said, had been responsible for launching the hit-and-run attack on the Japanese Defense Force—the PLA presence merely a reaction to the Americans violating the integrity of China's borders.

"Oh no," President Mayne said, "not this time. Those bastards can't have their cake and eat it, too. They started this. We'll finish it."

"What can we do?" press secretary and adviser Trainor asked. "Beatty made a complete hash of—"

"Reinstate Freeman!"

"But Mr. President . . ." the chairman of the joint chiefs of staff began.

"Unleash him!" Mayne ordered.

"Yes, sir."

"But Trainor—" the president added.

"Yes, Mr. President?"

"Tell him to end it as soon as he contains it. This isn't a fishing expedition."

"Yes, sir."

"You think that'll do it, Mr. President?" inquired Schuman, the national security advisor.

"We'll see," Mayne answered.

The president's advisers were not sure what he meant by it. What would they see? The end of the fighting, or how difficult it was to contain Douglas Freeman once he was unleashed?

CHAPTER TEN

Khabarovsk

"THAT SON OF a bitch tried to kill me." They were the first words Freeman uttered upon touching down at Khabarovsk.

"You mean Cheng?" Norton inquired.

"I mean Cheng. Monkey wants to make it personal. Well,

Dick, I won't fall for that piece of Sun Tzu about getting angry and then losing the battle because you lose your head. I'm not angry, Norton."

"No, sir."

"I'm mad as hell!" Freeman pulled on his leather gloves. "Weather's supposed to be warming up."

"It is, sir."

"Course, Dick," Freeman said, striding toward his staff car like an old athlete resurrected, "trick is not to stay mad. Be cool. Rational."

"Yes, sir."

"What's his disposition of forces?"

"We figure it at ten divisions minimum on the Manchurian border. More coming."

"They got that damn Nanking Bridge fixed over the Yangtze?" It was the bridge that the captured Smythe and the other SEALs had attacked and severed earlier in the war.

"Figure they must have, General," Norton said. "Either that or they've put a pontoon across—though that would take some making. It's at least three miles across there."

Freeman grunted, pulled up his collar, and buttoned it at the throat. "Should be warmer than this. We heard anything from that SAS/D troop?"

"No, sir."

"That's good news then." The commandos were on radio silence.

"We hope, sir."

"How far would they be from Ulan Bator?"

"They're flying in on a Pave Low now."

"What's the drill?" Freeman asked. "A burst radio message approximately forty-eight hours from now when they've completed their mission?"

"Yes, sir—if they do."

"Pray to God we get that message through, Dick."

"Yes, sir."

"Anything else?" He sensed there was—Norton had that look about him.

"Yes, sir."

"Spit it out!"

Norton slipped a folder from his flip-top briefcase as they entered the Quonset hut. "Bad news I'm afraid. Photos," he said, taking a steaming cup of coffee from the general. "All from Ofek-10." It was the Israeli high-resolution electro-optical camera satellite, one of those launched by IAI—Israeli Aviation Industries—using a Shavit, or "comet" rocket, known to Freeman's G-2 staff as a "Shove it!"

"Well," Freeman said, looking down at the whitish shape made by the microdot-size pixels that looked about half the size of a cigarette filter against a background of gray, barren landscape. "Sure as hell aren't Scuds."

"East Winds," Norton said. "Type four. Confirmed by the Pentagon. Conventional or three-megaton payload. Range three thousand miles. Has a circular error probability of around plus or minus two miles—so Tel Aviv says. But a CEP of plus or minus two miles doesn't matter much if they're after a big target like a city or—"

"An army," Freeman said.

"Yes, sir. They're theater-level offensive all right—not divisional. That's why I thought you ought to see them straight away."

Freeman sat down, patting his shirt for his bifocals, couldn't find them, and had to go to the makeshift bedroom where he retrieved a spare pair from atop a Gideon Bible, its pages held open by a box of buckshot cartridges for the Winchester 1200 shotgun he kept by his bedside. The general found he didn't need his glasses after all, for even without them Israeli and Pentagon intelligence reports had already concurred with Dick Norton's assessment, classifying the missiles in large, black capitals as INF—intermediate nuclear forces—from PLA's Second Artillery. He was shaking his head in disgust as well as alarm.

"I told them in Washington. I told them the moment those goddamned fairies signed that INF treaty with the Russians. While we were sending our Pershings to the scrap heap, and the Russians were doing the same—" He looked up at Norton, then back down at the missiles, a cluster of six of them. "Beijing, my friend, was grinning—ear-to-ear. Moment Gorby and Reagan signed the INF, China became the number one INF power in the world. You figure the fairies didn't think of that?" Freeman was getting madder by the second. "I tell you what, Norton, when I think of all that goddamn incompetence running around loose in Washington it makes my blood—" The general stopped midsentence, directing a wary glance at Norton. "These infrared confirmed?"

"Yes, sir." Norton knew that the general was remembering the humiliation heaped upon him by the press—the La Roche tabloids in particular—for the casualties Second Army had suffered earlier in the Siberian campaign, when Freeman believed, as intelligence had reported, that he was about to engage a division of enemy tanks hidden in the taiga. They had also been infrared confirmed, the Siberians having simply put battery-powered heaters inside the plastic mockups of the T-80s to give off a sufficient infrared signature to fool aerial reconnaissance.

As well as leading his armor into the trap, Freeman had sent Apaches on ahead to soften the Siberian armor up, only to have over fifteen of the Hellfire missile-armed choppers blown out of the sky by VAMs, or vertical area mines. Freeman knew that he'd been lucky that he'd lost only the battle on the Never-Skovorodino road and not the war. It was a lesson he'd not soon forget. "Any other confirmation?" he pressed Norton.

Norton reached over, turning past the photographs to page three of the typed report. "Yes, sir. Indentation. We can tell from blowups of the tire tracks in the desert approximately how many tons the carrier vehicles and loads are. The indentation weight equals that of a missile. If they're fakes, they're sure as hell heavy ones. And you know how the ChiComs are about fuel. It's damn near a capital offense to waste a gallon in the Chinese army. I don't think they'd be driving heavy fakes around for fun.''

From the coordinates, Freeman could tell at a glance that it was somewhere in Sinkiang province, Lanzhou military region. ''Missile sites at Lop Nor?''

''Further west than that,'' Norton answered. ''Past the Turpan depression—in the foothills of the Tien Shan range. Pentagon and Israeli intelligence figure the missiles were originally situated there because Moscow was well within striking distance. They still don't trust one another. Especially now. With the breakup of the old Soviet Union, Beijing's afraid the disease'll spread.''

''Maybe,'' Freeman replied, ''but the point is, Dick, their three-thousand-mile radius means they could easily reach us.''

''That's what the report concludes, General. Washington and Tel Aviv are agreed on that. Only need to hit us with two or three in the first salvo and that'd be it for Second Army.''

Freeman was tapping his teeth with his bifocals, a habit that annoyed Norton intensely.

''By God, Dick, what we need is a preemptive strike. Apart from anything else those missiles are so close to the border they're a gift to Yesov if he wanted to use them against us—if he and the Chinese are in cahoots. Remember in Siberia, Novosibirsk doesn't like Moscow any more than Beijing.'' The general saw Norton's unease about a preemptive strike.

''I know, I know.'' Freeman waved his hand impatiently. ''Fairies'll have a fit. Hopefully the White House will back us this time. I think that's why MOSSAD sent their report straight to Washington.''

''But if we move anything in there, General, we'd be in a much wider war with China. Sixty-eight divisions against our forty-four, and these're only the divisions on the Sino-Siberian border.''

Freeman didn't need the figures. He already knew that China's full-time army alone stood at over one hundred divisions—a million and a half men—and this ignored the two million men they had in the reserves. And Freeman knew the Chinese weren't Iraqis. It wouldn't be simply a mass of poorly led conscripts he'd have to face if it hit the fan. To a man, the Chinese were volunteers, and long-term volunteers at that. Like the German Wehrmacht, the PLA had taken pains to make sure that the members of any unit came from not only the same province, but wherever possible from the same village. It seemed like a small enough detail, but Freeman pointed out it was enormously important in terms of morale. You might bug out in front of strangers, but it'd be a long time before you'd let your own village down. Everyone in the village knew you and your parents. The disgrace would be total. It went a long way to making up for lack of sophisticated weaponry—the United States had learned that in 'Nam.

And, as they'd shown in Korea, the ChiCom commanders knew a few more tricks than the Iraqis, like slipping a division or two—over twenty thousand men—right under your damn nose. They'd wait for a thunderstorm to trip off all the ground-movement sensors, then move. And PLA officers, while paid more, were much closer to their men than the Iraqi officers had been to theirs. In this respect the Chinese were more like their traditional enemies, the Vietnamese. Still, Freeman was confronted by the brutal reality of the missiles. A massive attack on Second Army could take out its heart. The problem would be to get permission for a bombing mission to try to take out the missiles. It was so deep into China—2,300 miles—that if the bombers were to stand a chance of getting through to the target, the flight, given the fractures found in more Stealths, would have to consist of B-52s originating out of western Europe.

But most likely France wouldn't allow it—just as she'd refused permission for the U.S. to overfly French soil in the raid against Qaddafi in Libya. There was nothing for it but to ask the White House to ask the Brits. Still, Maggie Thatcher was long gone, and elements of the leftist Labour party opposition were bound to oppose such a flight as they had in the case of Libya.

In Beijing, meanwhile, the extent of General Beatty's unexpected response had made it clear that China was now de facto in a war with the United States. Both Premier Nie's and General Cheng's forcefully stated determination to defend China's borders ''against imperialist U.S. aggression'' immediately gave way to reawakening Asian memories of the humiliating defeat inflicted upon the Americans in Vietnam.

The Chinese hated the Vietnamese, who were continually arguing over border areas and the resource-rich islands in the South China Sea, but nevertheless Nie and Cheng had no qualms about invoking the Vietnamese victory over the Americans to remind the PLA that a much smaller Asian country had defeated the mighty U.S.A. Besides, the PLA was many times the size of the North Vietnamese army, and for the PLA to be victorious over the Americans along the Black Dragon River in the north would enhance China's reputation in all Asia, particularly given the vacuum left by the demise of the USSR.

CHAPTER ELEVEN

Britain

THE MINISTER FOR defense, Stanley Wright-Attersley, was sitting at the long cabinet room table at 10 Downing Street, a battered-looking red box of ministerial documents in front of him on the green baize-covered table. When the P.M. entered, Wright-Attersley rose. "Prime Minister."

"Is my information correct, Stanley—the French won't come on side?"

"Afraid so, sir. Elysée Palace issued a secret memo earlier this morning that the French cabinet deem it 'an inappropriate response to the misunderstanding along the Black Dragon River.' "

"Is that what they actually said—a misunderstanding along the Black Dragon, not the Amur?"

"Yes, Prime Minister. They're afraid that an American bombing mission would, to quote their president, 'inflame the situation further.' "

"Misunderstanding?" the prime minister huffed. "My God, the Chinese attacked the U.N. line. Any schoolboy could understand it."

Wright-Attersley nodded. "Quite so, Prime Minister. But we're dealing with the French."

The P.M. grunted, pulled out a chair, and his aide knew it would be a pot-of-tea decision.

"Darjeeling, Prime Minister, or Earl Grey?"

"Darjeeling," the P.M. said without turning, putting on his pince-nez to read the remainder of the French communiqué. "They're a fractious lot, the frogs. Sometimes I think it's against their principle to say yes to anything. They simply cannot tolerate any idea that doesn't originate with them."

"They no doubt feel," Wright-Attersley said, "that French-Chinese trade would be damaged if they allowed bombers to use French airspace."

"And do they think," the prime minister asked rhetorically, "that *our* trade with China would not be affected? And never mind the retaliation that the Communists may very well wreak on British passport holders in Hong Kong now that it's under the benevolent rule of Beijing—those of Tiananmen Massacre fame."

The defense minister said nothing. There was nothing more he could say about the French. In the world of self-interest theirs was the most self-interested. The French had always had a love-hate relationship with America—a love of Hollywood and a contempt for everything else.

The P.M.'s private secretary entered as tea was being poured. He had the latest poll results—the government was fifteen points behind Labour. He said nothing but merely laid the message slip alongside the secret French communiqué refusing to assist the Americans.

"Does Labour know?" the P.M. inquired. "I mean, has the U.S. request leaked?"

"No, Prime Minister," the private secretary answered. "Though I can't answer for the next twenty-four hours." Wright-Attersley sipped the Darjeeling and placed the cup down without a sound. "Be that as it may," he said, looking over at the prime minister, "I feel obliged to tell you that this kind of thing is extremely difficult to keep under wraps. Bound to get out sooner or later, Prime Minister."

There was a long silence. It was a trying decision for the British P.M.—already down in the polls and shortly to face a general election. A decision to assist the Americans could cost the prime minister not only personal popularity. He could well lose the entire election to Labour—a prospect infinitely more worrying to the government than French displeasure.

The P.M. took tea and thought upon the matter. His mind went back to the time during the Falklands War when he was but a junior in Whitehall. He remembered the clandestine operations made necessary by the Americans Haig, Secretary of Navy Lehmann, and U.N. envoy Jeane Kirkpatrick—especially by Kirkpatrick's hostility toward Britain and her support, along with that of Assistant Secretary for Latin American Affairs Thomas Enders, for Argentina against the British. The American who had saved the day was Caspar Weinberger, the U.S. secretary of defense, who arranged, at great personal political danger, secret transfer of U.S. weapons and spy plane intelligence on Argentinian positions to the British.

The air-to-surface Stinger missiles, which the SAS had used to such good effect in the Falklands, were just part of the massive aid supplied by Weinberger, which included everything from air-to-air missiles to KC-135 tanker aircraft used for the midair refueling of the British Vulcan bombers. The prime minister knew that without American help the British, with only one carrier, could not have defeated General Galtieri.

"Of course we'll help the Americans," he said, taking up his tea again. "I should never be able to look at myself in the mirror again if we didn't." He looked directly at the defense minister. "We're cousins after all."

"Quite so," Wright-Attersley answered.

"The polls, Prime Minister," the private secretary suggested, one eyebrow arched apprehensively.

"Damn the polls!" He turned to his defense minister. "A friend in need, Stanley. Isn't that right?"

"Absolutely, sir. Absolutely."

"Don't tell me the details, Stanley. Less they're discussed, the better. And perhaps they won't have to go after all. Media types get wind of this—slap a 'D' notice on 'em. That'll shut *them* up."

"Very good, Prime Minister." A Defence Ministry notice would mean anyone who published anything about the planned raid would be immediately prosecuted.

CHAPTER TWELVE

FRANK SHIRER WASN'T happy about the mission. It wasn't the danger. It was the insult—like being asked to drive the school bus after a BMW. He was a fighter pilot, born and bred. He liked living on the edge of technology and had done so in the F-14 Tomcats. There was nothing like the thrust of afterburner, the twin turbofans rocketing you to Mach 2.3, slamming you back into the Martin-Baker, and the feathery rush through your genitals. It wasn't a thing you could explain to anyone who hadn't done it, including Lana Brentwood, with whom he'd fallen in love while recovering from wounds at Dutch Harbor and whom he wanted to marry as soon as Jay La Roche, her husband, deigned to give her a divorce. Shirer knew more than he wanted to know about La Roche—Mr. Smooth and Successful on the outside—inside, a slimeball who rolled over people as though they were ants.

Lana had left La Roche, tired of his sexual madness, and had begun a new life for herself—gone back to school, finishing her nursing training and joining the Waves, winding up, through La Roche's malevolent influence in Congress, being posted to the naval hospital in what was called America's Siberia: Dutch Harbor, Alaska, off Unalaska Island in the Aleutian chain, where it could go from sunshine to full blizzard within half an hour. The foul weather was mitigated, however, by her falling in love with Shirer, and then Ratmanov happened.

When the small island, the bigger of the two Diomedes, smack in the middle of the Bering Strait between Alaska and Siberia, had to be taken by Freeman's paratroopers, Shirer had flown CAS, but close air support had got him downed, his RIO—radar intercept officer—captured by Siberian Spets, one of whose interrogators had stabbed Shirer's left eye from sheer bloody-mindedness and to make sure Shirer never flew again. But after Ratmanov was taken by Freeman's SAS/D commandos, Frank was sent to Dutch Harbor, where, with the help of "Mr. Doolittle," a streetwise Cockney and fellow patient, he'd learned how to do what Doolittle called an "Adolf Galland." Galland, who was the top Luftwaffe air ace of World War II, had only one eye. He'd cheated the charts, and Shirer likewise passed the eye test. But instead of being reassigned to fighter duty, Shirer now found himself "driving" a Buff—big, ugly, fat fellow—the acronym for the well-worn B-52. Rumor had it that he might get a crack at being posted to a Harrier squadron, but it was only that—a rumor. Besides, he wasn't that enthused—a Harrier was small stuff next to a Tomcat.

Murphy, his rear gunner, wasn't happy about the mission either, but in Murphy's case it was sheer unadulterated fright, though he tried not to show it. Murphy, for whom the mere mention of China evoked childhood images of San Francisco's Chinatown—mysterious smells and fearsome dragons, shot through with weird music—fervently wished the B-52s had had their turrets rigged for radar remote firing as they had been in the old days. However, with the new .50s with a higher rate of fire but not yet successfully slaved to the turret, the machine guns in the rear turret would have to be manned, albeit with radar assist whenever possible.

At Lakenheath in southeastern England, bemoaning the awful weather that swept in from the channel was de rigueur among the B-52 crews because it was the expected thing. Gunner Murphy always joined in, but secretly he couldn't think of anything better than bad weather. So it might mean a rough ride, especially over the European Alps and the mountains of south central Asia, which included the Himalayas, but gray cloud socking them in would keep them out of visible sight, and as a rear gunner, despite all the advances in infrared, Starlite vision, and radar, Murphy retained an old-fashioned belief that lack of visibility in the enemy's territory was your best defense. Besides, on the visual skyrange he'd brought down many more drones with line of sight than with radar assist.

Sometimes there were too many damn dials to watch instead of your sights. His big worry of course was that the bad weather wouldn't hold. In spring the stratus could suddenly clear, revealing vistas of sky and earth that would be an anti-aircraft battery's heaven. To be on the safe side, Murphy went again to the Lakenheath PX and stocked up on the new and improved Pepto-Bismol tablets, tearing open the cardboard packages and stuffing the cellophane-wrapped pink tablets into every opening in his flying suit he could find. He explained away the Pepto-Bismol on the basis of having some vague stomach condition undiagnosed by the doctors but due, he was convinced, to the service food.

The PX quartermaster was shaking his head at the quantities of Pepto-Bismol that Murphy was concealing about his person. "Murph, you fart up there, the sky'll turn pink."

"Don't be a smart ass. You got any more?"

"Christ, you've got the last six packs. You've bought enough for the whole damn flight."

"What if we go down?"

"Christ, you're a happy fella aren't ya?"

"Cautious," Murph said tersely. "I like to cover my ass. Rear gunner's motto—right?"

"Listen, Murph, if you go down you're gonna need a hell of a lot more than Pepto-Bismol."

"Cheery son of a bit—" Murphy began, then suddenly stopped. "When'd you hear about the mission?"

The quartermaster shrugged. "Yesterday, I think. Scuttlebutt is your wing's on call. Could be tomorrow. Could be next week. Right?"

"Right. 'Cept you aren't supposed to know. They tell you the target?"

"Nope."

"Well that's something," Murphy said, and was gone.

When he got back to the NCO's mess the buzz all over was that the mission had been scrapped. "Oh, shit!" Murphy said, as if he really meant it. "What's up?"

"Politics," someone said. "Some Labour congressman—"

"M.P.," another cut in. "Member of Parliament. They don't have congressmen."

"Yeah, well, some Parliament joker's heard about the request to launch a flight from here in England and threatens to raise shit unless the Labour shadow cabinet gets a chance to hash it over."

"Aw, shoot!" Murphy said, really getting into the disappointed flier mode now. "That could mean weeks."

"Could mean never," another rear gunner said.

"Aw, shit!" Murphy said.

Shirer was ambivalent about the news. On the one hand, a cancellation might mean a bit of time to grab a C17 cargo flight over the pole to Alaska to spend a few days' leave with Lana. On the other, he didn't like just sitting around waiting.

So what if the mission would mean driving a Buff? At least that was some kind of flying. Besides, the longer it took for the politicos to make a decision—to stop the Labour party from going public—the greater the danger that news of the exact target would leak out. At the moment hopefully all that would leak was a request for a U.S. Air Force overflight, the target unspecified.

But if Shirer was concerned about that, the one thing he had to feel good about was that Jay La Roche was about to go on trial in the States for "treasonable activity"—selling arms to China before the cease-fire, many of the weapons having been used in the slaughter of Freeman's III Corps on Lake Baikal. He'd been out on bail ever since his arrest on the last night of the presidential moratorium—an Emergency Powers Act that had allowed police to arrest on due suspicion only and without having to Mirandize or to release their prisoner if a charge had not been made. Although the moratorium was over, there was speculation that it might be quickly reintroduced by the president if hostilities increased—to combat any potential internal sabotage in the United States.

In any case, La Roche had been arrested twenty minutes before midnight, midnight having been given by the president as the end of the moratorium, and La Roche had been flown from Alaska for trial in Manhattan.

The newspapers were full of it—except La Roche's tabloid chains—and Frank was looking forward, like many others, to seeing La Roche put away. If La Roche had been locked up for what he'd already done against some of the underage boys and girls he'd had picked up to perform oral sex on him as well as beating them up he would die in jail. So far, however, his money and influence had thwarted any such charges. But now they had him cold on the selling of weapons to the PLA through his Hong Kong front men, one of the Hong Kong Chinese having "spilled his guts," in La Roche's words, in return for not being prosecuted and being under the protection of the government witnesses program.

CHAPTER THIRTEEN

THE PAVE LOW'S blades chopped the air, its FLIR—forward-looking infrared sensor—guiding it over the corrugations that on the radar were the ridges radiating out of the Hentiyn Nuruu Mountains fifty miles northeast of Ulan Bator. The helicopter's vibrations could be felt in the bone. Aussie Lewis and Salvini were asleep, Aussie snoring so loudly that, because of the Pave's relatively quiet rotors, he could be heard by the others.

David Brentwood and Choir Williams were reassured by their colleague's apparent cool, but David had seen it often enough before—something that civilians never believed, how men, going into harm's way, in this case flying over hostile territory, about to land on a dangerous mission, could manage to fall asleep. But they did. For like mountain climbers who were sometimes able to strap themselves to the pitons on a narrow ledge and take a nap, their nervous energy had been exhausted by the meticulous preparation, the adrenaline put in reserve as the body demanded rest before the final push. David had seen SAS and Delta commandos catnapping with only a few minutes before the descent or the drop. David shook the Australian awake, then Salvini.

"What time is it?" Aussie asked.

"Oh four hundred hours," David said. "Dark as pitch. No moon. Pilot must be sweating it."

Aussie Lewis began strapping on his gear: haversack containing his Mongolian herdsman's outfit, two three-and-a-half-pound Claymore mines, ten top-feed mags of 5.7mm ammunition for the P-90, a canteen of water, six hand grenades, folding spade, and furled "washing line" satellite antenna. They were still on radio silence and would remain so until they accomplished their mission and/or were back at the insertion point. Should their mission have to be aborted, a radio burst—an SOS giving their position—condensed into a fraction of a second would be permitted, plus any information on Siberian troop movements into Mongolia. The latter, often called the sixteenth Soviet republic, still had Siberian advisers and their units along the railroad from Ulan Ude near Lake Baikal south to Ulan Bator, the rail being a branch off the Trans-Siberian.

The stony terrain being too risky for a landing at night, the Pave Low would hover as Brentwood, Salvini, Aussie Lewis, Choir Williams, and Jenghiz fast-roped down with their heavy packs. Aussie Lewis was putting on rubber gloves to prevent rope burn.

In preparation for the mission that would take them through the foothills and down to the pasture-rich plain before Ulan Bator, none of the men had been permitted to wash or shave for several days, and the air in the chopper was, as Aussie Lewis put it, "like a bloody parrot cage." But better this than the smell of aftershave, which could cost them their lives. Jenghiz swore that a plainsman could smell foreigners a mile off. The cabin's red glow gave way to an eerie green, and the Pave Low's ramp opened, the rope uncoiling fast like a huge snake frantically descending into the abyss.

Jenghiz was the first to touch ground, and the dusty smell of cold wind and of a few spring bushes that had flowered high in the Hentiyn Nuruu, together with the rushing sound of water nearby, flooded him with a nostalgia that brought tears to his eyes.

"Right," David Brentwood said as they all regrouped. "Jenghiz, lead the way."

"Okay, roger," Jenghiz said cheerfully. David had told him several times that the double affirmative wasn't necessary, that either "okay" or "roger" would suffice, but Jenghiz would simply smile and still say, "Okay, roger."

CHAPTER FOURTEEN

PRAPORSHNIK—OR WARRANT Officer—Petrov, in charge of the seven-man Spetsnaz commando team, checked his gear: an AKS-74 5.45mm with noise suppressor, front pouch magazines, half a dozen RGD-5 grenades and five F-1 grenades, an RR-392 VHF transceiver, a "Dozhd" air mattress, ten-power B-N1 night binoculars, gas mask, canteen, map case, and 9mm Makarov pistol. Finally he checked his MR-1 throwing knife attached to his calf.

Next he turned to his radio operator, helping him to check his R-357 high-frequency burst transmission radio, AK-74, 9mm Makarov pistol, and RPG-22 antitank grenade launcher. The third man in the seven-man Spetsnaz commando team carried a 7.62 SVD sniper rifle along with 12cm-diameter contact-fused PMN antipersonnel mines. Like the other six members he also carried one of the MON-50 trip wire fragmentation mines that could destroy anything up to 150 feet away and which were now being collected in the middle of the squad.

The MON-50s would be used to "square off" the area where the transmitter had first indicated the American helicopter had stopped, either by hovering or landing to let off the four SAS/D commandos. Whether or not the American chopper had actually touched down, the Spetsnaz couldn't be sure, only that the transmitter had indicated the zone exactly. It had all been easier to arrange than anybody at the Glavnoye Razvedyvatelnoye Upravleniye—GRU—or military intelligence quarters—had had any right to expect. The guide, Jenghiz, was well known in Khabarovsk for his knowledge of eastern Mongolia and so his relatives in Ulan Bator were just as easy to trace. He had been given a simple choice by the GRU: Take the cigarette-lighter-size transmitter they gave him, or "we'll kill all your relatives." *Praporshnik* Petrov joked how he wished he'd been given the same chance to be rid of his mother-in-law.

The Spets had been worried that because of the rugged, mountainous area north of the capital the transmitter would at times be "blinded" by the natural terrain. For a while this had happened, but then they'd been in luck and picked it up again.

The seven-man Spetsnaz squad's orders were specific, for the guide Jenghiz did not know the purpose of the SAS mission, acting as guide only. The Spets had opted not to use their Hind A helicopter to overfly the SAS/D group, as this would only create a firefight, and the purpose of the SAS/D mission might die with the firefight between Spets and the SAS/D. GRU HQ had ordered Warrant Officer Petrov to take at least two of the SAS/D alive—if not all of them. Petrov, however, and the six men in his squad agreed that the only way you were going to take an SAS/D man alive was to get him in his sleep—overpower the guard and be onto him before he had a chance to know what was happening. For this too a chopper was ruled out—it could only be used at night, but even then only when the SAS/D team was far enough away not to hear its approach. The Spets were not worried about the SAS/D getting out, for when the American helo came back, in two or three days or whenever, it would set off the trip wire once it landed, the resultant fusillade of fragmentation pieces from the MON-50s' explosions so deadly that the American helo would look like a sieve.

As the Spets chopper, carrying only two Spets, rose then banked to fly due north for ten miles toward the map reference that marked the SAS/D drop-off zone from which the transmitter was now moving and where the Spets would plant the mines, the other five Spets spread out following Petrov, whose radio operator was locked onto the transmitter signal. The SAS/D commandos would almost certainly stop to hide and rest just before dawn rather than risk being seen approaching the capital in daylight.

In this assumption the Spets were not to be disappointed, for by 5:30 A.M., when the first hint of dawn presented itself on the horizon, David Brentwood gave the order to wrap it up for the night and go to cover. They selected a spill of auto-size boulders scattered about the end of the escarpment. There were several caves nearby in the foothills, but the SAS/D avoided them. A cave was marvelous for making you feel safe, but if anything happened and you were discovered there was only one way out and this could easily be curtained off by enemy fire.

"Jenghiz and Aussie—first watch. Okay?"

"Roger okay," Jenghiz said.

"Right," Aussie answered, and positioned himself between two of the biggest boulders, whose shadow easily hid him from the view of anyone on the plain. He felt his right leg itching, almost uncontrollably. The horse-hide Mongol pants beneath the herdsman's smock had been chafing his shin, and it took all his willpower not to scratch. If necessary he'd dump the horse-skin trousers and put on his SAS/D camouflage trousers for the journey back, but until they got there he'd have to put up with it.

He glanced back at the snow-mantled peaks of the Hentiyn Nuruu and then back south toward the pastureland plain before them that ran like a pale green apron down from the foothills toward the lonely capital of Ulan Bator now about forty miles away. A two-night march should get them to the capital of half a million. They'd been told by Colonel Norton at Freeman's HQ that once in the capital they would be less likely to be stopped, for it would be nighttime and there would be Kazakhs, Khalkas, Chinese, and Russian Mongolians all mixing and caring only about their own interests.

At first it was thought by Norton that they would take Freeman's message, his "preventive medicine," to the Mongolian president at Government House in Sukhbaatar Square, a message that had been entrusted only to the four SAS/D men. But this was dropped in favor of approaching him in the more public, less defended pagoda temple now visited daily by the suddenly converted "Communist" president. Should one of them meet any misadventure the other three would have it, and each had been given the message in the majority Kazakh tongue. Jenghiz had not been told, as his job was merely to get them there and to translate if and when necessary. Again it wasn't that anyone mistrusted him, but the SAS/D men had been following the old "need to know" rule.

David, Choir Williams, and Salvini were already out of it—dead to the world.

The six Shenyang far northeast armies, forty-three thousand men in each, specifically the Twenty-third based in Harbin, the Forty-sixth from Kirin, the Sixteenth from Changchun, and the three armies, the Thirty-ninth, Fortieth, and Sixty-fourth from near Shenyang city itself—over a quarter million men in all—were now moving en masse, crossing the Sungari and Nen Chiang rivers en route to the Amur River hump. But now, instead of attacking their traditional enemy, the Siberians, they were attacking the American Second Army, and Lin Biao's famous dictum during the Korean War—"So we lose a million or two"—was being broadcast through loudspeakers all along the Amur River crossings, trying to terrify the U.S. soldiers. The U.S. Army countered by reminding their men of American technological superiority. But to men who knew how the mightiest nation on earth—theirs—had been humbled by the North Vietnamese Army, a much smaller army than that of the Chinese, the Chinese broadcast had some success.

Freeman gave an order for every piece of "goddamn ice" from here—Khabarovsk—to Manzhouli in far western Manchuria to be blown out of the river. He knew of course there wasn't enough TNT in Second Army or in the Pacific convoys of resupply to blow up that much river ice, but it got the message across—the Chinese had to be stopped at the river crossings. And all bridges were to be blown as ice coagulated around the piers. CAS—close air support—was part of his strategy, but only part of it, as even the U.S. Air Force and carrier force in the Sea of Japan couldn't hope to lay down a "bomb fence" twenty-four hours a day, particularly given the vicissitudes of the weather in these latitudes and over eighteen hundred miles of winding river. Of course the major crossing points known from the long Siberian-Chinese hostility on the border might be taken out, but Cheng was known, like Freeman, for not being tied to the orthodox battle plans of others. He would make crossings wherever he willed.

Freeman looked at the vast front on his wall map, a front longer than the Wehrmacht had faced in Russia in 1942, a front along which the vast Amur River became the Argun further to the west. Still further west flowed the Herlen River, which came down from Mongolia's Hentiyn Nuruu.

"The west! Mongolia!" Freeman told Norton, his bifocals, used as a pointer, flashing in the Quonset hut's light. "Here—south of Chita on the Siberian side of the border— south of Mangut—across the border beyond the jumble of mountains on the Siberian-Chinese border. That's where we have to strike. Head south—hit the bastard on his left flank. Push him back, Dick—into the Manchurian fastness—keep him tied up there in the foothills on the Mongolian-Chinese border while our main force drives south.''

It seemed sound enough—giving your opponent a straight left while your right outflanked him south. Norton too was gazing up at the huge wall map. "How far south, General? You mean far enough to push them well across the Siberian-Chinese border—the DMZ?''

"South," Freeman said, and Norton felt a cold fear turn his bowels. It was unthinkable. Congress would have a blue fit. But then Freeman had made a career of thinking the unthinkable, and then doing it.

"But General," Norton cautioned, "if you drive due south from Mangut, to get at Cheng's left flank you'd have to pass through Mongolian territory.''

"And if we don't we'll have to move east of Mangut," Freeman retorted. "We'd have to make a detour through Chinese territory—a detour of hundreds of miles. With each M-1 tank guzzling two gallons for every mile that's one hell of a detour, Norton.''

"But it is in Chinese territory," Norton pointed out. "Going straight south from Mangut would mean taking a shortcut across Mongolian—'' He stopped, for it was at that moment that he realized precisely why Freeman had sent the SAS/D troop of four on their mission deep into Mongolia—the SAS/D troop, as Freeman's envoys, were to tell the Mongolian president in Ulan Bator that it might be necessary for American troops to cross from Mangut into China so as to hit the Chinese deeper on their left flank—go into the steppe country in the Gobi Desert—tank country—across which Freeman's echelons might race. Would Freeman's request for free passage be acceded to by the Mongolians? On the one hand, the Mongolians had a long and intense hatred of the Chinese. On the other, they were still in fact, if not in name, largely dependent on the whims of Siberia. Would Novosibirsk go along with letting Freeman take the shortcut across Mongolian territory? Or had Freeman told young David Brentwood something else to tell the commander of the Ulan Bator forces? Was it to be as much a warning as a request—let the Americans pass through Mongolian territory or else? Norton suspected it had been both—the carrot and the stick.

Suddenly Norton saw it—Freeman's real objective—and the general sensed disbelief in the face of his aide.

"Listen, Colonel," Freeman told him. "I didn't come over here to dance." His fist thumped Beijing, rattling the map. "Only thing these jokers understand, Dick, is defeat. We don't get this dragon where it lives, by the throat, the son of a bitch'll be hissing and spitting for another twenty years. We lost China once in forty-eight. Goddamn it, we're not going to lose it again. Trouble with you, Dick, is you're thinking like the rest of them. Monolithic China. Don't you see? It's just like we used to think of the Soviet Union—now what do we have?" He answered his own question, gesturing at the board north of the Siberian-Chinese border. "Thirteen new republics and they're still counting. China's the same, Dick. Rotten at the center. Old farts hanging onto power for grim death. Like tortoises in their shell."

"General, they could lose a million men and still have twice as many men at arms as we do."

"A tough shell, I'll agree to that, Dick. Damn tough. But Dick, with a little ingenuity and determination we can do anything."

Any excitement in Norton had waned, and now all he felt was a dull headache.

"A *little* ingenuity, General? Your southern strategy seems sound enough, but how about all these Chinese armies massing on the Manchurian border along the Amur? What if they suddenly come west against your flank attack?"

"Then my flank attack wouldn't work, Dick."

"Well, sir, we can hardly ignore them. There're over five armies along that river." He meant the Amur hump.

"We've got to keep them occupied," Freeman answered, with what seemed calculated ingenuousness.

"Yes, General, but how? Our CAS can only do so much, and given the bad weather—"

"Dick—you have that wolf dung I told you to get?"

"Lots of it, General. You know what they're calling us here in Khabarovsk?"

"What?"

"The shitheads."

Freeman let forth a belly laugh that could be heard in his communications room. "Shit stirrers, Dick! That's what they're going to call us. Stirrers!"

"Yes, sir. But what if the Ulan Bator mission doesn't go smoothly?"

"Why shouldn't it?" Freeman demanded. "No one knows they're there except us. Boys are well trained for exactly this kind of mission. Thrive on it. Their instructors were with Special Forces in Iraq. They'll be okay."

"I hope you're right, General. And then there are those missiles we have to worry about."

"Ah—I don't think we'll have any trouble with that either," Freeman responded confidently. "You're a good officer, Dick, but you have to guard against being too pessimistic. Stop seeing the glass as half empty. Start seeing it half full."

Sometimes the general's optimism frightened Norton more than the Chinese did. The worst thing about it was that if something went truly wrong the general could be prone to a depression so dark that few realized how perilously close his pride rode to the abyss—his depressions as intense in their way as his highs. Well, at least the general was right about the SAS/D mission. No one else knew about it but the four SAS/D troopers involved.

CHAPTER FIFTEEN

London

THE REPUBLIC OF China, or Taiwan, was a country worth
cultivating if and when the Labour party came to power. The
Taiwanese would have to do business with the government,
and Trevor Brenson, M.P., thought it might as well be with
him. Besides, there was no more excitement in living with
his wife. He'd grown tired of her—she spent all her time at
women's rights rallies, so much so that Brenson wondered
whether she was married to the feminist movement instead
of him. And when they did get to be together in bed she
began telling him what to do—"this way, not that way"—
"you're too rough"—"harder"—"slower." After a while it
felt as if he were learning to drive and she was the instructor.
More and more he just wanted to swerve off the bloody road.

Lin Meiling, however, was different, and she offered him
a way out. Like his wife she was outspoken, too, but she had
the Oriental sense of place—which in bed was to do what the
man wanted, anything to please. Besides, at their rendezvous
in a Hampstead flat, she never rushed it or talked politics,
and when she'd finished with him he felt so deliciously
drained, so completely relaxed, that he'd already missed one
shadow cabinet meeting because Lin Meiling had literally
squeezed then sucked him dry, and as he told her later, he

must have slept right through his alarm. In fact Lin Meiling had turned off the alarm, giving her ample time to go through his briefcase after they made love.

So far she'd found nothing of note, only some dry skulduggery against a conservative M.P. for having had personal use of government aircraft—taking his family on a hop across to France. They all did it, of course, and Brenson had absolutely no doubt that he'd be doing it when he got into power, but he wouldn't be as damned silly as the Tory.

And when he got to power he wouldn't tell Lin Meiling any more than he did now, which was naught. She could be a spy for either the ROC or the PRC. Whatever—she could detect his mood the moment he walked into the flat, and all she had to do was let him talk about the idiots and various assholes who were trying to run the government, and how he could do it so much better.

Here and there he'd unconsciously drop a hint about what was going on, but she never seemed interested. The trick, as Lin Meiling knew, was patience and knowing that it was better sometimes to know someone in the shadow cabinet than the real cabinet itself, for in order for the shadow cabinet to operate they had to know exactly what the government was up to. There was some brouhaha at the moment— something about the Americans—exactly what she didn't know. But she remained patient, knowing that in two or three days Brenson would be so horny again that he'd want her desperately. It would give her another opportunity to flick through his files and/or listen to his self-pitying frustrations about what a thankless job it was being a member of the queen's loyal opposition.

CHAPTER SIXTEEN

AUSSIE LEWIS, LIKE Salvini, Brentwood, and Choir Williams, had been well briefed in what to expect in the mountains northeast around Ulan Bator. Indeed, he'd been so well instructed that he was by now thoroughly disabused of the false notion, held by most foreigners, that Mongolia was nothing but desert. He knew that in its far west mountainous region there were lakes and streams and vegetation that reminded one of Switzerland, and that parts of the Gobi Desert that ran from southwestern Mongolia east, swinging up into Manchuria, weren't all desert. Much of it was semidesert pastureland capable of sustaining great herds of sheep, camels, and wild horses that roamed about, outnumbering the human population by fourteen to one—the population density of the whole country being no more than three people per square mile.

Because of his briefing on the flora and fauna of the once-mighty kingdom of Genghis Khan, Aussie Lewis was not surprised to see ermine, sable, and squirrels in the mountains, but because the briefing officer had not mentioned it, he wasn't at all prepared for the two roe deer that Jenghiz pointed out to him, one of which, in Lewis's inelegant phrase, "upset the bloody applecart." He glimpsed the deer only a moment before it descended between a smaller spill of the rocky outcrop, and stood stock still, its nose twitching in the hot spring sun, before it bounded across the open area be-

yond the blind side of a large boulder that protected their
southern exposure against a sudden sneak attack.

"No!" It was Jenghiz's panic-stricken voice from the other
side of the huge boulder, behind which he had suddenly flung
himself. In that split second Aussie visualized the whole
thing: The deer must have hit the trip wire, releasing the
spring-loaded firing pin—the Claymore mine set up on its
legs in dry grass so as to go off at chest height and so avoid
any accidental trip by small animals. He could hear its backblast hitting the protective boulders about their camp.

The Claymore's ear-stunning blast echoed throughout the
foothills, its eight hundred steel ball bearings screaming out
at supersonic speed—the equivalent of over eighty shotguns
fired simultaneously, deadly to anything within four hundred
feet of the perimeter. The deer was momentarily lost to view,
shrouded in clouds of gritty dust that looked like yellow
smoke, the sound continuing to roll down through the foothills and back up into the mountains. In an instant Brentwood
and Choir Williams were awake. Salvini, still open-mouthed
at their bad luck, was staring at Aussie. "Holy—"

David Brentwood, his eyes temporarily blinded by the dust
particles, staggered up, dabbed his shirt tail with his canteen,
and wiped his eyes. "What the—"

"Fucking deer!" Aussie said. "Must've tripped the wire."

"Let's go!" Brentwood ordered, and within two minutes
they'd broken camp, each man carrying a cigarette-pack-size
GPS—geosynchronous positioning system—his Browning
high-power 9mm pistol, and pack, Salvini humping the radio. All of them moved briskly, despite their heavy packs
and the unfamiliarity with their *dels*, the ankle-length, silk-
lined tunics of the Mongolian herdsmen. The echoes of the
explosions alone alerted everything and everyone within
miles to their presence.

Ulan Bator lay ten miles, several hours, ahead, and it would
be dark if and when they arrived there. In the daylight they
could be seen moving in the direction of the capital. Jenghiz,

however, Aussie noticed, looked strangely elated. It was almost as if the explosion had been received by him as a good omen, or perhaps his bright-eyed expression was nothing more than a sudden surge of fear.

Five miles behind, the Spets *praporshnik* was hurrying his men from their position and cursing his luck. Now the SAS/D team would know that someone would come to investigate the explosion and so they would be doubly vigilant. But then he slowed his pace, the small avalanche of rocks he was starting slowing to a trickle as another realization swept over him—namely that perhaps part or all of their equipment had accidentally exploded and wiped out the SAS/D troop, ending whatever mission they had been on. Nevertheless, he resumed his steady gait, the seven Spets hurrying down beneath the ridge line of one of the foothills. Whatever the situation, he had to make sure. And in any case there was still no reason for the enemy commandos to expect anyone so close on their heels. If anything the SAS/D team would probably expect a Mongolian-forces helicopter to investigate the explosion, and for a moment he was tempted to call the Hind now returning from setting the mine trap at the enemy's insertion point and have it sent south. But then he decided against it. The absence of a helo would give the Americans a false sense of security—just what he needed to catch up to them.

"*Speshi!*—Hurry up! We want to be close to them by dark—before they get into Ulan Bator."

Lin Meiling loved the storms in England. Some of her fellow Guo An Bu agents who, like her, also used the jobs at the Taiwanese consulate as the perfect cover for their PRC activities, complained unendingly about the weather, about the ever-changing skies, governed so much by the English Channel. And why the English Channel? they asked. Why not the French, the Dutch, or European Channel? But Lin

Meiling cherished the eccentricity and the vicissitudes of England, though in the larger sense she detested its political system.

The party had given Lin Meiling everything, including her university education in Marxism-Leninism and her unshakable belief in communism despite the vicious attacks from the running-dog lackeys in the Commonwealth of Independent States. Once these had been a brotherly Union of Socialist Soviet Republics, now long betrayed by Gorbachev and Yeltsin and the others, delivered up to the altar of western capitalism.

Oh, *they*—the West—had tried to topple the party, too, through the agents provocateurs in the Tiananmen Square incident of 1989 when the goddess of Democracy was paraded by the degenerate counterrevolutionaries down Changan Avenue. Well, the party had flexed its muscle and shown who ran China after all. It was flexing its muscle now against the criminal Freeman and his gang. And the party would flex it against any lackeys in England who dared to undo the work begun by the great helmsman, Chairman Mao.

One could see the chaos created in England by the capitalists. The problem was too much freedom—the English and American disease that so affected the young. It even affected Trevor Brenson, who called himself a leftist. The British Labour party was about as leftist as a Tibetan monk. They had no fiber, no toughness to clamp down on the religionist disease, on the free-thought disease of degenerate democracy. Self-indulgence was what they wanted. Trevor Brenson, the Labour party's much-touted shadow "defence minister," still claimed he was "socialist," said he greatly respected Mao, and yet in the bedroom his religion too was self-indulgence.

The party had warned Lin Meiling of what might be required of her to extract information from such a man as Brenson who, despite his Labour party protestations of brotherhood with the workers, was at heart a capitalist lackey. A woman to a capitalist was merely another thing, a plaything, and Trevor Brenson liked to play disgusting games, games that Lin Meiling was sure the great leaders of the party in Beijing would never indulge in. To have sex with Brenson it was necessary to remind herself that she was doing it for the party and greater socialism. If she could find out from Brenson what the Americans were up to in this war, then she could do the party a great service, and no matter her personal sacrifice.

He was late this evening and had rung to say he would not be back at the flat till ten. Liar! He pretended he was hard at work in the shadow cabinet when he was no doubt seeing his wife—the other *thing* he used from time to time.

Meiling undid the box he had sent her from Harrods—the great socialist store, no doubt. She brushed aside the soft, rustling tissue wrapping, as thin as rice paper, and saw a scarlet bustier and matching scarlet lace panties. He had signed the card, "To M, love T," careful, as usual, not to use his full name and to write in a hand distinctly unlike that which he usually used—in the event that she might accidentally leave the card around the flat. No doubt the people's store had thought he was buying the lingerie for his wife, and he would have been sure to pay in cash—no credit card traceable should he be under surveillance by the Tories or MI5. She shrugged off her status as one of his two women— or did he have more?—as easily as she crushed the tissue paper into a tight ball, pushing it into the recycling bag. He was very big on recycling. Well, Lin Meiling determined that when she got what she wanted she would recycle him. It was ten after nine.

When he walked in at ten he smelled roses and saw her sitting, legs drawn up seductively on the sofa beneath a low, soft lamp that turned the scarlet bustier and panties blood red, her long black hair combed forward, draped over the bustier like a tantalizing curtain. Beside her she had a tall drink, her fingers trailing up and down the frosted glass, her lips parting for a moment over the cherry, sucking it, caressing it with her tongue.

He dropped the briefcase and all but tore off his rain-splattered mackintosh, walking toward her, unzipping himself as he approached.

"No," she said, and turned away.

"Please!" he urged.

She shook her head like a petulant child, rolling the cherry between her lips, her hair a black sheen whipping back and forth over her breasts.

"I'll go crazy," he said.

She shook her head again. "You're too cold."

"What—"

"You're too—" Her hand closed over his erection and squeezed. "You're too cold."

"Christ—I'll—I'll warm up. I'll take a shower. All right?"

She smiled.

When she heard the torrential downpour and saw steam emerging from beneath the bathroom door, she got up from the sofa and, kneeling on the carpet, one eye on the bathroom, she went quickly through his briefcase.

CHAPTER SEVENTEEN

THE FIRST VISIBLE signs of Ulan Bator were its six high smoke stacks. Unlike the *ghers*, the round, canvas-skinned huts of the Mongolians that were kept warm by burning camel dung, the capital was heated by more modern methods, including coal and a nuclear power plant. The four SAS/D troops and Jenghiz paused to hide their packs, only Salvini allowed to take the small but powerful radio under his *del* along with his Browning 9mm.

They had a short rest and checked their flat-folding PVSs, or night-vision goggles, before beginning what they hoped would be the final ten-mile leg of their hike to Ulan Bator and to the capital's Gandan Monastery.

Since *perestroika* and *glasnost*, part of the Mongolians' determination to make their country their own was their determination to allow more religious freedom, though even in this, Mongolia aped Soviet example. The Communists, like those in Beijing, still hated religion for two reasons: Not only did religion pose an alternative to the only way, the party way, but in Mongolia it had encouraged males to take holy orders in the lama monasteries—over seventy of them—and because the monks were required to be celibate this had led to a drastic fall in population.

The Mongolian hordes, who under Genghis Khan had ruled all China and whose kingdom had included much of Europe, were now reduced to no more than 2.9 million in the entire country—a country twice as big as Texas. Freeman believed that this fact alone would play a decisive part in the secret request the SAS/D troop was entrusted with.

Though thoroughly atheistic, the Mongolian president, since *glasnost*, had made a practice each evening of going from the Great Hural, the People's National Assembly, to the Gandan Monastery to pray by either prostrating himself before the Buddha or spinning a prayer wheel on the Gandan Wall. It was unlikely, Freeman believed, that the president, with such a small population, would refuse to let the American Second Army have free transit across its territory into China. But Freeman held it as an article of his faith that the difference between doing it and asking to do it first marked a profound difference between totalitarianism and democracy, and for this he'd been willing to dispatch the four

SAS/D men to see the president. There was always the danger, of course, that the Mongolians could inform the Siberians of the American intention, but it was a chance Freeman was prepared to take in the belief that the Mongolian president would be loath to put himself in a squeeze between Freeman's Second Army and Marshal Yesov's army, which so far at least was abiding by the cease-fire.

The absence of any helos in the sky was taken by David Brentwood's troop as a good sign, and as Jenghiz led them through the silken dust on the outskirts of the flat Ulan Bator, the pale green foothills of the Hentiyn Nuruu took on a peaceful deeper mauvish hue beneath a darkening royal-blue sky that reminded David of the grasslands of the big sky country in Montana.

It was so peaceful that he was now viewing the accident with the trip wire as a blessing in disguise, for it had forced them to take the risk of a daylight hike out in the open, over the protruding fingers of the foothills down to the plain, a journey they would not have otherwise attempted till nightfall. It meant that they were now well ahead of schedule, and Brentwood thought of Freeman's quoting the ancient Chinese warrior Sun Tzu, that an army is like water, that it must adapt itself to the terrain and circumstance. It was exactly what the SAS/D team was doing, using the explosion of the Claymore not as an impediment that had set plans awry but as a new opportunity.

Brentwood fought the temptation to be pleased with himself, but Freeman's directive to approach the Mongolian president at the monastery in the evening fit in perfectly. If nothing happened to stop them they should reach it within a few hours, with Jenghiz leading the way across the vast Sukhbaatar Square in the center of the city toward the Gadan.

CHAPTER EIGHTEEN

CHINESE DIVISIONS CONTINUED to mass across the Amur, and with the weather clearing, though for how long no one knew, it seemed that only the threat of close air attack by the U.S. Air Force, particularly the presence of AC-130 Spectre gunships firing their deadly, seven-barreled Vulcan machine guns and 105mm howitzers, had stemmed crossings by the Chinese troops. But while the awesome power of the gunships was part of the reason for a pause in the Chinese advance, there was a much more pressing cause.

Chinese officers were reporting deficiencies in the small arms supplied to the northern armies—dozens of men having been seriously wounded, some having lost limbs and/or been killed when grenades exploded as soon as the pin was pulled, others having weapons exploding in their faces. Under such conditions of substandard equipment, an advance was deemed unadvisable by General Cheng and an investigation promptly launched. At first it was suspected that La Roche Industries had wilfully furnished defective munitions—that is, until several grenade fragments were collected and sent to Harbin for closer forensic inspection.

Cheng doubted that La Roche, already in trouble in the U.S., suspected of supplying arms to certain countries against congressional edict, would be likely to jeopardize his lucrative multibillion under-the-table arms business by shipping poor-quality arms and ammunition to his prime customer.

Confirmation that Cheng was right came when scientists, rushed up from Turpan's First Artillery Regiment—the name the PLA gave to its missile contingent—determined that while serial numbers made it clear that the defective grenades had indeed been American made, they were not from any of the La Roche batches.

Further investigation along the Amur revealed that the arms in question had been among those stolen from American soldiers in brothels along the river towns of the DMZ. Cheng immediately ordered all such arms and ammunition destroyed, but by now they were mixed up with standard issue and the testing was a hazardous, painstaking, and extremely time-consuming business, as in order to find a single round that had been tampered with, every round had to be examined carefully.

The incident told Cheng and Freeman something important about each other. Cheng learned that the American general's much-touted attention to detail was as great as it was reputed to be, while Freeman's intelligence services, fed the information by underground Democracy Movement agents like the Jewish woman, Alexsandra Malof, learned that Cheng was not as cavalier as, say, Lin Biao had been in the Korean War about sacrificing the lives of his men if he could avoid it. In fact Cheng would rather pause, even though it gave Second Army time to reinforce the crossing points, and make sure everything was in order before he would strike. Of course it also gave Cheng more time to reinforce his side of the river.

CHAPTER NINETEEN

IT WAS 1:00 P.M. Jay La Roche and his guards were met by a barrage of cameras and microphones as he made his way up the steps of New York's central criminal court building, his head held high, looking sneeringly at the blind statue of Justice as though confident that nothing could touch him.

It took only minutes for the charges to be read and less time for La Roche's lawyer to get him off scot-free—the reason stunningly simple. Jay La Roche had been arrested under the Emergency Powers Act, which ended at midnight, Washington time, on the day of his arrest, and under which a suspect could be arrested without being Mirandized. But having been arrested at 11:40 P.M. Alaskan time meant that he had in fact been arrested at 3:40 A.M. Washington time, that is, three hours and forty minutes *after* the Washington deadline, thus rendering his arrest "technically" invalid, as he had not been Mirandized. That is, Jay La Roche had been arrested and not advised of his rights under a law that no longer was in force.

It was pandemonium in the courtroom, and even more flashbulbs and TV crews crowding the corridors than had been on the steps when La Roche had entered the building. As he exited a free man, he walked down the steps of the courthouse unhurriedly, pausing halfway so that his picture in his own tabloid would show him released beneath blindfolded Justice, who had shown impartiality under the law.

He made a grave face about how he was of course innocent of the charges of trading with the enemy and he would have "much preferred" to have been cleared on other evidence but that in the "present political climate" during wartime he doubted that he could have received a fair trial.

Lana, still in shock, called Frank Shirer and as it was 1:30 P.M. in Dutch Harbor when she made the call, she woke him up at 10:30 at Lakenheath—all air crews having already turned in while waiting for a decision to come down as to whether or not they would be going on the China mission.

"Set *free*?" he asked Lana.

"Yes, absolutely—"

"I don't believe it," Frank said, and then made a remark about lawyers that all but turned Lana's face red with embarrassment.

"I know," she agreed. "I can't believe it either." She sighed. It was part pain, part resignation. "I suppose we were all naive in thinking they'd get him. The rich get richer and the poor—"

"The bastard!" Shirer cut in, his tone one of bitter resentment. It meant more than La Roche was free again. It meant that the divorce Lana had longed for—a divorce that would have been much easier to get if he'd been convicted—was now as far off as ever.

"I—I don't know what to say, Frank. I—" He could tell she was crying. In the Dutch Harbor Hospital she'd seen some of the worst injuries of the war: melted skin where once there'd been a man's face, a mangled stump of splintered bone and flesh that had once been a limb, and the smells— the vinegary stink of fear, the eye-watering stench of pus-filled gangrene. With all this she could cope, but the trapped feeling of being sealed in a marriage gone sour with no release in sight was too much.

"Hang on, honey," Frank told her lamely. "We'll beat it—Lana?"

"Yes," she replied, but it was so desolate a response that he felt it in his gut and was left too with that desolate feeling that only a telephone can give in its awful illusion of nearness shattered by the reality of being so far apart, the feeling that teased you into thinking you could do something against the cold reality of knowing you could do nothing. In his pain he selfishly wished that she hadn't called.

When he went back to his bunk he couldn't sleep. The thought of her thousands of miles away in the wind-blown loneliness of Dutch Harbor, a speck in the vast darkness of the world, brought tears to his eyes, and with them the animal urge to be with her, to feel her warmth, to give her his, to be in her, to possess her so that he tossed and turned, nothing but the low moan of a channel storm blowing about the eaves of the Quonset hut for company and the gray dawn creeping.

CHAPTER TWENTY

AUSSIE LEWIS DIDN'T think the day would ever come when he'd be happy to see a Siberian, but now in the gathering purple dusk the presence of other Caucasian faces, no doubt Siberian advisers and the like, afforded Brentwood's group added protection as they lost themselves in the crowds milling about the temple. Long shafts of golden moonlight shone through the pillars, the beams getting thinner and thinner as the moon passed in a golden wafer through cloud.

At the entrance to the temple several pilgrims were prostrate, while in the temple itself others moved so silently that all that could be heard was the wind sweeping down from the Hentiyn Nuruu, the shuffle of feet, and the soft whir of prayer wheels whose spokes, containing the little paper messages that the Buddhists believed would find their way to Heaven, spun about like small merry-go-rounds. The notorious Mongolian cold was already seeping up from the ground like dry ice, the change dramatic and particularly uncomfortable for Salvini, who had worked up a sweat during the long hike dressed in his *del*. The only firearm he, like the others, carried into the city was his 9mm Browning, and it was irritating his skin beneath the silk-lined tunic.

Soon the official presidential party arrived, the president's entrance to the holy place as low-key as they'd been briefed it would be. Now everything depended on Jenghiz handing the president Freeman's sealed note, the same size as those that were inserted in the prayer wheels, requesting free passage for the American troops in the hostilities against China. If anything went awry, David Brentwood knew that even with the 9mms hidden under their *dels* it would be "dicey," as Aussie was wont to say.

As Jenghiz, in a silent, respectful attitude of prayer, made his way closer to the president, the latter, acting as yet another pilgrim with no special prestige within the temple, bowed his head to the Buddha in respect. One of the bodyguards cast an eye over the crowd in the darkened temple, its candlelight casting huge, flickering shadows on the monastery's temple walls. The four SAS men moved into the throng of worshippers, trying to form a rough protective semicircle around Jenghiz as he faced the Buddha. Aussie Lewis said a prayer of his own—that there would be no fighting in the holy place. The Buddhists subscribed to the theory of nonviolence, but he knew the presidential guard wouldn't.

It was then, however, that Aussie felt strangely uncomfortable. Was it that, the Claymore explosion aside, everything had gone so smoothly—too smoothly, almost—that there was an air of unreality about it all, as if they were somehow going through the well-rehearsed motions of a play written by someone else? Perhaps, he thought, it was the relative silence of the monastery itself and the almost ethereal sight of the saffron-robed monks, some with small scarlet skullcaps on their heads, the whole atmosphere added to by the thick aroma of incense in the air. It had been only seconds since Jenghiz had pressed the piece of prayer paper into the president's hand, but now Jenghiz, having said his prayer, was talking to one of the bodyguards.

At the same moment David Brentwood saw a white face near a candle's flame, then caught a glimpse of Spets military fatigues beneath it, and yelled, "Abort!" into the darkness. In that instant Aussie saw Jenghiz's hand shoot out toward him, and Aussie fired through his *del*, an explosion of orange silk, dark in the dim light, filling the air, Jenghiz hit twice, falling dead, and the crowd into which the SAS men turned now surging in panic, all trying to head for the exits.

There were shouts from the Siberians, a burst of jagged red fire over the crowd's heads, but to no avail, the crowd moving even more frantically now, surging through the temple's entrance, passing around the Spets commandos in a dark river of *dels* and fur caps, a roar coming from the street as the panic spread like an instant contagion. Each of the four SAS/D team members was now on his own, separated from each other by the mob and being carried along by it, past the incongruous sight of animals that one moment had been wandering in, grazing peacefully around the square, now in stampede, each SAS/D man knowing that Jenghiz had betrayed them. Each of them had to assume that their insertion point and therefore extraction point was known, realizing they would now have to revert to the emergency extraction plan. The latter called for them to rendezvous sixteen miles southwest of Ulan Bator, just north of Nalayh, the actual EEP, or emergency extraction point, at longitude 107 degrees 16 minutes east, latitude 47 degrees 52 minutes north, in a valley between two mountains, one to the north, seven thousand feet high, the other to the south, five thousand feet.

With each man carrying a hand-held, calculator-size GPS, none of them had any doubt about finding the place; the GPS could get you within fifty feet of a grid reference. The problem was, would they get there alive? And if they got there, would they get there in time? Their "window," or time frame, was thirty hours. It was far too deep in enemy territory for a helo pickup, and so it would have to be a fighter-protected STAR—surface to air recovery—pickup. If they weren't picked up first by the Spets seen at the monastery.

It was only then that Aussie realized that it hadn't been a deer tripping the wire at all. It had been Jenghiz. All he'd needed was a piece of string, the resulting explosion no doubt pinpointing their position, whereas a transmitter would have been boxed in by the boulders. But right then neither Lewis, Salvini, Choir Williams, nor David Brentwood was burning with the rage of betrayal—survival being first and foremost in their minds.

CHAPTER TWENTY-ONE

England

MEILING HADN'T FOUND anything in the briefcase of any interest except a Xeroxed sheet notifying Brenson of a shadow cabinet meeting on the "China question." The problem was, *what* China question? Was it confirmation of one of Beijing's biggest fears: the possibility of a Taiwanese invasion on its east flank while the Americans invaded Manchuria? The PLA, with over four million in arms, counting the reservists, could more than cope with two fronts—could in fact turn them into victory. But its Achilles' heel was what foreign businessmen like Jay La Roche had euphemistically called its "internal distribution system," by which they meant a bad road system—one that was prey to monsoons much more than to enemy action.

In short, the difficulty for Beijing was transporting troops quickly from one part of China to another. Before the cease-fire, the double-decker road-rail bridge across the three-mile-wide Yangtze at Nanking had been hit by some of Freeman's commandos—SEALs—and the result was a catastrophic bottleneck on the southern shore of the Yangtze that had extended as far south as Wuhan. It had been the biggest single factor forcing Cheng to sue for a cease-fire.

Now the bridge was repaired and the waters about it thoroughly mined, patrolled by Chinese frogmen, the bridge itself ringed by a thicket of AA missile batteries and by two squadrons of Soviet-built MiG-29 Fulcrums. But this kind of protection could not extend to all of the convoy's rail links, and, taking heart from the resumption of the hostilities between the American U.N. line and China, the underground Democracy Movement was increasing its sabotage.

Cheng needed to know how deep they had infiltrated the party structure and what else they were planning to sabotage should the opportunity present itself. It was particularly important that his agent in London find out what it was about the China theater of operations that was preoccupying the British political parties. Oh of course, he told his comrades, it would most probably be an air attack if the British were involved—a European overflight perhaps, which would mean the attack would come from the west. But where along the thousands of miles to the west? Or perhaps it was to be a flight further north to sever the Trans-Siberian that forked off at Ulan Ude to become the Trans-Mongolian—to bomb it, hoping to thwart any Siberian assistance from the north. But railways were notoriously difficult to keep out of action for long by air attacks. Fake rails and quick mending by ground crew could make it a losing proposition for the enemy.

It might, of course, be an air attack on the missile complex at Turpan, but Cheng had to be sure. If he had to move fighters west, away from the east coast, this would weaken his coastal defenses. Once again he was struck by the fact that you could have all the SATRECON reports, have all the experts and all the computer enhancements you liked, but there were times when there was no substitute for a beautiful woman who was prepared to go to bed with the enemy, especially the ones like Lin Meiling who enjoyed it. She pretended, of course, that she was not promiscuous, and this only made the men more anxious to conquer her. Cheng sent a message to London that Meiling was to find out precisely what the Chinese question was, and to this end she must do whatever was necessary.

This time as Brenson was having a shower, Meiling drew the translucent shower curtain aside. Brenson's naked body was steaming, filling the bathroom with a dense fog. "Are you finished?" she said slowly, disappointedly. "Already?"

"I'm in a hurry," he replied, grinning, flicking the towel behind him, ready to dry his back.

"You sure you're clean?" she asked him cheekily. She had the cake of soap in her hands and caressed it and squeezed it, producing a ring of suds around her forefinger and thumb. "You need someone to wash you," she said, smiling. Demurely she got into the tub and, pushing herself into him, began massaging his buttocks, kissing his chest, sucking on him before her soapy hands slid between his buttocks, pulling him even closer against her damp, scarlet lace panties.

"Undo me," she whispered, and in a second the scarlet

bra fell to the side of the tub, her breasts rising, pressing—lunging forward.

"Aren't you going to turn the water on?" she inquired.

"What—oh—yes, of course. Oh, Meiling, you don't know how much—"

"Shh—" she whispered, and now a gossamer spray of warm water cascaded over them, washing away the soap as, one arm about her, Brenson slid down, licked her, and with the other arm pulled the suction rubber mat down from the side of the bath. "Don't want to break our necks," he said.

"Or something else," she giggled.

"Oh Lord—Meiling—"

Suddenly she stepped out of the tub, jerked the long fluffy towel off the bar, and wrapped it about her, prancing out to the living room, her panties still about her thighs where he'd pulled them down in eager anticipation. "What the hell are you doing?"

"Teasing," she shot back, giggling, pulling her panties up so high they seemed to be cutting into her.

"Why—you little slut," he yelled boyishly. "Wait till I get you."

"Have to catch me first!" She was glad to see him fully aroused. At his most vulnerable she would ask him. . . .

There was no time—he took her hard and fast and rolled off her, satiated and silent.

CHAPTER TWENTY-TWO

WHEN THE CIS—Commonwealth of Independent States, or what used to be the Soviet Union—was desperately short of cash in 1990, it sold a twenty-four-plane squadron of Mikoyan Gurevich MiG-29 Fulcrum jet fighters to the German Luftwaffe. The Germans, Americans, and others had seen the highly rated Soviet counterair fighter performing at air shows with its computer-controlled maneuvering flaps and the canton lever structure of its twin-finned tail unit demonstrating its agility.

But until now the West had never had a Fulcrum really to put through its paces, and all of the experts knew that airshow flying was one thing, air combat something else. The Fulcrum had demonstrated its ability, for example, to go into a tail-slide climb, a characteristic underscored in the hammerhead stall/tail-slide maneuver the aircraft was able to accomplish at a relatively low altitude of 2,500–3,000 feet, losing itself on radar in the near-vertical hover position.

But how dazzling would it be when put through the tight, gut-wrenching maneuvers dictated by a dogfight against, say, an F-14 Tomcat? The first up-close inspection of the Fulcrum by western experts didn't look that promising. The German engineers sent from Messerschmitt kicked the tires and felt the plane's skin and were frankly disdainful. One of them from Frankfurt contemptuously called the skin "Rice Krispies," the plane's bumpy surface, compared with the smooth surfaces produced for the American fighters, being the result of inferior rolling of the metal.

Then the Luftwaffe pilots took the Fulcrum up and were ecstatic. Some claimed the MiG-29 was the best fighter ever built. At Mach 2.3, or 1,520 miles per hour, the plane, which could pull eleven G's as opposed to an American nine, was a relatively small fighter. It was only 37 feet 4½ inches from wingtip to wingtip, and 57 feet long, as opposed to the American Tomcat's 64 feet 1½ inch width and length of 62 feet. The plane's box intake engines pushed the Fulcrum faster not only than the Tomcat but also the F-16 Falcon and F-18 Hornet, and it had a faster rate of climb than the Hornet. Only the F-15 Eagle could match its speed, but even then the Fulcrum was so good in its double S turns, loops, its flip-up midflight attack, and its spectacular dives on afterburner— its pilot equipped with an amazingly simple and cheap infrared "look-shoot" system—that the Luftwaffe quickly incorporated the Fulcrum squadron into its air force. And then the habitually skeptical engineers made the most intriguing discovery of all—namely that the inferior bumpy skin afforded the aircraft substantially more lift than the smoother, better-milled skin of its Allied counterparts.

Its two serious weaknesses were a comparatively small fuel capacity, giving it a maximum in-air time of only two hours without external tanks, which would have made it heavier, and, like all CIS-made fighters, it had been built to be directed by ground control and could take only one target on at a time. If ground control went out then the Fulcrum was effectively out, as opposed to the Allied pilots who fought largely independently of ground control. This factor notwithstanding, the speed and sheer agility of the Fulcrum made it a superb aircraft, and China, through the timely purchases of General Cheng, congratulated itself on gaining fifty of the aircraft from the CIS, all fifty planes stationed on airfields throughout the populous eastern half of the country.

One of the Siberian instructors who had come to China

with the fifty aircraft was Sergei Marchenko, the renowned air ace who had downed over seventeen U.S. fighters, among them Frank Shirer's F-14 Tomcat. Shirer had returned the compliment over Korea, but like him, Marchenko had managed to bail out to live and fight another day.

Shirer doubted he would ever get the chance to go up against Marchenko again. Even the talk of him possibly being given a try on the Harrier in Britain was no real consolation. Oh, the Harrier was a fighter, all right, but with a maximum speed of only 607 miles per hour, .5 Mach—not much faster than some commercial airliners—it was hardly a promotion to top-of-the-line. If flying B-52s was like driving a bus after the thrill of a BMW, then a Harrier was like getting a station wagon to drive after having handled a formula one racer. It would be a step up of sorts from the bombers, perhaps, but the Harrier was so damn slow compared to the Tomcat. And besides, he knew he was being asked only because of the shortage of Harrier pilots, most of them having graduated upward to the Falcons and Hornets.

Sergei Marchenko's reputation in Siberia as the *Ubiytsa yanki*—"Yankee Killer"—ace came with him, though in Beijing he was called the cat man, the man of many lives. Whatever he was called he was held in awe, for despite the fact that he was a long-nose—a Caucasian—the Chinese pilots knew they had a lot to learn from his experience. And even if he was aloof and sometimes distant toward his PLA hosts, his ability to take the Fulcrum into a hammerhead stall/slide—to go into a near vertical climb, reduce the thrust of the twin 18,300-pound augmented bypass turbojets, and then let the plane slide earthward, all under 2,600 feet—was legendary. And when the Chinese saw how this maneuver could play havoc with enemy radar—which because of the lack of relative speed momentarily lost the Fulcrum from its screen—Marchenko's skill was greeted with gasps of admiration.

Politically speaking, Marchenko, a Russian, son of the one-time STAVKA, or High Command, member Kiril Marchenko in Moscow, had no particularly strong beliefs one way or the other about the Chinese, the Siberians—or the Americans for that matter. But he was a Russian, proud of it, and, like Shirer, all he cared about was flying. If this involved killing Americans, so be it. All he wanted to do was to maintain his reputation as the top ace, and he was somewhat chagrined by the fact that unless the Americans crossed the Manchurian border in significant numbers of aircraft, it didn't seem as if he'd be doing any more than training Chinese pilots as part of the fifty-plane deal.

CHAPTER TWENTY-THREE

THE FACT THAT their journey to Ulan Bator had been on one of the nights of the *baraany zah*—the weekly three-day open-air market—meant it had been easier for the SAS/D four to escape the indeterminate boundaries of the flat city where the round, pointed-roofed, canvas-and-felt tent houses, or *ghers*, inhabited by the Mongolian herdsmen, stood next to modern buildings, the culture of the plains meeting, but not yet quite intermingling with, that of the city.

As Aussie Lewis quickly made his way past the new Mongolian stock exchange building on Sukhbaatar Square, he saw there were not as many Mongolian regulars roaring by in trucks as there were Siberians. It was stark enough evidence of Freeman's view that the Mongolians were caught in a squeeze between the Han Chinese to the south, whom they detested, and the Siberians, whom they were more fond of but not friendly enough toward to want to be dragged into a war by proxy because of them.

Even so, the political views of the soldiers hunting you, Aussie knew, didn't make any difference. A bullet from a Siberian AK-74 could kill you as easily as a bullet from the older Mongolian AK-47. His adrenaline up, Lewis didn't notice the cold until he was well beyond the city's limits, the khaki color of his blue-silk-lined *del* making him invisible against the dark foothills of the Hentiyn Nuruu.

By avoiding the main roads, such as they were, one leading south to Saynshand and China and the other east to Choybalsan, Lewis followed the course of the Tuul River for a few miles south, then headed due east, figuring that by skirting the base of the six-thousand-foot mountain he could be at the rendezvous point between it and the higher mountain to the north within the thirty-hour deadline.

All his senses were heightened, more intense, and he could smell the sweet spring grass and feel the cold that was now invading the warm wrap of the *del* and, as it had done with Salvini, was turning his perspiration to ice. He slowed the pace and got his second wind. He heard a truck coming in his direction about a mile behind him on the rolling grassland of the foothills, much of them still crusted here and there with patches of snow.

Often drivers on the steppes didn't bother about a road as such, the land being so amenable to vehicular traffic, even in the stonier southern regions of the Gobi, that a driver, providing he had a good compass and/or good sense of direction, could easily make his own road. In doing so, he scarred the topsoil for decades. The earth was so porous, the hold of the grass so tenuous, that once driven over it took decades to heal.

The truck, its headlights two dim orange blobs, was off to his left, following the course of the river, probably heading for some *gher* settlement of a few nomadic herder families. Often herders were told when and where to move to better pastures by the party, whether they liked it or not. Suddenly something moved in front of him. His hand dove for the 9mm but in a vibrant moonlight he saw it was a tarbagan, a marmotlike animal, scuttling down toward the river. It was then he heard the faint but distinctive *wokka-wokka* of a helo coming eastward from the city.

He scanned the sky for any sign of a chopper's searchlights, but in the cloudless black velvet sky of Mongolia, where stars were so clear that they seemed to spangle just above his head, he could see nothing.

He heard the helicopter sound die away and felt reassured by the fact that the SAS/D's greatest weapon was that they were moving south from the city to escape, before turning east. It was the exact opposite of the direction someone heading out of the city would take if he wanted to head back toward the Hentiyn Nuruu, closer to the Siberian-Mongolian border. All logic would tell the Spets to head north, into the mountains, to where the SAS/D had been inserted, and not to head south, *away* from the Siberian-Mongolian border.

There was only one hitch, however, to the fallback extraction point east of the city: Jenghiz had been given it, too. After he'd handed the message "prayer" to the president, had he betrayed the extraction point, or had he only had time to say a few words as he'd fingered Aussie Lewis and the other three SAS/D troopers before Aussie had shot him dead?

If Aussie was a betting man, and he indubitably was, then he would say Jenghiz hadn't had a chance to say anything else. But the thing that made gambling gambling was that you could never be sure. The outside chance was always lying in wait for you. Would the Spets be waiting? If Jenghiz had talked, though Aussie would still bet dollars to donuts that he hadn't, Aussie, Salvini, Brentwood, and Choir Williams would be hurrying into a trap—which might explain the present lack of local activity. The Spets wouldn't want to give their hand away. On the other hand, there might be no local activity because Jenghiz hadn't a chance to say much else.

In Ulan Bator the president was still badly shaken. This "business at the temple," he nervously joked with his advisers, "is what becomes of converting from the party to Buddhism. You go to the temples and you get killed." They all laughed at the irony of their chief, who, like so many others in the Communist world, had suddenly become a religious convert after *perestroika* and *glasnost*. On a more serious note, the aides pointed out that if the SAS/D men had wanted to kill him, he would have been dead. "They shot the man Jenghiz because he betrayed them, Mr. President."

"Yes," the president conceded. "You are right, comrade. I was not the target."

"Have you shown the Siberians your request from the American general?"

"No."

The aides understood the president's wisdom in this. If they gave it to Marshal Yesov's HQ, the Siberians would want to move even more Siberian divisions into Mongolia.

"But we have to give Novosibirsk something," another aide put in. "There were Spets in the temple. They saw the guide hand you the prayer strip. You cannot tell them it contained nothing. They won't believe you, and their suspicion could do more damage to us than—"

"Yes, yes, you're quite right, comrade," the president agreed at once, full of gratitude, more than he could explain, for the comfort and attendance of his friends after the fright he'd got in the temple. He asked the aide to look at the paper again, at the American general's request for free passage of American troops across eastern Mongolia should it become necessary. The American general had clearly meant the message to be seen only by the president. But the guide Jenghiz had added something else. At the end of the prayer there was another sentence: "Save my family" followed by seven numbers.

"What are these?" the president asked his aide.

"Coordinates, I believe, Mr. President. Map references."

The president had a moment of inspiration. "Should we give these to Novosibirsk? Tell them it was an assassination party against me and this is the enemy's escape plan?"

The aides nodded. They liked the idea. There was a danger of course that if captured, the SAS/D men would be tortured and confess Freeman's request, but the chief aide said that this was highly unlikely now that the SAS/D and Spets group were on the lookout for one another. There would be no prisoners if they met.

"Yes," the president said, brightening with the prospect. "Yes. Give the Siberians the coordinates. Let them think the SAS was on an assassination mission. Tell them the bullet was meant for me instead. Whether they believe it or not, they'll settle for an SAS/D troop. Yesov can do what he likes with them."

The aide tore off the coordinates and gave them to a messenger. "Have these radioed to Novosibirsk. Immediate."

Novosibirsk bounced the encoded signal off satellite, and within minutes the Spets squad was enplaning a Kamov Helix-B chopper armed with a four-barrel rotary 7.62mm gun behind a starboard articulated door and an array of antitank Spiral radio-guided missiles and two 80mm rocket packs on four pylon hard points. The Helix would take them to Nalayh, the extraction point for the SAS/D troop no more than five miles north of Nalayh township's center.

But even with the Helix-B the *praporshnik* and his six-man team knew they'd have to hurry, for the SAS/D was as well trained as they were. They knew that for a member of the SAS to be "badged" with the highly coveted Special Air Services beige beret with its cloth insignia of a blue-winged white dagger on a black shield, the SAS recruit had to go through a grueling regimen with everything from cross-country marches with full packs to the HALO—high altitude, low opening—drop with oxygen mask and full gear.

The SAS/D commando requirement for an "in-house" assault was that a man armed with a submachine gun must be able to burst into an embassy or enemy HQ and mortally wound three opponents using only one magazine from as far away as thirty feet. As with the Spets, no more than three shots were allowed on target, and in SAS close-quarter battle every SAS man, no matter what his previous incarnation—artillery, engineering, catering corps, or infantry—had to be able to achieve "minimum kill," taking out four men from a distance of sixty feet with no more than thirteen rounds of 9mm from his Browning pistol. If he had to go to a second clip he was disqualified.

Only after they'd finished their course in the Black Mountains on the Welsh-English border where the SAS "Sabre" combat groups were trained—eighty men in a squadron—would they be allowed to graduate with the coveted insignia, "Who Dares Wins." The Spets leader had studied the SAS minutely. He knew also of their tremendous esprit de corps, how hard they trained to "beat the clock," for when SAS men were killed in action the regimental tradition called for their names to be carved on the clock at Hereford HQ.

Since 1950, over 270 had died in action—not a lot compared to the casualty list of regular army line units, but for a small, elite unit like the SAS it was heavy enough. And among those had been twenty-one American dead from U.S. Special Forces who had served with and helped train the SAS in "field medicine" and LIT—language immersion techniques.

"Hurry!" the *praporshnik* told his six-man squad.

Aboard a Boeing E-3A Sentry AWAC—airborne warning and control aircraft—the thirty-foot-diameter rotodome picked up the green blip of the Helix-B chopper rising from the vicinity of Ulan Bator, and given that this was during the time slot allocated for the SAS/D mission into Ulan Bator, the AWAC crew automatically notified Freeman's HQ of its presence. But there was nothing more that Freeman, who'd retired for the night, or Colonel Norton, who'd received the "in-trouble" burst transmission from the SAS/D group, could do at this juncture. The drill was straightforward. If something had gone wrong, the radio burst transmission from the SAS/D troop would indicate this and they would have to rendezvous at the backup position near Nalayh. An MC-130 Combat Talon aircraft with fighter cover would be dispatched for a quick STAR extraction.

Such an extraction, Norton knew, as did everyone else who'd tried it, was highly dangerous. But first the SAS/D team had to reach the emergency extraction point. Norton, wish though he might, could do nothing. They were on their own.

Unfortunately this wasn't Norton's only worry. Even if the SAS/D team had got the message through to the Mongolian president, any American drive south in the coming days would be in high jeopardy so long as the Chinese could use their IMF missiles, which Israeli intelligence had confirmed were in the Turpan depression in western Sinkiang. Meanwhile all Norton could do was tell Second Army's logistics officers in the U.S.-held Siberian zone to get ready with as much matériel as was needed at railheads south of Ulan Ude and Chita, which would be the main supply hubs for any southward drive of Freeman's.

Meanwhile SATRECON showed the Chinese still massing troops on the border between their Inner Mongolia and Mongolia proper as if rushing to form a reverse-seven defense. Troops on the top of the reverse seven—in its northern sector—protected the Manchurian-Siberian border along the Black Dragon, or Amur, those units constituting the vertical section of the reverse seven forming the PLA's left flank.

Norton could only hope that the new whiz kid, General Jorgenson, a brilliant forty-five-year-old flown out from the States to take over as chief logistics officer after the previous one had died in the action around Poyarkovo, knew what he was doing. Jorgenson had been selected because of his experience in the Iraqi War. Even so, Norton knew that, given the distances and varied terrain here, it would take more than logistical brilliance to sustain an American counterattack either to the south or against the Chinese northern or left flank.

While General Cheng was taking care not to move his troops before the chaotic small-arms mess was sorted out at the front, he had used the time to bring up ten companies of self-propelled 122mm howitzers mounted on Soviet-style M-1967 amphibious fighting vehicles, twenty companies of Zil-151 launcher vehicles carrying sixteen 132mm rockets apiece with side-mounted reloads, and three hundred sixteen-tube Zil-157 truck launchers for 140mm rockets, along with three hundred of a PLA favorite—the twelve-tube 107mm rocket launcher. At four hundred pounds, the 107mm unit was heavy enough but sufficiently light that it could be man-handled—that is, pulled by a squad of Chinese infantry or, if they were lucky, by a BM-13 truck or mules as they passed through the Manchurian mountains under cover of strato-nimbus cloud that stretched like a thick, gray ceiling all the way to the Sea of Japan.

Colonel Soong, hero of the A-7 capture—A-7 being a mountain on the Siberian side of the Chinese-Siberian border that he had overrun earlier in the war—was honored to be placed in the breach at Poyarkovo. Cheng knew that Soong was under no illusion about the Americans. It was popular in Beijing to decry them as capitalist degenerates turned soft by a consumer-crazed democracy, and while this might have been true for some of the conscripts at the war's beginning, it no longer held for the soldiers of Freeman's Second Army.

For the most part they had already been blooded from the landings at Rudnaya Pristan on the coast to the battle for Lake Baikal, and their SAS/D troopers were the *jin rui bu dui*—the elite. Had there been more SAS/D troops atop A-7, Soong knew it would have taken another battalion as well as his own to dislodge them. And Soong knew that it was because of his experience with the SAS/D commandos that General Cheng had placed him at Poyarkovo, for the Americans, as the Iraqi War had shown, were prone to using their Special Forces as the tip of the spear. It was a spear Cheng wanted to first blunt then smash.

Nearing the rendezvous point in the valley between the two mountains east of Ulan Bator, Aussie paused to get his bearings with the hand-held Magellan GPS—global positioning system—2000. Using the folds of his *del* to hide even the faint greenish luminescent glow as one hand held the small, fat, cigar-size aerial, the other the GPS, he saw on the computer dial:

> USING BATT POW
> SELECT OP MODE
> QUICK FIX

And within seconds, via the GPS's MGRS, or military grid reference system, he had a readout and knew he was barely a half mile—867.3 yards, to be exact—away from the rendezvous point in the valley between the peaks. Suddenly there was an approaching thudding sound, and he dove to the ground, whipping out the Browning 9mm, swinging it in the direction of the noise, only to see a ghostly apparition as three shaggy wild horses, manes flowing, were momentarily and beautifully silhouetted against the cutout-moon sky above the steppes. They headed down into a depression off to his left.

The thing that struck him was how these wild, semidesert

Przhevalsky horses, as the briefer at Freeman's HQ had described them, had been spooked quickly, either by him or someone else already in place.

He donned the night-vision goggles, which, contrary to public belief, were not easy to wear—indeed they were notorious for giving the men, especially the pilots, who had to use them severe headaches from eyestrain, but at least now they were smaller and easier to carry than earlier models.

Aussie had no sooner put them on than he heard the distant drone of a plane, and above it a higher-toned sound of fighters. Obviously Salvini, Brentwood, and Choir Williams had already reached the rendezvous or perhaps, more accurately, were about to do so, having sent the SOS-AEP—alternate extraction point—burst radio transmission. Whether the AWACs had picked it up before Second Army signaled HQ, Aussie didn't know and didn't care. "You beaut!" was the only whispered comment he allowed himself as he made his way toward the pickup point. Then, dimly at first, he saw two shadowy figures moving about a hundred yards ahead of him. He went to ground, wondering if they'd seen him, and in that moment, for a reason he couldn't explain, he became acutely aware of the sweet smell of the early spring grass sprouting up between the ice crystals of crusty snow.

All his senses were on high alert again, an alert downgraded when he thought one of the figures was Choir Williams. It wasn't a front-on view he had, but it was one of those moments in which you recognize someone you know from the back. Choir had a lazy monkeylike slouch when he was in the head-down position, a slouch that Aussie unmercifully teased him about during maneuvers. Then both figures disappeared beneath a knoll.

Cautiously Aussie made his way forward, 9mm at the ready, toward the knoll. He had gone about thirty yards when his throat was so dry it felt like leather, a manifestation of his almost obsessive fear of being a victim of what the SAS called "blue on blue"—or friendly fire.

"Aussie bastard!"

It was said in a hoarse whisper, and he swung about to see a figure behind him and heard another voice in front. "Where the fuck you going?"

"Shit!" Aussie whispered in a surge of relief, the heavy, pulsating drone of a big plane—he guessed an MC-130 Talon—drawing closer. "You bastards frightened the friggin' life out of me." For a moment he felt the adrenaline draining out of him, a flood of weak-kneed relief passing over him as he gestured skyward with the 9mm. "Am I right? That the cavalry coming?"

"Sure is, boyo," Choir said cheerfully.

"Where's Sal?" Aussie asked.

"Up yonder!" Choir said, pointing to a sharp rise about sixty yards away and fifteen feet above the level grassland. "He's signaling the big bird—penlight code. How come you got lost in the temple?"

"Lost, my arse!" Aussie responded, still keeping his voice low. "I just got out o' there faster than you three."

"Can it!" David ordered. "Let's get ready for the FUST." He meant the highly dangerous but last-ditch STAR, or more correctly Fulton STAR, surface-to-air recovery technique, used only by commandos and SEALs, the pilot of the MC-130 Combat Talon on night vision devices, as were the SAS/D. Aussie of course called it the FUCK technique— the Fulton cock killer!

"We've been waiting for you for hours," Williams teased Aussie.

"What d'ya mean?" Aussie retorted, the drone of the plane making it safe to talk, albeit in low tones.

"Got a truck, boyo," Williams explained, "with a long bloody Ack Ack gun on it. Just drove straight out of the city and you, you poor sod, on your Paddy Malone."

Aussie now realized that it had probably been their truck he'd seen earlier. "And I had to bloody hoof it," Aussie quipped. "You bastards!"

The planes—the Combat Talon and fighter escort—were closer, but now there was another sound. At first it was as if firecrackers were going off, but it rose to a crescendo and the sky lit up, revealing the MC-Talon and fighter escort caught in the glare of a high flare, red tracer lazily crisscrossing the sky, seemingly filling the night with red and white dots.

"To the truck!" David Brentwood yelled, realizing that the attempted FUST rescue was over, the STAR technique dangerous enough when everything was going right. In this melee, it would be impossible.

It was David's quick thinking that saved them, for once they were in the truck, a Zil-151, he ordered them to fire the twin 37mm AA gun at an acute angle skyward, its spitting flame masking it for the Spets or whoever else had reached the pickup point, making it seem as if it were a friendly vehicle, a truck manned by Mongolian regulars perhaps, trying to aid their Siberian friends in trying to deny the SAS/D troop, wherever it was, any possibility of rescue.

Aussie was on the machine gun, Salvini driving, with Brentwood and Choir Williams feeding the 37mm that was spitting out eighty rounds a minute to a height just under ten thousand feet. Aussie's aim was well away from the U.S. aircraft yet in the general direction—enough to fool anyone watching nearby. But his tracer made an F-16 pilot mad enough to peel off and come at them with his 20mm rotary cannon blazing and dropping two of his six five-hundred-pound bombs from two hard points under the wings, the bombs whistling down into the night. Fortunately they were not laser guided, and exploded wide, but their combined shock wave almost knocked the truck over as the Zil jumped, sped up a small hillock, and came rattling down on the other side, the F-16's cannon unzipping the earth in a furious run, churning up clouds of dust behind the truck, dust that was now mingling with the enormous dirt cloud thrown up by the bombs, which in turn obscured the truck from the Spets who were firing with everything they had at the American planes.

"East!" Brentwood yelled to Salvini. "Drive east!"

"I'm *going* fucking east!" Salvini replied, and then the night turned red, the MC-130 exploding, breaking in half, bodies spilling like black toys into the orange balls of flame, the bodies now afire, screams lost to those below in the flickering shadows of the plain.

The Combat Talon was now nothing but falling pieces of burning fuselage after being hit by a Spets ground-to-air conical-nosed SA-16, one of the Soviet Union's most portable surface-to-air missiles. The truck with the SAS/D troop aboard, its lights out, continued to race over the flat grasslands, the Spets now being paid back in full by an F-16 dropping a napalm canister that turned the grassland to a long, bulbous rush of tangerine and black, incinerating four Spets, two of them struggling out from the fringes of the fire but so badly burned that the *praporshnik* drew his 9mm Makarov and shot them. He had no time to waste, for he now suspected that the truck he'd heard, its engine in high whine as it pulled out from the circle of flickering lights from the debris of the downed American plane, might well be carrying the SAS/D troop of which no evidence had yet been found.

By the time he had collected his three remaining men he knew the SAS/D troop must have had at least a fifteen-minute head start. But there was no need to be despondent. In a few hours it would be dawn and you could see the truck's tracks— even if they hid the truck somehow—etched clearly for miles over the hard yet fragile grasslands.

"Like Hansel and Gretel," he told the Spets troop, four of them now, including himself. "We'll just follow their path. Back to the Helix."

"We still have orders to take at least one of them alive?" one of the Spets asked.

"If we can," the *praporshnik* said, but he said it without

any real commitment. They—the Americans—had killed four of his best men, including the radio operator, and destroyed the R-357 KM high-frequency radio set with burst transmission system—the radio nothing more now than twisted and charred metal, its plastic components having melted over it like taffy.

"I say we kill the bastards," one of the other three troopers said.

"Yes," another said, "as slowly as possible."

"We have to get them first," the third member said. He was pointing at what remained of the Helix—a burnt-out shell no doubt caught in the F-16's napalm run, the dead pilot and copilot still strapped in their seats.

"We'll get them!" the *praporshnik* promised. "Whatever it takes."

CHAPTER TWENTY-FOUR

LAND'S END WAS hauntingly beautiful, the sky's saffron ripples spreading forever westward over the Celtic Sea, white streaks of foam from an exhausted storm flung in a golden lace about the ancient pink-brown rocks.

Trevor Brenson, M.P., had a soft spot for Cornwall with its moody air of romance and its legacy of smuggling, of defying the proprieties of the establishment. His ancestors on his mother's side had come from Cornwall, and though he'd been born and raised in London he liked the idea that the genes of Cornish smugglers were in his blood. It didn't stop him from having his own grand plans for taxing the populace when Labour got into power.

Meiling didn't comment on this more obvious hypocrisy of Brenson's. To do so would have upset the mood as Brenson and she walked atop the cliffs, their hair blown roughly by a gusty southerly, the salty air of the sea both invigorating and relaxing at the same time. Turning from the Celtic Sea in the west south toward the Atlantic and the channel, Brenson held her hand with what was for him an uncommon show of affection for his mistress.

"I feel like I'm whole down here," he told her, his gaze fixed on the horizon where there was nothing but sea. Meiling knew what he meant. The closeness of the sea, the enormity of it, gave them at once a feeling of insignificance and yet integration with the whole world, with one another, with all things. And it was then, as in a quiet moment with a friend, that he apologized for not seeing enough of her lately, for coming to her flat burdened with files and cares of the day. What he said next surprised her, because she had thought that when it happened it would be in the quiet exhaustion of having made love, the most unguarded moment of all.

"We've got the Conservatives where we want them," he explained. "They're sucking up to the Americans as usual."

"Oh?" She was careful not to ask why, and looked out to sea, affecting disinterest, listening more out of politeness, her focus fixed on the vista of sea, land, and sky.

"Yes," he continued. "Yanks want to overfly Europe— bomb China. I don't know why London didn't tell Washington to go take a—"

"Is that a petrel?" she asked suddenly, in what she considered a flash of brilliance, even more to convey a profound indifference that only encouraged him.

"What?" he asked. "Oh, yes, I think it's a petrel. Stormy petrel."

"I'm sorry," she said. "I interrupted. What were you saying?"

"Americans want to send bombers to China."

"Which China? Not Taiwan, I hope," she said flippantly.

"No. Of course not. In the far west apparently."

The west—the "far west." She felt her heart racing—it had to be the missile site at Turpan. It was the only target of any real military significance. She took his hand. "It's all right," she said of his apology for not seeing her enough. "You're with me now."

"Yes," he said, and stopped, looking down at her.

"What is it?" she asked.

"I love you," he said.

"I love you," she lied, and kissed him. She would have to keep seeing him after she'd passed the message to the Chinese embassy via the dead drop near Hampton Court. Besides, it occurred to her that if she complained about him not seeing her enough over the next week, she might get the actual target, though she believed she probably knew enough already.

On their way back to London they stopped for tea at Penzance, and when she went to the ladies' room she had the urge to phone but had enough control to stem her excitement, her trade craft quickly reining in her emotional high, reminding her that in a world of beam-fed directional microphones that could pick up a conversation through glass across a street, you were never to use the phone to contact the *te wu*—the resident or head of station. Instead, that night she worked off her nervous energy by letting him try a half-dozen positions before he finally settled on one—rear entry, mounting her like a dog.

"God, I love you," he gasped.

"You too."

CHAPTER TWENTY-FIVE

HAVING SPED EIGHTY miles east across the plain with dawn only two hours away, David Brentwood, Aussie Lewis, Salvini, and Choir Williams knew they would soon have to abandon the truck, for come first light the Spets would be looking for them.

In fact the Spets, whose chopper had been gutted—all but vaporized in one of the F-16's napalm runs—had had to walk back to Nalayh before calling in helicopter gunships, among them a Hokum, and this gave David Brentwood's SAS/D troop more time. But they were still three hundred miles from the northeastern Mongolian-Siberian border, and to be in the truck come daylight would be asking for certain death. The trouble was that, because of the distance from the nearest American chopper base, a helo pickup in time was out of the question, even given the possibility of in-air refueling. The most they could hope for was a drop of heavier weapons and supplies.

In the early hours of dawn, before the pale gray was transformed into cerulean blue, the four SAS/D troopers approached a group of *ghers*, the round felt-and-canvas dwellings of the Mongolian nomad herders a welcome sight. They had deliberately chosen a group of six or seven *ghers* south of where they had abandoned the out-of-gas Zil, assuming that any search party would naturally fan out north of the abandoned truck, which had been heading northeast toward the Mongolian-Siberian border and not south. It was a calculated risk to buy time, for if the Siberians and/or Mongolians who were looking for them came to the *ghers* before any U.S. aircraft could reach them for a drop, it would all be over for the four men.

Apart from the chance of a resupply drop to aid a possible escape, the SAS/D's only confidence lay in what they'd been told about Mongolian herdsmen at Second Army's HQ briefing. For the Mongolian, long used to the vast emptiness and often rocky harshness of the steppe, to refuse a stranger hospitality was to be regarded as a cur—not fit for the company of humans. The problem, as Aussie Lewis reminded the others, was that in every group there was the possibility of a cur, or, as he more colloquially put it, the danger that some "son of a bitch" who'd had a "bad day on the range" might take his frustration out on the strangers rather than on the expensive camel or mare who'd kicked him. Or, if any one of the herdsmen was a good party man, he might saddle up and bring down the wrath of the authorities on the small group of long-noses.

The four men were now half a mile from the *gher*, walking down a ridge, careful to avoid its summit lest they silhouette themselves against the brightening dawn. A gust of wind quickly gathered itself into a spiraling eddy like a miniature tornado and David Brentwood hoped it wasn't an omen, like the first trickle of a grain of earth that starts a smothering avalanche.

He tried to dismiss his fear as unworthy of the SAS/D team, but he remained distinctly uneasy, and as if to confirm his suspicions, spiraling clouds of dust could be seen weaving their way through the knee-high spring grass with surprising speed, lifting the topsoil with them, at times hiding the *ghers* from view. Brentwood hoped he hadn't made a mistake, that soon they would be safe and he could have Salvini send a transmit requesting a drop.

* * *

If Brentwood hadn't made a mistake, Freeman had. Assuming that Cheng's orders for the air conditioners indicated a summer, not a spring, offensive, Freeman had allowed a battalion of lighter, tougher Block 3 M1 tanks with their new gun and modular armor to be given a lower priority on his Sea-Lift resupply convoys, so that the newest and latest tanks were only now leaving the U.S. west coast for the Siberian and Manchurian theaters.

Meanwhile, Freeman knew Cheng would be building up his echelons of tanks, Freeman's G-2 estimating the Chinese T-59 to American M1 ratio at four-to-one. There was no doubt that the M1 was the superior weapons platform, with its see-through smoke and laser range finders, but no matter how good a range finder was against a T-59 and no matter how much better the M1's 120mm cannon was against the T-59's 105mm, the best tank commander in the U.S. Army knew that if you had to kill four tanks against the enemy killing just one of yours just to stay even, you were in deep trouble.

But first the M1s had to come up to strength, which meant the convoys had to get through unmolested. This was considered a cinch—after all, while the Chinese had seventy-five submarines, only two were nuclear. Besides which the U.S. SOSUS—sound surveillance system—underwater microphone network along the U.S. coasts could, it was said, pick up a whale's fart and classify the whale by species, which was a gross exaggeration, but was a measure of the confidence the Pentagon had in the SOSUS. It could certainly classify any ship from a threat library of known prop cavitation sounds in the same way a mechanic could tell the make of a car by its engine sound printout.

CHAPTER TWENTY-SIX

MANHATTAN'S LIGHTS SPREAD out below his penthouse like spangled jewels, Jay La Roche was celebrating his court victory—already drunk on champagne and ordering one of his covey of lawyers to go get some "chicken," by which La Roche meant young boys whom he could play around with later.

Francine, who'd started as a bar girl in La Roche's Il Trovatore and who had been "promoted" to his stable of "fillies," as he called them, wasn't amused. It wasn't that she cared much one way or the other about the kids that La Roche would be having it off with, but she saw his request as a rejection of her that night. She knew that for her it was a love-hate thing with La Roche, but she couldn't help it. The things he made her do sometimes turned her stomach, but for the security his money and position brought her, she figured being humiliated every time they had sex—he'd urinate on her—was a temporary inconvenience. Animal that he was, he was the one man who was untouchable in the city—as in the way his lawyers had beaten the "treason" charge, for example. However cruel he was, and he was, if you were with Jay La Roche you were protected from "out there."

Now Jay, slowing down his drinking, eyes bright from a snort or two of angel dust, was announcing a new plan to the assembled party. He was atop the grand piano, boasting that La Roche Industries was going to go ahead and do what it had intended to do before the "buffoons" from Washington "falsely accused me"—that La Roche Industries wasn't going to be put off going to visit the guys and gals at the front to show La Roche Industries' continued support for the American war effort. There was a lot of yahooing and clapping. Francine noticed a face in the crowd that she'd seen in the newspapers—some politician or other. She remarked on the fact to Jimmy, the barman, who was wrapping a towel around another bottle of champagne.

"What's that senator doing here?" she asked.

"Congressman," Jimmy corrected her, running the bottle along a line of sparkling tulip glasses. "He wants to be seen with Jay. Don't we all."

Francine still didn't get it. Oh, she didn't mind what Jimmy was doing with Jay La Roche, ready to go up and have it off with La Roche whenever La Roche rang for him, but she told Jimmy she didn't know the congressman was gay. He wasn't, and Jimmy was shaking his head at her. Francine was an all right kid but naive as a babe—mostly about herself. More than once, as when Jimmy had to go up to the penthouse when La Roche had pulled a knife from the drawer and cut off her bra, it had taken him half an hour to calm her down before he realized that she sort of liked it. The danger, not knowing the rules, somehow made it more exciting.

"Isn't he running a risk?" Francine said. "What if he's photographed by—"

"Don't worry," Jimmy assured her, his voice all but drowned out by the party. "The congressman won't get his picture in the paper. See that gorilla by the door?"

Francine sipped some champagne. "Yeah."

"Wears size thirteen—D. Specializes in stomping on cameras. Congressman's safe so long as he does what he's told. Votes the way La Roche tells him to and as long as he keeps La Roche's wife stationed up in Alaska."

"He can do that?" Francine asked.

"Jesus Christ, Francine. When you gonna learn La Roche

has these guys' IOUs all over the friggin' place. Remember that guy—'' A hand came out of the crowd and snatched four glasses of champagne without a word.

"And thank you, dear—" Jimmy said. "That congressman who shot himself." Jimmy reminded her. "Hailey— 'bout a year ago?"

"No."

"Hey, Francine. You stoned or what? Anyway this congressman was asked to do La Roche a big favor. Congressman didn't want to do it, so La Roche showed him a few Polaroids of the congressman with a page boy." Jimmy paused, pouring the champagne. "Pretty, too. Anyway, the congressman was caught between a rock and a hard place as they say. Couldn't pull off the favor. Couldn't bear the photos coming out for all his kids in college to see. So bang! Funny thing is, La Roche's papers gave him the front page: 'Tragic Death,' blah, blah, blah!''

Francine wasn't listening. She was anxious to get to the powder room to take another snort. It made it easier to go down on him and lick him behind, which is what he really liked after he got his load off. He was still up on the piano, singing "North to Alaska," the flunky congressman standing in the crowd of flunkies with that fixed "I'm-having-a-great-time-Mr.-La-Roche" stare on their faces. Reelection cost ten million these days, and without La Roche Industries it would be a near impossible run.

Francine saw a TV starlet take off her high heels, now gyrating, shoving pussy at La Roche atop the piano like she was trying to break down a door with it. It made Francine jealous, mad, and smug all at the same time. Jealous because she knew she wasn't the only one he could give security to, and smug because she knew something the others didn't— that Jay La Roche, when he gave you the strap to beat him before he did his thing with you, before he used you like a piece of toilet paper—kept calling out "Lana," the name of his estranged wife. He'd had something beautiful in her and had lost it. The starlet—even if the bitch got to lick him all way round—would be strictly a one-night stand. So long as Lana La Roche, née Brentwood, stayed in that outhouse of a burg, Dutch Harbor up in Alaska, Francine would be first filly in the stable.

Colonel Soong's soldiers weren't taking any chances. It was bad weather all over northern Manchuria—excellent cover from enemy photo reconnaissance, but any unnecessary sound, such as the mules' braying, could travel across the mist-shrouded, snow-patched valleys, and so Soong's men were thrusting their arms down the mules' throats, severing their vocal chords as they continued moving men and equipment and many heavy one-hundred-pound, 81mm mortars up along the east-west ridge lines that ran like an extension eastward of the Genghis Khan wall, much of it, like the Great Wall, still intact.

General Cheng, deciding that whatever happened, the Americans would not use gas, had made a decision that, though small enough in itself, allowed each man to carry extra rounds and rice in place of the cumbersome biological and chemical warfare protective suits.

"How can you be so sure?" Chairman Nie had pressed him. "That the Americans won't use gas?"

"Because the Americans have bourgeois notions of war, comrade," Cheng answered. "No matter that they have tons of VX and Sarin—they've never used the nerve gases. They proved that earlier in Korea, even when the NKA almost pushed them into the sea. They didn't use it in Vietnam or Iraq. They won't use it here."

"But," the commander of the Shenyang armies cut in, "what if they do, General?"

General Cheng's reply was as even as that of a schoolmaster who had been asked a simple mathematical problem. He had thought he had made this clear earlier in the war. "We run away, comrade."

Cheng knew that gas attacks depended much on local conditions, and rather than lose precious time climbing into a suit so heavy that many more pounds of supplies could be carried in its stead—and never mind the cost of the suit—it was better to have the men simply flee the field. Oh, certainly you'd lose some, but the ratio of the PLA to the U.S. Second Army was fifteen-to-one. The PLA could afford to take the risk.

Also orders whether or not to suit up for chemical attack were so dependent on local conditions that a chaos of countermanding orders could affect an entire offensive anywhere along the Black Dragon River. That a major war was in the offing there was no doubt, for as in the great Russian empire of the czar in 1914, once general mobilization was ordered in China, the scale of the call-up was so vast that it became an unstoppable bureaucratic juggernaut that, under its own momentum, all but demanded a clash of armies.

The man who emerged from the first *gher* reminded David Brentwood of Eskimos he'd seen—the same broad-boned, tanned face, clear, almond-shaped eyes, and a smile of teeth white as ice. The man's thick sheepskin *del* reinforced the impression, for the sun was still not fully up and the deep, creeping-up cold of the semidesert had yet to be driven off, nor had the wind whistling down from the Hentiyn Nuruu abated, the air gritty with the dust and infused with the pungent odor of burning camel dung, its smoke escaping from the *gher*'s roof vent, causing Salvini's eyes to water uncontrollably so that he appeared to be weeping.

According to the ancient custom, the Mongolian opened the wooden door of the *gher* and welcomed them into the round canvas-and-felt house. As they'd been briefed at headquarters, the four men were careful not to walk on the door's low board frame but to step over it so as not to bring the *gher* bad luck.

Inside the *gher* it was an island of sheepskin and other hide rugs on the floor, the walls of canvas and felt supported by wooden poles no more than five feet six inches high, spars of wood leading from these to the center where the stove pipe from the stone-based oven met the vent. Again as was customary the four guests were bidden to sit on the westward side, their backs to Nalayh, their faces to the east, the door directly to the right of them, their feet pointing to the stove where camel and cow dung kept smoldering, providing heat not only against the cold but to warm the *arkhi*, an alcoholic drink of fermented mare's milk.

The head man of the *gher*, careful to sit opposite the four SAS/D troopers, waited until all had partaken of the light orange cheese his wife had passed around. This was the best insurance the troopers could have, for by custom once the cheese had been shared there could be no conflict between host and guest. But as Aussie braced himself for another sip of the *arkhi*—a small streak of melted yak butter giving it a taste like sour milk—he was ready to reach for the nine millimeter if anything went wrong.

A wide-eyed child watched him from atop one of the two metal-spring beds, a dark red and Persian blue carpet of silk and wool draped behind the beds on the *gher*'s wall. Adhering to custom once more, David Brentwood, consulting his phrase book, knew he should avoid "disputatious" subjects—politics especially—and wondered how he might confine himself to generalities about the weather and such. At first this had struck him as being as peculiar to the Mongolians until he realized how during his own childhood he, his two brothers—Robert, the oldest, an SSN commander, and Ray—and his sister, Lana, had been told by their father never to talk about politics or religion. It was no different with the Mongolians' headman, he decided, except he knew that *perestroika* and *glasnost* had worked some magic here, too, and that the party was finding it tougher these days to control the herdsmen or what they spoke about.

But whatever the customs Brentwood also knew he didn't

have time to pussyfoot around, and so started with the weather, using it to come at the main point from an oblique angle. What he wanted to know was whether they could seek shelter here from the sun till nightfall.

Whether it was the heat from the vodka-spiced *arkhi* or from the stove itself, the cold was being driven off, and he felt sweaty about the neck as he finished his question, trusting he had used the correct Mongolian phrase. The headman smiled and, pointing to himself, said, "Little English, me."

"Struth!" Aussie said. "That's good news, mate."

" 'Struth'!" The headman didn't understand, but he knew what David Brentwood meant about "bad weather."

"Not to be moving—" the old man said, "in bad weather."

"Right, mate!" Aussie put in, relieved. "No bloody good at all."

"Shut up, Aussie!" David said in an intentionally stern tone. "We're not out of the woods yet."

"No friggin' woods here, mate," Aussie said, then saw the child. "Sorry."

The painfully slow conversation between David and the headman was really not necessary, however, for the Mongolian had understood the moment he had seen them come in from the plain that they were on the run from authority. It was all he had needed.

"You rest," he told them.

"We'll move tonight," David Brentwood promised.

The old man nodded, his hand pointing to the sheepskin rugs on the bed as he talked to his wife.

"Just till tonight," David promised again. David took a chance and gestured back toward Nalayh. "Communists." He knew enough already to know that the herdsmen didn't like the Communists—they told the herdsmen where to go and when, striking at the very heart of the nomad's life: his freedom to move when and where he wanted.

CHAPTER TWENTY-SEVEN

IN NEW YORK, Alex Miro, a tall, thin man, pulled up the fur-lined collar of his brown suede topcoat as he made his way past the Plaza Hotel toward the Columbus Circle entrance on Central Park's southwest corner. He liked the park—it had brought him luck, and he was as convinced of his purpose as he had been on the very first day those years before when, as a bearded young man, his future before him, he had arrived as one of the thousands of Russian minorities allowed to emigrate to America in the heady days following Gorbachev's and then Yeltsin's *perestroika*.

The reception committee in those days consisted mostly of older emigrés who had managed to flee the Soviet Union before Gorbachev, and Alex could still recall the day when, as one of about thirty new arrivals, he had been taken on a tour of the city by one of these older emigrés. The group had paused for a moment across from the Plaza near the horse-drawn cabriolets.

The wealth of the people entering and leaving the famous hotel overwhelmed the new arrivals almost as much as their first sight of a supermarket. One babushka, from the Ukraine, had kept clicking her tongue and shaking her head beneath the black head scarf at the sight of such opulence. After going north on Fifth Avenue, seeing the stately stone townhouses on the East Side and being told by the guide that only one family lived in each house, Alex had seen the woman's disbelief, her tongue clicking again as she gazed at the stately buildings, her husband, however, skeptically informing several of the group that the guide was as bad as the old *Pravda*—"*lozh*"—"all lies." It was probably just a Potemkin "village," he said—made exclusively to impress visitors just as the fake Potemkin village had been for the czarina—why, any fool could see there was enough room for six families in any one of the townhouses.

One of the emigrés asked the guide to take them to Harlem—*insisted* they see Harlem, the place of the *gigantskie basketbolisty*. Alex's beard was so full in those days it had hidden the tight-lipped grimace of satisfaction he'd allowed himself on seeing that what the party had said was true— here was the grinding poverty, the rampant disorder, the half-naked black children, the awful, discordant noise of democracy, the look of hatred and despair in the eyes of the blacks who stared resentfully at the bus of tourists like caged animals, the putrid smell of garbage overpowering.

It was still so vivid in his mind, particularly the loss of dignity he had seen in these faces—a poverty that was horrible to Nikolai Ryzhkov, Ryzhkov being his Russian name before he had taken the oath of allegiance to his newly adopted country and changed Ryzhkov to Miro. It was the lack of dignity in the blacks' eyes that struck him as being more crushing than any he had known in his youth in Russia. For there, though people had been poorer in material things than their American counterparts, there hadn't been the burning rage and spiritual deprivation that he saw in these faces.

The memory of this, his first experience of the vast disparity in wealth between rich and poor in America, not only stayed with him but all his life had acted as a spur to his single-minded goal, the memory of Harlem as troubling and as clearly etched on his mind as was that of the immigrants' first visit to Central Park. There, in the green, ordered world that accepted everybody, it had been completely different, surely what the great Abraham Lincoln had in his mind—a place that did not depend on whom you knew, on special party shops accessible only to the powerful, but was a refuge for the common people. He hated the zoo, though—hating anything being put in a cage—anything that was hemmed in.

As a boy he had loved the Moscow Circus, which he had seen illegally, sneaking beneath the tent flaps of the traveling troupe when it had visited his town. But when they had brought on the bears, the huge, muzzled beasts reduced to playing big babies for the amusement of rude peasants like his father, Alex had felt immeasurably sad—not only for the bears but for those like his father whose sensitivities had been so brutalized by poverty in old Russia, in Siberia to be exact, that they could find the sight of the leashed bears only amusing.

As Alex had grown older, he learned that to liberate such people from such brutality no effective appeal could be made to sensibilities deadened by the constant crush of circumstance. Throughout history, he was convinced, there had been only one way. One had to *fight* indifference and prejudice, as Lenin had said, not submit to it. But Gorbachev had warned that you would get no thanks for trying to improve the lot of the people—those in chains did not always thank those who set them free. Look at what had happened to Gorbachev himself, and how vividly Alex remembered the Muscovites demonstrating in Red Square, telling the American announcer Mike Wallace, who was doing his open-mouthed "surprise" act, that they'd had enough of *perestroika*, of *glasnost*—of how they pined for the order, the comfort of predictability that Stalin's postwar years had given them.

"I'd like to take the muzzle off that bear," young Alex had confessed to his father at the circus. "*Osvobodit*—set him free."

"Ha!" his father had laughed, "you are the first he'd kill—bite your head off." But if that's what his father had said, Lenin had told every younger generation, *"Bud'smel.*

Bud'terpeliv''—Be brave. Be patient—yes, the party had made serious mistakes, but at heart the party was still right.

Lenin was gone now, reviled by some as some atheists reviled Christ, but Alex had not deserted the party, nor had the other members of his "sleeper" cell, as firm as ever in their conviction that capitalism was at heart evil—that its enemies were their friends.

This wintry afternoon, Alex's returning again to the park seemed propitious. Presently he was joined by a short, stout man, Mike Ricardo. Parks had always been a favorite meeting place for the Soviets, and still were in what was now the Commonwealth of Independent States, or CIS. Last time they met they had set Operation Kirov's Ballet in action, knocking out Con Ed's Indian Point plant, poisoning the city's water supply at Hillsview Reservoir with one Thermos of PCBs, and taking out the cesium clock in Hillsboro, Wisconsin, the pacemaker clock for all the computers in the country, including the Pentagon's.

"What d'you think?" Mike asked, walking up, helping himself to a chestnut from the packet Alex was holding, tossing the nut from hand to hand, blowing on it, his breath short, coming in sharp puffs of mist in the chilly air. "You think the Chinese'll cross?"

"They always have."

"Yeah, I know, but I mean all along the line?"

"Who knows?" Alex replied. "I can't even figure out how they do embroidery."

"Embroidery?"

"Double-sided stuff. They'll do a picture on a silk screen. You swing it around—same picture on the other side but no knots, stitch marks, or loose thread. Beats me where they hide the ends. Must go blind."

"Time," Mike explained, peeling the chestnut, its steaming wisp in the air joining that of his own breath. "Chinks are in no hurry, Alex. They're building up their strength."

"Chinese can't wait forever or Freeman might cross the line."

Mike rolled up the *Post* he'd been carrying and stuck it under his arm, hands thrust deep in his topcoat pockets. "What's in it for us?"

"Novosibirsk wants us to give Beijing as much help as we can. Beijing can't start sending their operatives into New York. 'Frisco maybe but not here. So we do our job and turn this thing around we'll be on top. Chinks'll make a deal with us on the disputed border areas along the Amur."

"The Black Dragon," Mike said.

"The Amur," Alex said. "Anyway, this way Novosibirsk stays out of it—ostensibly—but if we do our job, shut things down here, hit Con Ed again, slow up the sea lift resupply, sow panic in the population, we'll have Beijing's IOU."

Mike took one of the chestnuts from the bag, noticed it was too sooty, pulled out another, and saw a squirrel keeping pace with them in short, quick dashes by the snow-dusted path leading down past the puppet house toward the dairy.

"Son of a bitch is with the CIA." He threw the husk at the squirrel. "You sure we'll pull it off?"

"Look, we did Con Ed okay," Alex reminded him tartly. "If we do this thing right—Christ knows we've been training for it long enough—Washington'll shit its pants. Americans don't have the stomach for it. You know that."

"We Americans are tougher than you think," Mike said.

Alex didn't like the "we" but figured it was probably a good sign. Mike always got right into the part. Mike pointed out that some of the others, though neither he nor Alex met them very often, had gone a bit soft—not on the strategy, but they'd been waiting so long they'd started going to seed. "Donut guts!" Alex called them. They liked the blue-collar affluence they enjoyed—plumbers eighty bucks an hour! But if they'd gone soft it didn't mean they'd gone over. Anyway, most still had at least one parent back in the CIS republics, and grandparents, even brothers and sisters—whatever Siberian Intelligence's KGB Chief Chernko had decided he needed to keep everyone committed to the *semya*—family.

One of them had gone off the rails completely—started playing around with street women, spending most of his time screwing and spending. Paid out more at the track than he made on his job as subcontractor for New York Port Authority's HERT, the harbor emergency response team. They'd found him, a floater, in the East River off the South Street Seaport, blood alcohol count of 1.6 and his testicles sewn in his mouth.

The *Post* had run a story that the man, a diver for HERT, had been humping one of the mob's tarts. It had shaken everybody up except Alex, who, Mike thought, might have done it. The thing was, you never knew who was Chernko's iceman in New York or anywhere else. Before the war, the *rezidents* in the U.N., UNICEF, or in the embassy in Washington would have handled it. Now you never knew who it was. Alex said it didn't matter who whacked the big spender, that the Americans would do the same to any one of their people who started screwing anything in sight. You couldn't afford the risk of who they'd blab to when they'd gone that far off the rails.

"Oh yeah?" Mike said in an accent as flawlessly American as Alex's. "What about Kennedy? He screwed anything in a skirt."

"And they whacked him," Alex said.

Mike got the message, though he'd never bought the idea of a conspiracy theory—some big organizational plan to get Kennedy—even though he did think for one man to get away three shots at a moving target in a few seconds was tough to do. He, Alex, and every other "apprentice" at Spets training school in Novosibirsk had tried it. Alex had been the fastest and most accurate, blowing Kennedy's head off three times in a row. But that wasn't why he'd been chosen as the "foreman," nor had he been chosen because he could do a floater if needed. No—Alex's outstanding quality was his ability to sustain the long view, to bide his time through all the Gorbachev-Yeltsin turbulence and to hold the others to it.

Whoever shot the floater, Alex told Mike, was unimportant. The point was, he couldn't keep his pecker in his pants and he paid for it. "Drew too much attention to himself. Put everybody at risk."

They saw Stefan, a wiry man well over six feet with what the doctors had told him was poor posture—stooped "from ducking doorways," Mike joked. Stefan was a tradesman, too, an electrician from upstate, but he always wore a jacket and tie that made him look like a small businessman. He was standing by the monkey cage watching one of the animals sitting high on the loops, the monkey ignoring them, peering down into his crotch, grooming himself. Alex could smell Stefan's breath as he approached him and tried not to make a face. Here Stefan was, living in the most advanced industrial country on earth, the home of the brave and dental floss, and he wouldn't take care of his teeth. But it was a subject that Alex, for all his hard-nosed Spets training, couldn't bring himself to broach, though he did move around Mike so that he was upwind as they stood either side of Stefan.

"Look at his red ass!" Stefan said.

"Yeah," Mike said. "He's a party monkey."

"How big's the park?" Alex asked flatly, and he wasn't smiling at Mike's little joke. Stefan, immediately sensing Alex was in his usual all-business mood, answered, "Eight hundred and forty-three acres." Then Stefan asked his question. "How many blocks?"

Despite being upwind, Alex had to turn away from Stefan's bad breath before answering. "Fifty-one blocks."

Chernko in Novosibirsk, obsessed by the possibility of infiltration, insisted that every cell go through the formality of such a preset exchange after an American look-alike years ago had penetrated the Walker ring in Vienna on appearance alone.

The formality over, Alex suggested the three of them walk down to the reservoir.

"Christ, if I'd known that," Stefan complained, adjusting the porkpie corduroy hat that made him look strangely elfish despite his height, "I could have met you at Eighty-fourth Street."

"I like to walk," Alex said, and offered Stefan a chestnut—maybe that'd help his breath.

"No thanks—makes my throat itchy. Listen, I know this is *it*, but which one do we take care of? Eeny, meeny, miney, mo?"

"What do you care?" Alex asked, unsmiling. "All you need to know is how to work your end."

"Don't worry about me, Alexi," Stefan said. "Could do it with my eyes closed. Just like to know how many are going down, that's all. We're lucky Johnny Ferrago didn't get to tell them anything." Ferrago had been the foreman of another cell. They'd done their job poisoning the New York water supply earlier in the war, but Ferrago had ended up being taken out in a SWAT team firefight.

Alex quietly stepped to his left on the pathway to let a weaving ghetto blaster with skateboard attached fly through them. Closing the gap, he told Stefan, "All four of 'em," his tone unchanged. "Rush hour's the best time for eeny. Meeny, early morning between two and three. Miney and mo anytime after that. Have you got the rats ready?" he asked Stefan.

"Yeah. Listen, Alex—you sure all four are going down? I mean—man, it's gonna be an asylum."

"Well," Alex said, watching another ghetto blaster approaching, "it wasn't meant to be a tea party, was it?" Not waiting for an answer, he continued. "By the book, remember. None of your families leave. That's the first thing they'll be looking for—a sudden move to another city. All you've gotta do is just follow the instructions to the letter and you'll be okay."

"Alex?" It was Mike, trying not to look as worried as Stefan, but he was bothered, too. It had come as a bit of a shock. They'd been living with a secret for so long that by now they'd stopped worrying about it ever getting out. And now suddenly they were going to do it. Their lives would never be the same—not after a job this big.

They were approaching Bethesda Terrace, the sun already lost to the skyscrapers. "It'd sure help to know there were others in the same boat," Mike said. "I mean, I know—yeah, sure we shouldn't ask."

"No, you shouldn't," Alex said. "Are you nuts? Christ, it's basic. Right, Stefan? Only one of us knows two others—ever. That way we could lose a cell but not the whole group." Alex cupped his hands to warm them against his mouth. "What is it?" he asked them, sensing a sudden reluctance. "You all want to hold hands? Your wives? You going *soft*?" He was looking at both Stefan and Mike. "We've had perfect cover for over fifteen years, and now you're going slack-ass on me? Like Gregory?" Gregory was the floater whom the police had found in the East River. "Too old for it?" Alex pressed. "Is that it? Mommy's boys?"

"Jesus—" Stefan said. "Jesus, Alex. It was—we were only asking."

Alex turned on him. "Well don't. Just do your fucking jobs. Or I can send your request for 'layoff' to Cheerio." "Cheerio" was the name they used for Chernko. "He's got the master list. Knows where everybody lives. We can replace you two quick as I did Gregory. You aren't the only fish in the tank. We've got understudies all the way."

"Okay, Alex," Mike said. "Relax. We're ready to go. No problem."

"Stefan?" Alex snapped.

"Yeah. Fine, no problem."

Alex was so angry with Stefan he was about to tell him to clean his goddamn teeth.

When they reached Bethesda Terrace, where the footpath

they were on, an extension of East 72nd Street, wound westward, a silence reigned over the three as they approached the winged statue fountain, the water falling from the tapered tier in an uninterrupted veil, the air remarkably clean, a small boy kneeling, trying to crack a thin crust of ice at the edge to put in a sailboat. Alex watched him, automatically looking for any sign that the older man reaching down holding the boy's jacket was carrying a parabolic pickup mike, using the kid as cover. Even though he knew Mike was carrying a detector, there was always the possibility that its batteries were on the fritz. But then he realized his sudden anxiety was merely a result of Mike and Stefan asking too many questions.

"This is the last meet," he told them quietly. "After it's done you fade back into the woodwork." He told them, if they hadn't already seen it for themselves, that the ad, like the one for a man in his "early thirties desiring a live-in companion, sexual preference not important, must like cats—no Republicans," which had activated the Ferrago cell earlier in the war, was now appearing in every major newspaper across the United States. It was Chernko's "go" signal for Spets "sleepers," who had so easily infiltrated the U.S. during the KGB's *vershina*—"high summer"—of the West's honeymoon with Yeltsin and the CIS.

Before they parted, they spoke a little longer about incidental family concerns, Alex trying to ease things up a little, showing he understood how they felt, complaining about his kids' dental bills. "Christ—they'll break me," he said, smiling.

"You'd be covered by the Con Ed benefits?" Mike said.

"Yeah but not 'preexisting conditions.' "

"What the hell does that mean?" Mike asked.

Alex shrugged. "Anything they don't want to pay for, I guess."

Stefan nodded toward the boy across the pool. "That kid'll fall in if he's not careful."

"The weather should help us," Alex said. "They say there's a cold front moving down from Canada."

He was half right. There *was* a cold front moving down from Canada, but it was the storm brewing over Virginia and moving up the coast that would help them most of all to shatter American morale.

"Oh shit," Stefan said, and started off around the edge of the pool—the kid with the boat having fallen in and the old man frantically reaching for him.

CHAPTER TWENTY-EIGHT

OVER THREE THOUSAND miles away, on the other side of the world, the old Mongolian herdsman entered his *gher*, reached down toward the four sleeping SAS/D men, first grabbing David Brentwood by the collar, then shaking Choir Williams, Aussie Lewis, and Salvini. Instantly Aussie slipped his hand beneath the *del* for his pistol. The Mongolian stopped him. "Dogs," he said quietly.

"Dogs?" Brentwood asked sleepily. "What do you—"

The old man put his finger to his mouth and motioned to listen. "We tell you dogs. They are—"

"Jesus!" Salvini said, whipping the sheepskin cover off him. "Tracking dogs."

It wasn't yet dark—no way could they risk a daylight trek from the *gher* through the desert.

"How far away?" David asked.

The old man made a circling motion with his hand. "Helos. Minutes."

"Bastards are probably searching every settlement," Aussie said.

"Right," David instructed. "Sal, get on your blower and call in our map reference for a FUST—we've got no choice. We're in too far for our helos to help."

Within a minute Salvini had his whip aerial up through the *gher*'s smoke opening and broke radio silence, giving their position for a FUST.

"Choir," Brentwood instructed. "You go first."

"Ta!" It was an ironic Cockney thank-you.

"Aussie, you and I'll provide covering fire if any Spets show up to intercept. Sal, you stay here. Aussie and I'll fan out outside the *gher* and see whether we can spot them first." Suddenly Brentwood turned to the old man. "How do you know there are helos and dogs coming?"

The old man was astonished that the American didn't know. "Herdsmen," the old man explained—one camel herdsman told another and so on. Then the old man had a stroke of genius for Aussie and Brentwood if they were to make a reconnaissance outside the *gher*. Camels.

Dressed in their *dels* high atop the animals, they would be able to see for miles across the plain toward the mountains, and this way everyone else could stay under cover in the *gher*. Salvini was inside the *gher*, manning the radio. He'd only used a burst message, and hopefully there had not been time for any enemy intercept to backplot him. No sooner had Brentwood and Aussie mounted their respective camels than a bulbous-eyed Hind E passed low overhead, heading further to the northeast, Aussie waving up at them.

"Silly bastard!" Choir called out.

"Gotta play the part, 'aven't we, squire?" Aussie said.

"What are you going to do," Choir asked, "when they come back and let out some dogs sniffing for us? Thanks to that bastard Jenghiz they'll have scent from stuff we handled back at the drop-off.''

"Not to worry, sport," Aussie said flippantly. "The old CT'll be here in a jiff." He meant the Combat Talon aircraft.

But for all of Aussie's patter, they knew it was more bravado than certainty. The "old CT" or MC-130 Combat Talon wouldn't be over them in a jiff, and the best hope they had now was the low-flying F-15 Eagles coming in in fluid four formation, screaming low overhead to avoid radar, the first pair closer together than the second pair, the wingman further apart, all four releasing four packs from their hard points.

As quickly as they had appeared over the Mongolian desert, the Eagles were gone in a screaming U-turn, with the high Hentiyn Nuruu as a backdrop. Only when the Mongolian herdsmen from the *ghers* had retrieved the four drum-size packages and like excited schoolchildren were feeling the silk canopy of the bundles did Brentwood think they might have a chance. Problem was, you didn't even get a chance to practice a FUST it was considered so dangerous—it was only ever used as a last resort. The best they could do in training was to use dummies to show you how it should be done.

"Go check the helium tanks!" Brentwood called out to Choir amid the excited chatter of the Mongolians as they gathered around to see what was inside the cylindrical-shaped helium canisters. One canister was already open, a FUST harness spilling out. Afraid that some of the FUST tackle might get tangled in the herdsmen's excitement, Brentwood asked the old man to call his herdsmen off. It took one command, the headman smacking the butt of his slung rifle for emphasis, and they were gone, leaving only Aussie and Brentwood, still on the camels, as Choir checked the packs.

"Bloody lovely in't it?" Aussie complained. "Bloody lovely. There they are, opening the packs, and I'm stuck up 'ere having my ass reamed out by this bloody great beast while Sal's inside having a cuppa!"

"Looks like you got a bum rap!" Brentwood jousted.

"Oh, very droll. Very fucking amusing I'm sure. Let's see what your ass looks like after—" He stopped as Salvini burst from the *gher* to tell them the fighter-escorted Talon would be there in twenty minutes.

"You beaut!" Aussie said, slapping the camel's rump in his excitement, the animal immediately taking off, throwing Aussie two feet in the air before he came crashing down and saw three specks coming out of the eastern sky: Spets helicopters, one of them probably the one that had previously passed overhead. The enemy helos looked to be losing altitude, coming straight for the *ghers*.

"Only one chance," Aussie said, calling out to Brentwood, who had just spotted the approaching helos.

Within minutes Aussie and Brentwood, devoid of the *dels*, showing only their light SAS/D camouflage drill uniforms, were tied together as the headman waved at the three helos. One helo peeled off, the other two fanning out toward other settlements some miles to the south of Nalayh. As the helo came down, blowing up dust of such intensity it was as if the whole settlement had been momentarily obliterated, Aussie could barely see the black rotor spin of the Hind.

The headman holding on to the rope that was tied to Aussie and Brentwood waved up again at the Spets pilot, who saluted back and who could see several of the other herdsmen now jeering at the two Americans, one of the herdsmen throwing patties of camel dung at the two bound SAS/D men.

As the high whine of the Spets chopper's two 2,200 SHP turboshafts decreased, making a chunky sound in the gritty sand cloud, Aussie could hear the rear door opening where the eight-man assault squad would be soon filing out to take aboard their prisoners and setting loose the dogs. As the door was opened, the head herdsman, in a swift movement that belied his age, shot the pilot point blank with his range rifle, while Brentwood and Aussie, with one pull on the bowline knot that bound them, quickly tossed six stun grenades into the rear cabin. The explosion was loud, yet the sounds of the dogs and men screaming and dying was muffled as if inside a great boiler.

The rotors began to cough to life, but not before the headman had also taken out the copilot, the undernose 12.7mm multibarrel rotary machine gun immobilized by a maneuver that would have done any American rodeo proud, as ropes from two camels, one pulling hard left, the other hard right, prevented it from moving, even if the operator above was still functional enough to try for a traverse. Aussie, David, and Choir went inside the cabin, where four of the Spets were already dead from the concussion, the others in such a state that they fell quickly beneath the enfilade of small-arms fire.

"Bloody waste!" Aussie said, reloading the Parabellum mag, then grabbing a fire extinguisher to put out a small electrical fire that had started up forward. "And a bloody shame none of us can drive one of these friggin' things." It was a singular deficiency that none of them had ever thought much about before. They were men who had been trained to survive in the harshest environments in the world, wherever they were dropped, and it was a matter of no small pride that at least one of them could get by in the local language, but piloting a chopper had not yet been added to the course, and for a moment they all felt less for it. But if that was the case, they would soon have ample opportunity to show what they were made of should the Combat Talon and its fighter escort appear.

Already Salvini had received a burst message that ChiCom fighter units were being scrambled to intercept the incoming American F-15 Eagles. And it was only now that Aussie Lewis and the others realized what an extraordinary sacrifice the Mongolians had made for them and how it answered Freeman's question about whether or not the Mongolians would stand in his way if Freeman drove south. Everything the SAS/D team had seen showed clearly that the Mongolians had no intention of trying to stop the Americans from reaching Mongolia's hated Chinese neighbors.

* * *

For Freeman, however, this might not be that much help after all, for he could not move south with any confidence so long as the missiles in the Turpan depression in western China were still intact. The British Labour party was playing black-mail with the Tories: We'll support an overflight if you will agree to higher capital gains tax. It was a question of who would give in. Meanwhile Frank Shirer was being summoned to the wing commander's hut at Lakenheath. Here a Captain Fowler-Jones, from the British navy air arm, was accompanied and introduced by a Captain Moore of the USAF. Fowler-Jones did most of the talking.

"So you're not satisfied?"

Frank was taken aback—wasn't the British officer corps supposed to be known for its polite reserve?

"Haven't time to waste, old boy," Fowler-Jones pressed. "You're not satisfied flying the big jobs?" Fowler-Jones indicated the nine B-52s on the rain-slick tarmac.

"Well," Shirer began tentatively. "I'd rather be flying Cats."

"He means Tomcats," Captain Moore put in.

"Yes, yes, I know. F-14s. Good plane, but we have all the fighter pilots we need, at least for that caliber weapons platform."

There was a long pause.

"Shot down, weren't you?" Wing Commander Fowler-Jones said bluntly, opening a file and studying it. "Twice."

"Yes, sir."

He looked up at Shirer. "Learn anything?"

Shirer shrugged. "A MiG-29's a lot better than we thought it was. In the stall slide it can—"

"Yes, quite, but your nerves, and I want gospel on this. Up to snuff?"

"Yes, sir—I believe so."

"Believe so? Know so?"

"Know so."

"Well then," Fowler-Jones said to the U.S. captain. "That's that."

"May I ask—" Shirer began.

"Harriers!" Fowler-Jones said. "We're very short of men on Harriers. Vertical takeoff and landing. Old carrier pilots like yourself often get quite good at it in a short time. Short takeoff and landing, that is. You game?"

"Yes—yes, sir."

"You sound hesitant!"

"No, sir, I'm just—"

"Yes, yes, I know. You just expected a top-of-the-line combat fighter. Well I'll tell you this, Shirer, we need good Harrier men right now. Can't go into all the whys and wherefores at this time. Need to know. Follow me?"

"Yes, sir," Shirer lied. The man talked like a telex machine.

"Quite frankly they're the only aircraft in any supply we have left in this theater. Idea is that if this mission to China goes off then we could give Harrier escort. In-flight refueling of course."

The Harrier, Shirer thought. Jesus—it might be better than jockeying the Big Ugly Fat Fellows, but it had always been the ugly duckling of production lines with its funny ferry tips or swivel jet nozzles at the end of each wing that made it look more like an aspiring fighter blighted by dropsy than a revolutionary new aircraft.

"Not the new Harrier Two, mind you," Fowler-Jones explained, to show there was no misunderstanding. "It's the Harrier One. Single-seater job we're offering you people."

"People?"

"Yes," Captain Moore put in. "The idea is to put in a flight or two of Harriers to go in with the B-52s."

"Yes," Fowler-Jones cut in. "Riding shotgun, I believe you chaps call it. If we get the word go, it would mean two Harriers per bomber. As I say, in-flight refueling—in Pakistan before you go over the Hindu Kush to join the big chaps on the raid in. I assume you're in-flight qualified?''

Shirer still hadn't shown the kind of enthusiastic response Fowler-Jones had been looking for, and he snatched up his cap and gloves. ''Well of course if you'd rather not. I just thought that some of you people were itching—''

''No, sir,'' Shirer began. ''I mean yes. I'd be happy to go, sir.''

''Good. Your combat experience—just the thing we need. But you'll have to get used to the Harrier in short order. That's up to you, I'm afraid.''

''Yes, sir. What field?''

''They're squadroned in Peshawar. You'll join them there.''

''Yes, sir.''

With that, Shirer saluted and Fowler-Jones was gone.

''Is it anywhere near Lakenheath?'' Shirer asked Captain Moore.

''What?''

''Peshawar.''

''You're joking! Other side of the world! You heard him— Hindu Kush and all that. Harrier squadron is based in Peshawar. At the moment Pakistan is in bed with Washington and London. You see, this way they don't have to move fighters around where they'd be noticed by the Chinese.''

''Oh? How about moving nine B-52s around? They'd notice that, wouldn't they?''

''Sure would, but we've been flying C-15 relief planes from the military's air transport command during the spring floods, dropping urgent food relief. At least that's one reason why planes have been flying back and forth from London to Pakistan for the last two weeks. So when the B-52s show up on Chinese radar they won't know the difference. That is, until they start turning in toward the Turpan depression. That's when they're going to need you boys.''

"Oh," Shirer said, "and what do you think the Chinese'll do then?"

"Don't worry, pal," Moore cut in. "All their top-of-the-line fighters—Fulcrums especially—are in eastern China. Right now they're trying to bottle up Manchuria and keeping one sharp eye on Taiwan. They can't have their jets all over the place at the same time."

"No, but when the B-52s start crossing that old Hindu Kush or thereabouts, buddy, they'll move a few."

"Sure they will, but by then the mission'll be half over. You guys in the Harriers probably won't see anything more exciting than an avalanche."

"This is all assuming that the Chinese don't figure we're going to hit them."

"Right. Where's your faith in Intelligence? Look how we pulled the wool over old Saddam Insane's eyes."

"Maybe, Captain, but the Chinese aren't the Iraqis. Besides, once bitten, twice shy. Anyway," Shirer continued, "what the hell are British Harriers doing in Pakistan?"

"They aren't British, they're Pakistani. But don't worry. By the time you go up there'll be Old Glory on the tail."

"Jesus," Shirer said, "this is all politics."

"So what's new? All you need to know is you'd better get a handle on the fuckers in case you're going in. Brits'll make the decision yea or nay anytime now."

"Yeah, well I hope the Chinese fall for your relief flight routines."

"Don't worry. They're too busy trying to lock up Manchuria." Then Moore hit him with the bombshell. He'd have ten days from the moment he reached Peshawar to train on the Harrier. To brighten him up, Moore told Shirer that the older single-seater went faster than the newer Harrier Two.

"How fast?" Shirer asked, the veteran of Mach 2.3 Tomcats.

"Around point nine," Moore said.

"Point nine!" Shirer stopped in his tracks.

"Not all the time," Moore assured him. "Sometimes it drops to Mach point eight."

"Jesus Christ! Has it got enough power to take off?"

"Well, it hasn't," Moore said, adopting Shirer's ironic tone. "You see there are these four guys, good runners, one under each wingtip, one under the nose, the other under the—"

"Up your ass!" Shirer said.

"Not if I can help it."

Shirer couldn't help laughing. Well hell, at least he'd be flying again—a lone eagle.

Pulling out the coil of strong ply nylon rope and the tight roll of twenty-three-foot-long polyethylene balloon, Aussie clipped on the first of the Thermos-size pressure tanks and pulled the safety pin, releasing a hiss of helium gas, the balloon inflating in an obscene condom shape until the second tank kicked in and filled the twenty-three-foot-high balloon that now, with its flanged tail also inflated, took on the shape of one of those tethered AA balloons used during the German air attacks over Britain.

Within five minutes the white balloon, trailing its white nylon rope like some gigantic tadpole tail, rose to five hundred feet, the end of the rope trailing earthward, already attached by means of a ring bolt to a wide strip of canvas harness that was now clamped tightly against Salvini's midriff. The Combat Talon's dull rumble could be heard before the sudden scream and sonic boom of the F-15 fighters that were well ahead of the Talon passing over them.

Even though the dust had settled, it was still difficult for Aussie to see the horizontal V that extended from the Talon's nose like a pair of scissors, one blade projecting left, the other right, the idea being that the Talon, using the balloon as a fix above it, would fly its V into the nylon rope like someone extending two index fingers in front of him, snaring the line, which would then jerk the man off the ground as the Talon kept going, winching him up.

Should the Talon miss catching the cable with its nose V, the cable, instead of endangering the props, would slide off the V against a taut protective wire strung from wingtip to the forward fuselage, thus buffeting the balloon rope along the protective wire away from the props. At least that was the theory. It was tough enough to do without interference, but with the knowledge of Siberian MiGs now scrambling aloft to meet the F-15s, everything, as Aussie said while checking Choir's harness, was "a tad tight!" Next Aussie made sure that Choir's chute was firmly attached in front of him and head held up.

"You ready, Mr. Williams?"

"No—Mother of God," Choir replied.

"Ah! You'll be laughin' in a few minutes. Here she comes. Come on, Choir, legs straight out, hands palm down, head up—atta boy."

The rope looked like a thread of curving cotton stretching between him and the four-tailed balloon. There was a line of orange tracer arcing from the east and then two orange streaks: Sidewinders from the F-15s. Aussie could see the slack taken up as the Talon's V snared the line, then suddenly Choir was jerked violently aloft. It was the most dangerous moment, for if the Talon hit a wind shear or lost altitude for any reason, Choir would smash into the ground at over 130 m.p.h. But the Talon kept climbing, and slowly they could see the arc that was the balloon's line with Choir at its end reducing in angle as the Talon crew continued winching him up, the line growing tauter. Salvini was the next to go, his balloon already hissing loudly, inflating with the helium and rising heavenward.

Aussie glanced at his watch. It was 1005. Smacking Salvini's boots together, making sure he was in the correct position, Aussie joshed him. "Bet you ten bucks they winch me aboard faster than you."

"What?" Salvini asked, his anxiety, for all his SAS/D training, suddenly betraying itself.

"Bet you ten bucks," Aussie repeated, "that they take longer to winch you in than me."

"Oh yeah? And how do you figure that?"

"Easy," Aussie retorted. They could hear the tracer getting closer. "You're heavier than I am."

"I'm as fit as you are."

"Course you are. But you're heavier. Come on, pay up or shut up."

"You're sick," Salvini said, his anxiety written all over his face.

"All right, five bucks. I can't do better than that. Right?"

Salvini nodded, thinking that the Australian was now asking him if he was in the proper position for the jerk. He was, but Aussie always liked to make sure of a bet. "Five bucks, okay?"

"Yeah—five bucks, all right, all right. Where's the Talon?"

"She's making the turn," Aussie said. Just then a small sandstorm broke locally and they could see nothing.

"Damn it!" Salvini said.

"Don't sweat it, sport," Aussie encouraged. "The Talon'll pick it up. We can't see them, but they can see the rope up higher. Just you get ready for the—" Before he finished, Salvini simply disappeared into the dust, Aussie barely glimpsing his boots as he was jerked aloft.

"Two up, two to go," Aussie said cheerfully. David Brentwood was thanking the Mongolian herdsman who had risked his life and family to help them. Already the herdsmen were gathering up their *ghers* and packing, ready to move, to avoid any punishment patrols that might be sent out from Ulan Bator.

"Come on, Dave!" Aussie yelled. "Or you'll miss the friggin' bus."

Within two minutes Brentwood was in his harness, Aussie having already released the balloon from its small bedroll-type wrapping. As it expanded, disappearing into the dust, it looked like some fantastic ghost in a mustard cloak.

"Palms down," Aussie instructed him. "Davey, you want to make a wager?"

"No."

"Ten bucks they winch me in faster than you?"

"No. You've got some scheme to help pull yourself up a few feet on the cable and beat us all, is that it?"

"No way," Aussie said. "Look, I've never been on one of these things either. I just figure my luck's in. What do you say—ten bucks."

"All right—anything to shut you up."

"That's my man."

"Where's that damn Talon?" Before Aussie could answer him, there was a loud explosion, followed by another.

"I hope to hell that's one of theirs," David said.

"We'll soon know if the Talon doesn't reappear."

"How will we know in this dust storm? Lord, I've never seen anything like it."

"Huh," Aussie said, "locals tell me this is only a bit of a whirly. In the Gobi they say you can't see your hand in front of your face during a dust storm."

"All very educational, Aussie, but how the hell can we tell where the Talon is?"

"Keep your bloody head in position. Don't want a case of whiplash on top of—"

Suddenly Brentwood was being dragged along the ground, swearing, bumping on pebbles, then he too suddenly disappeared into the whirling dust storm.

Next Aussie, already in harness, pulled two helium tanks to fill the balloon, and within minutes could hear the Talon off to the north, making its circle, his balloon now ascending. The old herdsman shook his hand, and around them, like shadows in the darkness of the dust, he could see the various odds and ends of the herdsmen's life, as the canvas-and-felt homes came down to be loaded onto a wagon, a small TV being wrapped carefully in a carpet, and camels laden with bedding and harness, the Mongolians wishing him well with their Eskimo-like smiles and golden teeth.

There was a crash like thunder, either a Siberian or American jet hitting the desert floor, then in less than a second, Aussie, his arms now crossed tightly in against his chest, was airborne, the spring in the nylon cord making the initial ascent smoother, faster than he'd anticipated. But then the spring was at its end, and this was followed by a sudden jolt, so fierce that Aussie felt his head was about to come off.

Once above the two-hundred-foot-high dust storm that had invaded the *ghers*, Aussie could see far above him the three, now small, balloons that had been severed free once the V-shaped scissor clamp had got hold of the previous three lines. Now from the tail of the aircraft another vertical line descended that would hook onto the rescue line and haul it up and into the belly of the plane. The Talon was flying higher than usual because of the loss of visibility due to the dust storm. They liked to see their man as quickly as possible before engaging the winch.

With wind and dust screaming about his ears, Aussie could hear the staccato of machine gun fire off to the west where the American and Siberian fighters were engaging, and now and then he caught a glimpse of tracer as one of the Siberian fighters would try to break out of the American fighter's box to try to bring down the Talon. A Fishbed-J MiG-21 was visible for a moment when Aussie, dangling like a toy at the end of the enormous rope, was six hundred feet above ground, but as soon as he'd seen the Fishbed-J with its green khaki camouflage pattern he saw an F-15 Eagle on its tail and the spitting of fire from its 20mm, six-barrel rotary cannon. The Fishbed immediately started making smoke, rolling into evasive action, its twin barrel GSh 23mm cannon firing from its belly pack. Suddenly Aussie knew he was in free fall, the line severed.

He had less than a second to make the decision that was

no decision at all: either pull the key ring release on his chute or smash into the ground. His right hand grabbed the key ring and jerked hard. There was a flurry of air about him like a hundred pigeons being released, and suddenly his downward thrust was slowed as the chute filled and he descended back into the dust storm. The Talon, already having overstayed its welcome, was forced to turn back northeastward across the Mongolian border into Second Army territory before the Siberian MiGs got lucky again.

Aussie used swearwords on the way down he thought he'd forgotten. Whether the line had somehow fouled in one of the props despite the safety wire rigged in front of them or whether it had been a lucky tracer bullet didn't really matter. Whatever severed the line, he wasn't going back with his three buddies. But, like all members of the elite SAS and Delta Force commandos, he was trained in how to turn a losing situation into a winning one.

Cold reason also told him, though, as he entered the gritty dust storm and hit the ground harder than he had wanted, that the Spets helicopters and patrols would soon head out from Nalayh and possibly Ulan Bator looking for him. And right now he had four hundred miles of grassland and desert between him and the safety of Second Army. It seemed impossible, yet the only thing he could think of was the motto of his unit: "Who dares wins," or, as General Freeman, echoing Frederick the Great, would have said, *"L'audace, l'audace, toujours l'audace!"* But meantime Aussie was stunned by another realization: that he had just lost fifteen bucks cold.

CHAPTER TWENTY-NINE

NEXT AFTERNOON, A Friday, when Mike Ricardo walked into Con Ed's eight-story-high fossil-fuel Astoria Station for his four-to-midnight shift, he paused for a moment to look up at the five sets of high twin stacks belching their white smoke, in sharply etched columns, against the cerulean blue. He'd been working at the Astoria fourteen years, his job a member of one of the maintenance crews for the six giant white log-cake-shaped turbines that sat on an immaculately kept rust-red-painted boiler-room floor over a hundred and twenty feet below the 217 miles of piping that bent and curved like the exposed innards of some enormous refrigerator. But here it was far from cold, temperatures soaring to 120 degrees Fahrenheit as the fossil fuels, coal mainly, burned twenty-four hours a day to drive the turbines that helped feed the enormous appetite of the New York grid.

At the same time that Mike was beginning his shift, at Indian Point in upstate New York, thirty miles north of Central Park, Stefan, the third member of the cell, was donning a blue surgical cap. Slipping his ID/lock card into the slot, he passed first through the turnstile and the blue-green protective door, on through the second shielding door, and into what the men at the two plants at Indian Point called the "blue room." Here the fuel rods lay in an innocuous honeycomb arrangement twenty-five feet beneath the blue water shield.

In Albany the computer monitoring the flow of electricity was showing above average power being consumed in Manhattan and Queens, so that up to half of it had to be drawn from the grid fed by the enormous hydropower complex at La Grande in Quebec, the "juice" coming down on the 345,000-volt lines from the roaring spillways of La Grande One and Two. Manhattan's eight substations' transformers, like those throughout the rest of the city, downstepped the voltage so that David's father, Admiral John Brentwood, in the World Trade Center's offices of the New York Port Authority, could keep track of the highly complex business of coordinating convoy loading, departure, and arrivals, and, when he had time, brew the coffee that kept him and millions of other New Yorkers, from brokerage houses to subway drivers, working the extended war hours.

Northeast of the Bronx, on the calm waters of Croton Reservoir, the water-police helicopter was carrying out its normal patrol to insure that no powerboats were churning up the bottom. If left undisturbed, the water would be aerated through the action of the sun's ultraviolet light, and, once rid of impurities, would pass through the aqueducts and tunnels built a hundred years before and become part of those one-and-a-half billion gallons of water that New Yorkers consumed every day. The chopper came down as it spotted the quality-control men on the only powerboat allowed in the lake lowering the seki disk—which they saw was visible down about three and a quarter meters, much deeper than the two meters required by law.

In New York, the fourth Spets who was replacing the "floater" Gregory walked as casually as he had for the past ten years into Con Ed's orange-carpeted ECC—energy control center. The controller glanced about at the twelve-foot-high, half-moon-shaped wall beaded by quarter-size lights that traced the lines on the hundreds of flowcharts, making it all look like the massive circuit board of a railway network rather than that of New York's electric flow.

The weather report was now predicting variable overcast conditions preceding the storm moving up from Virginia. The overcast was responsible for more afternoon lights than usual being turned on in Manhattan. The operator, pushing himself back in the high, gray, luxurious chair at the center of the control room, glided quickly and deftly to the tracking ball control, his palm moving over it as blue and amber readouts on the computer screens told him backup alarms were about to ring. The indicator for the substation at West Forty-ninth and Vernon was flashing, overloaded at nine hundred megawatts, about to trip and set in motion a "brownout." This was averted by the controller siphoning off extra power from feeder line eighty—the line which brought the hydro-power down from Canada. Still, overload threatened.

"If it goes above two thousand," the controller called, "start shedding," which for the men on the four-to-midnight watch meant that they weren't to wait until substations started tripping out. "Call Kennedy, hospitals, medical, fire, ambulance—they'll have to go to EGs." But the Spets man knew that the controller didn't suspect any crisis building up. He was merely taking strict precautionary measures, confident that Con Ed's BJGs—backup jet generators—could kick in at a few moments' notice if necessary. What the chief controller didn't know, however, was that the jet-engine generators had over ten pounds of sand thrown into their innards. It had been as simple as a child throwing sand at a beach. The moment they kicked in, they'd overheat and burn out.

While the controller watched, alarm lights started to flash all over the circuit board.

Twenty-seven minutes later, the huge spillways of La Grande in Quebec exploded, causing massive flooding racing at unprecedented speed over the vast Canadian tundra. Feeder eighty and all other transmission lines from Quebec went dead. Four-point-seven minutes later both the nuclear plants at Indian Point reported explosions, not in the restricted rod pool area inside the plant but in the control rooms themselves. Six operators were dead—more than twenty critically injured.

Now, devoid of nuclear power, its hydro feeder and fossil-fuel generating plant capacity out, over 90 percent of New York City was plunged into darkness—only hospitals and control towers at LaGuardia and Kennedy functioning on their own emergency generators.

The lightning forked blue over New York so that at first New Yorkers believed the power lines and substations had been hit by the storm moving up from Virginia, and they blamed this for stopping everything from their TVs to the subway—over two million people caught in rush hour, the port loading facilities immobilized, auto accidents by the thousands, and in Flatbush, looting worse than during the blackout of '77.

In Mount Sinai and other hospitals from New York to New Jersey and in Westchester County, over forty-three patients died during the delays before emergency generators kicked in. At Bellevue a new orderly, eager to help, struck a match, creating a flashback along the oxygen feed line to an oxygen tank, which became a rocket, tearing through two walls and killing four elderly patients waiting to go into OR, and two more in the recovery room, the explosion also creating a massive fire. Oxygen feeds were quickly cut off to prevent other explosions, but this meant that dozens of emphysema patients, most elderly, went into respiratory distress, eleven of them dying despite heroic efforts under emergency battery lights to resuscitate them.

Ambulance crews did their best but were plagued by motor accidents, fourteen in Manhattan alone, which prevented them from responding to emergency walkie-talkie calls. Many civilians were struck down in Times Square as they were pushed off curbs by the sheer force of crowds panicking in response to the gunfire of a mugging at the corner of Forty-second and Broadway.

Two women were dragged off near Central Park West between West Ninety-third and Ninety-fourth and raped. One was left dead, her throat slit by her attacker. There were quiet, heroic actions too throughout the city, but these were isolated cases that couldn't hope to arrest the war-spurred fear, which climaxed around 7:15 P.M. that evening when a radio station, broadcasting weakly but broadcasting nevertheless via its own emergency generator power, relayed a conversation with a ham radio operator claiming the police had found evidence of coordinated sabotage against the city. Furious, the mayor, having to drive through the terror-filled streets first to Con Ed's ECC and then to the radio station, finally countered the report by announcing that he had been assured by Con Ed that the blackout was an "unusual confluence of forces" and that power would be restored as soon as possible.

Many people took refuge in churches, and some caught by the blackout near Fifth Avenue sought protection in the Metropolitan Museum of Art and the Guggenheim. But nowhere was it totally safe, several people mugged in the western chapel of St. Patrick's, while on Sixth Avenue a visitor to New York, driving north, took a right onto Fifty-seventh Street, and was sideswiped twice before being hit and killed by a city garbage truck, the accident creating a solid traffic jam four blocks east to Lexington.

While most others had been heading home when the power went out, some had been on their way back to work in the New York Port Authority's convoy-coordinating center in Trade Tower One when the power went out, and found themselves trapped on an elevator between the sixtieth and sixty-first floors. All telephone lines were out, the only news being relayed by the emergency-generator-run radio stations, the mayor's assurance sounding thinner by the minute, with one station reporting heavy gunfire in Flatbush between blacks and "Little Seoul," and several shootings in the Midtown Tunnel.

By 8:17 P.M. the New York radio stations operating on their own power had grown to half a dozen, their lights, like those of the hospitals, pinpoints of illumination in the canyons of darkness, several more stations broadcasting unconfirmed reports of sabotage against the feeder lines coming through Westchester County and from the East Rockies mountain grid. The mayor did what he could to disavow these rumors as well, and indeed several of the stations refused to run them, but those that did were no longer relying on the unconfirmed reports of ham radio operators but on FM "Radio du Canada" broadcasts out of Montreal and CBC stations in Toronto, picked up by truckers on the interstates from Chicago to the Adirondacks. The mayor again appealed for calm. "Now's the time," he told the population of eleven million, "for New Yorkers to stick together."

For the most part they did, but the widespread random acts of violence had not yet abated, and by the time the mayor returned to City Hall he was already trying to compute the political costs to him of having told a barefaced lie earlier on, having dismissed the rumors of sabotage as "patent nonsense." One of his aides told him that he was wanted on the phone.

"Better be the president of Con Ed!" His Honor snapped.

"No, sir. It's the president of the United States."

The mayor held his hand over the receiver for a moment to compose himself. "Mr. President?"

The president's voice was competing with static on the radio telephone. "Mr. Mayor. I'm sending Al Trainor up to see you."

The mayor wasn't sure what to say. What he needed was electricity—and fast—not presidential aides. "Well, Mr. President, he won't be able to . . ." His voice disappeared in the sound of an enormous explosion and a ball of crimson flame curling in on itself, followed by the sound of crashing glass. A chopper, all but out of gas, had tried for a last-minute landing atop one of the skyscraper pads, but instead, buffeted by wind shear into the darkness, the pilot momentarily disorientated in the pitch black night, a rotor had hit the water tank.

"We don't want to get in your way, Jim," the president was telling him, switching to an informal tone, impressing the mayor's media aide who was close enough to pick up the conversation. He could hear Mayne cough briefly, then continue. "I ordered Fort Dix to give all possible assistance." The mayor knew he was alluding to the riots but was being nonspecific as they were on an open line. "Al Trainor'll fill you in with the details of assistance. I want him to be with you to see at first hand, then report back to me. Help you coordinate recovery efforts. We don't want Washington bureaucrats standing in your way. He'll be bringing the Apple Two contingency plan with him. Get rid of any red tape."

"Thank you, Mr. President."

Putting down the receiver, the mayor seemed even more puzzled by the president's last comment. He turned to the clutch of aides. "What in hell was that all about? Contingency apple—two? What the hell *was* that? Marvin?"

"That'd be the emergency response plan, Mr. Mayor. 'Apple' for New York."

"We've got our own contingency plans," the mayor replied tartly. "What we need is electricity and money, not goddamned—"

"It's not just for New York," the aide explained. "It's a plan that ties in New York with the feds. With the rest of the country. Ah—you signed it, Mr. Mayor."

The mayor raised an eyebrow. "You mean we're only going to get what's left over—after Washington gets finished allocating it to—"

"No, sir," Marvin said. He liked the mayor—had worked for him for five years—but His Honor had a tendency to see the whole world in terms of political clout and money.

"No, sir. Apple *Two* means that it's not just us involved. It's all over the country. The West Coast has been hit, too."

"Who the hell else is going to get in on it?" the mayor pushed. "We don't need Trainor up here to tell us that. I don't want Jersey and the rest of them riding on our coattails. New York's my priority. My responsibility. If Trainor's coming up here to slice up the pie I—"

"Until Trainor gets here, Mr. Mayor, we won't know."

The mayor took a breather and relaxed as much as the situation would allow before turning to another of his aides. "What d'you think, Frank?"

"Well, Mayne's fresh from reelection. No cause for him to go grandstanding with us to win votes—long as he doesn't send us a Quayle."

For a moment the mayor thought his aide meant a bird. "Trainor's no Quayle," put in the mayor's stenographer, a petite redhead who up till now hadn't said anything, preoccupied with worry that her parents had been caught in the tunnel. "Trainor's very well thought of in Washington."

The mayor grunted. He was always skeptical of Washington—no matter what the situation, Washington always wanted something in return. If he wasn't careful, the mayor of the Big Apple knew that the president would get all the glory. "Jennifer," he said, looking across at the stenographer, "I want air time booked—prime time. Soon as Con Ed's got the power back on."

"Can't right now, Mr. Mayor. Phone lines are down again."

"What—Jesus! Well, send someone by car. Send a smoke signal—anything. If we're not on the tube first Washington'll steal all the bases."

Jennifer dispatched messengers—some by bike. For some strange reason in the flashlight-lit hallways her voice seemed to echo more than it ever did in the bright night light.

When the messengers returned an hour later, one of them bleeding badly from a fall, they apologized to Jennifer that though they'd booked time for the mayor, the White House had already requested air time ahead of them.

"Damn it! I knew it," the mayor thundered. "Washington wants all the glory. It's a grandstand play."

It wasn't.

Electrical-distribution networks right throughout the United States had been hit, including and especially the West Coast ports, where sabotage throughout the Rocky Mountain grid caused a "back jam" of ships urgently needed to resupply Second Army over five thousand miles away.

It was the president's decision in the face of such overwhelming sabotage to once again broadcast a reintroduction of the Emergency Powers Act of the kind that had allowed them to pick up the likes of La Roche, though in that instance their timing had been all wrong.

To assure the nation that the government was still intact, the top Washington bureaucrats were already en route to Mount Weather, forty-nine miles west of Washington, its hub a massive bunker dug into the mountain that was operated by EMA—Emergency Management Agency—with four-foot-thick, blast-proof, reinforced steel doors, a complex that had its own underground water supply, cafeterias, hospital, TV and radio communication center, and, particularly vital in such situations as that created by the blackouts, its own power plant and sewage facilities.

That evening as Washington's bureaucratic convoy moved through Virginia's Loudoun County along County Route 601, slowing near Heart Trouble Lane to no more than ten miles per hour, they saw the barbed wire atop a ten-foot cyclone chain fence that ringed Mount Weather's four hundred acres. Above the bunker, amid the rich Virginia foliage, barracks and microwave relay antennae were already alive with activity. It might take only several days for the total power failure to be put partially right, but until then Mayne was playing it safe. What Mayne desperately needed for the American people was not to give them any more humiliating communiqués from a superhardened bunker but a victory—the feeling that despite their trials and tribulations at home, at least America was winning.

What in hell was Freeman doing?

What Freeman was doing was waiting for the brand new M-1 Abrams-1 Block 3 automatic loader, modular-armor, main battle tanks, which at fifty-one tons versus the old sixty-plus could go faster and fight harder but which were now sitting cluttered dockside, the U.S.A.'s power failures meanwhile paralyzing communications not only from the Pentagon to the West Coast but even within the Pentagon itself.

Meanwhile Freeman's G-2 was informing him that General Cheng's ChiCom buildup along the Manchurian border was continuing unabated, that Second Army must expect an all-out crossing of the Amur within seven days. There was another "minor" impediment, as Freeman, with calculated understatement, put it.

"They can hit me from the Turpan depression with intermediate missiles if I move south to engage the Manchurian west flank."

"Yes, they can," Norton confirmed.

"Your estimate, gentlemen?" Freeman asked, looking about the forward headquarters Quonset hut at Chita.

"We're between a rock and a hard place," a young colonel proffered. Norton waited for the explosion to come for the officer having stated the obvious, but it didn't.

"Colonel's quite correct," Freeman conceded, his face drawn and tired from looking at the maps. "Well, gentlemen, there's only one thing to do!"

"Sir?" Norton asked.

"Take a walk." And with that Freeman buttoned up his winter coat and pulled on his gloves.

"Sir?" It was Norton.

"Yes?"

"Think you'd better have two minders."

"Whatever you think, Dick, but if the good Lord says your time's come, so it has." And with that, two nonplussed marksmen were sent out after him.

"Give him at least twenty yards," Norton advised them. "Otherwise he'll start giving you the gears for being goddamned nannies. Got it?"

"Yes, sir. Ah, Colonel Norton, sir?"

"Yes?"

"I sure hope he thinks of something to get us out of this—"

A clump of needle ice crashed from a pine onto the roof of a Humvee.

"So do I," Norton said.

Freeman hadn't even turned at the ice smashing on the Humvee; he was already doing what Norton called his "Napoleon": head down, walking stick behind him, trudging through the crisp spring snow. The PLA was south and east of him along the Manchurian hump, and no word yet from the SAS/D team he'd sent in to sound out the Mongolians' disposition.

East of Nalayh, over four hundred miles south of the confluence of the Manchurian-Siberian-Mongolian border, the wind was increasing and Aussie Lewis, after having floated down into the gritty dust storm, had to rely entirely on his GPS to know exactly where he was. He lost sight of the Talon completely, hearing only its fading roar as it, together with its fighter escort, withdrew, heading back north to Second Army's territory.

Aussie wasn't bitter—had he been David Brentwood he would have done the same thing, ordering the Talon to withdraw, not having enough time to try another FUST.

As Aussie unclipped his chute, the head herdsman moved quickly over to him, yelling excitedly. Perhaps he had heard a chopper, but no, now the Talon had gone, the dogfights had ended, and all he could hear was the banshee howl of the wind. Then he saw it, suspended by two parachutes, a blurred orange image at first in the dust but its archetypal image more definite now as it struck the ground, bounced, and flipped on its side.

"You bloody beaut!" Aussie shouted, immediately running to and unharnessing the Talon's farewell gift. It was no guarantee he'd get away, but at least there was a chance. The headman recognized it of course as a motorcycle, but he had only seen some of the motor and sidecar units of the Chinese army in earlier skirmishes with the PLA over southern borders—not one like this.

"You bloody beaut!" Aussie repeated. It was a khaki-painted Kawasaki-250D8, which had won out against the Harley-Davidson and Yamaha for the marine corps and army contract. Used mainly in Desert Storm for recon and courier service during radio silence among the most forward units, the Kawasaki had performed well. Aussie cut the chute straps with his ankle K-bar knife, heaving the 296-pound bike up onto its stand, and could hear the tight slosh of a full tank, another jerrican of gas strapped to the left side of the pinion seat, a carbine in a right hand reverse cavalry leather holster.

With a liquid-cooled engine, the Kawasaki could give him eighty-plus miles per hour over the rock-strewn plains, the motorcycle modified for the army so as to have wider, better-grip tires, especially in sand, with a forty-six-tooth rear-tires sprocket, giving it two better than the standard forty-four and so reducing its gearing. And the biggest plus of all, given Aussie's position, was that the Kawasaki had a liquid-cooled engine. This made it not only more environmentally friendly in reducing fuel emission but more importantly for Aussie made it about the quietest bike in its class.

Aussie figured if he could average fifty miles per hour through the dust storm that had now enveloped him and the enemy alike and could drive on through the night, he could make the border in eight to ten hours. But first he went back to the bullet-riddled Spets chopper and helped himself to a Makarov pistol, an AK-74 with six clips, and a dozen Spets F-1 grenades. He stuck two of them in the pockets of his *del* and the others in the right saddlebag with a water canister and the dried camel meat the herdsmen had given him.

Using a canvas strap from the parachute he made a sling for the AK-74, the Makarov 9mm in his belt beneath his *del*, a pair of ten-power night-vision binoculars around his neck, and packed on—or rather, packed around—the pinion seat more cargo from the immobilized chopper, namely an RPG-7D antitank rocket launcher with five rockets. Then, courtesy of the dead Spets chopper pilot, he took off the man's Spets uniform, including the telltale blue-and-white-striped T-shirt, rolling it into a bundle that he stuck between the seat and gas tank. The herdsman was grinning appreciatively and shook Aussie's hand vigorously as if it were a water pump.

Two minutes later, Aussie was lost to the herdsmen's view in a muffled roar as the Kawasaki headed east from the *gher* caravan that itself was already on the move. Checking his GPS, Lewis knew exactly where he was within ten meters because of the satellite triangulation. What he couldn't tell was what he'd meet along the way, and soon he was too far from the *ghers* to see what happened a half hour later when a Spets chopper out of Nalayh blasted the moving caravan of *ghers* to a stop, then landed and took prisoners.

In the swirling dust storm they asked them which route the American had taken and how was he traveling—by camel, by foot—how! The Siberian fighters, probably Fulcrums, though having driven off the Americans, had reported the three dirigibles that were part of the single-line extraction technique. Where was the fourth? Was he heading north or east for the border—along the Indermeg road or even further east towards Choybalsan on the Herlen River before turning north?

The terrified Mongolians reminded the Spets that the

Mongolian People's Republic was a friend of the Siberians and told the Spets that they did not know what direction the fourth American took. The Spets loaded them all aboard the Hind, flew it to two thousand feet above the dust cloud, where it looked like a huge, bug-eyed dragonfly, and threw all of them—seven adults and three children—out, then headed toward Choybalsan. Flying through the dust storm they could see nothing, but one never knew—a sudden shift in the wind here and there might suddenly reveal a break.

The Spets were in no mood for any more noncooperation, especially by Mongolians whom they no longer thought of as the master race that had terrorized and subdued their world under Genghis Khan but as mere lackeys of Siberian will. They glimpsed another *gher* village during a break in the dust cover, landed, and asked about the Americans. The herdsmen, eleven of them, had nothing to tell them and were quickly shot. Then two Spets held the youngest female—a girl of about thirteen—while a third Spets raped her by locking his arms about her neck, barely able to enter her because she was bucking so much, the other two Spets laughing until finally she was exhausted and groaning like a wounded animal, bleeding, having no option but to submit to his will. Then they shot her.

It was clear they'd get no information from the Mongolians, who were obviously more favorably disposed to the Americans, but at least from now on word would spread quickly through the *ghers* that if the Spets wanted information you'd better give it to them. The Hind took off through the dust cloud. "What are we looking for?" the Spets pilot asked. "Is he on a camel, horseback, walking, or what?"

"We don't know," the *praporshnik*, an Afghanistan veteran, snapped. "We'll shoot anything that moves. *Anything*. Understood?"

"*Da!*"

* * *

Frankly, Aussie told the wind, he would have preferred a Harley MT-350cc—better suspension. Besides, he'd always fancied himself a bit of a rake on an Electra Glide in blue and like Fonda—not his commie fawning sister—out on the road on the old Harley-Davidson. Still, the Kawasaki's whine was just fine and, head down, goggles firmly attached, he was making good time, though learning that driving virtually blind—visibility down to fifteen feet—took more courage than he'd thought. Man, if his Olga by the Volga with the big tits could only see him now—whoa! Through the dust he could see a darker dust, looking like a huge scab, a stationary Soviet-built armed personnel carrier—a BMP-1.

Aussie knew the odds immediately: a crew of three, three passengers with assorted nasty small arms, a main turret gun—73mm, killing range twenty-five hundred yards. Also armed with a coaxial 7.62mm and antitank guided weapons. Stifling inside, most of its infantry resting outside. Its hull armor plus or minus 19mm. Only thing in his favor was that the Kawasaki was almost twice as fast as the BMP-1, and if they'd seen him, by the time they'd loaded up with their full complement of infantry, he'd be a quarter mile ahead anyway.

"Say bye-bye to Ivan!" Aussie told the Kawasaki and gave it full throttle. The next minute he was airborne, the bike skidding furiously in front of him, the right side of his *del* shredded to pieces by the gravel rash, the spill driving the Makharov hard into his groin. He had the bike up, its wheels still spinning, and was resaddled in a matter of seconds, pride a little punctured, the earth exploding about him with small-arms fire. But then he was flat out again, into the curtain of dirt.

The BMP's 7.62 started chattering as if it felt left out, followed by the steady *thud-thud-thud* of the 73mm, but the shots were wild and well behind him. But of course now the word would be out: the lone SAS was on a motorcycle heading east for Choybalsan. The BMP didn't even start its engine, no doubt radioing his position to the next roadblock as he rode parallel to the Herlen River road.

Aboard the Talon combat aircraft David Brentwood, Salvini, and Choir Williams were grim-faced at having had to leave Aussie behind. The only good news they could give Freeman's headquarters was that from what they'd seen, the Mongolians were clearly anti-Chinese, and that Marshal Yesov, if he did have any plans of attacking the Americans from the west, wasn't going to get much help from the Mongolian militia or the regulars; otherwise the Mongolian president would have had the foothills and the flats around the Hentiyn Nuruu swarming with patrols looking for the SAS/D team. Instead, he'd left it entirely up to his Siberian "guests."

CHAPTER THIRTY

THE THING THAT struck Frank Shirer immediately about Peshawar was the smell of the northern Pakistani town—one of smoke, dust, dung, gasoline, and spices that he was unfamiliar with, which arose from the town's bazaars, where one could wander down the Street of Partridge Lovers or the Street of the Storytellers, looking at the famed Persian carpets and watching the coppersmiths beating out their wares in the time-honored way. But if he thought he was in for any more sightseeing he was in for a shock, as within an hour of landing at Peshawar he was being familiarized with what had once been the Cinderella of the fighter production line: the

Harrier vertical/short takeoff and landing close-support/reconnaissance fighter.

"Now, see 'ere," a British NCO said with the same kind of accent as that of the man called Doolittle who had managed to help Shirer fake his way through the eye chart exam at Dutch Harbor earlier in the war. "See we've placed two 30mm cannon—hundred rounds per gun—under the fuselage. Can carry up to eight thousand pounds of disposables if you like, but if you're going up over the Hindu Kush, mate, it's not bombs you're gonna need, it's height. So apart from the air-to-air missiles we'll put on your underwing hard points, most of your weight'll be extra gas and thirty-millimeter rounds. Okay?"

"Suits me," Shirer said.

"Now, how many hours have you had in 'em?" the NCO asked.

"None," Shirer said.

The NCO looked at him aghast. "*None?* Blimey, mate, I 'ope you're a quick learner."

"I can fly anything from a Tomcat to a B-52."

"Yeah—maybe so, mate, but you got runways there, 'aven't you?"

"Well before the instructor gets here," Shirer said, "why don't you show me round the kitchen?"

"Crikey, you're keen, I'll say that about you."

"Thanks."

The NCO began with the ejector seat. "Martin-Baker Mark Nine—just in case. Right?"

"I like your sense of priorities, Sergeant." The sergeant grinned, loosened up a bit. "There you've got your HUD—Smith's—can't get 'em better than that, and a Smith's air data computer. It comes to radar warning, we hand you over to old Marconi here, and if you get lucky you can lock on with the Ferranti laser range finder and target seeker. You're strapped on top of a Rolls-Royce Pegasus vectored-thrust turbofan, maximum speed at low altitude plus or minus point nine, maybe Mach one if you fart.''

"I'll remember.''

"This little baby's big winner is the old Viff. Those two tits''—he meant the ferry tips or low-drag jet nozzles—"are little marvels, they are. Wivout them you might as well leave 'er parked in the garage. That's what you'll be spending most of your time on—how to control those little buggers. Up, down, and around. Handled right can make a faster attacker look bloody stupid. Hopefully of course you won't have anyone attacking you.''

"You mean there's a good chance the mission might be off?'' Shirer asked.

"Oh—I dunno about the politics of it, mate. But I mean the chows'd'ave to get their crackerjack fighters west in a big hurry in time to intercept any bombing raid, wouldn't they?''

"I keep thinking they might have thought of that,'' Shirer said sardonically.

"Only if they know about the mission, and with these dummy runs we've been making they probably don't have a clue.''

The ground crew sergeant had no sooner finished talking than Squadron Leader J. Williams came out excitedly on the tarmac to exclaim, "It's on! Just come through from London HQ. Turpan.''

"When, ma'am?'' the sergeant asked.

"Four days time—five at the outside.''

Shirer was in shock. Squadron Leader Williams was a petite blonde.

"Christ!''

It was out before Shirer could stop himself.

"You're Major Shirer, aren't you?'' she asked tersely, taking her mood from his.

"Yes,'' he said.

"We've heard quite a lot about you. You and your nemesis, Marchenko. How many times did he shoot you down?''

Bloody hell, thought the sergeant, if he didn't get in between them there'd be blood on the tarmac. "Squadron Leader Williams'll be leading the Harrier cover."

"I take it that doesn't meet with your approval, Major?" she said tartly.

"What—er, no. I mean—fine. That's fine."

"I hope you're a better flier than you are a liar." She flashed an angry smile.

"I'll try."

"Good, because you've only got four days. Think you can handle it?"

"I'll handle it."

"We'll see."

Shirer knew rationally that there was no reason a woman shouldn't be a combat pilot, no reason her reflexes shouldn't be as quick as his, that she didn't need a man's physical strength to fly by wire, so what was his problem? He didn't like it, that's what.

"Ah, Major Shirer?" the sergeant tentatively said.

"Yes?"

"Ah, we don't call the ferry tips 'tits' when the boss is around."

"Anything else I ought to know?"

"Yes, sir. She's a damn good pilot. Can turn this little gremlin on a dime. One more thing—she's a stickler for discipline."

"Sounds like fun."

That night Frank sat down to write a quick note to Lana at Dutch Harbor. He had to be circumspect about what he said, and his letter was terse, not only because of what the squadron censors would take out or because he was fatigued from ten hours straight on the Harrier without yet having taken it up, but because he simply could not bring himself as a once-household name in America—an American ace, a Tomcat veteran—to tell Lana that his boss was female and younger than he. "My boss is English," he said, and left it at that.

He knew he should be more broad-minded, more magnanimous, but damn it—he'd flown Tomcats, hooking the three-wire in zero visibility on a rolling deck, when she'd been going through puberty. No way he'd let on to Thompson, his replacement on the B-52, that he was under the direct command of a woman. Damn, now he knew why that toffee-nosed Fowler-Jones had talked him into it. They were so short of Harrier pilots they were having to use skirts. It was humiliating, that's what it was. All right, so he was a male chauvinist pig, but hell—it just didn't seem right. One thing for damn sure, he was going to learn every possible thing about the Harrier—this "little gremlin," as the NCO had put it—that he could. He'd live on coffee alone in the next few days, if that's what it took, and go over the gremlin inch by inch until he knew every part of it.

Why was it, he wondered, that men always called their ships and their aircraft "she"? He pushed it out of his mind and buried himself in the manual for the Ferranti 541 inertial navigation and attack system, the Smith Head Up Display much the same as he'd seen before.

Red-eyed and determined, Shirer mastered the vertical takeoff and landing over the next twenty-four hours and was ready for high-altitude tests. What was it she had said? "Your *nemesis*, Marchenko."

Cheeky bitch! And whether it was her or some of the other pilots in the Harrier squadron, a rumor was going around that Marchenko was now stationed somewhere in eastern China as an adviser on the MiG-29s.

CHAPTER THIRTY-ONE

AS THE CRUNCHY ice gave way beneath his boots, Free-man had pondered his strategy. To go south while the missiles remained intact at Turpan to the southwest would be suicide, yet to wait much longer for Cheng to build up his forces in Manchuria east of the bulk of Second Army would be equally disastrous. Yet to mount a frontal attack on the Manchurian border—all along the Amur—would also be suicidal.

He watched the small trickles of water formed by the stamp of his boots flattening the ice and was reminded how at night images of rivers had kept running through his dreams—not in a gurgling, hypnotic, sleep-giving way but more as impediments to his sleep. In childhood, rain falling on the barn roof in the Midwest and later on the barracks at Fort Ord and his home at Monterey had always given him comfort. So why not now? What was the running water trying to tell him?

Often before, a problem had resolved itself for him while he had been asleep, but, to date, the dreams of water were elusive in their message: If the ice suddenly melted on the Amur, his tanks would sink without a trace, but anyone knew that. The more he thought of the message of the water, the more he thought of the work of the ancient Chinese warrior whose book on the art of war had been beside his bedside along with the King James version of the Bible. What was it that Cao Cao, one of Sun Tzu's lieutenants, had said to him?

"The military has no constant form, just as water has no constant shape—adapt as you face the enemy."

"Adapt," Freeman told himself, and now another of Master Sun's lieutenants spoke to him. "Use deception to throw them into confusion. Lead them on in order to take them." Freeman stopped suddenly in the snow, more rivulets running from his boots like streams finding the easiest runoff path, the line of least resistance. Often the most obvious answers were hidden because of the maze of detail. What was it? You couldn't see the woods for the trees. Well Freeman had suddenly seen through the trees into the heart of Sun Tzu. As he turned back to his headquarters hut, his "minders" found it difficult to keep up with him, he was walking so fast.

Aussie Lewis knew he was on the horns of a dilemma. The Spets knew he was headed east in the direction of Choybalsan, where he would no doubt turn north, but now all the river crossings that would take him north to the U.S.-controlled Siberian border would be manned—if not blocked—by BMP-1s. And the river was deep, wide, and particularly dangerous now; great lumps of ice were piling up at the bends in the river.

It was a strange landscape, the temperature rising daily, sending up forests of mist, dropping to freezing and below at night, and now the dust storm was beginning to abate. It was 3:00 P.M. Come morning the storm would probably disappear altogether, a fresh easterly overcoming the west wind that had brought on the storm. He saw a blur up ahead, then another. For a moment they seemed, in his fatigued, saddle-sore state, like sheep, but in fact they were the outlines of two or three *ghers*.

The question was, had the Spets had time to reach this settlement and spring some kind of trap? Shutting down the Kawasaki then lowering it with some effort to its side to break any possible silhouette, he took out his K-bar knife and moved forward into the dust storm. It was only as he got a hundred yards or so closer that he realized what had happened, why the settlement of the three or four *ghers* had looked like sheep, shrunken in size.

The smell of wood smoke now mixed with the dust, and he guessed in a moment what had happened. As he came stealthily upon the first *gher*, his guess was proven right. The *ghers* had been burned to the ground, and in a small depression in the middle of them lay the murdered bodies of the few families who had been there and who could not tell the Spets that they had seen the escaping American.

Lewis had seen some painful sights in his time, but this turned his stomach, one of the children disemboweled. He could feel the bile rising within him as he saw another small child's body, its head crushed by a rock, a rag doll held tightly. Lying still in the dust storm that was howling eerily about him, the sand smattering on his goggles, Aussie could see a circle of sand and pebbles that had been thrown up by the Spets helicopter.

The butchery had all the signs of a ferocious haste, one of the *ghers* still smoking, one Mongolian, an elder, probably the head herdsman, having been struck halfway down between two of the *ghers* surrounded now by bleating sheep. It was clear the chopper had gone, but Lewis, taking no chances, crept slowly toward the wreckage of the first *gher* and smiled, whispering, as if Choir, Brentwood, or Salvini was by his side, "The stupid bastards."

With the canvas, felt, wooden doors, and slats, Lewis went to work with his K-bar knife, stopping now and then to make a quick circuit of the burned-out *ghers* in the event that anyone had returned, but he was alone in the dust storm.

When he had finished it wasn't pretty to look at, but if he didn't get caught between two chunks of rogue ice, the rough raft he had fashioned would get him and the Kawasaki across the river to the northern side. He kept two sturdy roof poles apart and now put them in the center of the raft as he hauled it back toward the Kawasaki. As hard as this was, the most difficult part, he knew, would be getting the raft into the water once it was loaded with the Kawasaki, using the two poles as the raft's slipway. Suddenly he stopped, for he thought he heard a noise nearby. He whipped out the Makharov .9mm but saw nothing, thinking it must be the bleating of one of the sheep.

The other side of the river, which he could see only dimly now and then in the dust storm, was about a hundred yards away, and if his guess was right, the current would carry him swiftly toward a left-to-right bend in the river that would push the raft into a jumble of ice that had collected at the turn there, but that would allow him to leap ashore and anchor the raft before the swirling eddies about the bend once again took it out into the river.

CHAPTER THIRTY-TWO

THE RADIO MESSAGE coming in to Canadian Forces Base Esquimalt on the southern tip of Vancouver Island, just north of Washington State's Olympic Peninsula, was garbled: "Panicky," reported the U.S. coast guard who was also picking up the message off Whidbey Island.

As well as being an SOS, the signal, patched together, made it seem that the *Southern Star*, a fish-processing factory ship out of Seattle, which had headed out to beat its competition with four small, fast trawlers, was saying something about an "enemy submarine." It sounded highly improbable, given the extensive SOSUS—underwater hydrophone or microphone—array network along the West Coast. For this reason, neither Esquimalt nor the submarine base at Bangor, Washington, was inclined to take the report seriously.

There was no storm that, as in the case of torpedoed tankers at the start of the Siberian war, could have masked the sound of an enemy sub attack. Besides, with the Sea Wolf-class USS *Aaron Peal*, the dual-purpose attack and ICBM nuclear sub, egressing through the degaussing or demagnetizing station on Behm Canal further north on the British Columbia–Alaska border, it was considered extremely unlikely that the Sea Wolf's sonar wouldn't have detected any large enemy sub movement.

Further out in the North Pacific would have been a different matter, with enemy subs expected to be nosing about the perimeter of the old Soviet buffer zone that stretched, half-moon-shaped, from the Bering Sea south to southwest toward the Kuril Islands north of Japan, lying in wait for the vital convoys en route to Freeman's Second Army. But going by the radio message, the *Southern Star* was within the well-patrolled two-hundred-mile zone off the Canadian–U.S. mainland.

"Ah—" Washington State coast guard pronounced, "they probably saw one of our Hunter-Killers going out on patrol—started shitting themselves."

"Or a school of fish," the second officer added. The sudden shifts in water color caused by the quicksilver-like veering of near-surface feeders could suddenly alter the pattern of water, giving it a shivery "patch" look, a patch often mistaken by fishermen, especially in wartime, for the change occasioned by rapid temperature shifts at the water-air interface caused by a sub's venting excess fresh water, a side effect of its abundant nuclear power. A suspicious-looking patch could also be produced by the upwelling of hydrothermal vents, or hot springs, on the sea floor, whose spouting columns racing up through the cold layers produced a "bubbling'' effect on the ocean's surface akin to a huge globule of oil popping and expanding on the surface in less dense water.

The MV *Southern Star*, her listing on the coast guard's manifest showing that she was a fish processor of 15,000 tons, was asked politely, calmly, whether she could have been mistaken.

"No way," the immediate reply came, this time unencumbered by any kind of static.

"Nothing garbled about that," the coast guard duty officer said. "Must have seen something, I guess. Notify Whidbey Island. They can send out a chaser."

Within twenty minutes a P3 Orion, replete with sonobuoys and other ASW equipment, including eight Mk 54 depth bombs, eight 980-pound bombs, six Mk 50 torpedoes, and six two-thousand-pound mines on underwing hard points, was being dispatched on full alert speed at 470 mph. After the saboteur attack on a Trident sub by an antitank missile earlier in the war as she had egressed Hood Canal, the duty officer wasn't about to take chances, even though he believed the lookouts on *Southern Star* had seen no enemy sub but perhaps a whale breaching.

With its MAD—magnetic anomaly detector boom, an extension of the plane's tail—on active, the Orion made for the last reported position of the *Southern Star*, and within twenty minutes of crossing the surf-fringed ribbon of Vancouver Island's Long Beach saw the factory ship, the dots on the *Southern Star*'s forward deck waving frantically up at the aircraft, more crew members spilling out by the second, as if by sheer force of numbers they could somehow convince the aircraft to shepherd them into port.

"What are they worried about?" the Orion's radar operator asked. "No one's gonna go after a fish boat."

"Yeah," the copilot wryly said. "But figure it's you down there, buddy boy. And you thought you'd seen a hostile. You'd want protection, too." From the *Southern Star*'s position, the copilot gave the captain a search pattern for possible Hunter-Killers in the area that, taking the *Southern Star* as its center, extended in a circle two hundred miles in diameter.

The only anomaly the MAD picked up was metalliferous deposits around sea mounts where superheated water from the unstable sea floor southwest of Vancouver Island had streamed up, causing minerals to be leached out as the hot plume hit the colder water of the northeast Pacific. But these anomalies were already marked clearly on the oceanographic charts.

"Unless," the radar operator proffered, "a hostile has nestled in all cozylike against a sea mount, using the magnetic mineral deposits as a cover?"

"Siberian or Chinese sub wouldn't know the sea bottom that well around here. You'd need to have it laid out like the back of your hand, buddy boy."

"Maybe they do."

"Don't think so—our navy didn't put up with any of the 'oceanographic research' bullshit the Soviet trawlers tried to pull. Goddamn things had so many aerials sproutin' from them they looked like anemones. Kicked their ass out of here years ago. Anyway, tricky business hanging around sea mounts—all those canyons running off the base, turbidity, currents galore. Sub could end up gettin' buried in a friggin' great mudslide."

"I dunno, they might try it, 'specially if they're ChiCom diesels." The senior ASW officer took the point. Everyone was thinking about Siberian subs, a cold war habit. But the Chinese had subs, too, and, being diesel electric, they were often more dangerous than nuclear subs. The nuclear boats, though faster, always had to have the water pumps going to cool the reactor and so gave off sound. The diesel electrics, just as capable at firing torpedoes or ICBMs, could go on battery and remain completely silent.

"Hey—I'm easy to get along with," the senior ASW officer said. "Drop a deuce and see what we get."

"You got it." With that, two chute-born sonobuoys were popped out of the left side of the aircraft. The sensitive mikes that would unravel twenty feet below the air-sea interface would send back any abnormal sound from the noisy world of the deep. Freeman's convoys couldn't afford to lose one ship. Even so, the best ASW equipment in the world told the ASW crew aboard the P-3 Orion that the *Southern Star* must have seen a ghost, as when everchanging cloud patterns threw light and dark shapes on the sea. There was a tendency at sea to see what you feared most, like a child at night imagining that a coat hanging in a dark hallway was an intruder.

CHAPTER THIRTY-THREE

AUSSIE LEWIS DRAGGED the long ten-by-six-foot raft of wooden slats and canvas down to the river's edge at a point where he estimated the current would take him diagonally across to the other side, where the bend in the river was jammed with floes of ice, coagulated where the current had narrowed. With darkness approaching, he fed the two long poles that he was going to use as a slipway into the water and firmly anchored the raft by means of ten tough hide straps, which in turn were held fast by wooden stakes that he'd driven into the sandy soil with the butt of his AK-74.

With slipway and raft held steady, he went up the bank to bring down the Kawasaki. He saw movement near it, dropped, and heard a noise, the same low moan he thought he'd heard before. It was a Mongolian herdsman lying next to the bike. He must have made his way down to the river as Aussie had done a last-minute check around the *ghers*. Aussie switched the AK-74 off safety and, going low, crawled about to the right of the Kawasaki so as to come up behind the man. If the man had punctured his gas tank, Aussie swore he'd take his head off at the neck. When Aussie was only a few feet from him he could see the old man had done nothing of the sort. Aussie could see the man's *del* blood-soaked to the chest. He had been one of those who had been shot by the Spets who were punishing them for not knowing anything of the SAS/D. When he saw Aussie in the tattered *del* he gestured with what little energy he had left for the SAS/D trooper to come closer.

Lewis moved his finger off the safety of the AK-74 and could tell from the old man's chest wound that he was not long for this world. It was a miracle he had managed to crawl so far from the rubble of the *ghers*. Aussie Lewis knelt beside him and gave him several sips of water from the motorcycle's canteen. The man made as if to talk but could only gesture, the same kind of moan coming from his throat, but it was as clear as a desert day in that dark, dust-riven twilight what he wanted—begging Lewis to finish him off, to see that his agony might not go on.

Aussie couldn't use the AK-74 for fear of the shots being heard, but the old man was reading his thoughts and drew his hand across his own throat. Aussie Lewis nodded, and with an agnostic's hedging of the bet, made the sign of the cross on the old man, whose hands now stretched out from his side. Perhaps the old man would understand, perhaps not. Aussie took out his K-bar knife and quickly drew it across the old man's throat. The blood spurted then gurgled like a crimson brook, and it was done. Aussie then dug a hole in the sand and covered the old man, leaving a hastily rigged cross from two of the *gher* slats, then he lifted the

Kawasaki. It felt twice as heavy as before as he wheeled the bike aboard the raft and again had to lower it before cutting the leather straps that had held the raft in place.

Immediately he began pushing on the stern oar—a long slat—hard to port to catch the current. A piece of jagged ice about four feet square bumped into the raft, sent a shudder through it, then another hit it amidships. "Bloody hell!" was Lewis's response, but in the swift current he was now already a third of the way across the river with only seventy yards to go, desperately working the rudder hard to port lest he be sucked into the fast-flowing midbend channel. But the length of the raft took care of that, for it couldn't make a sharp turn and its front end was already crashing and splintering into the packed ice of the bend.

In a flash, Aussie was racing through the ice jam with the painter of hide and anchoring the hide rope to a stake he was driving hard into the ground. Then without pausing for breath he hauled for all his might, the ice jam now helping him slide the raft, albeit bumpily, a few feet forward, acting like glider wheels beneath the raft, but then one or two pieces obstructed him. Suddenly he could pull it no further. He felt the impact of several more lumps of ice hitting the stern of the raft but paid no attention, going back and starting the Kawasaki on its side, holding it in neutral then lifting it up and in one movement pushing it hard forward and accelerating in gear. He was off the raft in a second and up the side of the riverbank, heading north of the river through the tractless Dornod depression, not toward the Great Wall, which was hundreds of miles to the south, but instead toward the still-existent wall of Genghis Khan. He estimated it would be about 150 miles to the border—three to four hours if he made good time, barring any other impediments. Certainly the Spets would think he was still on the southern side of the Herlen River, heading east toward Choybalsan, rather than north.

Now and then he had to slow down on the rock-strewn

stretches, but at others the firm grassland, still hard despite the thaw from its winter hardness, gave him a surprisingly fast and relatively comfortable ride. "No problems," he assured the Kawasaki. "Not to worry."

CHAPTER THIRTY-FOUR

"AN ATTACK ON the Chinese front?" Norton said. "General, I thought you said—"

"Never mind what I said, Dick. Get my corps commanders here for a meeting at oh nine hundred hours." The general listened intently to what David Brentwood had to say—namely that it seemed quite clear from everything they'd seen that the Mongolians were in no mood to die on Marshal Yesov's behalf, that the Mongolians, in short, had taken *perestroika* and *glasnost* as seriously as the Eastern Europeans. The Mongolians wouldn't be a problem, but from what they'd seen of the Spets behavior, Yesov couldn't be trusted.

"Never did trust that son of a bitch. How about this Lewis?"

Brentwood said they just didn't know. He was as resourceful in the desert as any other clime that the SAS had been trained for. And they had dropped him a Kawasaki.

"A what?"

"Kawasaki."

"Jesus Christ!" Freeman said. "You mean we couldn't even get him an all-American bike?"

No one knew quite what to say.

"I'll tell you something, Brentwood," the general said, his eyes glowering. "Someone back in Detroit needs their ass kicked for letting Japan take over like that. Goddamn disgraceful!"

"Yes, General."

"Course," Freeman said, "it was Doug MacArthur's fault. Got to thinking he was goddamn king of Japan. Gave women the vote then helped Japan build up new factories to out-industrialize us. I tell you, Brentwood, that's what happens when a man gets too far from the good old U.S. of A. and he starts going native and NATO on you. Eisenhower was the same, damn it—kept holding Georgie Patton back on a leash. Patton could've stopped the cold war before it began."

"Yes, sir."

"Yes, well long as the son-of-a-bitch motorbike gets him here. He got a rescue beeper, purple flare?"

"Yes, sir."

"Well I want every chopper outfit west of Manzhouli to keep on alert so that we can go in and pick him up soon as he's close enough. If he gets close enough."

"Yes, sir."

"Now, if he gets back he'll be part of 'Operation Front Door,' the door, gentlemen, being the Amur or, as the ChiComs call it, the Black Dragon. Brentwood!"

"Sir?"

"I want you to take a squadron of your men in here . . ."

As Norton listened to the plan unfold, a smile began to replace his earlier apprehension. It was brilliant. Vintage Freeman. Daring all right, but still there was always the question, Would it work? After the general left the Quonset hut to relieve himself someone remarked, "I'm glad our helos are American made."

"Right," another said. "But the friggin' beeper isn't, and half the electronics aboard the chopper are Japa—"

"Quiet, here he comes."

As Freeman began to go into more detail, Salvini, Brentwood, and Choir found it hard to concentrate. They were thinking of Aussie Lewis, alone in the Mongolian expanse. Special Operations had already lost one man earlier in the war in a commando raid near Nanking—Smythe—and he was now rotting away in Beijing Jail Number One. A Chinese jail, they said, was unimaginable. The Jewish woman, Alexsandra Malof, had been in the Harbin jail. To stay alive she had to lick the walls for moisture and pick out tiny pieces of undigested food from her feces. When she escaped, they said she was thin as a rake.

CHAPTER THIRTY-FIVE

IN BEIJING, GENERAL Cheng was about to switch off his reading light above the antimacassar-topped lounge chair that was the only luxury he allowed himself. He was reading transcripts of General Schwarzkopf's press conferences during the Iraqi War. Most of it was routine stuff—silly questions by silly reporters who had no idea of the complexity of war, but one answer of Schwarzkopf's was burned into Cheng's memory, and he had it marked for the red box—the documents that would be taken to the military Central Committee. Schwarzkopf had said,

There's black smoke and haze in the air. It's an infantryman's weather. God loves the infantryman, and that's just the kind of weather the infantryman likes to fight in. But

I would also tell you that our sights have worked fantastically well in their ability to acquire, through that kind of dust and haze, the enemy targets. And the enemy sights have not worked that well. As a matter of fact, we've had several anecdotal reports today of enemy who were saying to us that they couldn't see anything through their sights, and all of a sudden their tank exploded when their tank was hit by our sights.

Cheng had made an immediate rush order via La Roche's front companies in Hong Kong for the infrared night vision, particularly the thermal-imaging sights that could cut through smoke and dust, plus additional supplies of smoke thickener that had caused Freeman's tanks so much trouble when Yesov had used it up around Lake Baikal before the cease-fire. The other thing Cheng was banking on was that delivery of the newer Abrams M1A2 tank, which had two gun sights—one for the gunner and one for the tank commander, to track two targets simultaneously, unlike the M1, in which both commander and gunner had to share the same sight. The delivery had been delayed by the widespread sabotage carried out in the United States from dockside to communications.

CHAPTER THIRTY-SIX

THE TWO U.S. destroyers, 430-foot-long Knox-class warships of 3,900 tons each and manned by 280 seamen, along with a Canadian Tribal-class destroyer, whose previous twin, angled stacks were now one in order to reduce her line-of-sight infrared signature, moved at flank speed on patrol, slicing through long Pacific swells. They were heading toward the last-reported SOS position of the disabled factory ship, the MV *Southern Star*, which had reported earlier that she might have seen a submarine in the area being fished by her four trawlers.

The three investigating destroyers were three miles apart, seventy-one miles out, southwest of Long Beach on Vancouver Island on the main egress, or navy exit, "track" for U.S. and Canadian warships coming out of the Pacific Northwest. Suddenly there was a feral roar, enormous mushrooms of foaming water, both Knox-class destroyers ripped apart, sinking within minutes. The only reason some survivors, thirty-seven in all were plucked up from the oil- and debris-scummed water was that the Canadian destroyer was slower and running three miles astern of the Americans when the pressure-activated mines blew, gashing the destroyers open, the modern ships' thin armor plate a concession in the constant tug-of-war between more equipment and speed. Five hundred and seventy men and twenty-six women aboard the U.S. ships perished.

Tragic as it was, the loss of the destroyers to the U.S. Navy was hardly something in itself to undo the strategy of the chief naval officer in Washington. But the damage was far worse than at first supposed, for the entire egress channels for the northwest were now an unknown factor, meaning that each cargo vessel, submarine, or U.S. warship setting out to sea off the Pacific Northwest had to make a one-thousand-mile southern "detour" loop to avoid the suspect area, thus effectively bottling up and/or delaying large sections of COMPAC's West Coast fleet.

The sinkings became a crisis because of the cluster of questions pressing the CNO. Why didn't the U.S. Navy know about the mines? How could a submarine, recalling the *Southern Star*'s sighting, mine such a huge area, if it *was* huge and not merely local? Just as alarming, how could an enemy submarine get so close in undetected? If enemy submarines could do this with impunity, "within a stone's throw of our coastline," the *New York Times* had asked, what were the implications for the desperately needed resupply of Freeman's Second Army?

The CNO's spokesperson gave a terse "No comment at this time" to the scrum of reporters dogging her and the CNO as the admiral prepared to enplane the helicopter in Washington to report directly to the president at Mount Weather.

As he was whisked across the line into Virginia, CNO Admiral Horton was now giving much more credence to the *Southern Star*'s initial report, and ordered COMPAC— Commander Pacific—to have his chief of naval intelligence send someone immediately out to the *Southern Star* to interview her captain and crew before she limped back to dock and before airborne "experts" were rushed out by the TV networks and La Roche's tabloids.

This proved impossible. There was no difficulty locating the *Southern Star*, despite the failure of the navy and the factory ships' four trawlers to make radio contact in surges of static afflicting the northwestern states. The problem was that the ship wasn't where she was supposed to be, the southern-flowing Californian current taking the disabled vessel to a point sixty miles off the Olympic Peninsula, the swells lethargically moving the big ship to and fro like a wallowing whale who had lost all sense of direction.

When Lieutenant Eleanor Brady, a vivacious redhead who COMPAC's intelligence officer craftily gauged would elicit much more response than her male counterparts, was lowered by harness onto the *Southern Star*'s aft helicopter deck, there was no one to greet her. *Southern Star* was far from a ghost ship, however; the bodies of the two hundred men who had crewed her were painfully visible—strewn all over the ship in the galley, walkways, others having been shot down in midmeal, others murdered in their bunks, the officers on watch and the lookouts found sprawled amid the debris of shattered glass on the bridge, the ship's telegraph still set for "Full Ahead," though the engines, while still warm, were dead. The commandos, who, Eleanor Brady supposed, had obviously taken over the ship, had moved with grotesque swiftness and thoroughness. In the cavernous engine room, over twenty men, many more than usually would be on shift, had sought frantic refuge and now lay dead.

To say Lieutenant Brady's discovery shocked her would be an understatement. When other naval intelligence officers arrived aboard the ship from Bangor, they found her ashen-faced. The ammunition used was quickly ascertained to be depleted-uranium–tipped 7.62mm of the kind used by Spets.

At first the theory was that Spets aboard some other merchantman had somehow taken over one of the four trawlers and, once aboard the *Southern Star*, had been the ones to radio in the sighting of a submarine—in order to lure the Americans into the mine field, thus inciting a massive panic attack amid the navy brass and precipitating an equally massive lack of confidence in the navy throughout the country. Pressure mines, the CNO informed the president, would not have shown up on the sub-chasing Orion's magnetic anomaly detector, as the mines were often manufactured of nonmagnetic plastic composite.

The supposition that the Spets had sent out the message to lure the Allied ships made sense, but then questions were asked about where they had come from in the first place. Satellite pictures showed no other surface vessel within a hundred miles of the *Southern Star*. Had there been a sub as the *Southern Star* first reported? A sub carrying Spets commandos?

All the theories fell apart, however, when the four trawlers were found between a 110- and 130-mile radius from the *Southern Star*'s last position. Furthermore, none of the four trawlers had seen any other vessels—the other common agreement among the four skippers being that they had been unable to contact *Southern Star* after midnight.

With the certainty of ice turning blood cold, the truth began to sink in, and the director of naval intelligence, along with the CNO, knew he would have to inform the president without delay.

The DNI, his gold rings catching the velvety firelight in the deceptively calm atmosphere of the president's Mount Weather lounge, gave the president the bad news that contrary to first suspicions, the Spets had certainly not come from a submarine. The undersea sound-detection network was working fine—both U.S. and Canadian ships out of Bangor and Esquimalt respectively having run PROSIGs—prop signature recognition tests—in the hours following the *Southern Star* incident. And to show that everything had been working properly, it was pointed out that the shore SOSUS stations had plotted the Canadian and U.S. warships' exact positions and given detailed computer visual recognition of the ships and their armaments within twenty seconds of first noise pickup.

A sub would likewise have been picked up by SOSUS with the same ease. Even if a sub had been hiding near a hot spot, using the sound of thermal vents to mask it, once the sub made any move to attack or release mines, SOSUS would have picked it up.

"If there were no subs in the area," the president asked, "then where the hell did the Spets come from?"

"Mr. President," the DNI replied, "they were already there." He paused. "Aboard the *Southern Star*. Sleepers. *Southern Star* laid the mines. It's difficult for the layman," the DNI began, stopped short by a warning glance from the CNO.

"I'm sorry, sir," the DNI corrected himself. "I mean for nonnavy personnel to realize, but a ship that size, fifteen thousand tons, while not a big vessel in navy terms, is plenty big enough to hide a couple of automobiles without anyone noticing—if the parts are brought aboard piece by piece. Pressure mines would be a cinch. ChiCom agents among the crew could have been stashing them aboard for months, even years, waiting to be dumped in the event of war. So far," the DNI continued, "we've listed thirty crewmen not accounted for. All Chinese names. Out of San Francisco. But in all honesty we'd have to search the vessel for days to be absolutely certain. There are so many nooks and crannies a body might have been dumped in."

"They would have killed the crew—before dumping the mines," Mayne proffered.

"That's what it looks like, Mr. President. What puzzled us for a while is how they got away, but we think we have the answer for that one now. The factory ship's helicopter is gone, so it's pretty clear they escaped to shore, flying low, taking advantage of wave clutter to avoid our radar."

"But could thirty men—I mean against two hundred?"

"Mr. President, it would have taken only ten commandos from the Guo An Bu—Chinese Intelligence—or anywhere else against unarmed men. They used grenades as well."

For Mayne this was the last straw. The attack on Hillsboro's cesium clock, the sabotage against the huge electric grid, the water poisoning in New York and other cities—and now his entire West Coast sealift—shipping having to be rerouted, losing days, possibly weeks, in reaching Freeman. He and his cabinet decided he had no alternative but to extend and widen the Emergency Powers Act: curfews and empowering the police to arrest on mere suspicion, and suspension of Mirandizing suspects. He turned to Trainor, whose gaze during the crisis seemed morbidly attracted to the flickering of the fireplace.

"Trainor—cancel all my appointments in the morning."

"Wha— Ah, yes, Mr. President," Trainor answered, embarrassed at being caught daydreaming, his attention having momentarily been drawn to the crumbling symbolism of logs collapsing in the fire.

Suddenly there was a bang. The door flew open, the two Secret Service men already either side of Mayne, one of them his Uzi drawn, the other knocking the president to the floor, crouching protectively over him. "Everyone down!"

Somebody in the marine corps detachment guarding Mount Weather had goofed and inadvertently thrown a couple of cypress logs in the stack of firewood, a knot in the wood having exploded.

"Enough!" the president said. "Damn it!"

CHAPTER THIRTY-SEVEN

Taiwan

IN HIS HOME port of Kaohsiung on Taiwan's far southwest coast, Admiral Kuang was waiting. He had been waiting for twenty years, and another few weeks here or there didn't matter if his dream of personally leading an invasion across the straits came true, after which he would personally go to Hangchow—which Marco Polo believed to be the most beautiful place on earth—and there cross the West Lake to raze Mao's hallowed villa to the ground.

But Kuang knew that in Taipei the War Council would not release him until they saw the American Freeman was fully committed to an attack from the north. Kuang knew his lieutenant had promised the American general his full support when the time came, but it was a half truth—a promise based on the assumption that Freeman would lead off and so draw the bulk of Cheng's army northward away from the Straits of Taiwan.

But now Kuang's agents had told the admiral about the ChiComs' sabotage via the *Southern Star* on the American west coast, which would seriously delay resupply for Freeman. Kuang was anxious. It involved his word as an officer to help Freeman. He had, as the Americans would say, stuck his neck out, knowing that only if Taipei was willing to move could he. Had the admiral known, however, the full measure of the growing pressure against Freeman by Cheng's northern buildup in Manchuria, he would have relaxed. For Freeman, in the face of Cheng's buildup, would have to do something, and quickly, or be crushed by the Manchurian colossus. Still Freeman, in view of the sabotage on the United States, particularly that on the West Coast delaying his sealift, might be tempted to hold back. Kuang sent an encoded signal to Freeman's HQ that, decoded, read simply "mercury."

Freeman could move or not, but Kuang's message would tell him the ROC navy was ready to invade the beaches of Fukien, and thus take pressure off Freeman. After Freeman read the message there were tears in his eyes. He pulled out a tissue and blew his nose hard. "Damn dust in this hut! Doesn't anybody clean it?"

CHAPTER THIRTY-EIGHT

"YOU DUMB BASTARD!" Aussie castigated himself in the near-dawn light. He was less than a hundred miles from the border and was ready to use the beeper to bring in an EVAC when he heard the ominous *chud-chud-chud* of a bug-eyed Hind coming from behind him to the south.

It had been the cross probably. A Spets chopper or ground patrol for that matter had probably come across the cross and then, once alerted, they might have seen the leftovers and signs of his raft making. In any case, he told the Kawasaki they were in deep shit and he'd have to think fast. He picked one of the narrow gullies up ahead that went into an S-curve, probably following an old, dried riverbed, given the size of the boulders and sand dunes between them. He pulled the Kawasaki into the gully, laid it down on its side, took off his *del*, scooping sand underneath it, quickly sculpturing it into a body shape by the collapsed motorcycle, sweat streaking his blue-and-white Spets undershirt as he pulled out the fifteen-pound RPG-7 and two of its five-pound rounds and scrambled further down into the gully amid a small island of dunes and boulders scattered along its base.

The *chud-chud-chud* of the five-rotor chopper not yet visible was coming closer, and then suddenly its shadow passed over the gully and went into a turn. The pilot, no doubt having seen the splayed figure by the bike and realizing that the gully was too narrow to land, turned the helo about, coming down as close as he could to inspect the scene in the indistinct light, the rotors blowing sand every which way, obscuring his view.

The chopper suddenly rose, turned abaft, further away from the fallen Kawasaki, then lowered its rope ladder. Two Spets, AK-74s slung across their backs, were already descending.

Aussie knew the RPG-7 well enough from enemy arms training. He knew there'd be no backblast to give him away as he moved behind the rocks further away from the Kawasaki. With the chopper about 170 meters away, he was well within range of the RPG-7's five hundred meters.

Unlike with the controls of the Sagger or Spigot antitank weapons, he would have no toggle by which to steer either horizontally or vertically. It was strictly line of sight: aim—hit or miss. The chopper was drifting now about 180 meters away.

Leaning against a boulder, Aussie inhaled, exhaled half his breath, held the rest to subdue any nerve tremor, saw the lower Spets about to jump from the ladder, and fired, feeling the strong jerk backward. The pilot must have seen something coming at him and banked hard right, but with the warhead traveling at two hundred meters per second, the helo couldn't escape the antitank round hitting it below the left engine intake, the Hind exploding like some huge airborne animal, pieces of shard metal, much of it aluminum, looking like flaccid skin as they flew through the air, falling to the earth like so much tin among the stones, then the deafening roar of the gas explosion spewing out bodies like toys.

The man who had been at the bottom of the ladder had been blown to the ground by the downdraft and was now walking, or rather stumbling, around, holding his head. Aussie immediately raced forward. The man saw him coming and fumbled for the AK-74, but Lewis had three shots off, each one hitting the Russian. The man was still alive when Lewis reached him, holding his head as if in pain, as Lewis pumped another into him. "That'll cure your headache!" Aussie said. "And this one's for those kids back there in the pit. You bastard!"

Aussie was back on the Kawasaki and took off, pushing the beeper, mad at himself again. He should have been able to fell the Spets with one shot and not got mad when he was doing it. His old instructor in Hereford would have chewed him out for that, but then the old instructor wasn't dog tired and on the run.

"No excuses!" he told himself. "No bloody whining, Lewis. Now come on, you air cav. Where the fuck are you?"

They—two Blackhawks—were locked onto the beeper via an AWAC feed, and they were coming in low over the Mongolian sand with .50s nosing out the doors and four F-15 Eagles flying cover, and within eleven minutes a Blackhawk's rotor was stinging Aussie with small stones the size of marbles.

"Jesus Christ!" he complained as he jumped aboard. "Fucking near stoned me to death!"

"Welcome aboard," the corporal said.

"Thanks, mate," Aussie said, shaking his hand. "You saved my bacon."

The corporal, shouting over the roar of the rotors as they headed across the DMZ to the U.S.-Siberian territory east of Baikal, handed Aussie two envelopes. One was from Freeman's headquarters, telling him to report there to Major David Brentwood immediately upon his return. The second was from Salvini and Brentwood. The note was terse: "You owe us a bundle. We were hoisted aboard Talon quicker than you."

"Bastards!" Aussie said.

"Who?" the corporal yelled, his voice barely audible.

"My mates," Aussie answered.

David Brentwood had suggested to Freeman that Aussie Lewis be excused participation in "Operation Front Door."

"He wounded?" Freeman asked.

"No, sir, but he's been on the run for—"

"Then he'll have his second wind," Freeman said. "This isn't a lunch break. Operation's so important, every man designated is needed, especially with a commando's experience. Is that understood?"

"Yes, sir."

"Well I want you to go over the plan once more—fill in Lewis once he gets here or en route to the target. I'll leave the decision to you. He'll have six hours to sleep before the mission."

David Brentwood was about to say that Aussie would appreciate that but his discretion got the better part of cheekiness with Freeman. One thing you couldn't fault Freeman for: work. And one thing that drove Washington up the wall was the general's determination to lead his own men into action. He'd done it at Pyongyang, over Ratmanov Island, at Nizhneangarsk, and now he was willing to do it again. Like Patton, Rommel, and MacArthur before him, he had a fatalism in the face of fire that either awed men or struck them as bone stupid.

When Aussie Lewis showed up, his blue-and-white Spets shirt was filthy, torn to shreds; also his *del* was missing.

"What happened to your dress?" Choir asked.

"Yeah," Salvini said. "You can't come like that."

"I can come anywhere," Aussie said. "Where we goin'?"

"Little job on the old rampart," Salvini answered.

"What fucking rampart?"

"Genghis Khan's, you ignorant man," Choir said. "Not the Great Wall—another one in Manchuria. Only a couple of hours flying from here."

"Christ, I haven't had breakfast!" the Australian replied.

Choir Williams tut-tutted. "It's breakfast he wants. Should've kept up with us then, boyo—'stead of playing silly buggers on that bike."

"Yeah," Salvini added. "And you owe me five bucks."

David Brentwood smiled inwardly at the esprit de corps among the commandos, at the unemotional emotion of welcoming Aussie back.

"All right," Lewis said, as someone threw him a towel and a bar of soap. "What's it this time? Mongolian gear or Wall Street bankers?"

"In our own kit, mate," Choir Williams said. "Full SAS."

Aussie was impressed. "Must be serious then."

"It is," Brentwood confirmed, pointing down at the computer-enhanced, three-dimensional map of northern Manchuria. "Simulated attacks all along the line."

"Simulated?" Aussie asked. "You mean we just yell out at them? Frighten 'em a bit?"

"Real attacks," David answered. "Half a dozen places, from Manzhouli in the west to Fuyuan in the east near Khabarovsk. Right across the Manchurian front."

"But if we go full frontal—" Aussie began.

"That'd be crazy," David Brentwood finished for him.

"Agreed," Aussie said.

"The general knows that," Brentwood assured him. "What we have to do is create so much racket—make it look like a full frontal attack—do more than yell at them, Aussie. Tie down Cheng's troops all along the Manchurian border so that our Second Army can make its dash south of Manzhouli into the Gobi where Freeman can hit them on their left flank."

"If it works," Sal said, "we'll be halfway to Beijing before Cheng wakes up and can withdraw any of his forces from the north to reinforce his left flank."

"All right," Aussie said, "but how are we going to convince the Chinese it's a full-out attack when it isn't? Don't you think they'll twig to that?"

David Brentwood looked up from the three-dimensional mock-up. "You know Freeman goes to sleep reading Sun Tzu."

"Who the hell's Son Sue?"

"An ancient Chinese general," Brentwood said. "Very big on the art of war. Very big on deception."

"Right," Aussie said. "I don't suppose it occurred to any of you blokes that old Cheng might read this Son Sue—you know, being Chinese and all that."

Salvini looked worried.

"I think," Brentwood said, "that when you have the chance to see the plan in detail you'll see how Freeman'll outfox Cheng." David Brentwood paused. "By the way, Aussie, everyone is to bring a lighter with him—there's a box of Bics over on the counter—and one quart bag of this." He nodded toward a cardboard box packed with quart-size plastic bags, each bag filled with what looked like gray powder.

"What the hell's that?" Aussie asked.

"Wolf dung," Brentwood answered matter-of-factly.

"Don't bullshit me!" Aussie riposted.

Brentwood shook his head at Salvini and Williams. "He's a hard man to convince."

"Ten bucks it's wolf dung," Choir Williams proffered.

Salvini couldn't suppress a snort of laughter. Aussie eyed them suspiciously. "What are you bastards up to?"

"Go on," Brentwood told him. "Clean up, have breakfast, and hit the sack. We'll fill you in en route."

"All right," David Brentwood said, "it's AirLand battle, right?"

"Right!" came the chorus of twenty SAS/D troopers. There were a million details for any AirLand battle, and for the twenty men to be led by David Brentwood, the first was weapon selection and uniform. Weapon selection was very much an individual affair among the commandos, but the uniform wasn't—not on this predawn attack that hopefully would penetrate the ChiCom line in enough places to convince Cheng that a full-scale frontal attack was in progress.

There would be many more SAS/D troops along the Amur

together with regular elements of Second Army involved. Most of the SAS elected to arm themselves with the American 5.56mm M-16 rifle rather than the three-pounds-heavier British 7.62mm, particularly with the M203 grenade launcher fitted beneath the barrel of the M-16 rifle.

Others, like Brentwood, who had seen Freeman in action on Ratmanov Island, opted for the military-modified Winchester 1200 riot gun with five shotgun shells, one up the spout, four in the tubular magazine, the pumping effected by the forestock going back and forth, the range of the shotgun increased from 150 to 900 yards by fléchettes, twenty high-quality steel darts. Lead-slug shells were also carried, these being capable of passing right through an engine block at over fifty meters or blowing a door out of its frame. And almost every man carried at least several "soup cans"— smoke grenades—and the smaller palm-size SAS special, the stun grenade. But because it would be an attack in darkness and could well be at close quarters in the town of Manzhouli, the uniform was the all-black SAS antiterrorist gear, including the SF 10 respirator in case the Chinese used gas, black leather gloves for rappelling down or climbing up the Genghis Khan wall, or any other wall for that matter, Danner lightweight firm-grip boots favored by U.S. SWAT teams, and each man's black belt kit holding magazine pouches and grenades and thirteen rounds of 9mm for the Browning automatic.

"All right, fellas, now let's go over the AirLand prayer. One?"

"Maneuver!" the chorused reply came.

"Two?"

"Fire support!"

"Three?"

"Command and control!"

"Four?"

"Intelligence!"

"Five?"

"Combat service support!"

"Six?"

"Mobility—survivability!"

"Seven?"

"Air defense!"

"Eight?" Aussie shouted.

"Best of fucking luck!"

Brentwood grinned. "Now our short-range fighter-bombers and Wild Weasel jammers will penetrate as deeply as they can at points all along the line to simulate full frontal attack. Main battle tanks will go in where possible with Bradley fast-fighting infantry vehicles behind and with Apache helos as antitank cover. This will be followed by Hueys—eleven men apiece, some helos carrying a one oh five millimeter howitzer and crew. Now behind all this there's the Patriot missile defense should we be bothered by anything from Turpan. But remember, the Patriot is great but is overestimated. Unless it hits the enemy missile's warhead and explodes it midair, it simply blasts the body of the incoming missile, and the warhead still comes down. It isn't a great deal of help to us—no matter what you read in the papers. Got it?"

"Got it."

"Now," Brentwood continued, "there'll be SAS/D-Green Beret, Special Operations squadrons hitting Fuyuan near Khabarovsk, another SAS/D team hitting at Heihe—halfway along the Amur, a third commando force targeting Shiwei, and the fourth team, us, will be paying a return visit near our old friend A-7."

There was a groan from several of the veterans who had vivid memories of the fighting atop the 3,770-foot mountain just north of Manzhouli in the Siberian Argunskiy range. It marked the most northwesterly point or corner of the Manchurian arc defense line that stretched from Khabarovsk up around Never-Skovorodino and down into western Manchuria. A-7 had been the very spot where the war had started before the so-called cease-fire, and so would now be heavily fortified, its high ground having a commanding view of the American side of the line.

"Don't worry," David said, anticipating his men. "A-7 will be left to our air force."

"And about time," Choir Williams quipped.

"So give us the bad news," Aussie said.

"We'll be going southeast beyond A-7 into Manzhouli," Brentwood answered. "Just east of Manzhouli. We're to secure the railhead there so Cheng can't move troops west out of northern Manchuria and hit Freeman's left flank."

"Old Cheng won't have to move anything," Choir Williams said, "if those chink missiles aren't taken out in Turpan."

"That's the air force's job," David said.

"Well they better get on with it, boyo, or else we'll be in range while we're in bloody Manzhouli."

"Question!" It was from one of the young American SAS/D troopers. "Look, I know our short-range bombers can't take out Turpan, it's just too far west, but why can't we use them against Manzhouli? I mean, just go in and blow up the tracks?"

David gave a wry smile—the trooper was one of the latest recruits, not yet blooded. "If we'd been able to blow up train tracks and trails we'd have won the Vietnam War in the first two years. Only way to make sure that railway stays ours is to go into Manzhouli. There are a hundred different ways of the enemy making it look as if you've destroyed their train lines from the air and the next morning they've passed a thousand tons of munitions over it. Only way is to go in on the ground and make sure. Besides, they've got a communications tower there so we'll have to hit it with C charges. Aussie, that'll be your troop's job."

"Thanks very much."

"Well, hell, Aussie, you can't ask for everything," someone shouted.

"Jesus, I wish I was with that Fuyuan crowd."

A few of the newer men didn't understand and weren't as confident as veterans like Aussie or Brentwood, Salvini or Williams in knowing there was no shame in saying you'd rather be somewhere else.

"Ah," Choir Williams said, nodding his head toward Aussie. "Pay him no mind, lads. He misses Olga, he does. He likes the titty!"

"Bloody right I do," Aussie said.

"Why are we all black?" Aussie asked. His question wasn't meant as any kind of joke, for normally SAS were allowed some leeway in the choice of uniform, but all black—antiterrorist—usually meant close-quarter combat.

"Freeman doesn't want Manzhouli bombed, so if we're to clear it it'll be house to house," Brentwood said tersely.

"Right," Aussie said, quickly exchanging an M-16 for a stockless Heckler & Koch 9mm MP5K submachine gun. You aimed it by jabbing it toward the target and adjusting your aim according to the hits.

The last thing that every man checked was the black gloves, for quite apart from the rappelling down and climbing up that might be necessary, word had come down that it would be a "fast rope" descent from the helos. H hour was set for 0500 hours; the pilots aboard the Pave Lows would be flying on night vision and by hover coupler, which would orchestrate gyroscope, radar, altimeter, and inertial guidance system readouts to keep the helo steady and very low.

"Apart from anything else," Salvini reminded one of the newcomers, "the SAS black antiterrorist uniform is meant to frighten the enemy."

"You don't need one then, Sal," Aussie quipped. "You're ugly enough already. We show them Salvini and it's instant fuckin' surrender!"

"Up yours!" Salvini told Aussie.

"Promise?"

"All right, you guys," Brentwood said. "Let's move out.

Four of you attach yourselves to myself, Lewis, Williams, or Salvini.''

"Hey, Davey," Aussie asked Brentwood as they went out onto the Chita strip. "What's all this crap about Freeman not wanting to bomb the towns and villages?"

"Don't know, Aussie. Part of the strategy."

"He gone soft in the head or something?"

"Freeman? I doubt it."

"So do I. So why the hell—" Brentwood couldn't hear Aussie's last word as a brisk wind was blowing east off of Lake Baikal, a bitter edge to it as the Pave Lows began warming up, their stuttering now a full roar, their warm wash felt through the all-black uniforms.

As those sectors of Freeman's forces designated to simulate an all-out attack on the Manchurian front started to move out, Freeman received word that at long last the Labour opposition in Britain had conceded to the B-52 overflight over Britain. France still wouldn't agree, however, and this would mean a diversion around Spain, but at least the mission of the big bombers was on. The problem was, would it come in time? Yet he could wait no longer with the north Chinese buildup of men and matériel about to burst upon him from the Manchurian fastness. Besides, Admiral Huang would tie up the southern forces.

CHAPTER THIRTY-NINE

Lakenheath, England

AS HE CLIMBED into the rear barbette of the lead B-52, Sergeant Murphy, or "Pepto-Bismol," as he was now known, was very unhappy and festooned with packets of the "new and improved" antacid tablets.

"Crabbing it," their wheels angling into the crosswind, compensating for their natural tendency to drift to one side on takeoff, the nine B-52Gs forming the nine-plane wave of stratofortresses from the Forty-second Wing of the U.S. Sixty-ninth Bombardment Squadron thundered along the runway and roared into the night sky over southeastern England. Each of the eight thirteen-thousand-pound-thrust Pratt-and-Whitney jet engines on the Big Ugly Fat Fellows was in high scream as the bombers, tops painted wavy khaki green, undersides white-gray, headed across the channel at the beginning of their 4,700-mile mission half a world away to attack the missile sites at Turpan.

Traveling at forty thousand feet plus, each of the nine bombers that made up the three cells—Ebony, Gold, and Purple—carried in its bomb bay and beneath its 185-foot wingspan the conventional bomb-load equivalent of fifteen World War II B-17s. Due to recent malfunctions in the normally remote-control console of the rear barbette with its four 12.7-millimeter cannon, the guns were manned, Murphy being the rear barbette gunner in Ebony's lead plane. The heavy ordnance aboard the B-52s included thirty eleven-hundred-pound FAE, or fuel air explosive, bombs, each bomb of jellied gasoline over four times as powerful as the equivalent weight of high-explosive. In addition, each plane carried twelve five-hundred-pound free-fall high-explosive iron contact bombs with Pave conversion kits that turned them into smart bombs.

"Wish we were carrying cruise," the radar navigator aboard Ebony One's leader commented.

"You and me both," added the ECM—electronic countermeasures or electronics warfare officer, a technician who when the war broke out had been selling the superfast Cray computers.

"It was a political decision," answered Ebony's captain, the air commander of the nine-plane wave. "Washington doesn't want us carrying cruise missiles anywhere near the Mideast. Wouldn't give us a 'weapons free' release even if we were packing them. Too risky. The Iranians are the worst. They pick up a cruise missile, think we're popping off nuclear warheads, and bingo! The balloon goes up."

To make especially sure that no such interpretation would be made by any one of the countries they'd be flying over, each one of the nine planes in Ebony, Gold, and Purple had been fitted with the special flared-wing fairings, which, if the B-52s were picked up by satellite, would identify them as being "cruise free."

None of the six-man crew aboard Ebony One—the pilot and aircraft commander Colonel Thompson, copilot, navigator, radar navigator, EWO—electronics warfare officer— and gunner—was at all happy about the decision, but neither were they anxious about starting what was euphemistically referred to in air force manuals as a "nuclear exchange." Even so, the EWO, in the cramped, windowless electronics recess of the tiny lower deck, had confided to the navigator and radar navigator forward of him on the lower deck that if he was to be downed, he'd just as soon go out in a "mushroom" as in some Iranian prison camp—the sight of the POWs in Vietnam and of the American hostages of the eighties and nineties was still a chilling memory for the American fliers. Several of the crew, teenagers then, could still recall the terrifying images of the Ayatollah seen on television and the humiliation of the Americans.

Above the EWO, the air commander and his pilot were carrying out visual checks, using the erratic wash of moonlight to make sure that all the contact bombs on the extender racks beneath the wings were well in place. The fine wires that would extract the safety pins of the primers could not be seen in the moonlight, but none of the bombs looked askew to the AC as he scanned the huge 185-foot wingspan that, supporting the four pods of the twin engines and the bombs, rose slowly as they gained altitude though the line of the wing was still below that of the fuselage, the tanks "loaded to the gills," as Murphy, the rear gunner, was fond of putting it, with over thirty-five thousand gallons of kerosene.

As the English Channel, now a silver squiggle, receded far below them, the three cells disappeared in cloud, the navigator on Ebony One already going over his trace with the electronic warfare officer, who would have to coordinate his "jammer" pod against any ground-to-air missile batteries that protected the mobile sites around Turpan. Reading the coordinates from the computer, the navigator drew, as manual backup, the intersect lines with his protractor. The EWO circled in the last reported satellite digital photo relay showing the missile shelters around Turpan, but there were now seven additional "tents" showing up on the computer-enhanced photo.

"Are they more CS-2s, Ted?" the radar navigator asked. "Or SAMs?"

"Don't know," the EWO replied. "All I know is that we're going to have to drop our load from as high as we can and I'll be using every jammer we've got. Are we spot on the track, Charlie?'' the EWO asked the navigator.

''No sweat,'' the navigator answered, giving their position over the Bay of Biscay as they were heading over Spain for Turkey, Iran, and Iraq, their flight taking them over the bay because as with the American raid on Qaddafi's Libya, they were not allowed to fly over French soil. Also, AC Thompson wanted to keep as far away as possible from the trigger-happy new Soviet republics. Hence the southern crescent-shaped detour. Also time had to be allowed for Phantom-4G Wild Weasels to go in just ahead of the bombers to jam as much ChiCom ground-to-air communications and radar as possible.

In Freeman's AirLand battle opening up all along the Amur front, first the medium-range bombers and fighters went in, shooting up everything in sight, including superbly camouflaged oil-lamp-heated dugouts, which their infrared targeted as tanks in defilade position. Even so, the Chinese were struck by the ferocity of the American offensive.

Colonel Soong, north of Manzhouli, had his troops well dug in atop A-7 but was paid a return visit by a C-130 Spectre gunship whose crew's infrared night-vision capacity enabled it to pour down a deadly rain of fire. But whereas during an attack on A-7 earlier in the war a C-130 had finally fallen prey to a surface-to-air missile, this time the SAM sites had been raked by F-15 Eagles.

Each Eagle dropped sixteen thousand pounds of smart ordnance from its underfuselage and underwing hard points, so that the C-130 was left unthreatened save for small-arms fire. As it continued in its devastating counterclockwise spiral, spewing out its deadly fire, if any of the Chinese troops lifted a rifle or RPG, or any other weapon in a desperate attempt to down it, they were immediately' sighted on the infrared screens and targeted.

From Fuyuan in the east near Khabarovsk to Manzhouli

in the west, the night was rent by fire. In Fuyuan the Americans received unexpected help from the Jewish underground in the nearby Jewish Autonomous Oblast and actually succeeded in pushing the Chinese four miles back across a frozen section of the river.

The advance, General C. Clay reported, was getting out of hand. One of the most aggressive groups was a Jewish contingent led by Alexsandra Malof, the woman who had been tortured by Siberian and Chinese alike and who was determined to help the Americans. It was she who, with other Jewish women, had been forced to fraternize, who had been the *poprosili*—the requested ones—for the pleasure of the Siberian fliers in Khabarovsk before the Americans came. Aleksandra had been a favorite of the ace, Sergei Marchenko. But she was only one, and so many had scores to settle against both Sibirs, as they called them, and the Chinese that General Clay had to order a slowdown in order for his logistical tail to catch up with his forward troops in the rugged ravines of the Manchurian fastness.

Up around Never and Skovorodino, sites of one of Freeman's fiercest-fought battles earlier in the war, the Chinese gave as good as they got. The ChiCom regulars wouldn't yield even to the marines' M-60s, whose 105mm guns, atop the tortoiselike appearance of the tanks caused by blocks of reactive armor all over them, blasted PLA infantry positions across the river. Salvos of expensive, at least for the Chinese, RPGs were fired at the M-60s, but the reactive armor blowing up as it was struck neutralized the Chinese attack in the main and the M-60s kept up a deafening fire that resounded like thunder through the still–snow-dusted hills and along the flats of the river at the foot of cleft-hewn mountains.

Cheng could tolerate the situation so far, but what he was asking his aides for was any reports coming in from around Manzhouli to the west on his left flank, where Chinese positions stretched along the wall of Genghis Khan, and beyond to the south, where the country became flatter—and would be much more suitable for the American Abrams forty-five-mile-per-hour main battle tank.

"Nothing, General."

"What do you mean, nothing?" Cheng asked, though his voice was subdued and suprisingly calm.

"Only static, General! The American Wild Weasels' electronic interceptors are jamming all radio communications."

"We don't know what's going on anywhere," another said. "They're attacking on so many points we don't know where their main concentration lies."

"Freeman's no fool," Cheng said. "He knows better than to spread his forces that thinly from Manzhouli to Khabarovsk—over a 1,200-mile front. No army in the world can attack equally along such a lengthy front. If our radios are jammed we'll have to rely on our motorcycle couriers."

"But General, it would take them hours—in some cases, days—before they could reach—"

"Not to us here in Beijing, you fool. I mean between regimental commands. We have good men up there. They will use their initiative."

Indeed they were, one motorbike signal company already moving couriers out along the narrow roads through the mountainous cold. They might as well have been carrying a neon sign, however, saying, "Here we are," for the F-16s and F-15s, while they didn't kill all of them in the narrow defiles, did get most of them.

As the Pave Low banked, Aussie felt his Bergen pack shift despite its tight rigging, and now they were coming into the darkness of Manzhouli, the rail lines ribbons of steely light beneath the moon running east of the wall, which was now being breached by the Pave Lows.

"Bloody great orb!" Aussie said, cursing the break in the clouds. "Might as well send up a flare." The Pave Low took a whack and seemed to skid in midair, but it was shrapnel from AA fire hitting the second chopper and perhaps the third.

"Second chopper's going down!" someone said.

The red light went to green and they felt the icy rush of air.

"Go!"

And one by one they went down the rope, the big Pave in a clearing not a quarter mile north of the railway station. The choppers would return in forty-five minutes.

Aussie felt the heat through his black gloves as he descended on the rope and fell back into gritty snow. Within a minute he had the 9mm Heckler & Koch MP5K in one hand, shucking the chute with the other, then joined the other nineteen men from the three Paves. The chopper that had been hit had landed, albeit bumpily, and discharged its six SAS/D men but was now unable to take off, the other two choppers already up and away.

"Right!" David Brentwood called out to the crew of the damaged chopper. "You're with us. Keep in the center." There was a chance—just a chance—that the Pave Lows, some of the best nap-of-the-earth fliers in the world, had come in so low via their ground-sensing radar that despite the AA fire that could well have been directed at the helos' sound, none of the ChiCom guards atop the wall several hundred yards in front of them, or at the railway complex a quarter mile ahead of them, had actually *seen* the choppers. Then again if the ChiComs had been trying to make regular radio calls to units up along the Genghis Khan Wall they would have quickly realized that the static jamming their lines was so intense as to be more than merely atmospheric in origin.

In fact, the whole garrison of 120 Chinese troops at Manzhouli was alerted, having seen one of the Pave Lows pass like a bulky chariot across the moon, and the garrison's commander, an unafraid twenty-three-year-old Captain Ko, made the eminently sensible decision to go out straight away to meet his attackers head on rather than do half the job for them by staying bottled up in the railway station. Surprise was to be met by surprise. To begin with, the small town of Manzhouli had been evacuated by all its citizens, and only the military remained.

CHAPTER FORTY

THE NAVIGATOR IN Ebony One informed Air Commander Thompson, the pilot of Ebony One, "We're coming up on Büyuk Agridome. Otherwise known to you peasants as Mount Ararat."

"Which one?" the radar navigator asked, crammed in next to him. "There are two peaks."

"The big one, dummy," the navigator replied. "The 'dome' is a sixteen-thousand-foot massif, the twelve-thousand-foot twin is four miles to the southeast. Four point two to be exact. Iraq and Iran to your right."

"How far to target?" Ebony's captain asked as he glanced out to try to pick up the two arrowhead formations of Purple and Gold, assuming they were carrying out precisely the same computations, but not absolutely sure as all cells were on interplane radio silence, the only conversations allowed being those within each aircraft.

"Damn!" Thompson said.

"What's up?" his copilot asked.

The captain was looking out the port side. They were out of cloud, though mountainous cumulonimbus was all around them, the captain indicating the long contrails that in the moonlight had taken on a sheen that could be seen for miles as the three cells progressed in perfect formation. "Should be cloud pretty soon," the copilot said reassuringly. He'd barely finished speaking when the entire wave was swallowed up by more cumulonimbus as they approached the mountains of northern Iraq and Iran. "What'd I tell you, Cap?"

"Yep. God's on our side, Captain," cut in Murphy, at the rear gun controls.

"Never mind that, Murphy," Thompson responded. "Keep your eyes peeled. Radar nav—anything on the scope?"

"Just our eight compadres, Captain. A milk run."

"Right," Thompson said, encouraged by the esprit de corps after his concern about the contrails. As air commander as well as captain, he shouldn't have said anything about the vapor trails that might have induced anxiety in his crew, but this was his third combat tour and sometimes he just felt jumpier than others. Besides, like the other fifty-three men in the wave, he had an abiding hatred and fear of the religious fanatics who inhabited so many of the Islamic countries over or near which they would be flying.

One of the most vivid memories of his childhood was the nightly broadcasts of the Iranian-held American hostages, and even though he was too young then to fully understand what was going on he well understood the humiliation of the blindfolded and tortured Americans as they were daily taunted and paraded before the world. His great-grandfather had told him the Iranian fanatics reminded him of Hitler's SS—they weren't simply fanatical but were fierce fighters, and their hatred of America knew no bounds.

So intense were the crews' feelings about falling into the hands of Muslim fundamentalists that everyone aboard Ebony One had opted to carry "the pill" in his first-aid kit just in case.

"Hey," Murphy said from the rear barbette control above and aft of the swivel-mounted cannon. "Ara— Whatsit?"

"Ararat," the navigator told him.

"I've heard that somewhere before," Murphy said.

The electronics warfare officer leaned forward over his plot, shifting his canvas-holstered service revolver further around on his belt to keep it from digging into his pelvis.

"Yeah," Murphy said eagerly. "Ararat—isn't that where they had some winter Olympics?"

The navigator drew a line on his plastic overlay from Ararat to the Hindu Kush and from there to the Turpan depression, a red circle the size of a dime on Ararat. "Olympics?" the gunner responded. "Not unless Noah was a hotdogger!"

"Noah?" Gunner Murphy said. "Noah who?"

"For Chrissake—" the copilot chuckled.

"You know, Murph," the radio nav cut in. "Noah—*Raiders of the Lost Ark*."

"I saw that," Murphy triumphantly said. "I don't remember any Noah."

"You jerkin' us off, Murphy?" the copilot asked.

"What? No," Murphy said. "Why?"

"He's jerking us off," the EWO said. "Right, Murph?"

Freeman waited for word that Cheng had fallen for the bait and was now moving the Shenyang army and other northern reserves up to the Amur front. Once this happened, if it happened, Freeman could launch his armored attacks south across the Chinese nose that poked into Mongolia, then across the eighteen miles that comprised the Mongolian toe of land that likewise stuck into Manchuria, and then onto the semidesert plains of the Gobi and China's Inner Mongolia.

With the B-52s having taken off from Lakenheath and traveling around six hundred miles per hour, depending on the altitude, it would take them seven and a half hours before they hit Turpan, and Freeman knew that if he was to take advantage of faking out Cheng by his Amur front deception he might have to order his armor south *before* the missiles at Turpan were taken out. What was it the British had said to him during the battle of Ratmanov Island between Alaska and Siberia? That "it might be a near run thing!" But before it could be anything, Cheng had to take the bait.

CHAPTER FORTY-ONE

"AUSSIE!" BRENTWOOD WHISPERED hoarsely. "You got the bag?"

"Got it!" Aussie answered, referring to the plastic bag of wolf dung.

"He's full of it," Salvini joked. Brentwood ignored him. "Choir, you there?"

"I'm here."

"Salvini?"

"Here."

It was in that order that if Aussie was hit, the wolf dung would be passed. It was not to be lit before dawn—about a half an hour away—and in Freeman's words, "God help the son of a bitch who doesn't keep it dry!"

The advantage of the ChiComs having seen the Pave Lows come down was offset now by the fact that as the PLA company spewed out across the rail line and briskly made its way toward the areas where it thought the three choppers had landed, the SAS/D teams were invisible in their black uniforms against the dark forest. And the ChiComs were making the mistake of bunching up, a natural tendency of men facing danger, and their harder, cruder boots made more noise on the ties.

David Brentwood, his ear to the rail, having picked up the first movement of men coming toward him, quickly had the SAS/D team fan out left and right of the tracks. The natural move for him was to have his commandos melt into the woods either side of the track; but he resisted the temptation because it would mean the danger of them crossfiring into their own men, and so they went to ground instead and stayed there, those closest to the rails packing C charges against the rails wherever they could, waiting. Then everything went wrong. They heard the *whoosh*. Night became day, the line of SAS/D men exposed in flare light showing up like slugs against the patches of snow. Immediately the rattle of AK-47s filled the air, snow flicking up like a swarm of white insects.

"The trees!" Brentwood shouted, and as he did so crushed the acid timer ampoule for the nearest C-4 plastique charge. The bravery of neither the ChiComs nor the SAS/D troops was in question, but Captain Ko's decision with an advantage of six to one that offense was in this case the best form of defense overlooked a vital component: that once in the trees the SAS/D commandos became the defenders and Ko's men were exposed. In order for Ko's men to uproot the commandos, who, as well as having the natural defense of the woods, were still making their way through the woods either side of the railway up to the rail yard and control hut, Ko's men would have to go in after them.

"Scopes only!" Brentwood yelled, and a burst of AK-47 fire erupted in his direction, shredding some pine bark. It was an order that referred only to those SAS/D troops who had longer rather than shorter range submachine guns, the longer range weapons having been allocated infrared night-vision scopes. With only scopes firing, "blue on blue," or, in other words, being shot by your own men in the dark, could be avoided. It was a classic case of the Americans adapting to new circumstances quickly, and in the process suddenly turning a dangerous situation to their advantage.

"Right," Salvini muttered, "here we go!" And with that he rested his AIS rifle against a low pine. The accuracy of the international supermagnum sniper rifle came from its Kigre KN 200 F night-vision image intensifier. Through the scope he could see a PLA cap and torso crouching. He squeezed the trigger and the torso was lost amid an explosion of green flecks as the depleted-uranium bullet tore right through him and kicked up the snow back of him. Within seven seconds Salvini had felled three more ChiComs in the green circle of his night scope, and he could hear the single whacks of the Heckler & Koch MP5K submachine gun and an occasional quick rip of it set on three-round bursts, which meant that some of the ChiComs were reaching the edge of the wood and could still be seen in the fading flare light so as to be easily targeted without night-vision optics. The last thing Ko wanted was another flare light now he'd seen his strategy backfire on him, but Brentwood yelled, "Choir! Flare!"

Choir lifted his M-203 grenade launcher that was attached to his M-16 so that its skyward flare shot would not come back at him from overhanging branches, screaming aloft instead, well clear of the timber. There was a quick sound like the belch of a sinkhole emptying, and moonlight went to daylight again as the magnesium sun floated slowly down.

Ko ordered his men into the woods, and the Chinese, about fifty yards on either side of the snow clearing, charged into the woods to fight it out man to man. There was a roar of fire, AK-47s, AK-74s, 7.62 bayonet-equipped type-56 Chinese carbines, type-43 and -50 7.62mm ChiCom submachine guns, and from the woods either side the eruption of the SAS/D's Heckler & Koch 9mm Parabellums streaming out at over eight hundred rounds a minute, the crash of grenades, and the terrible whistling of fléchettes. These steel darts, fired by the SAS/D Winchester 1200 shotgun, twenty darts for each shot, drove through ChiCom helmets at a hundred yards as if they were butter, those without helmets falling, their heads exploding, spraying blood everywhere.

Ko was not to know that the enemy was the SAS/D elite, otherwise he might have elected to withdraw, but close-encounter warfare was what the SAS/D called a "specialty of the house." For the SAS this meant the CQB—close quarter battle—practiced at the house in Hereford, England, and what the Delta men referred to as the "shooting house" at Fort Bragg, both houses training the commandos for everything there was to know about CQB. Adding to this, the Varo flip-up/flip-down night-vision goggles supplied to the SAS/D men helped reduce what had been a six-to-one ChiCom advantage to a three-to-one advantage during the firefight. And now, the fight being closer in, SAS/D cold steel found bone, ripping the ChiComs to pieces.

Ko's contingent fought bravely, and it wasn't until the first light of dawn after the C charges had blown, injuring two SAS/D men with shrapnel, that the full extent of the carnage could be gauged, the snow pocked red with the dead, the wounded, and the dying. The victory for the SAS/D was somewhat hollow, however, when it was discovered that as well as four SAS/D men killed, all of the Pave Low's crewmen had died, despite the best efforts of the SAS/D men to protect them.

"Damn!" David Brentwood said with an uncharacteristic vehemence. "I should have told them to wait with the chopper."

"Ah, rats!" Aussie said. "None of us knew whether the Chinese would find the chopper and—"

Commandos were now setting charges in the railway control boxes and on other lines. With radios unable to get through the jamming of Freeman's Wild Weasels, the SAS lit orange and purple flares for pickup. The wall of Genghis Khan had clearly been breached by the SAS/D team, but to make it official two SAS/D men—Salvini and Aussie—were dispatched to light the wolf dung fire by the base of one of the watchtowers atop the old wall.

"What the fuck's all this about?" Salvini asked Aussie.

"Don't ask me, sport. Davey's the only one that knows, and he's apparently under orders to keep it mum till we're out of here."

The arrival of the Pave Lows was interrupted for a minute or so by a Chinese sniper hiding out in the woods, but he was taken out by a scope-mounted M-16 and the helos came down and took aboard the living and the dead.

"So?" Aussie yelled as the Pave Low rose with the dawn, heading away from the tall but distinctly gray-white trail of wolf dung smoke. "What's all this business with the wolf shit?"

"Wait till we get a few hundred feet," Brentwood said, his face still grim after the loss of the crew from the Pave Low, which they had blown to pieces with a C charge before takeoff, denying any of the helo's weapons or electronics to the ChiComs.

"Why?" Aussie began, and then he and all the other commandos saw it: All along the front for as far as they could see, spirals of the same grayish smoke could be seen rising straight, high into the dawning sky.

"What's the idea?" Salvini asked.

"It's the traditional Chinese signal," Brentwood explained. "For some reason the chemical composition of wolf dung makes it burn thick and go straight up—straighter than any other kind of smoke."

"Yeah, but signal for what?" Salvini pressed.

"The wall—China's defenses being breached."

"I get it," Aussie said. "Cheng and his buddies can't get squat info from his radios, so with the smoke signal they'll think we've broken through all along the line."

"We have," Brentwood said. "But what they don't know is for how long. Hopefully Cheng'll be rushing fresh troops— all his reserves—up north instead of westward."

"While Freeman's armored spearhead heads south," Salvini said. "Brilliant. Meanwhile, we go back to base. I love it."

"That crafty bastard!" Aussie said, and everyone knew he meant Freeman. The wolf dung smoke trails could be seen along the entire length of the Black Dragon River by the Chinese reserve battalions miles back from the front but already moving northward to counter what they saw as the enemy's penetration of the Black Dragon line.

Cheng was not completely sold on the reports—slow in coming because of the radio jamming—that the wall had been breached everywhere. He guessed there must be some copycat panic down the line. But what sold him was the intelligence reports further south of the front amid the villages and towns along the few roads that snaked through the Manchurian vastness.

While all ChiCom military targets—at least those not camouflaged well enough—had been hit, not one single town or village on the sparse roadways through Manchuria had been destroyed. This was not, Cheng believed, because of any humanitarian gesture on Freeman's part not to bomb civilians, but because bombed-out villages and towns in such mountainous terrain caused so much rubble on the narrow roads that it would be a major impediment to any armored columns snaking through the steep valleys, and indeed would bunch up armor, making it much more vulnerable to attack by small guerrilla bands.

Ironically, while the high columns of wolf dung smoke had alarmed other commanders along the line, it was the care that Freeman had taken not to create such rubble rather than the wolf dung that convinced Cheng it was an all-out deep attack by Freeman's army against China's northern defenses.

* * *

By now Freeman's armor was well underway west and south of Manzhouli, his M1A1 tanks leading, his Bradley infantry vehicles following, at times on the flank. Reports kept coming in to Freeman that Chinese troops were still taking the bait and on the move northward in Manchuria from Shenyang toward the Amur or Black Dragon River.

"By God, Dick!" Freeman told Norton exuberantly. "We've done it. Wolf dung. Norton, how about that for high tech? By God, we've done it!"

And so they had—until, as the position became clearer to the northernmost Chinese commanders, a very low tech carrier pigeon arrived at Shenyang HQ informing the PLA's Northern Command that the ferocity of the American attacks that had been assumed to be a major offensive now appeared to be no more than well-coordinated probing actions. Cheng was about to order the northern bound troops westward, but this would take time, especially with rail links like that of Manzhouli now broken. Instead he ordered the reserves to reverse direction and head south back down out of Manchuria as fast as possible and *then* westward into Inner Mongolia and the Gobi. So, Cheng thought, the great American general believed he had outwitted the PLA!

Suddenly the EWO in Ebony One saw an amber blip on his screen. "AC," he said, notifying the air commander. "Unidentified aircraft. Two o'clock high. Fifty miles."

The captain acknowledged. "Stay with them, Murphy— must be one of our Harrier escorts."

"Got him in the cone, skipper."

"Countermeasures ready?" the captain asked as a precaution.

"Ready, sir," the EWO confirmed. Four seconds had elapsed since the first radar contact.

"Range?" the captain asked.

"Forty-nine miles. Speed, Mach one point eight," which meant that whatever it was was traveling in excess of nine hundred miles per hour. Most probably a fighter, all right, but not a Harrier.

The captain banked left, beginning evasive action, hoping that Purple's and Gold's EWOs would have seen either the contact on their screens or his "radio silence" evasive maneuver. Hopefully they had seen both. Beneath them the great peaks of the Hindu Kush rose majestically in a sea of moonlit white peaks. "Range?"

"Forty-eight miles. Closing. Mach one point three. Three others joining him."

The first four-thousand-mile East Wind 4, which western experts thought had been discarded in favor of the longer eight-thousand-mile-range CSX-4, landed on the right flank of Freeman's armored column racing south of Manzhouli. It did no more damage than blow up enormous blocks of ice from the twenty-mile-wide Lake Hulun, which still, mostly frozen, was providing Freeman's armored columns with a shortcut south. The second and third missiles, however, hit the ice in the middle of the column, and an M-60 tank and Bradley fighting vehicle rolled at speed and disappeared.

Immediately Freeman in the lead tank saw other columns slow. "Full bore!" he yelled into the radio. "Keep moving, damn it! And everyone stay buttoned up." The clang of cupolas and hatches shutting could be heard echoing along the ice as the tracked vehicles continued to throw up a curtain of fine white ice particles that glinted beautifully in the early dawn.

"Where the hell are those B-52s?" Freeman mused, while looking through his commander's periscope for sign of any enemy activity in the Manchurian foothills far off to his left, his tank's remarkably quiet gas turbine blowing the snow aft of him like castor sugar.

Over the Hindu Kush it was not yet dawn as the nine B-52s adjusted their course northeastward for Turpan. The mountains' snowy peaks, like the B-52s themselves, were still moonlit, with some clouds bunching up, shifting in from the west as the four ChiCom fighters, Shenyang J-6Cs, wings swept back, nose intake reminiscent of older MiGs, were swooping down at Mach 1.3 from thirty-six thousand feet toward the B-52s, two of the fighters armed with four air-to-air missiles, the other two with eight 8.35-inch rockets, together with their deadly NR-30mm cannon.

The electronics warfare officer in Ebony One and those in the other eight bombers that made up Ebony, Gold, and Purple were watching their own radars, each plane's quad 12.7-millimeter machine guns in the rear barbettes shifting with the bogeys' approach, but the ChiCom fighters were still too far away, beyond the effective one-kilometer range of the guns.

The three B-52s of Purple were now in thick stratus, their exhaust heat signal weakened by the clouds' moisture, the Shenyangs shifting their attack to the six planes of Ebony and Gold. It told Ebony's captain that he could expect heat-seekers, so that when he saw the pinpricks of light from the Shenyangs he yelled, "Release flares," knowing the B-52s could not turn in time. Even if the six B-52s did manage to swing toward the ChiCom fighters, denying the B-52s' engine heat to the rear-entry infrared-seeking missiles, the bombers' guns, their only external antiaircraft weapons, would be facing away from the Shenyangs.

The sky was suddenly aglow with phosphorus flares, like shooting stars, the ChiComs' four 120-pound, Soviet-type Aphid missiles streaking toward Ebony and Gold at over 2,800 meters per second, to reach the B-52s in 6.5 seconds.

Murphy, controlling the rear barbette of Ebony One, his heart thumping so loudly it was the only thing he could hear, cheered as he saw the ChiCom missiles curving off into the thickets of burning flares aft of Ebony and disintegrating. But now another four rockets were streaking toward the B-52s.

"Active! Active!" Ebony's EWO yelled, indicating these weren't Aphids—heat-seekers—but were emitting radar beams, using the reflections of these from the B-52s to home in on.

"Chaff!" Ebony One's captain yelled, his order, as he was also air commander of the wing, immediately obeyed by Gold and Purple so that now the sky twinkled in the dying light of the flares, the millions of strips of aluminum, cut to various wavelengths to cover the band, "fuzzing" the ChiComs' radar-homing missiles.

"Ha! You bastards!" Murphy called, elated by the Chinese's failure to sucker the B-52s into thinking the second set of missiles was heat-seekers instead of radar-homing air-to-air Apexes—which, though heavier at seven hundred pounds, were one and a half times faster.

These four missiles began curving away, but unlike the heat-seekers before them, each missile's flight path wasn't so much a single curve but rather a series of jerky movements, crisscrossing one another's smoky trails like hounds confused by the fox's scent, tearing into the chaff clouds at over one thousand meters per second. "Foiled by foil, you fools!" Murphy shouted.

Then he heard a rapid thudding noise, one of the Shenyang's NR-30mm cannon raking Ebony One's port side. But the big plane had seen worse than this, its upgraded wet—that is, fuel-carrying—wing having a remarkable ability to soak up self-sealing punctures created by the ChiComs' machine gun fire. The Shenyang swept past, going into a tight turn. The B-52s were in cloud, out of it, then in again. Then as quickly as they appeared, the bogeys were gone, obviously on bingo fuel or because there were SAM sites ahead that might not distinguish between friend or foe. Murphy was ecstatic, but not so Air Commander Thompson. They had yet to reach the target and get back again. And where in hell were the Harriers?

* * *

Freeman's lead division of five hundred and forty tanks was advancing in column, broken up into three brigades of 144 M1A1 and M-60 tanks each, and the brigades in turn were broken down into three battalions of sixty tanks, companies of fifteen tanks each, and finally platoons of five tanks. The lead tank had two aerials instead of one, one for intertank communication, the other for air strikes if necessary, and was followed in column by the second tank covering an arc of fire on the right side of the column, the third tank covering the left side, and so on down the column.

Once over the ice and onto land, the visibility was still good on the low, flat country but not as open as it was on the lake. Freeman moved to wedge formations, the lead tank of each platoon as the point, the others flanking it left and right a hundred yards apart to form the triangular advance.

The dust trails, it was hoped, would be dampened somewhat by the still scantily snow-covered terrain and by the early morning dew, but in the fragile ecosystem of the semidesert around the Gobi, the dust rose like mustard-colored flour, forming an enormous cloud south of Lake Hulun, and Freeman's M1A1 leading the way, cruising at thirty-five to forty miles per hour, was followed not only by the remainder of his M1A1 and M-60 tanks but by scores of Bradley infantry fighting vehicles.

The Bradleys' diesels were in a high whine, as opposed to the more muffled, lower-toned roar from the gas turbines of the M1A1s, the Bradleys' turrets mounted with 25mm chain guns with a 475-round-per-minute capacity. Run by crews of three, they also carried a "deuce" of TOW—tube-launched, optically tracked, wire-guided antitank missiles. The twenty-five-ton, forty-one-miles-per-hour amphibious vehicles carried nine infantry men with port firing automatic weapons, riding it out in the armor-protected cabin.

Out forward of the main armored force, relays of three lightly armed but fast Kiowa Warrior reconnaissance choppers were darting about like dragonflies, searching for any sign of impediment, either enemy troops or natural barriers, that might have to be dealt with, as map references could not always be relied upon. In the Gobi the shapes of dunes could change overnight following a storm from the west, and in selected sites not yet on the maps, forests had been planted and watered on the desert's edge in a desperate attempt to stop the ever-encroaching sand.

Behind the Bell two-seater Kiowas and in support of the armor were the tank-killing Apaches ready to shoot forward and kill with either laser-guided Hellfire missiles, rockets, or their below-the-nose-mounted 30mm cannon, which could deal with any enemy tanks or other targets of opportunity pointed out to them by the Kiowa spotters.

"Incoming!" the warning came as another East Wind with conventional warhead exploded overhead, taking out three tanks and a Bradley, over twenty men and over twenty million dollars worth of equipment lost in a few seconds.

Freeman knew he couldn't take this too much longer before his force was decimated, and standing up in the cupola he lifted his ten-power binoculars, looking for possible revetment areas in some hilly country off to his left, a continuation of semidesert and dune.

Everyone was asking where the hell the B-52s were. Some were yelling in their tanks that the old man should have waited before moving, but other voices countered by arguing Freeman's point that to keep the initiative he had to drive south quickly if he was to outflank the Manchurian reserves.

The Manchurians reserves, in particular Shenyang's Sixteenth Group Army of fifty-two thousand men, were moving faster than Freeman had anticipated. In part it was because they had been bored, and no matter what the danger, soldiers of any army welcome some activity after long, dull hours at the rear. Besides, in the sparse grasslands and semidesert, the PLA's motorcycle and sidecar battalions could move at speed, each pinion seat carrying another soldier in addition to the rider and the machine gunner or antitank missile operator in the sidecar. Simultaneously, all trains and civilian traffic had been commandeered by Cheng, who was using Freeman's deliberate policy of not bombing the villages and towns to his, Cheng's, advantage, by using every route that led south and west to Erenhot.

Because of the absence of serviceable roads leading west out of Manchuria, Cheng knew, and he knew that Freeman must know, that no substantial PLA flank action could be mounted against Freeman's southward-headed column until he got further south. Cheng would have to stop him further down in the Gobi's dunes around the railhead of Erenhot, and so it was to Erenhot, the railhead on the border of China's Inner Mongolia and Mongolia, that many of the reserves from Beijing's Sixty-fifth Army Group were now being sent.

The Shenyang armies, including towed artillery, were able to reach the dunes faster by being able to cut directly west through Chifeng and Duolun. Meanwhile Cheng was receiving the news that Freeman's armored division was being pounded by the missiles from Turpan. Anticipating the coming battle, Cheng allowed himself a rare smile of satisfaction. Did the American general think he was the only one who read Sun Tzu and understood how all war is deception? Did the American think that he, Cheng, was asleep?

CHAPTER FORTY-TWO

UNFAZED BY THE nonappearance of the Harriers, keeping the big planes on course, Ebony Leader, now that his flight had been attacked, switched from in-plane to intercell radio. It was 0753 and there was a strong headwind against them. "Ebony Leader to Gold and Purple," Air Commander Thompson called. "Will start 'to-go' count at one hundred twenty seconds before ERT—at oh-seven-five-six plus twenty-one seconds. I will release bombs at end of radar nav's fifteen-second count and on his—"

"We've been hit!" a surprised voice came over the intercom, Thompson ignoring it, carrying on, his tone tense but controlled.

"Targeting radar's out!" the same voice cut in.

Again the AC kept talking, refusing to be interrupted, even as he took account of what he'd just heard. "We'll be visible bombing then," he instructed the other two cells. "Drop on my 'pickle' signal. Acknowledge!"

"Bogeys . . . three o'clock . . . coming in high. Mach one point two. New bandits. Configurations MiG-29s. Repeat, MiG-29s."

"Gold Leader to Ebony Leader. Acknowledge." The lone plane in Purple also acknowledged.

"Radar nav," Ebony Leader called. "You read me? We drop on your call and your call only. Okay?"

219

"Affirmative, Skipper!" But the air commander had difficulty hearing him over the thundering of the engines and more hammering as the bandits' cannon tore into several of the other B-52s, the latter continuing to jettison flares, radar-emitting dummies, and chaff to foil the MiGs' heat- or radar-seeking missiles.

"Bogeys closing . . ." Ebony One's electronics warfare officer yelled. "Splitting. Two for our nose, two for the tail. Get 'em, Murphy!" The tails of six of the remaining seven B-52s seemed to explode, tracers arcing out from them in long, easy, orange curves, the curves closer now in a cone of fire against the oncoming ChiComs, one barbette out of action, its gunner dead.

Then the bombers were out of cloud again.

"Angels—five o'clock! Angels five o'clock! Harriers!"

" 'Bout fucking time!"

Far below, the pilots could see the rugged, deep defiles of the Tien Shan Mountains, crooked-edge wedges of black, fringed with ice cream snow, the silver streaks of streams seen one moment, lost the next, then flat, mustard-colored desert terrain far to the northwest around Turpan, the four MiGs making another turn.

At 0753 plus eleven seconds, the SAM missile radars—twenty miles away around Turpan—were picked up by Ebony's EWO. The fighters were coming in from the starboard side from a distance of four miles, firing air-to-air missiles, the slower but higher Harriers coming down to meet them. Ebony One's copilot took over chaff and flare control, Thompson, as air commander, keeping Ebony One steady, leading the rest of his wing, flashes of light all about him, and the powerful stench of sweat.

At 0753 plus sixteen seconds Ebony One's navigator informed the radar navigator, "Final GPI—counters are good."

"Roger."

The navigator checked his indicators. "A half mile off track, pilot. Make five-degree S turn to right."

"Roger, navigator," Thompson acknowledged. "Taking five degrees S turn right." They felt the plane suddenly buffeted, momentarily rising in a gust, and thought they'd been hit, but it was the shock wave of the explosion of Ebony Three, hit by an Aphid, the flares it had dropped for decoy degenerating in the cold, fleeting cloud. Either that or the flares had malfunctioned. That left six planes out of the original nine.

"FCI . . . is . . . centered," Thompson advised, his voice vibrating along with the rest of Ebony One, the aircraft having been hit somewhere on the starboard tail plane near the actuators.

"Stand by for initial point call," the navigator announced. There was a burst of orange light—a Harrier gone. Ebony One's navigator had the infrared scope on the area just south of Turpan where the missiles were supposed to be. For a moment he thought they weren't there, but the next second saw them coming within range, spread out over a wider area than the Israeli satellite photos had indicated but still in the "target grid" that was two miles long by a quarter. The navigator waited, waited, then centered for the initial point call. "IP—now, crew."

Ebony One's navigator grabbed the stopwatch, index finger resting on the stop button as he heard the air commander: "Stand by, timing crew. Ready . . . ready . . . ready . . . hack!"

The radar navigator pressed the button on the stopwatch, the navigator, trying to keep his voice as calm as possible, reporting, "Watches running." A computer could suddenly go on the fritz in the melee of electronic war—a stopwatch was preferred.

It was 0754. "Time till release, three minutes twenty seconds. Captain to Nav. Understand. Three minutes twenty seconds."

"Cross hairs going out to target area," the radar navigator advised, watching the cross hairs of his sight flicking in and out, then in, in, in, closing over the target area like a rapid slide show, each slide showing more detail as Ebony One, still shaking, closed distance south of Turpan, the desert around the Turpan depression being held at bay here and there by orderly oases of irrigated reforestation.

They heard a muffled explosion nearby, their cockpit momentarily lit up as brilliantly as if a flashbulb had gone off. The captain made a mental note to check out why the flares and chaff hadn't worked as well the second time around—though he suspected that it was due to the four MiG-29s, probably the only four Fulcrums in all western China, coming in behind the B-52s' engines' exhaust, risking the 12.67mm fire from the barbettes in hopes of getting a lock-on with heat-seekers.

There were five B-52s remaining, and no matter what the MiGs did, Thompson had irrevocably committed all remaining B-52s to the bomb run. The only good thing, he thought, was that there'd be no SAMs coming his way as long as he had the fighters mixing it up, trying to bring the five bombers down. Then again—

"Sixty seconds gone!" he announced.

"Target area," the radar navigator reported, "at zero one niner degrees, twenty-eight point one miles." A scream all but jolted Thompson out of his seat, but by the time he'd intuitively grabbed for his volume control the scream had gone and in its wake he could hear the crackling of fire aboard the stricken B-52 off to his right, and through the headphones a dull, persistent hammering of 30mm raking it before the fighter was over them, already a mile off to the port side, Murphy trying without success to nail him.

"Looks good direct," the captain's voice came to the radar navigator.

It was 0754 plus forty-eight seconds, ninety-three seconds

still remaining until the air commander could give the TG—
to go—signal, at 0756 plus twenty-one.

Suddenly they had lost the fighters.

"You bastards!" Murphy yelled excitedly. "Too good
for ya!" But nobody paid him any attention, and three seconds later they saw the first white trails of the "telephone
poles" becoming silvery in the moonlight, the first of the
SAMs climbing toward them now the fighters had gone. Earlier the Wild Weasels, F-4G Phantoms, had taken out their
share of SAM radar sites, but there were too many clustered
about Turpan for the Phantoms' Shrike air-to-ground missiles to get all of them. Besides which, the Phantoms were
now mixing it with the ChiCom MiG-29s, getting the
worst of it, so much so that soon all four Phantoms were
gone, either blown up in midair or crashed—no chutes visible.

The two wingmen of the four remaining B-52s started to
fall away, one to starboard, one to port, amid a static-broken
stream of orders, the other two B-52s above going into sharp
banks, one to the right, the other to the left, below Ebony
One. They didn't bank too quickly, otherwise the SAMs
would have time to change course, and not too slowly or the
SAMs would hit, but in any case both of them acting as bait
for the ChiComs' surface-to-air 12A missiles—four of which,
"pairing," were streaking up for the lowest aircraft.

Ebony One's radar navigator reported, "I'm in-bomb now,
pilot. Center the FCI." He meant the aircraft–to–bomb site
director system.

"Roger. FCI centered." In a sudden gust Ebony One
yawed then slipped to port before Thompson got it back on
track. The radar navigator was now speaking to the navigator. "Disconnect release circuits."

Suddenly Thompson saw the "tents," the missile silos,
bright as day, lit up by one of the two flaming B-52s as it
exploded, without sound, over fifteen thousand feet below.
"Release circuits disconnected," the radar navigator con-

firmed. "Connected light on . . . 'on.' Light on . . ." Now they heard the noise of the exploded B-52 reaching them.

"Bomb door control valve lights?" the navigator asked.

"Off," the radar navigator said, the electronics warfare officer ready to drop more flares should the bandits return.

"To go," Thompson called. "Driving one two oh seconds."

The navigator was checking the Doppler as the plane rose slightly then settled down, the radar navigator waiting anxiously till zero minus fifteen when he would take up the final count. He heard Thompson counting: "One one five to go . . . one hundred TG . . . seventy-five TG . . . sixty TG . . . fifty TG . . . thirty TG . . . FCI centered."

"Bomb doors coming open," the navigator called, the radar navigator now hunched over the visible sight, oblivious to the buffeting of increasing AA fire and taking up the count. "Fifteen seconds . . . thirteen . . . twelve . . . eleven . . ."

The plane rose sharply again, this time the result of a wind gust in the bomb bay.

"Nine . . . seven . . ."

Thompson flicked up the safety cover on the bomb button, hearing the navigator: "Four . . . two . . ."

Thompson pressed the button. "Pickle! Pickle! Pickle!"

There was another explosion as a SAM, its electronics successfully interfered with by Ebony's EWO, detonated somewhere off to their left even as Thompson heard his counterpart in the remaining B-52 releasing his load.

The bombs released, Ebony One rose like a thing suddenly freed from bondage, the bay door closing. It was only several minutes later that they could see the roiling fires and enormous shock waves moving through the explosions that made the land look as if it were boiling. Along with destroying a line of missiles, the bombs had more importantly for Freeman's Second Army also wiped out the Turpan missile control center. But as the two huge bombers turned, the three remaining Harriers above them, they knew that the ChiComs might yet come after them—or would it be that because fuel was so precious to the ChiComs they wouldn't waste it on a pursuit? The two EWOs scanned their scopes. All they could see was the three Harriers and each other. They thought they might escape any further enemy interdiction.

CHAPTER FORTY-THREE

LA ROCHE WANTED Francine and fast. He rang down to the Il Trovatore bar. "Get up to the penthouse," he told her.

"I'm wanted upstairs, Jimmy," she informed the barman.

"Be a good girl," he said. What he meant was, do as you're told if you don't want trouble.

When she arrived the air was cloying with the perfume of roses, as if a bucket of it had been spilled, and he was already in his robe, flashy gold silk with dragons rampant.

Wordlessly, roughly, he walked up to her, pulled off the tight black blouse and, taking the knife from his private bar, he cut the bra off her. The first time he'd done it she'd frozen in panic, but now she knew it was part of the ritual. "You bitch!" he told her, pulling the bra off and throwing it to the floor. "You're all the same, right? You all want it. Go on!"

It was her cue, and wordlessly she slapped her hands beneath the folds of his robe, grabbing it firmly, pulling him gently toward her, her tongue wetting her lips.

"That's enough!" he commanded, and told her to get into the bedroom where she could see the strap and photograph of his estranged wife, Lana Brentwood, on the side table.

Francine hated this part, but she feared La Roche more. She doubled the strap over and almost lethargically smacked his buttocks. She would have to wait until he told her to do it harder.

"More," he commanded, lying facedown on the Chinese brocade bedspread, his hands clenching and unclenching as her whipping aroused him. "Come on!" he called urgently. "Come on!" Quickly she dropped the strap and felt under him. "Now!" he told her, and she brushed her hair quickly aside as he rolled over on his back and she went down on him, her tongue flicking back and forth then sucking and flicking back and forth again and all the time him gasping, "Lana . . . Lana . . ." until his back arched and fell, arched again and again in spasm, his whole body shaking until he was satiated. He lay there, exhausted, arms out, staring at the ceiling.

"Get me a beer!" he ordered. "Then clean me up!"

As he held the beer, Francine, in order to complete the routine, had to take off her panties and lick him dry.

"A new deal?" she ventured. She'd been with him long enough to know that the routine, his fantasy of being back with Lana Brentwood, was always triggered by some financial orgasm he'd had, but she'd never asked him anything until after—otherwise he wouldn't pay her the five hundred on top of her weekly take at the bar.

"A new deal!" he said. "No, sweetie, it's an old order that was renewed three hours ago. We're rushing it in from Hong Kong to my benefactor, Mr. Cheng. Jesus, three million—just like that!"

"For what?" she asked idly.

"For *what*? Hey, Francine, what are you—fucking cub reporter?"

"No, I was just wondering—"

"Well don't. It'll hurt that pretty little head of yours." He took another long pull at the beer, then arched his back again in the ecstasy of her tongue between his legs darting in and out like a snake. It wasn't just the money she did it for—Francine liked the sense of power, however transitory, it gave her.

"Cheng's gonna have a big surprise for that fucking Freeman, I can tell you that."

She didn't press for details. Besides, she'd learn about whatever it was when the time was right; the La Roche tabloid chain would spread the word from coast to coast and overseas of any great American defeat.

She had asked him one time, when she was a little drunk, whether it bothered him that what he did was against the law.

"Fuck the law. That's why I've got lawyers."

"No," she'd said, "I mean against—you know—against our boys. Against our country."

"Fuck the country. What's it done for me? When are you gonna learn, Francine, that you have to look after number one?" He'd paused, a slatternly look on his face, as he'd raised himself on his elbows from the bed. "In your case that means looking after me—right?" She had nodded obediently.

Now he ordered, "Give me the donut. Nice and slippery."

She rounded her lips into the shape of an O and worked it back and forth on him, careful that her teeth didn't touch.

"Oh Christ, that's good. You're a good kid, Francine." He reached down and tousled her hair.

By midmorning Freeman's advance column, his logistical tail following, was seventy miles south of Lake Nur, having now crossed the blunt arrowhead of Manchuria that sticks out into Mongolia, taking the vital sixty-to-seventy-mile shortcut across the Mongolian territory, swinging to his right, southwest toward the desert regions of the Gobi rather than due south, which would have led the columns into the swamps of Huolin Gol on their left flank.

The only report Freeman received that morning apart from Washington's insistence, which he ignored, that he not be at the head of his troops but back at headquarters where he belonged, was an intelligence report that the Jewish underground, led by the woman Alexsandra Malof in the Jewish Autonomous Oblast near Khabarovsk, had been waging a pitched battle with ChiCom regulars. They were trying to sabotage their own flatcars near Khabarovsk so as to deny Freeman transfer of the hundreds of lighter, automatic-loader 3 block M1A2 tanks en route from the United States but held up because of the SS *Southern Star*'s delaying tactics of having mined the seas off the West Coast's bases.

"How's this Malof lady doing?" Freeman asked Norton, who had come up alongside in a Bradley IFV. Sometimes Freeman's phrases—"this Malof lady"—conjured up an old world charm that seemed strangely arcane coming from a general of high tech ordnance. Norton liked it.

"Pretty well, General. You remember she's one tough lady."

"Remember?" Freeman asked, nonplussed, his face now a mustard color from the fine dust.

"Yes, sir, she was the woman the Siberians arrested in Khabarovsk early in the war and shipped out to Baikal. When we hit Baikal before the cease-fire she escaped. Wound up in Harbin for a while where she got the message through to us about Cheng moving everything over the Nanking Bridge."

"Ah!" Freeman said in happy admiration. "I remember. We decorated her!"

"Yes," Norton confirmed, "but I'd have thought that after what they did to her at Baikal then at Harbin she would have had enough."

"Woman after my own heart," Freeman said, his goggles now completely coated by dust so that he had to take them off, the dirt caked about his mouth and eyebrows. Only his gentian blue eyes seemed visible. "Onward and upward! Right, Norton?"

"Yes, sir."

"Well, tell our boys to give her underground lot what support we can, and tell that new logistics wizard, Whitely, at Chita that no matter how many tanks get through to Chita I want them shipped down via Borzna and Manzhouli ASAP!"

"Yes, General."

"Norton," Freeman added, "keep close liaison with all those logistic boys. I'll need up-to-the-minute estimates of just how far back our tail is. I don't want it too stretched out and have to do what the damn Siberians do—follow their supplies. We don't go to our supplies—they come to us. Understood? I want our ammo to be near my tanks wherever the tanks are."

"Yes, sir," Norton yelled out from the cupola of the Bradley. "I'll tell them."

"Make sure that Whitely knows he mightn't get enough flatbeds coming from Khabarovsk if the Jewish underground can't stop the Chinese sabotaging those flatbeds. He's to use his initiative."

"Will do, sir."

"How about those light fast attack vehicles?" Freeman asked.

"The FAVs are three miles back, General, with the SAS/D teams if we need them."

As Norton's Bradley fell back to convey the general's orders, Freeman began "coattailing," sending a dozen twenty-three-ton Bradleys running out at thirty-five to forty miles per hour either side of the main column, creating a huge dust wall like a smokescreen, certain to obscure the column and creating the impression of having much more armor than they actually had. No Chinese had been spotted so far. Indeed, there was nothing ahead but the long, pebbled semi-desert, taking on a brief, luxuriant green color here and there from the spring runoff. But beneath the light cover of grass the dirt was like talc powder and the further south they would go, the hotter it would get. Everything seemed to be going well, and it made Dick Norton nervous.

* * *

There were no ChiCom fighters attacking the remaining two B-52 bombers on their return flight, that is, until they reached Shache at the edge of the vast Taklimakan Shamo, or desert, of southwestern Sinkiang, the great dunes east of Shache looking like some vast, undulating brown sea glimpsed beneath flitting cloud.

"Bogeys! Four—six o'clock!" the EWO called. "Mach one point three. On your tail, Murphy." It meant that the four MiGs had gone back to base, refueled, and come back to kill the two remaining B-52s. Three Harriers led by Squadron Leader Jean Williams entered the fray, and now Murphy saw something few men or women outside of war games pilots and test pilots would see, and it happened so quickly that Murphy and the EWO watching the dogfight on the scope barely had time to notice. On paper there should have been no contest, the supersonic MiG-29, 2.5 Mach against a pedestrian Harrier whose top speed was .9 Mach, a cheetah running a dog to death, the lead MiG piloted by Sergei Marchenko getting on the tail of Williams, her wingman yelling, "On your tail . . . on your tail!"

She went into a right turn. Marchenko turned with her, got into her cone, and fired a 120-pound Aphid heat-seeker. She had already released flares, and with the Harrier's vectored thrust, "viffed"—suddenly dropping like a stone three hundred feet, the MiG flashing by overhead and turning left. She rose and saw the Fulcrum going into its world-renowned "flip-up," when the plane, in a virtual tail-slide, is raised up, and Marchenko was ready to fire straight into Williams's gut, with his thrust-to-weight ratio so good he actually increased speed in the straight-up-the-wall vertical climb.

But this time the Harrier moved abruptly to left, dropped again, as if punched by some unseen force, and turned slowly compared to the Fulcrum but with the turn much tighter. Shirer's Harrier had caught up and was behind Marchenko. He heard his Sidewinder missile "growl," showing he could lock on and shoot, but then Marchenko went to afterburner for a split second, rising high above and off to the right. Shirer and his Harrier worked their magic, the Harrier viffing, its vectored thrust slamming it to the right for a split second in the Fulcrum's cone, and he fired his two 30mm Aden underfuselage cannon. The MiG gave off a lick of flame from the exhaust which rapidly spread, briefly showing the "Yankee Killer" motif painted in black forward of the port box-intake.

Shirer saw two things simultaneously: Marchenko ejecting and another MiG taking fire from Williams's Harrier, exploding into Marchenko, swallowing him up in its own flame, due in no small measure to Williams's having been in the right place at the right time.

"Splash one!" Shirer yelled triumphantly.

"Splash two!" Williams's voice came.

The other two MiGs, flying "welded wing," almost touching and so flown by inexperienced ChiCom pilots, immediately broke off.

"Nice shooting, Major!" Williams's sweet voice came.

"Your assist on mine," Shirer answered. "Thanks."

"Don't mention it."

"Man!" Murphy said excitedly. "Did you see that—"

"SAM—gainful—five thousand," the EWO cut in. It meant that there was a twenty-foot four-inch–long, 1,230-pound surface-to-air type-6 missile with a warhead of 176 pounds streaking toward them, and no matter how high they tried to go, the SAM's thirty-seven-mile range could outreach their envelope.

With no foil, or chaff, left to scramble the missile's radar guidance, the air commander in Ebony One and the pilot of the other B-52 had to take whatever evasive action they could, but now the second EWO announced there were more "telephone poles" coming at them, and suddenly there was an explosion a hundred meters to the right of Ebony One and a sound like hail as the shrapnel from the SAM now struck Ebony One. The plane was shuddering violently. Whether he'd only been clipped by missile debris or by AA fire he wasn't sure and didn't care—he only knew that everything was vibrating so badly he could hear the ping of rivets coming out and could no longer talk to his copilot on the intercom, warning lights dancing madly in front of him. Thompson fought the yoke with all he could, barely managing to keep the plane aloft, losing hydraulic fluid and knowing one of the wing tanks had been hit. He did a magnificent job of keeping her aloft as long as he did, but he knew he was losing the battle, his altimeter needle telling him the end was near.

It was just beyond Tabriz in the far northwestern corner where Iran meets Iraq that Thompson knew he could no longer control Ebony One, its yoke now fighting him like a thing possessed. Thompson thought of his wife and two youngsters, ages two and four, back in Toledo, Ohio.

"Everyone out!" he yelled, indicating the top hatch to the copilot. The copilot unstrapped and, stepping below, holding the radar's console for support, yelled with all his strength at the navigator, radar nav, EWO, and Murphy to get out.

Both Thompson and the copilot ejected down out of the nose hatch. After them came Murphy, the EWO, radar nav, and navigator.

The copilot hit the fuselage of the remaining B-52 behind and to the right of them, traveling at 560 miles per hour. They knew this because his head had penetrated the aluminum sheeting on the port side of one of the eight Pratt and Whitney engines' intakes, the fan decapitating him.

Thompson tried to work his chute, but wind drift took him into the long tongue of fire now licking the starboard side, his chute becoming a roman candle within seconds as he disappeared into the swirling gray abyss beneath. The navigator, radar navigator, and EWO also drifted into the inferno, their chutes torched long before their bodies, like blackened matchsticks, disappeared from view.

As Murphy the gunner descended, his chute intact, he felt frantically for his survival pack and his .45 service revolver, and all he could think of was the pictures he'd seen as a child of the American hostages and hearing parts of the tape the Iranians had sent to the CIA, with the screams of an American on it whom the Iranians had slowly, methodically, tortured to death.

He had absolutely no doubt they'd see him coming down under the burning inferno of the aircraft, its flames casting enormous shadows off low clouds as he passed through them, drifting downwind in the overcast dawn.

Over a thousand miles east the sun had already risen and the Inner Mongolian sky was as blue as lapis lazuli but turning mustard as a moving wall of dust twenty miles wide proceeded south like the great invasions of the Khans centuries ago. With no enemy in sight and his Bradleys still "coattailing" back and forth to create the impression of a bigger force than he had, Freeman, his columns no longer falling victim to Turpan's rocket offensive, felt the tension ease and was giving a running commentary to his tank crew, whether they liked it or not, on the tactics of the great Khans.

As his body fell through the cold darkness of heavy cloud and his feet hit the dry dirt of the Kurdistan foothills, Murphy heard another explosion to the north behind him and wondered if it was the last B-52 caught by AA fire or downed by one of the SAM batteries. Quickly he punched for the release clip, the chute dragging him along over the dusty, stony terrain, but he missed and succeeded only in winding himself. He smacked at it again and felt himself slow as he scrambled out of the harness and began to walk back toward the billowing canopy of silk, rolling it up as he went, falling over stones the size of baseballs, skinning himself.

He began cursing, but not too loudly lest anyone hear him, though he seemed to have landed in a remote area, there being no sign of village lights of the kind he'd seen sprinkled below the bomber. As best he could figure it, he guessed the B-52 had been struck well south of what the navigator had earlier told him was Kvoy, one of the ancient cities in Kurdistan region whose unofficial borders had moved back and forth in the towering mountains of eastern Turkey and Iraq to the west and in Iran's northwestern frontier.

The towering bulk of the mountains, great bastions shrouded in fog, frightened Murphy—the wildness and vastness of them unimaginable twenty-four hours before, before he'd ever heard of Mount Ararat, let alone about these mountains that seemed to cover the world for as far as he could see.

Bundling up the parachute, he began to scrape a shallow trench with his knife to bury the chute, but the ground was unbelievably hard, like baked clay on the Utah salt flats, and he was worried about making too much noise. He stopped and listened, heard nothing, aware only of the sound of dry, cold wind sweeping down from the mountains. Moments later he heard running water and, as his eyes grew more accustomed to the gray dawn, he could make out a small ditch, possibly an irrigation channel, only ten feet or so away from him.

Thinking that it might mean a village nearby, Murphy drew his .45, the handle frigid, and made his way cautiously toward the stream. When he reached it he stopped, listened again, and stared into the fog to see whether there were any buildings nearby. He could see nothing, hear nothing but the water. He scooped up a handful—it had a surprisingly metallic taste, and he guessed it was artesian water rather than runoff from the snowcaps—

''*Befarmaid!*—Please!''

Murphy swung about, but the pistol was knocked from his hands. The Iranian, an officer of the Third Corps, was a short, thick man, like the four other soldiers now surrounding Murphy, their rifles pressed hard against his chest.

When the officer shone the flashlight directly into his eyes, Murphy instinctively put up his hands and saw his right hand was bleeding from where they'd kicked the pistol out of it. The officer gave an order and one of the men, a faded picture of what looked like an ayatollah on the butt of his Kalashnikov, bent down and retrieved the .45. The officer laughed. "You are idiot," he told Murphy. "Safety strap is not released." He meant the safety catch, but Murphy was in no mood to correct him.

"Where did you come from?" the officer asked, his tone sharp, bullying.

"The sky," Murphy said ingenuously, but the officer took it as sarcasm, whipping the revolver across Murphy's face. There was a crunch of bone, and Murphy tasted blood, like warm aluminum, running over his lips.

There was a shot—the officer pitching forward, knocking Murphy over. Another shot—a flare. There were several more—sharper rifle shots. Two of the soldiers near him dropped, the other two taking off. A submachine gun chattered, followed by a scream.

Out of the grayness beyond the fringe of flare light, one of the two soldiers who had run off was returning, or rather was being led back, hunched over, begging for mercy, the still-falling flare revealing the fiercest looking man Murphy had ever seen, dragging the soldier by the ear. He was a giant of a man in a white turban, not the kind Murphy had seen worn by East Indians but a turban like those he'd seen among Afghans. The man was wearing a rough, dark green lamb's-wool vest over a loose-fitting khaki smock, his khaki trousers wrapped about the ankles with puttees, chest crisscrossed with bandoleers, his eyes ebony black, his beard and mustache as white as his turban.

As he pointed his Kalashnikov to the sky, his other hand, holding the prisoner's ear, flexed, forcing the Iranian soldier to the ground. "Plane?" he asked Murphy, his gun still pointing at the sky. "American?"

Murphy knew he was supposed to give only his name, rank, and serial number, but right now he was willing to give the tall man his Instabank access number and anything else he wanted. "Yes," Murphy said, "Americ—" His voice gave out, the effort to speak creating a searing cramp from his lower jaw up to his nose where the revolver had struck him. When he tried to "peg" his nose with his fingers to staunch the flow of blood, he felt a mulch of skin and smashed bone, the strange thing being that it was the rest of his face rather than his nose that ached indescribably. What remained of the nose felt numb.

The man in the turban flung the cowering Iranian soldier to the ground next to the dead Iranian officer and offered Murphy his Kalashnikov while spitting on the soldier. Murphy waved the rifle off, not sure he could stay on his feet if the pain didn't ease up. The Kurd drew his dagger, the Iranian now scrambling backward like an upturned crab but unable to turn over quickly enough to get up and run. The Kurd, muttering an oath, barked out an order, and the man stood up. With one slash, the Kurd disemboweled him, then kneeling and with a few more quick strokes, the dagger flashing in the dying flare light, castrated the still-screaming Iranian, the next moment stuffing the genitals in the now-dead man's mouth and returning Murphy's .45 to him.

Murphy had heard now and then of Kurdish rebels, the bane of the Iraqis and Iranians alike, who, like the Afghans far to the east, had never given an inch in their fierce determination to keep the mountains as their own.

"Americans," the Kurd said, "friends. Stingers."

Murphy thought he must mean Stinger air-to-air missiles, which the United States had given the Afghans years ago after the Russian invasion.

"Friends!" the Kurd declared again with the same kind of ferocity with which he'd killed the Iranian. "Friends!"

"Yeah," Murphy said, still holding his nose, his voice nasal. "Very glad—" He tried desperately to think of something else to say but couldn't. Instead he sat, or rather collapsed to the ground, dimly aware of other figures, Kurds moving in toward him, as he fumbled in his emergency kit with the insane idea that he must get out his phrase book. Instead, his head weaving like that of a drunkard, he began holding the Hershey bar out to them and offered his .45 to the fierce one, who smiled, holding the .45 aloft as treasure. He said something, but to Murphy, though he knew the man was very close, the Kurd's voice seemed far off, lost in a swirling vortex of explosions and the air commander telling him, screaming at him to bail out. Murphy thought he saw the tall warrior once more—holding up the strip of three condoms from the kit—then blacked out.

CHAPTER FORTY-FOUR

FREEMAN HAD KEPT his word. With Cheng having violated the cease-fire the American general had unflinchingly struck back. Now it was Kuang's moment. Turpan had been destroyed, and late the next day the Taiwanese admiral gave the order.

At 0100 hours, the moonless night wreathed in mist, Admiral Kuang's ROC—Republic of China—task force, on radio silence, set out from Kuang's home port of Kaohsiung on the far southwest coast of Taiwan. Steering a course on a northern tack into the Formosa Strait, as if the battle group of one helicopter carrier, two cruisers, two destroyers, and four frigates were following routine maneuvers up the 240-mile-long west coast of Taiwan, the task force proceeded under the electronic umbrella of two Grumman E-2Cs early-warning patrol planes.

The battle group steamed twenty-two miles north-northwest before Kuang, after being joined by one hundred invasion craft that were waiting under camouflage nets off the mouth of the River Hsilo midway up the Taiwanese coast, would steam due west past the Pescadores twenty-nine miles off the coast.

If all went well, this course would take the task force toward the mainland where the landings would take place on the peninsula north of Xiamen Dao (or Amoy Island). The invasion would be supported by other ROC regiments already dug in on Quemoy Island, which had long been part of the Republic of China, and which lay less than ten miles from the Chinese mainland and which Chiang Kai-shek had festooned with high-explosive cannon. The ROC cannon on Quemoy would lay down heavy artillery barrages on mainland China's near shore islands less than two miles to the west of Quemoy.

For so long, Kuang mused, so many people in the world had seen Taiwan as the permanent home of the Kuomintang, after they had been pushed out by the forces of Mao Zedong in '49. But through the mist of the hundred-mile-wide Formosa Strait, Chiang Kai-shek had fled the mainland to Taiwan to carry on the fight. It was here that the next Asian "miracle" occurred when Taiwan joined Japan and South Korea as the three most prosperous countries in all of Asia. Admiral Lin Kuang, a one-time captain of a guided-missile frigate, did not remember this time of the economic miracle so much as the stories told by his great-grandfather—stories of how Taiwan was not to be viewed as home—never could be—but was an island garrison that, through the blessings of Matsu, the sea goddess, had been given to the Kuomintang on the condition that one day they would return, leaving the indigenous Taiwanese, who resented them so much, behind and reclaim their beloved homeland.

It was not enough, Kuang's father, grandfather, and great-grandfather told him, to be content with the luxuries the Kuomintang had wrought from their industry and the labor of the indigenous Taiwanese, and the wealth the millions of Chinese emigrés had produced. Nor was it sufficient to dwell on the fabulous wealth of the treasures they had brought with them—"plundered," the Red Chinese said—from Beijing's Forbidden City. Such treasures must one day return to China, or else how could the spirits of their ancestors who had borne such travail ever rest in peace?

Lin Kuang remembered how his great-grandfather recalled the humiliation of having been driven into the sea by Mao's forces and of everyone in the world sounding the death knell of the Kuomintang as the beleaguered refugees clambered ashore on Taiwan. Even the Americans who had given them so much aid finally did not believe they would ever see the Kuomintang on mainland China again.

But then when the North Koreans had invaded the South, the American response to the invasion resulted in Beijing suddenly having to shift its military away from Taiwan in order to meet the threat of the Americans in Korea, and quite suddenly made the old Kuomintang dream realizable. Not only were the descendants of the Kuomintang keen to act, but all those who suddenly saw the vast prize of China before them. And to carry out the promise, the superbly equipped Republic of China forces were ever ready, and now poised to attack the Communists' eastern flank across the straits. With Freeman in the west and the ROC in the east, Cheng would find himself in a two-front war—a three-front war if you counted the stalemate along the Amur to the north.

The Communist Chinese navy was primarily a coastal defense force and did not have big ordnance or the superior training of the American-tutored Taiwanese navy. Nor could the Communists' Shenyang F-6s—updated versions of the old MiG-19s—pose any real threat.

"Hawkeye radar report, sir. Unidentified vessel. Bearing two seven zero. Range seven zero miles. Proceeding south."

"Any others?" Admiral Kuang asked the officer of the watch.

"Nothing yet, sir."

"When we rendezvous with our landing craft off Hsilo River we will know. Meanwhile, tell me if the unidentified turns."

"Possible hostile," the operator said, receiving the Hawkeye feed. ". . . Hostile confirmed."

"Type?" Kuang asked.

"Huangfen. Missile attack boat—two hundred tons. Speed, twenty knots. Four HY2 surface-to-surface. Two twin 30mms—one forward, one aft."

"Radar capability?" Kuang asked. "It cannot be more than twenty miles."

"Less than six, sir, and there's a haze. He won't have us on passive sonar either. Unless he stops. His three diesels are twelve thousand horsepower each. That would wash out any of our sound."

The admiral nodded. "Quite so."

If all went well, he knew they would be off the mainland peninsula an hour before dawn. Then it would be no longer possible to conceal themselves—unless the goddess Matsu was still with them and kept the curtain of mist wrapped about them. Kuang prayed fervently. He held fast to his vision—his private vision—of him personally on behalf of the ROC accepting the Red Chinese surrender at the war's end. He would go to the beautiful city of Hangchow, the home of his ancestors, his dream to be consummated the moment his limousine drove through the garden-surrounded gates of Mao's villa on the West Lake, whereupon he would alight in triumph to personally remove the stain of Mao's house from the earth.

CHAPTER FORTY-FIVE

THE FIRST SIGN was a hazing over of the sun so that only a dull, purplish corona of it showed through the mounting turbulence. It was one of the great Gobi storms without rain, one of the terrible gritty and blinding storms borne westward in the desert, this time of year, April, being the worst month, and added to by the sand-pregnant winds out of the Tien Shan Mountains in China's westernmost province of Sinkiang, where the line of the mustard sky could be seen eating up the blue before the banshee howling and the pebble-hailing assault enveloped all.

Cheng was pleased. He had prepared without the hope of a storm though he knew it was the time of the year for them, but now he could see the massive storm gathering he welcomed it; it would make his trap so much more terrible for the Americans. Oh, the Americans had done well in the desert in Iraq, Cheng told his subordinates, and the incompetent Hussein helped them by being such a fool of a tactician. Besides, Cheng reminded his commanders, the PLA had had time—months, years—to prepare for any invasion from the north down the corridor between the great sandy desert to the west and the harder semidesert to the east—the corridor Freeman was heading for about ten miles in width and twenty-three in depth.

"You must understand, comrades," Cheng reassured his HQ staff, "that the Vietnamese defeated the Americans because they realized the falseness of an American adage—that the jungle was neutral, that it was equally difficult for the Americans and North Vietnamese alike. This, of course, was an incorrect assumption because the Vietnamese used the jungle as their friend. As we will use the desert. Remember we are on home soil and have had more time to prepare than Iraq.'' He paused. "Is everyone in position?'' His commanders assured him that they were.

"If anyone breaks camouflage he is to be shot immediately. Understood?''

They did, each platoon officer having been supplied with a noise suppressor on his revolver so that such a shot would not be heard.

Driving south, Freeman planned to take the path of least resistance between the great sand dunes around Qagan Nur or Qagan Lake and the salt lakes south of it, the corridor extending from the dunes on his left or eastern flank to the railhead of Erenhot on the Chinese-Mongolian border. Freeman's objective was the capture of the rail spur line that stuck twenty-three miles out northward from the east-west main line and which stopped at the small settlement of Qagan Lake, even though the town was actually ninety-five miles south of the lake it was named after.

Cheng's strategy owed something not only to the Vietnamese, whom the Chinese detested, but also to the Egyptians' highly successful foxhole strategy against the Israeli tanks in the Yom Kippur War. And he had elaborated upon it, not with a tactic from Sun Tzu but from the Turks of World War I.

There had been no way to gain satellite reconnaissance during the dust storms that Cheng had used as cover during the weeks of the cease-fire. No way for U.S., or any other satellites for that matter, to discover that beneath this corridor, the most obvious funnel to the south, he, General Cheng, had used only a fraction of his three-million-strong army to dig a vast interlocking system of reinforced tunnels.

Unlike the Viet Cong tunnels, they were not elaborately built insofar as they were not elbow- or S-shaped, nor did they have the misleading cul-de-sacs or sudden angular changes in elevation that in the darkness might trip any enemy brave or foolish enough to descend into them. Rather it was a honeycomb of tunnels that led to hundreds of foxholes easily concealed and manned by an elite infantry division from Shenyang's military district Group Army 40 and some elements of the infamous Beijing military district's Thirty-eighth Army—of Tiananmen Massacre fame. After firing an antitank missile from one foxhole, a PLA team could quickly remove itself to another, and in most cases the angle of depression of the M-1 or M-60 tank's big gun would be useless against them at any close range—only the tank's machine guns could effectively come into play.

"Son of a bitch!" commented the pilot of one of Freeman's Kiowa scout choppers, which had come low behind the protection of boulders the size of bungalows. "Can't see a friggin' thing." The chopper's copilot pushed the button that raised the periscopelike "two-eyed" mast-mounted sight still higher above the rock.

Still nothing.

They were in the fog of war wherein even the best commanders become confused by a lack of information or too much conflicting information. The chopper went higher, but they still couldn't see through the dust, the chopper's intake filters in danger of clogging, when they began getting radar blips, which were duly reported to Freeman but which could not be identified. Freeman ordered the Kiowas forward, and already mine-detector equipment and antimine blades and flails on mine-clearing tanks were called up from the columns as he ordered them to go into single file formation.

No mines were reported, but one Kiowa came in with a

report of dozens of what its crew believed, but could not be sure, were Red Arrow 8 antitank-missile-tracked vehicles. A small screen in Freeman's command tank selected the Red Arrow from the computer's threat library, telling him that the vehicle had an effective range of three thousand meters, a rate of fire of two to three missiles per minute—warhead diameter 120mm. Hit probability greater than 90 percent. But they were still a good six thousand meters off.

Then there came SITREPs—situation reports—from another Kiowa of what they thought were T-69II main battle tanks equipped with laser range finder, though the dust should render the laser useless in the storm.

Freeman realized that the Chinese probably could not see him either, but the noise of the Kiowa scouts alone must certainly have alerted the Chinese to his presence. No doubt Cheng, like the Americans, wasn't going to fight blind—it would be a matter of who would be seen first by whom, and Freeman's tanks could outreach the T-59s by three thousand yards and the T-72s by two hundred yards as they had in the Iraqi desert, standing back beyond the range of the enemy's T-59 105mm and T-72 125mm cannon while using their own 120mm to deadly effect.

But in the midst of the blinding storm that was still not anywhere near its zenith, Freeman was haunted again by what had befallen his tanks along the Never-Skovorodino road earlier in the war when Second Army had fallen into a trap baited in the taiga by dummy tanks, inflatables that looked like the real thing from only a hundred yards away, and with cheap oil lanterns in each to give off enough heat for an infrared signature; when he'd sent in the Apaches, the Siberians had unleashed their VAMs—vertical area mines—whose sensors were triggered by the sound of the approaching rotors and lifted off, spewing up submunitions that cost him a third of his Apaches and their crews.

"Slow to ten miles per hour," he told the driver.

"Slow to ten."

Sitting there in the turret, the gunner seated just below him, the loader to his left and the driver well forward beyond the turret wall, down under the 120mm gun and coaxial 12.6mm machine gun, Freeman wanted to send Apaches forward, but the dust storm was so thick it was unlikely they'd get a clear shot at anything.

Besides, if they were so close to the Chinese, only a matter of a mile or so, there was always the danger of a blue on blue when you could easily mistake the outline of one of your own tanks for one of theirs. Any visible insignia, in this case a black arrow stenciled on the M1A1's cupola sides, front and back, would be almost impossible to see in the sandstorm. He could not afford to go ahead blind and so ordered several Apaches in to try to find and blast a hole through the Chinese armor, which was still nowhere in sight.

The air, however, was now thick with smoke as well as dust, the smoke additive just one of the items purchased through La Roche Chemicals and something Cheng had paid particular attention to after remembering Schwarzkopf's boasting about how the Americans could see through the dust much better than the T-59s.

"But we saw through this crap in Iraq," Freeman said.

"Not the same crap, General," the gunner replied. "They've somehow made it so thick that we just can't pick up anything—infrared or laser. We're running blind."

"Well so are they," Freeman said, but he was right only up to a point. The flail tanks had as yet reported no mines. There was a string of profanity followed by "Back up! Back up!"

"What the fuck—"

Over his radio network Freeman could hear the gas turbine of a flail tank roaring.

"We struck some kind of berm or—"

The next minute Freeman's ears were ringing. He couldn't hear anything for the explosion transmitted by the radio of the flail tank before it went dead. In an instant Freeman made his decision, ordering the entire armored column, which prudence had just made him form a single file, to withdraw. "Don't deviate a millimeter from your incoming tracks!" he ordered.

Of course this was impossible, as most of the tank tracks were blown over or already half filled with sand, but each tank commander and driver knew what he meant: turn your tank on its own radius and get the hell out of here.

The full realization of what might have happened had all his tanks been aligned for a frontal attack now hit him—that every one, or certainly most, would have suffered the fate of the flail tank that had crashed through what appeared to be some kind of tank trap, the chains from the flail tank digging up the sand deep enough before it crashed through in what Freeman now realized might be a tunnel-strewn corridor, each one of them allowing two-man RPG 40mm type-69 antitank grenade launcher teams to take on his tanks.

He was wrong—the tunnel had in fact been dug so as to bear the weight of the M1, not to collapse as had happened in this case, and to allow access warrens for RPG teams.

During Freeman's hasty retreat, several more tanks were lost to teams who, realizing the American column had failed to take the bait at the last minute, had come out of their holes prematurely, most of them being killed at such close range by the M1s' .50 Brownings. Nevertheless two of Freeman's tanks were lost to RPG teams, the tanks' four-man crews cut to pieces by the Chinese as they tried to exit the burning vehicles. At the very least the Chinese had mauled Freeman's column and caused him to give the uncharacteristic order to pull back. Cheng was furious that Freeman had not come on in a frontal battle charge, but the storm had brought caution to the Americans' tactics and confusion to both sides.

"Very well," Cheng said. "Now he retreats, where does he go? He must either come through the corridor or—"

"Go eastward to the dunes that border the corridor," his

aide suggested. Cheng uttered an ancient oath. With the corridor mined as well as honeycombed by tunnels, there was only one place Freeman could go: toward the dunes. But it was impossible to tunnel the dunes. Sand had the insistent habit of falling in on you the moment you tried to dig a foxhole in it.

Very well, Cheng thought, returning to Sun Tzu's axiom: "The military has no constant form, just as water has no constant shape—adapt as you face the enemy." It must adapt. Freeman had, and so would he.

"Colonel," Cheng ordered, "get me Shenyang air army HQ immediately." The drop he had in mind would be a little haphazard and it would have to be done in execrable conditions, but it was the only way to stop the Americans. Besides, it gave Cheng a sense of perverse satisfaction to know that the very weapons he'd be using against Freeman had been provided by an American, La Roche, out of Warsaw Pact surplus. Cheng recalled how hard he had to fight the Central Committee for the allocation funds to buy the weapons. Now he would be vindicated.

If there was one thing Freeman hated it was retreat, and already a CBN reporter well in the rear of the logistical tail of the armored column, hearing that Freeman's armored spearhead was withdrawing, was in immediate contact with his Tokyo affiliate via his "four wire" satellite dish phone.

Within the hour the La Roche tabloids around the world were spewing forth FREEMAN ON THE RUN. Freeman was flipping over the leaves of his satchel-size operational map pad, assuring himself that you either went through the corridor between the dunes to the east and the Mongolian border to the west where SATRECON in one photo out of fifty had peeked through a brief clearing in the storm and spotted hundreds of heavy ChiCom field batteries—or you could try a fast end run across the dunes on his extreme left, then wheel about southwest in the sand. But if he knew this he knew that Cheng must know it, too, so if you were Cheng you'd try to stop the Americans at the dunes or better still try to take them out before they reached the dunes.

Freeman knew his M1A1s had a distinct advantage over the Chinese T-72s and T-59s in that the M1 was much faster. Then he got the bad news that the most forward of his tanks, which were now withdrawing from the antitank tunnel corridor and swinging east toward the dunes, were already reported as being under attack by swarms of ChiCom motorcycle and sidecar battalions, many equipped with Sagger optically controlled antitank missiles. It was difficult enough to deal with antitank ordnance normally, which is why Freeman had ordered the withdrawal from the tunnel-honeycombed corridor. But mobile Sagger antitank teams were a much more dangerous threat, even though Freeman knew it would probably be as difficult for the ChiCom sidecar units to spot his tanks in the blinding dust storm as it was for the tanks to see them.

Despite the blinding sandstorm, however, the quick turning ability of the motorcycle sidecar units was a distinct advantage for the ChiComs. There was the muffled *crump* of yet another tank as the explosion of fifty rounds of its ammo went up, and for a minute .50mm tracers from its machine gun ammunition could be seen flying madly in all directions as faint orange streaks in the dust-choked battlefield. It was at that point that Freeman realized from the reports of two drivers from the knocked-out tanks that it wasn't mines that were planted in the corridor but the much more dangerous mobile antitank RPG units that had stopped them. The general immediately ordered a battalion of his tanks to race at maximum speed for the sands, and the bulk of 205 tanks to re-form for an echelon attack, five tanks to an echelon, forty-one echelons in all heading forward again toward the tunneled corridor, but not until he ordered his three squadrons of SAS/D men—210 men—to race ahead of the tanks in their seventy three-man FAVs, or fast attack vehicles—"dune buggies" built for war.

The battalion of American tanks racing for the dunes on Freeman's left flank were told not to enter the dunes the moment Freeman had received a report from the forwardmost tank that aircraft could be heard there above the dust storm.

"You sure they're not our Apaches trying to get a look see?"

"Positive—definitely fixed-wing aircraft, General."

"Right," Freeman acknowledged, "then we must assume the ChiComs are dropping mines—thousands of them—onto the dunes."

It left him with no choice. He would either have to retreat fully or hope his FAVs as outriders could somehow navigate a safe passage through the corridor.

As he re-formed the tanks for another attempt on the corridor, the first FAVs appeared, the lead vehicle being manned by Aussie Lewis as driver, David Brentwood as codriver and machine gunner, with another SAS/D trooper on the back raised seat behind the TOW missile tube. Brentwood ordered the seventy FAVs to spread across the ten-mile-wide, twenty-three-mile-deep corridor. This meant that there were approximately seven FAVs to a mile of front, but while they tried their best to keep no more than a 200-yard spacing between them it was impossible to be sure because of the visibility being no more than twenty feet.

"What the hell's he doing now?" a CBN reporter demanded of Norton.

"Attacking," Norton replied tersely, uncharacteristically adding, "What the hell's it look like?"

"Well, we're too far back to see."

"Exactly," Norton commented. "Didn't report that to your paper, did you—that Freeman was in a lead tank?"

But right now the CBN reporter was more alarmed than insulted. "But Jesus, he's trying to drive through the corridor before the chinks turn their big guns from the Mongolia border on him. Shouldn't take them long to tow them into position."

"No," Norton said. "It's a race all right. He's running for gold and they're coming in from the flank."

"Jesus Christ! It'll be nip and tuck, won't it?"

Norton waved over a FAV.

"Yes, sir?"

"You fellas got room for an observer?"

"Sure, in the back," said Salvini, who was driving with another SAS/D man on the machine gun in the codriver's position and Choir Williams in back, manning the TOW. "Next to Choir—you can get a grip on the roll bar."

"Ah—listen," the reporter said. "If you guys are pushed for space—"

Norton had his sand goggles up and winked at Salvini, who waved encouragingly at the La Roche reporter. "Hell, no trouble, man. Always glad to help the press."

The reporter hesitated.

"Don't want me to tell the New York office you're chicken, do you?" Norton pressed, only half-joking.

The CBN reporter smiled weakly. "No—"

"Right, off you go then." And within thirty seconds they were gone, Choir Williams advising the reporter against the sound of the wind and the whine of the ninety-four-horsepower engine, "You hang on, boyo. When we get to those holes it'll be bloody murder!"

"What holes?"

"Them bloody manholes that Cheng has popped here and there atop his nest of tunnels. Throw you clear off if you're not careful. You just get a grip on the roll bar here like Mr. Salvini says. Okay?"

The fear in the reporter's eyes was hidden by the goggles.

"We'll be testing for mines," Choir informed him, having to shout over the FAV's engine.

"Testing?"

"Aye. Freeman doesn't know if the chinks 'ave mined the corridor as well as tunneled it. We doubt it—but the ChiComs sure as hell are having mines dropped on the dunes now that Cheng thinks we're taking the dune route on our left."

"Until he *sees* us," the reporter said, "coming back to the corridor."

"Aye," Choir said. "But he'll be getting reports of our tanks over by the dunes and he'll have to decide where he wants to concentrate his strength."

"Why can't the tanks test the mines?"

"Don't be daft, laddie. M-1 costs four million dollars. Fast attack vehicle comes in around twenty-five thousand."

"Thanks," the reporter shouted. "That makes me feel better."

"Oh it's a fine dune buggy is the FAV. Your readers might be interested," Choir said. "Thirteen and a half feet long, five foot high, six foot wide—tubular steel frame, can negotiate almost any terrain, and faster than a bloody tank. Seventy mile an hour attack speed, boyo."

"Is there someplace I can get off?" the reporter asked.

Choir smacked the newsman good-naturedly on the shoulder. "Ah—you're a cool one, boyo. Stand-up comic we have here, lads!" But Salvini and his machine gunner couldn't hear him in the wild banshee sound of the storm.

The next minute they were airborne at fifty miles an hour, the reporter's legs off the steel floor, his knuckles bone white on the roll bar. Choir pulled him down. Salvini saw a blur on the enormous blur of the mustard-colored dust storm. The blur seemed to be turning, or rather spinning, and looked about the size of a baseball.

"Sagger!" he yelled, yanking the wheel hard left while his codriver, manning a .50 machine gun, fired in the general direction of the Sagger. He couldn't see the man firing it but knew that the operator had to remain in line of sight of his target in order to guide the Russian-made antitank weapon to its target. And the U.S. soldiers had learned from POWs taken before the cease-fire that machine gun fire coming in your direction had a way of unsettling your concentration on the Sagger control toggle. The Sagger kept coming toward them, and Salvini turned hard right. The Sagger couldn't make the acute turn and passed them by.

A quarter mile on, Brentwood saw another Sagger's back-flash. "Two o'clock!" he yelled at Aussie. "A hundred yards." The FAV was doing fifty-five, and Aussie pressed his boot to the floor. The two-man Sagger team, though they needed only one man to guide the missile, was scrambling back into the manhole. The first one made it. Aussie braked hard to prevent engine damage and hit the second man full on, rolling him under the car, fast like a big, soft log. Aussie backed up to make sure and David fired a long burst into the manhole cover, its sandy wooden top flying apart like cardboard, then he dropped in two grenades, and they were off again. "No mines so far!" Aussie told Brentwood.

"No," Brentwood said, "but we're only five miles into the corridor—another bumpy seven straight ahead." The next two miles were not the hard-baked semidesert terrain that they'd been bouncing through so far but a mile-wide spill of sand, and in this the FAV was superb, up one side of a dune and down the other in its natural element. Aussie's FAV was still in the lead when he slowed and pointed off to his left. "TMD."

"Shit!" the response came from the usually moderate Brentwood.

"What is it?" the SAS/D man behind them on the TOW asked.

"Wooden-cased mine—bloody worst."

"So metal detectors wouldn't pick it up," the man on the TOW said.

"Right," Aussie answered, "and we're only running

on seventy pounds overpressure. Which is why we mightn't have set off any—if we ran over them. They could be the TMD-B4 type. Only go off under a main battle tank—won't waste them as antipersonnel. Need something really heavy to detonate them. A buggy probably wouldn't do it."

"How can we be sure?" David said.

"Everybody out," Aussie said.

"I'm in command here, Aussie. I'll do it," Brentwood said.

"Fuck off!"

"This is an order," Brentwood said. "Get unbuckled. I'll drive."

"*I'm* the fucking driver. I'm not moving till you're out."

David looked up at the man on the TOW. "How about you, Stansfield?"

"I can't get out," he lied. "Something's wrong with my buckle."

"You stupid bastards," Aussie said. "All right, hang on!" With that, Aussie drove through the howling, spitting wind directly at the 28cm wooden-cased mine. As he saw it looming up he shifted uneasily in his seat and, driving over it, cupped his left hand under his genitals and closed his eyes. Nothing happened. He put the FAV quickly in reverse and ran over it again. Then he pulled the pin on a five-second grenade, dropped it by the mine, and put his boot to the accelerator. A hundred feet from it the explosion sent out a shock wave through the sand that was like a ripple through water.

"Well," Aussie said, "we know they're not dummies. Bastards are genuine enough. But they won't be set off by a FAV's overpressure. That's something anyway."

Brentwood grabbed the radio phone to tell Freeman he would again have to slow his advance to single file or as many files as he had flail tanks that could go ahead, whipping the ground with their heavy chains to detonate the mines. He asked Freeman what they should do next, though he and

Aussie and everyone on the FAV radio network guessed it already.

"Boys," Freeman said to tank crew and FAV alike, "we're slowing down and our tanks'll have to get behind as many flails as we can. Cheng's going to have time to move his guns across from the right flank, maybe directly in front of us. There's a ridge at the end of the corridor where it narrows. They'll use this high ground for their artillery. M1's range is damn good at three thousand meters but it can't overtake their thirteen-mile-range artillery. You boys in the FAVs are going to go in ahead of us."

"Holy cow!" a FAV driver said. "If an M1 tank can't outshoot Cheng's artillery, how the hell are we going to?"

Freeman knew well enough they were in a tight spot, made worse by the lack of attention paid to detail by his new logistics whiz, Whitely. Up in Chita Whitely had been through every detail, from the size of every bolt to water decontamination pills, but he'd assumed that the rail gauge of the Trans-Siberian, which the Americans had to use when supplies were unloaded at the port of Rudnaya Pristan, would be the same as that of China. It wasn't. And to change troops and their equipment from one train to another was infinitely more complex than the average person realized or could ever imagine. To move tanks, especially those fitted with flails and so vitally needed down south, was a logistical nightmare. Whitely had no contingency plan for how to get U.S. cargo moved quickly from Trans-Siberian gauge to Chinese gauge. Freeman had fired him as soon as he'd found out, but that didn't change the situation.

What would change it was Freeman's knowledge of the minutiae of war that yet again would contribute to the Freeman legend. It was nothing mysterious, and quite simple once explained to any soldier, or civilian for that matter, and it had to do with angles of fire.

"Now listen up," Freeman said to the FAVs. "Quickly

now! We don't know exactly where Cheng's guns are at the moment.''

Freeman had no way of knowing it in the blinding hell of the Gobi storm, but Cheng was about to let him know with the biggest artillery salvo since the Sino-Soviet wars of the sixties. It would be the opening barrage—over two hundred guns—of what was to become known as the battle for Orgon Tal, or "Big Dick" as it was known to Freeman's Second Army, the tiny settlement of Orgon Tal being near the rail-head Freeman hoped to capture midcorridor and so sever Cheng's supply line from the east.

Cheng, nonplussed by reports of sightings of Freeman's forces attacking both at the dunes to the east and regrouping in the tunneled area, had to decide now whether to rush down more troops from the northern armies on the Manchurian front. This attack of Freeman's might well be a feint like that used against Hussein in '91, with the main body of the U.S.'s Second Army's AirLand battle strategy yet to strike all across the Manchurian border as Freeman had done before shifting his attack south.

It was then that Cheng decided he needed more up-to-date intelligence, and the truth was General Cheng believed that no one could deduce more from interrogation than he could; this Malof woman, for example, the Russian Jewess who had led the underground resistance in the Jewish autonomous region on the Manchurian border and who had just been recaptured north of Harbin after several months of freedom following the cease-fire. She had been a great help to the Americans with her band of Jewish bandits harassing China border traffic all along the Black Dragon.

Whether or not this harassment was itself part of a larger set piece in the Americans' overall battle plan would tell Cheng a great deal about Freeman's strategy. Cheng knew that they also had, in Beijing Jail, an American SAS/D trooper, Smythe, who might be of use as well, knowing how the SAS/D worked as auxiliaries to main attacking forces. Accordingly, he ordered them both rushed to the Orgon Tal railhead with any other prisoners who had been captured within the last week or two. By four P.M. he should have at least sixteen POWs—mostly Chinese June 4 or Democracy Movement members—and saboteurs caught around Harbin, including the Russian Jewess.

Meanwhile he assumed Freeman was attacking on two fronts locally: upon the dunes to the east of Orgon Tal and through the sandstorm-blasted corridor, and accordingly gave the order that his heavy guns, especially the towed M 1955 203mm with its eleven-mile-range, 2,200-pound shells, his three-mile-range Attila Mk11 multiple rocket launchers and his D4 122mm seventeen-mile gun with its rate of fire of six to seven rounds per minute, be moved as fast as possible into the middle of the southern end of the corridor. Cheng's troops positioned the guns on an east-west axis atop a hundred-foot tongue of clay that ran east to west for several thousand yards a few miles north of Orgon Tal railhead, so that the artillery and the railhead line formed a rough T, the artillery in effect protecting the railhead.

Cheng envisaged his trap now as a dragon's mouth. The teeth would be the mine fields atop the network of tunnels that the American tanks would have to negotiate first, while at the back of the dragon's mouth came the flame of the artillery, the latter's mobile dish radars sitting like clumps of high ears atop the ridge not visible beyond thirty feet in the dust storm.

Cheng entered the Orgon Tal railway station's waiting room, as bare of human comfort as anyone could imagine, looking more like a barrack that had been opened to the searing breath of the Gobi. But at least it afforded some shelter from the storm. The sixteen prisoners were told to stand. They ranged from a small, wiry student, shaking so much

Cheng could actually hear his teeth chattering, to an old man in his seventies, his face creased like leather.

"It's hot in here!" Cheng told the student contemptuously. "Why are you shaking?"

"I'm cold," said the boy, about fourteen years old.

"You're guilty!" Cheng said, his arm and hand rigid, fully extended, tapping the boy's shoulder with such single-minded and increasing force that the boy looked as if he would collapse. The boy had already wet himself in fear.

"You are *all* guilty!" Cheng said, looking about like an angry schoolmaster. In his experience it was the best possible way to break down a prisoner's resistance. Criminal or not, everybody was guilty of something, all the way from murder, to petty theft as a child, to sexual fantasies they could not possibly confess to those they loved, to resentment of the party. Yes, they were all guilty.

"You!" Cheng said to a man in his mid-forties, a worker in a fading blue Mao suit. "What instructions do you get from the Americans?"

"None, Comrade General."

Cheng looked at him and believed him, but it didn't matter. Often they knew more than they realized. Cheng was still unsure if this corridor attack was merely a feint to hide the fact of a massive U.S. attack south from the Amur to grab all Manchuria. He walked behind the prisoners.

"Look to your front!" a major bellowed. There was a shot—a worker's face exploding like a melon, parts of his grayish brain scattered on the sandy wooden floor.

One prisoner, the boy, gave a moan and collapsed. Cheng pushed him gently with his boot. "Wake up. Get up!"

The major kicked the boy. "Get—"

"No!" Cheng told the major. "Don't hurt him. Help him to his feet."

The boy tried to get up but dry-retched and stayed on his knees, looking strangely like a wet cat. There was another shot, and the boy's torso crumpled and seemed to melt into his arms before he fell sideways with a bump into a pool of his blood.

It was imperative to Cheng to be unpredictable in such circumstances. This held more fear than most people could bear. "I will return in a half hour. I want to know what your orders were from the Americans. Tell the major—word for word. If you tell the truth you will receive reduced prison sentences. Whatever you say will be carefully checked, and if it is found that the information you have given is incorrect, you will die—more slowly than these two." He indicated the worker and the student.

As Cheng walked out he told the major, "I want those reports in half an hour."

"Yes, Comrade General."

The major had only four guards and so asked who of the prisoners could read or write.

A man in his late fifties, though he looked much older, and Alexsandra Malof indicated they could.

"Very well," he said to Alexsandra. "You take half the group—the old man the other six. Take their statements including your own."

"I have no pen or paper," the old man said.

"Neither have I," Alexsandra said.

The major ordered one of the guards to go to the nearest HQ tent along the rail line and get pen and paper.

"Major," Alexsandra asked, forcing a smile despite the grim circumstances, "may I confer with the old man as to how we might—"

"No." The major looked at her, the hostility in his eyes so intense that she fully expected him to slap her. "You think that I am an idiot?"

"No," she said, feigning surprise.

"You are awarded the Medal of Freedom by the Americans and you think this will protect you?" he asked bitterly.

"No—I just thought it might be helpful if—"

"You *thought*," the major said, "that you could influence the old man and the others."

"No, I—"

"Be quiet!" The major strode out of the room quickly, looking for the guard he'd sent. Alexsandra coughed and tried to say something to the next prisoner, but her beauty, her dark, silken hair, dark eyes, and a figure whose curves not even a Mao suit could hide intimidated the prisoner, another young male student.

All four of the guards were staring, gawking, at her. "*Nimen hui shuo Yingwen ma?* You speak English?" she asked them pleasantly. They shook their heads. Still looking at them, she made a writing motion against her hand, but she was talking to the prisoners either side of her. "This is the only American attack. They won't attack along the Amur," she said, still looking and smiling at the guards. "This is the real attack here. If anyone in the line speaks English pass the message down. The Americans aren't going to attack from the Amur. This is the real attack."

One guard started to wave at her, shaking his head censoriously side to side. Another, getting the same idea, jabbed ineffectually at the air in front of him with his bayonet. Their message was clear and they could see the major coming back, but by then the prisoners had been whispering among themselves, barely audible in the wind, the guards moving toward them threateningly, yelling at them, "*An jing yi xia!* Be quiet!"

The major and the guard accompanying him had two sheets of paper and pencils and immediately gave them to Alexsandra and the old man. The old man thanked the major but said in broken but very clear English, "I do not think we know so much, Comrade."

"Talk in Chinese," the major yelled at him, "and get on with it."

* * *

Backfiring, the FAV leapt into the air at an acute angle, and for a moment Aussie, Brentwood, and the TOW operator thought they'd been hit.

"Did you fart?" Aussie yelled over at Brentwood, who ignored him, David's eyes looking hard through the goggles for any enemy movement up ahead. He saw another mine, directed Aussie to it, where they dumped a grenade and took off again, followed by the unusual hollow sound audible even above the wind, which betrayed the existence of a tunnel exit near the detonated mine. Aussie made a quick U-turn, saw a "manhole" half exposed, like a trapdoor spider's web, and braked the FAV as David gave the manhole several bursts of machine gun fire until it was perforated like the top of an old beer barrel given to the ax. They dropped two flash grenades and, following their *boomp!* tossed in their "skip" antipersonnel mines. These steel-spring-legged, spidery-looking mines were preset to go off when approached, filling the air with enough shrapnel to kill anyone up to ninety feet away. In the tunnel it would be even more devastating.

"No more diversions!" Brentwood ordered Aussie. "Let the guys in the tanks deal with the manholes. Besides, they can follow our tracks. Freeman wants us up front, *fast.*"

"I know," Aussie said, his lips stung by the sand. "Just didn't want any bastards popping up behind us."

"I'll keep watch!" the TOW operator shouted.

"You watch your front!" Brentwood corrected him. "You've got the extra height. I want you to see the guns before they see us."

"Bloody charge of the Light Brigade!" Aussie called out, recalling the famous and doomed charge of the British cavalry against the Russian guns at Balaclava.

"FAV's better than a horse!" Brentwood retorted. "And we have—"

"Sagger!" the TOW operator yelled. "Eleven o'clock low!"

It was coming at them like a curdling, spinning glob of gray spit through the mustard-colored air, and Aussie began his evasive driving, willing his nerves to hold till the last possible moment before going into a turn that hopefully would be too acute for the Sagger. But Brentwood got lucky—a bullet or two from the long burst of his .50 machine gun hit the Sagger. There was an explosion like molten egg yolk, a stream of blackish white smoke, and the whistling of shrapnel, one piece hitting the FAV's front bumper. Aussie felt his left thigh was wet and feared one of the jerricans of gas had been hit. But the cans were all right.

"Oh Christ!" It was Brentwood. "Stop!" David downshifted and braked, and an even denser cloud of dust enveloped them from behind as the vehicle shuddered and slewed to a halt. Brentwood was looking back. The TOW operator still clung to the shoulder-height roll bar, but his head was gone, the shrapnel having decapitated him, his torso a fountain of warm, spurting blood.

They only had time to unbuckle him—his dog tags were gone—and lay him on the sand. Aussie got back into the driver's seat while Brentwood used two standard-issue condoms to tie down the Browning .50 for the rough ride ahead and then mounted the wet bloody seat of the TOW operator and buckled up. Without a word Aussie set off again down the corridor—four miles to go and only God knew what lay ahead. He was struck again by the sheer bloody confusion of war. At this moment neither he nor, he suspected, any of the other FAVs, Bradleys, or M1s, knew whether they were winning or not. Now the scream of Cheng's salvos passed overhead to create havoc amid Freeman's columns.

"Well, Major?" Cheng asked. "What have you found out?"

The major handed him the sheaf of interrogation papers. "It's a jumble of patriotic assurances," the major said, "but several of them said that this attack of the Americans around Orgon Tal here is the major attack. This means the Americans' actions along the Black Dragon are only diversions to keep our troops up there—that they will not attack any further along the Amur.''

Cheng looked at the four reports that made more or less the same point. ''Where are the prisoners now?''

''In their cells,'' the major responded. What he meant was that they were in four-foot-square, four-foot-deep holes in the desert earth covered with spiked bamboo grates weighed down by rail ties so that the prisoner, not allowed to sit, could not stand properly either. The guards watched three or four cells each and could do so at one glance. Already there was the smell of human excrement coming from some of the holes as Cheng waited for the major to play the small, cigarette-size cassette tape recorder that had been given to one of the guards. He turned the volume up, but the sound of the storm was too powerful, like a frying-fish noise covering the conversation—or whatever the Jewess had said to the guards. The major pushed ''rewind'' and slid the little volume stick back to the mid position. Now they could hear her—not well but enough to make out that it was she telling the others to say that this attack against Orgon Tal was the full AirLand attack.

The major saw Cheng smile at the information. Even a neophyte in Intelligence listening to the tape could tell what she was up to. She knew that everyone would give up sooner or later under torture and most would give up much sooner than that. She was a veteran. And so she'd concocted the idea that this assault against Orgon Tal was the only attack in the hopes of persuading him, Cheng, to move his northern armies south away from the river. She had asked the guards whether they had spoken English—which none of them did— then she'd proceeded to tell the others what to confess, but not all of them—just enough—four—hopefully to convince Cheng that this was the real attack.

''She's been too clever by half,'' Cheng said, with a smile of deep satisfaction. ''The Americans obviously have a plan to attack from the north. The incidents along the Black River and Amur and around A-7 have *not* been diversionary. She's told us precisely what Freeman is up to, Major. The Americans are going to do exactly the opposite of what she told them to tell us. There *will* be an attack from the north, and so we must reroute some of our southern divisions northward.''

There was a tone of urgency when Cheng asked the major, "Is our towed artillery in place?" He meant had there been time to move the artillery that had been sent to the dunes east of them back to Orgon Tal?

"They should be ready within—"

The heavy thumps of ChiCom "Pepperpots," the long, muzzle-braked 203mm howitzers, gave him the answer, with their seventeen-mile-range, two-hundred-pound shells tearing through the sandstorm above the U.S. tanks. Because there was no reliable radar guidance for the Pepperpots due to the storm clutter it was strictly harassment fire, but soon Cheng's underground tunnel troops could hear the M1A1 Abrams approaching and could give the approximate quadrant as the fifty-ton tanks proceeded slowly overhead behind the terrible din of chain flails setting off the mines. But soon, Cheng knew, when all of the tanks became visible to manhole positions, quadrant vectors would be much more precise, and his artillery would cut the Americans to pieces. It was all a race against time, but the ChiComs could afford to wait for the M1A1s to come forward, the M1s' effective range being three thousand meters, the Americans' 105mm howitzers' seven-mile range hopelessly outreached by the six giant seventeen-mile-range Pepperpots.

To be on the safe side Cheng had kept his armor well back behind the rail line spur at Orgon Tal, to be deployed only should any of Freeman's armor break through the artillery-pounded corridor. To further bolster his confidence there was the fact that his T-59 and T-72 main battle tanks outnumbered the Americans four to one and, as he'd told his superiors, were manned by China's best, not by demoralized Iraqis.

"What about the prisoners?" the major asked Cheng. "Shoot them?"

Cheng shrugged. "Now or later. But I'd prefer the Americans to do it."

The major was puzzled.

"Keep them in the cages for now," Cheng instructed.

"Yes, General."

Cheng, they said, had a use for everything. In a winter campaign against the Siberians many years ago he had used the frozen corpses of his own dead strapped together to make up sleds so as to pull more ammunition and supplies across the frozen lakes and through the snow.

Reports were coming in that some of the light American fast-attack vehicles were in advance of the tanks. Saggers had hit three or four, but they were still coming. Cheng was perplexed. It was so un-American—why on earth was Freeman sacrificing relatively lightly armed vehicles, compared to the M1 tanks he had, at the front? Another one of Freeman's feints perhaps?

"But if these 'buggies' get through to the guns," the major suggested worriedly, "they could cause havoc with our gun crews."

Cheng looked at the major as if he were mad. "Our Pepperpots would blow them to kingdom come before they got anywhere near us, Major."

"*If* we could see them," the major began, "and if—"

"All right," Cheng said, "we'll surprise them." With that he gave the order for all tunnel troops to exit—to forget about the tanks, which could be dealt with by the big guns. To exit and make their priority targets the American "dune buggies."

* * *

Then, one of the American FAV drivers said, it was as if God had suddenly intervened—on the Chinese side. The storm suddenly began to abate, making the ChiCom infantry and the American FAVs more visible and allowing the dish antennae of the ChiComs' radar to start picking up some of the FAVs.

"Take them out!" Brentwood yelled above the storm into the FAV radio net. "Fast!"

With needles quivering on their 4,400 rpm dials, the Chenowth Fast Attack Vehicles, souped up to hit seventy-five miles per hour in battle conditions, hadn't been seen before by the Chinese troops.

The FAVs had extraordinary firepower, with an M-60 machine gun fore and aft and assault rifle for each of the three men strapped into the vehicle, a 40mm grenade launcher, laser target designator, and an antitank missile launcher with steel-webbed side compartments for casualty litters if necessary or for extra ammo and boxes of explosive. They were moving much faster than the tanks. The air-cooled FAV engine was well muffled and rear mounted, its cooling fins low down so that its infrared signature would be low to the enemy ahead.

The Chinese poured out of the tunnels, and for the first time in the newspaper reports the phrase "swarms of attacking Chinese" was appropriate. There was no doubt that the ChiComs, with their Red Arrow antitank missiles and machine guns, would take out at least a third of the 70 FAVs, others already starting to be attacked by saturation mortar bombardments. The buggies were often picked up off the ground by the concussion only to disappear in explosions marked by oily orange smudges in a rain of dust. It was not known whether the Chinese would have time to stop all of them.

One FAV came up over a rise at forty miles an hour, and ran down five ChiComs just as they were emerging from their tunnel exit. Another FAV—its engine hit, stalled in the sand—became a magnet to a platoon of ChiCom infantry, like ants encircling a piece of meat. The three Americans were cut to pieces, but there was no longer a Chinese platoon of thirty men—only half of them remained to claim a passing victory, and several of these were fatally wounded.

Back further, an M1 Abrams stopped, its front right track spinning off under the blow of shrapnel from a Pepperpot high-explosive shell hitting the earth only yards away. Then coming from the south through the gaps in their artillery at the Chinese end of the corridor came several companies of ChiCom motorcycle- and machine-gun-mounted sidecars, every fifth motorcycle and sidecar unit carrying a Sagger.

"One o'clock in the dip!" Aussie yelled to Brentwood, his face creasing momentarily from the sickly sweet stench of burning bodies. But even as he spoke he felt the hot rush of superheated air from the TOW's backblast. The pinion occupants of the motorcycle and sidecar unit were firing frantically and in the sidecar another ChiCom was working the toggle on his Sagger when the motorcyclist, still on his bike, was lifted skyward, and, in a somersault, was aflame, the sidecar no more than a hunk of burning metal sixty yards away from where the burning motorcyclist landed and broke in half, his body shriveled black, pieces of him peeling off in the high wind like sheets of burned newspaper.

Driving with his left hand, his right firing his assault rifle, which he had braced against the passenger's side M-60, Aussie was heading for another motorbike and sidecar coming straight at him, the sidecar machine gunner having only a ninety degree front-to-left arc in which to fire, otherwise there was danger of him shooting his driver. Aussie pulled the FAV hard left, giving the machine gunner on the sidecar even less of an angle as Brentwood popped off four 40mm grenades from their launcher. None actually hit the motorcycle and sidecar unit, but the shrapnel cut into the motorcyclist, who looked down, saw blood, and for a second lost concentration. The front wheel of the bike jackknifed, and they were over, the sidecar man crawling out, drawing his sidearm.

"Keep going!" Brentwood shouted, conscious that it was still a race to the Chinese guns before the storm cleared enough for the ChiCom radars to be effective against the M1A1s. There was the zing of small-arms fire off the "cage" of the FAV's roll bar frame.

"Cheeky bastard!" Aussie yelled. "I oughta go back and run 'im over."

"Keep going!" Brentwood shouted.

"Yes, sir! Righto, sir!" Already everything was mustard looking, visibility twenty feet maximum. "Jesus, we're doing sixty!"

"Faster!"

The sand-blasted desert was now taking on the aspect of a moonscape caused by everything from the explosions of the big PLA 160mm, 100mm, and the 82mm mortars to the huge Pepperpots, their HE shells screaming overhead louder than normal because of sand blown onto hot metal, the sense of a hot moonscape added to by the explosions of SAS/D TOW missiles, though Brentwood could be heard yelling above the sandstorm on the FAV radio network that they should conserve TOW rounds for heavier targets. He meant PLA armored personnel carriers type 82 and multiple rocket launchers mounted atop type-85 APCs, as well as the Hongjian 8 missiles carried by the type-531 APCs.

As he repeated the order, a "pic" stick or stick grenade bounced off the spare tire and exploded ten feet behind the FAV. Another Chinese twenty yards ahead of them pulled a cord fuse of another "pic" grenade, but it blew up instantly, taking his hand off. David Brentwood didn't know why but the ChiComs had a fixation about picric acid. It had cost them quite a few hands, the acid-packed grenade becoming dangerously unstable if any moisture was allowed to accumulate in the grenade boxes. But then picric acid was cheap, and the PLA had three million men to arm. Cheng probably figured the odd hand was worth it; the cast-iron shrapnel from the stick grenade when it worked had been the cause of many American casualties in Southeast Asia, American medevac choppers being called in to carry out the wounded.

Whenever the Americans were hit they had the habit of stopping until their wounded were taken care of. To wound an American seriously, in Cheng's view, was better than killing him—for it tied up at least a dozen men, from first-aid types to chopper crews who could have been more useful carrying the battle forward. Indeed Freeman was already ordering troop-carrying Hueys, "Blackhawks," up forward, not in an evac role but to see whether it was yet feasible to use them in an offensive role in the storm. But nap-of-the-earth flying was well-nigh impossible because of the ground clutter caused by the bouncing of millions of pieces of silica, the sand reflecting radar rays in a dancing static.

Besides, banks of PLA type-77 and W-85 12.7mm AA machine guns were radar linked, and once the helos rose above twenty or thirty feet some of them were coming under fire, for at this height they were out of the radar clutter that prevented them from flying nap-of-the-earth but it took them high enough to be picked up on the most powerful of the ChiComs' radar. Freeman ordered them to land and wait till the high winds and sandstorm abated enough to reduce the "bounce-back" clutter on their own radars. It was a mistake.

Chinese infantry streaming out of the holes had taken out four of Freeman's helos with "corncobs," the name given by the Americans to the conical shape of the 40mm type-69 antitank grenade round. Freeman quickly ordered the helos to get airborne, at least those that were not shot up too much, to return to their hover positions behind the tanks four miles back.

Freeman cursed himself for such a dumb move, which the La Roche tabloids would have called "brilliant and daring" if it had worked out and opened a hole in the ChiCom defenses but which even now was being described by one of CBN's "four-wire" phone-in rear observers as "Freeman Reeling before PLA!"

The only bit of good news Freeman got that day was that Admiral Kuang—true to his word—was apparently en route to the Chinese mainland off Fukien province and so, Freeman hoped, was effectively bottling up the PLA's Army Group One and Group Twelve in the Nanjing military district that served Fukien province.

Freeman had already lost fourteen M1A1s—and most of their crews—to the Pepperpot harassment fire. It was to be expected under such odds, and he was confident that once out of the corridor bounded by high dunes right and left of him he'd have room to move, and then he'd show Cheng what the M1s, free of a mine field, could do. But against this he had a morale problem, his troops' earlier enthusiasm already hemorrhaging with the loss of fourteen tanks and their crews. And he knew that if they broke through to the end of the corridor they would still be facing four to five tanks for each of the M1s and that those odds would go higher every time Freeman lost another M1 while being forced to proceed in column behind the flail and other antimine grader tanks. Yet to retreat would be to suffer the same kind of attrition among his tanks, as the Pepperpots would not let up.

"Problem is," he told Dick Norton, who was now aboard a Bradley APC running close alongside him in the lee of one of the grader tanks, "our guys got a bit spoiled with Saddam Insane. For all our smart bombs duly reported by a tightly controlled press—you know 75 percent of all bombs dropped failed completely to hit their targets?"

Norton nodded. Actually the general was wrong. It was even worse: Over 77 percent of all bombs had missed their targets in Iraq, but the army had controlled the press in a way it had never been able to in Vietnam, and the few spectacular successes with the smart bombs made the whole

Iraqi campaign seem a walkover that Freeman and others
should be able to duplicate.

"And they're wondering why I'm not sending in the air
force," Freeman thundered. "Christ, there's already been
four choppers taken out in this pea soup. This isn't Iraq—it's
a damn sight tougher." The general closed his eyes, took off
his goggles, wiped them clean, and put them on again, announcing to Norton, "Well, if Huang gets to Fukien he'll
keep them bottled up in the south."

"Yes, sir. Met boys say the storm will pretty much die
down in an hour or so."

"That's what they told me an hour ago. By God, where's
Harvey Simmet? He's the only weatherman who knows anything. Get him up here."

"Yes, sir."

Harvey Simmet, the meteorological officer for Freeman's
HQ, was a man whose patience and dedication had been
sorely tried by Freeman in earlier Arctic battles, Freeman
calling on him half-hourly, sometimes every five minutes in
the heat of the battle. Everyone thought Freeman had been
acting strangely, but he knew that once the temperature hit
minus sixty the waxes in the poor-quality Siberian lubrica-
tion oils would settle out and clog the hydraulics, stopping
the Siberian tanks in their tracks. Then he could counterattack. And he did.

"Where the hell's Simmet?" Freeman demanded.

"We're having him brought up the line soon as we can,
sir."

Freeman grunted. "This damn storm has been sent to try
us, Norton. It's hell-sent."

"Yes, sir." Norton wasn't about to contradict the general
who had very specific ideas about hell and often viewed the
vicissitudes of nature as heaven-sent omens. In this the general was as superstitious as the Chinese.

* * *

"Fellas!"

Neither Salvini nor Choir could hear the CBN reporter as Choir was busy blazing away at a motorcycle and sidecar unit with his M-60, Salvini using his M-16 on anything that moved in the dark day of the sand.

"Fellas!" the reporter repeated. "Let's head back—"

There was no answer.

"Look," the reporter said. "A thousand bucks—okay? You've been very good. I've seen enough . . ."

"No, no, boyo!" Choir yelled without turning his head, starting a new belt for the M-60. "You haven't seen the big stuff, laddie. 'E 'as to see that now hasn't he, Sal?"

"Oh, definitely," Salvini agreed.

"What's that?" the reporter asked, ashen faced in his goggles, the goggles giving him a mad look.

"Pepperpots," Choir explained. "Biggest fucking gun in the world, boyo!"

It wasn't, but it *was* big, and Choir knew that with its sheer size it would be an awesome sight—if they reached the guns alive.

Sal shifted down as they went up a small hill, changing up as soon as he felt the two rear Wrangler tires grip. The reporter was holding a fistful of notes. "You keep your money, chief," Sal said. "When you see those Pepperpots you might need some toilet paper."

"You're both mad!" the reporter yelled. "SAS is fucking insane!"

"Hang on!" Salvini yelled, then hit a series of deep potholes, the FAV sounding like a junk shop amid an earthquake.

Out of the original seventy FAVs only thirty now remained, and not one had failed mechanically. Then Salvini saw another go up in flame, hit by a Sagger. "Twenty-nine now," said Salvini.

Cutting in on the FAV network, Freeman informed Brentwood and the remaining FAVs that a Kiowa helo's mast radar had picked up a high, stationary blob on his screen before returning to hover position over the M1A1s. His explanation: a high radar tower that once the storm died could give the exact positions of the M1s.

"That's your second job," Freeman ordered the FAVs through Brentwood.

The reporter, with Salvini and Choir, sallow with fear, asked what the first job was.

"To follow Aussie—under the guns," Salvini said. "Haven't you ever heard of that, under the gun?"

"I thought it meant, you know, having a gun on you," the reporter said nervously.

Salvini shook his head. "Not here, chief. Freeman got us all together back there and told us the Pepperpots have an elevation of plus fifty-five and a down angle from the horizontal of minus two. You see he knows they can't lower their barrels beyond minus two. So once we get into their no-shoot zones—under the guns, like the cavalry used to, that is, beneath the lowest angle of their dangle—they can't use the artillery on us anymore."

"So what will you do?"

"Are you serious?" Salvini yelled, shifting down again. "Shoot the fuckers. The gun crews. Think we're out here for a picnic?"

There was a loud bang—the right front tire. The FAV skewed in the clay, or rather in what seemed to be hard soil much like clay. Salvini was out and unstrapping a spare— Choir covering him with the M-60 before the La Roche reporter knew what was going on. In the distance, a half mile to their left, there was a terrific salvo hitting and shaking the earth, and four more FAVs were gone. Only twenty-five remained.

By now some FAVs had taken more than twenty prisoners and returned them to the head of Freeman's column, where the general himself directed the interrogation.

"Ask them who are party members."

There was no response, though clearly several of the prisoners were frightened.

"Is it a shame to be a party member?" Freeman pressed through the interpreter. "Is there no honor?"

After a few seconds one of the Chinese POWs raised his hand. *"Wo shi dang yuan, wo wei ci er gan dao jiao ao"*— I am a party member and proud of it.

Another man, then another, raised their hands, signifying that they too were party members. It was a surprise to the Humvee driver who'd driven Freeman back from his M1 to the mobile APC interrogation unit. Like so many American soldiers, he didn't understand that the actual membership in the party in China, as in the CIS, was no more than 10 to 15 percent of the entire population. Most of the population in China merely obeyed because to do otherwise was to risk prison, torture, or death—beheading now reintroduced by Cheng and the Central Committee as a much cheaper alternative than wasting expensive bullets.

Freeman had the Communist party members removed from the APC. One of them glowered back threateningly at the others. Freeman's calf-gloved hand shot out, his forefinger jammed hard against the man's forehead. "Now don't worry about it, Jack—it's none of your business."

Outside the APC a grunt was puzzled, asking another, "How come Freeman called the prisoner 'Jack'?"

"Always does when he's mad at you," the older veteran replied.

"Where we got to take them?" the first grunt asked.

"Take them down the line and give them an MRE." He meant one of the prepacked "meals ready to eat."

"Constitution says we can't do that," the other grunt complained.

"Why the hell not?"

"It's cruel and unusual punishment. One taste of that crap and—" They all flattened beneath the scream of incoming, the explosion of a Pepperpot's shell seventy yards off creating a crater and a rain of sand.

Back in the APC, Freeman took his gloves and helmet off, the close atmosphere thick with the smell of oil, sweat, and cordite. Everyone was perspiring in the cramped quarters, including the general, but he looked fresher and suddenly became more informal, which helped ease the tension between him, the interpreter, Norton, and the POWs. Looking directly at the remaining prisoners, he nevertheless spoke quickly to the interpreter, the echo of his voice fairly booming inside the APC. "Tell them I admire the Chinese people. Magnificent fighters for thousands of years."

Some men showed no emotion, looking impassively at him. Others had their faces down. One, unable to wipe his nose properly because of the plastic strip that cuffed his hands behind him, was wiping his nose on the shoulder of his loose-fitting, olive green "pajamas." Freeman ordered Norton to cut the plastic cuffs off them.

"I like the Chinese," Freeman repeated. "But I hate the party. The party exploits the people. A man needs more than an iron rice bowl." Nearly all of the prisoners now looked up at him because he knew of Mao's promise of the iron rice bowl—a promise of a strong agricultural revolution that would feed all China.

"A rice bowl is good," Freeman went on, his hands resting in front of him in a relaxed, yet authoritative manner. "But is this all a man and his kin desire? Why can you not get into the foreigners' hotels? The luxurious friendship stores—serving foreigners while you must work to make goods you cannot buy even if you had the yuan, which you don't. Why is this?" No one answered, but he had their undivided attention.

"It is," Freeman told them, "because the party keeps everything for itself. While you slave they sit in their baths at the Zhongnanhai and dine on succulent delicacies, and their chauffeurs drive them in Red Flags while *you* ride a bicycle.'' The general paused. He knew they knew he spoke the truth.

''There must be another revolution against the party,'' he added. ''If you are to be free. But now you are like the cormorants who fish on the Yangtze with the rings about their necks so they can catch fish but are not allowed to swallow them. Do you wish to have the ring about your throat all your life?''

The interpreter finished, but there was no answer.

With that, Freeman took a large manila envelope from Norton, tore it open, and tipped it upside down—bundles of hundred-dollar bills spilling out on the bottom of the APC. ''We suspect,'' Freeman said, ''that the party has a large radar tower and complex immediately to the south of us. We need to know its position because the storm hides it from us.'' He put a thousand-dollar bundle in front of each man. He did not expect anyone to take it but merely wished to whet their appetites. But as he was putting his helmet and gloves back on, a hand dashed out and took a thousand, the man's expression defiant. He spit and yelled.

''What did he say?'' Freeman asked.

''It's a little indelicate, General.''

''What'd he say, God damn it!''

''He said, 'Fuck the party!' ''

''By God!'' Freeman said, sitting fully up and grinning, looking like George C. Scott. ''I like that. By God I do!'' He extended his hand in friendship and the PLA soldier took it.

''Take the particulars from him, Norton. Once you've got the grid references—'' Another man took a thousand, then another, and another. Soon only one bundle was left, and the last man—the others all looking at him—shrugged, then took the bundle before him.

''When you have the references, Norton,'' Freeman repeated, ''give them to the FAV leader. I want those towers and whatever buildings are around them taken out, and *fast*—before this storm stops!''

''If the FAVs get through the guns, sir.''

''If they don't,'' Freeman said, lowering his head to get out from the APC's rear door, ''I'll kick ass from here to Kentucky. And Norton?''

''Yes, sir?''

Once outside, Freeman indicated the two of them should keep walking. Freeman pulled his gloves on tightly, then squinting while adjusting his sand goggles, told Norton, ''Tell those dirty little rats in there that if the information they give you doesn't jibe—if we don't find a goddamn tower where they tell us there's one—I'll shoot every one of the sons of bitches—personally!''

''General, may I say something off the record?''

''Go.''

''Sir, what you've already done contravenes the Geneva Convention. Paying taxpayers' money to—''

''And what about shooting them?'' Norton couldn't tell whether Freeman was bluffing—couldn't see his eyes clearly enough through the goggles—but the general was just unpredictable enough. . . .

''That'd be murder, General.''

Freeman leaned over, his voice barely audible above the storm. ''Yes, but they don't know that.'' There was a trace of a grin, but then it was gone, the general saying, ''Soldiers ratting like that on their own men deserve shooting.''

''I thought you didn't like the party either.''

''I don't. But to risk their own men's lives by telling us. I don't go for that. That's despicable.''

''But,'' Norton said as the general mounted his M1 and stepped into the cupola, ''you're glad they did.''

As Freeman stood, his head out of the cupola, binoculars raised in the hope of seeing something in this forlorn wasteland, he rapped on the tank for the M1 to start off. There was a subdued growl from the gas turbine engine. ''I'm a general, Norton. Not a fool. You get those coordinates to Brentwood, or if his FAV's gone give them to the next in command, but it has to be done or we'll have us a massacre out here once it clears and their radar starts working.''

"By last report we only have twenty-four FAVs left, General.''

"Get it done, Dick!'' Freeman yelled back.

Norton was incorrect, for as they spoke there were only eighteen FAVs left out of the original seventy.

Harvey Simmet arrived and told Freeman that the met forecast was actually wrong. Freeman was delighted, thinking that the storm would last until he could get past the Chinese guns.

"No,'' Harvey Simmet said. "The storm is about to abate.''

It meant the FAVs had less time to take the guns and to do anything about the radar complex.

"Damn it, Harvey, what kind of forecast is that?''

"I can't change the weather, General. I'm not God.''

Freeman suddenly remembered Patton's relief of Bastogne when bad weather had delayed him until he ordered a prayer for good weather and got it. Freeman sent for the padre and told him to get rid of "this appalling bitch of a sandstorm!'' Harvey Simmet and Norton exchanged glances but said nothing.

"By God!'' Freeman thundered. "We have to start killing Chinese—soon as we can.''

Aussie watched the needle on the 4,400 rpm dial quivering, his right foot jammed so hard down on the accelerator he thought he'd push it right through the floor as the Wrangler's tires gripped and kicked up sand on a thirty-degree slope, hauling the two-thousand-pound vehicle and exerting 165 pounds per square inch as its ninety-four-horsepower engine gave all it had.

It mounted the summit of a dune, and was immediately taking fire from no more than thirty yards away. Brentwood responded with a long burst of tracer from his front-mounted 50mm machine gun. There was an explosion—a burst of lemon-colored light in the dust storm. Only now did he see he had committed a "blue on blue"—fired on a friendly FAV, the latter rearing up like some wounded metallic monster, its cage engulfed in flame, its TOW controller already afire, the driver still strapped into his seat as it came down with a thump, the right-seated gunner, Brentwood's opposite number, having released his seatbelt and been thrown clear. There was no time to mourn—everyone knew "blue on blue" was a high danger in the dust storm and was the very reason Freeman could not yet commit AIRTAC to the battle.

Aussie drove toward the burning vehicle, the flame giving the afflicted FAV the appearance more of a skeletal, tubular frame than the fighting vehicle it had been seconds before.

Brentwood was out of his FAV before Aussie had brought it to a complete stop and was rolling the burning TOW operator over and over in the sand, extinguishing the flames, the gunner, who had been thrown free and only slightly wounded, trying with Aussie to douse the driver with the extinguisher, but soon the foam was exhausted, the driver dead. The TOW operator had been saved, but the man was horribly burned, his face looking as if half of it had simply melted and slid away. It immediately reminded David Brentwood of the seemingly endless plastic surgery that had had to be performed on his brother Ray, who had received third degree burns aboard a Perry-class guided frigate at the beginning of the war. David turned his attention to the gunner. "How about you? Okay?"

"Yes, sir—sorry, sir, we thought you were a ChiCom motorcycle/sidecar coming over the rise and—"

"Never mind," Brentwood said. "Stay with your buddy.

I'll radio your GPS position back to the main column for medics."

"Yes—" He hadn't even got the "sir" out before Brentwood was back in his seat and Aussie was driving off, Brentwood realizing he'd killed two of his own men—his silence now infused with tension.

"They fired first, mate," Aussie said, moving the FAV from zero to forty miles per hour, despite the poor visibility.

"I know that, damn it!"

Two other FAVs were lost in other "blue-on-blue" engagements as they passed from the big guns' killing range into the zone where, because of the declination of the guns being only minus two degrees, and because the guns themselves were on the clay ridge, the shells could no longer bother them. The remaining fifteen FAVs, as Freeman had hoped, like those horsemen in the last great cavalry charge in history—the Australian Light Horse at Beersheba in 1917— were *under* the guns, the fifteen FAVs racing up toward the looming enormities that were the ChiCom's Pepperpot batteries.

ChiCom infantry and APCs came out to meet them. But here the sheer mobility of the FAVs, with their relative lightness and stunningly accurate TOW missiles, took a deadly toll of the slower Chinese personnel carriers, and the much heavier firepower of the FAVs was creating a hosing fire that ignited one APC after another.

"Go for the gun crews!" Brentwood shouted on the FAV network. "The gun crews!" he repeated. "Then go to the flanks. Repeat, gun crews, then the flanks. Do not engage their tanks." Conscious that "flank" might sound like "tank" in the confusion of static and explosions, David repeated, "First the gun crews, then find the radar. Repeat, first the . . ."

Salvini swung hard right, and there were two sudden bumps and screams as he ran down two ChiCom infantry exiting one of the manholes, his TOW operator exhilarated by having taken out three APCs and now "pissed off," in his own words, that they had to stick to the original plan to take out the gun crews first. Choir yelled back at the La Roche reporter. "Lively enough for you, boyo?"

The reporter didn't answer, couldn't answer—his tongue stuck to the roof of his mouth, dry as leather, his grip on the roll bar so hard that his body was rigid, despite the swaying motion of the FAV as it went over several corrugations of sand where a dune flattened out before the incline to the guns.

"What the—" Aussie began, but Brentwood had already seen it: a dozen or so civilian prisoners and captured American soldiers lashed to the wheels of the big guns. Aussie could see that one was a woman. Somebody came on the air, wondering what they should do.

"Take out the crews, for Chrissake!" Brentwood shouted, and the FAVs—now only fourteen remaining—drove resolutely toward the guns, the ChiCom infantry firing from behind them. Every time a gun went off, the prisoners ran around on their rope tethers like crazed rats in a cage, unable to get away from the crashing thunder of the guns, unable, like the gun crews, to block their ears from the earth-shattering sound.

"Smoke!" Brentwood ordered, as Aussie began a weaving pattern to throw off the Chinese small-arms fire. Soon all along the line the smoke from the 40mm canisters being fired from the FAV's rear-mounted gun was so thick that the FAV drivers had to gear down, then go quickly for the gaps created by the out-pressure of the guns still firing on Freeman's advancing tanks two miles behind.

The FAVs wheeled around behind the guns, taking out the crew with machine gun and, in a few cases, TOW fire. Half the hostages died as a result of either American or ChiCom fire. It was a chaotic battle lasting only minutes, the FAVs' rear gunners often literally throwing fragmentation grenades down a Pepperpot barrel or otherwise spiking the big guns so that they could no longer be used against Freeman's main battle tanks.

There was a stomach-churning rumbling sound, like an earthquake, and the noise of the FAV ChiCom infantry battle was pierced by the high-toned squeak of metal on metal as the first echelons of Cheng's main battle tanks now lurched forward, starting their advance toward the overrun Pepperpot artillery this side of the mines that had slowed Freeman's echelons, which were now turning into right and left "refused" formation—three of the five tanks in an echelon having their guns aimed straight ahead, the remaining two, to one side. Cheng's MBTs contained everything from laser-sight, up-gunned T-59s to T-72s.

Two of the FAVs were turned back by Brentwood with only a driver and gunner, the rear "cage" section with the spare wheel and the side compartments that normally carried ammo and other supplies now used to hold those few civilians who had survived the attack on the guns, one of them being Alexsandra Malof.

"Jesus Murphy!" Aussie said as the FAV carrying her and others passed him. "Would I ever like to mount—"

"All right," Brentwood snapped. "Turn to the right flank and stay well out of range of their MBTs."

"I can't fucking well see the MBTs," Aussie replied.

"You will soon enough."

There were only ten FAVs remaining.

Freeman knew that now the big ChiCom artillery batteries had been silenced he would soon be engaging Cheng's main battle tanks, and he knew that while the laser-ranging M1A1, with a top speed of fifty miles per hour and 120mm cannon, was considered the best MBT in the world, this was not enough to win. The American MBTs of World War II had been as inferior to the Nazis' Tiger and Panther MBTs as the ChiCom T-59 was to the American M1A1, but the then inferior U.S. tanks had won the day through their sheer weight of numbers, ironically validating the Soviet maxim that "quantity has a quality all its own."

It was not clear enough yet for SATRECON to see how many Chinese tanks were now aligned against Freeman following the collapse of the Pepperpot line, and the padre's weather prayer, though stated clearly, had done no good at all. Freeman estimated Cheng would have had time to marshal at least a three-to-one MBT advantage. And if the radar station could not be found and taken out quickly enough to render the ChiComs' triple AA defenses ineffective against the slower but deadly U.S.A. Thunderbolt and Apache tank killers, Cheng could still quickly overwhelm the Americans.

Further, once the ChiCom and American echelons mixed it up it would be near dark, and IFF—identifying friend or foe—would become increasingly difficult. The MBTs of both sides would be so close in the dust-churned night that even with friend or foe recognition not being a problem, the danger of blue-on-blue fire on the ground and from the air would become a certainty, yet only TACAIR could help redress the odds against the Americans. And so it was imperative that the ten remaining SAS/D FAVs take out the radar that would otherwise identify the incoming American planes once the weather cleared.

Freeman's lead tank, identifiable by its two aerials rather than one, received a burst-coded message of the latest intelligence estimate out of Khabarovsk of the enemy MBT strength based upon rail movements along the southern Manchurian mainlines and from Beijing to Erenhot.

"What are the odds, sir?" the loader asked.

"I was wrong," the general said. "It's not a three-to-one advantage after all."

"That's good—"

"It's *five* to one," Freeman said.

"Visibility's increasing to fifty yards, sir," the driver reported. "Dust storm seems to be falling off a little."

"Huh," Freeman grunted. "Maybe we'll just pass one another—eh, Lawson? Like two ships in the night."

"Unlikely, General."

"Damned unlikely, son. Anyway, you wouldn't want to miss it, would you?"

"No, sir," lied Lawson, who was now berating himself for all the times he'd been grumpy at having to put his two kids to bed at night and knowing now he'd give anything to be doing that at this moment, and if he died, would God, if there was a God, forgive him? "Visibility increasing," he said. "Sixty yards."

A minute later he reported that the dust had closed in again—visibility back down to forty yards.

The other bad news was that Freeman's earlier hope that the ChiCom radar complex was a fixed installation—which once the weather cleared might be an ideal smart bomb target—was dashed by a recent burst of radar waves from the ChiCom side that came in on a different vector. This meant that the radar unit was mobile, yet another reason why an air strike would yield nothing in a sky through which the American pilots couldn't see. A reconnaissance Kiowa had been sent out to test infrared visibility through the dust, but no radar target could be found, which puzzled Freeman's HQ. In any event, even if the weather had cleared in time, Freeman was remembering how most ordnance dropped in the Gulf War missed its targets—what the public saw on CBN were the relatively few hits. He knew it was up to Brentwood and his FAVs to take out the ChiCom radar. If they didn't, Freeman would lose any TACAIR advantage he might otherwise have.

CHAPTER FORTY-SIX

HIS PRIVATE JET approaching Dutch Harbor from Anchorage, Alaska, Jay La Roche was reclining in his Spanish calfskin chair, a bevy of "gofers" attending his every need. He had lost only one deal in his life, and her name was Lana, née Brentwood, now, in his view, wasting herself in some berg of an island, "playing at nurse," as he derisively put it. He'd kicked her out in Shanghai years ago, he told Francine and anyone who would listen, and, for the kind of money La Roche had, a lot of people did. He neglected to tell the whole truth: that in Lana's case *she* had been the one to leave *him* when, in a frenzy of his orgiastic sadism, he'd beaten and choked her till she was near death—the climax of his sexual passion often, as Francine could attest to, being to urinate and defecate on his partner.

At those moments he was uncontrollable, but he consistently viewed such forays as occasional lapses, a self-deception that even now allowed him to think he could get his wife to come back to him. He had tried, through Congressman Hailey, to get her transferred out of Dutch Harbor nearer to New York. Hailey had tried but failed, even though urged on by La Roche's color stills of the elected official's dalliances with several congressional page boys.

"What happened to him?" Francine had asked, trying to be nonchalant but remembering the congressman's name had been mentioned once or twice to her by Il Trovatore's barman as a warning about never crossing La Roche.

"Had an accident," La Roche explained. "Gun went off in his mouth." What disturbed Francine wasn't so much the story of the suicide—she'd seen enough of those in her time—but the way Jay told it. He enjoyed it. A lot. And she knew what was bugging him about Lana. Though Francine had never met her, only knowing what she looked like from the photo he kept in the New York penthouse and from some of the old magazine photos of the wedding before the war, Francine figured it was Lana's very resistance to La Roche that drew him to her. She was the only "piece of ass" next to his male secretary, La Roche had told Francine, who had been "stupid" enough to run away from him. By "stupid" Francine knew Jay meant Lana had been the only woman who'd had the guts to try to run from him. But to an ego like Jay's, the very fact that somewhere in the world, in this case in Dutch Harbor, there was somebody—*anybody*, especially a woman—whom he couldn't own "tit-to-toe" and "right through," as he delicately put it, wasn't merely galling, it was intolerable.

Now he was telling the stories of how he'd beaten Uncle Sam—how though he was the largest supplier of chemical warfare agents to the United States, he was also the sole supplier of GB, Sarin, and VX nerve gas to Asia. Chinese, North Koreans, Vietnamese, Japanese—La Roche didn't care who he sold it to, and when the Congress passed legislation forbidding U.S. citizens to trade with the enemy, La Roche's army of lawyers had gone on the march, as he gloatingly explained it, finding, Jay boasted to Francine, "as many loopholes" as "chickens in a barnyard."

If La Roche's metaphors were mixed as he told the story, everyone on his private jet knew that "chickens" meant child prostitutes, of either sex, whom Jay frequently used as "dawn breakers." Just as his lawyers had found a way out of Congress's restrictive legislation by the use of "front" nonenemy

Asian companies, primarily in Burma, through which to ship
the poison-gas-producing liquids to Iraq, North Korea, and
China, so too had the lawyers protected him from the slightest
whiff of ''chicken'' scandal. The lawyers' hands were
strengthened by La Roche's ownership of his tabloid chain
in North America and western Europe. If a decent paper
went up against La Roche, as his wife had once done when
she told him she'd sue for divorce, they would soon find
themselves, as she had, up against not only La Roche's
battery of experts but against threatened tabloid ''exposés'',
of their families. Lana had been so naive at first, La Roche
boasted to Francine, that she actually believed that if the
stories he'd threatened to publish about her parents weren't
true, the papers couldn't print them.

''How about this for a headline?'' he'd threatened her.
'' 'Retired Admiral Brentwood Denies He is Homosex-
ual!' '' Occasionally, he'd told Francine, ''someone like that
fool Hailey,'' who couldn't use his influence in Congress to
have Lana transferred, would snuff it rather than have his
family smeared across the tabloids. But usually it worked.

''That's enough,'' he said, pushing the hair dryer away,
checking the back and sides of his lean, darkly handsome
face in the mirror, pulling out his gold mouthwash nebulizer,
squirting it, rolling his tongue around and showing off his
immaculate white teeth.

As the plane began to descend, Francine's sulkiness increased. Till now she'd been under the illusion that she was
what he called his ''number one pussy''—with all the lavish
goodies and status that attached itself to the scrum of syco-
phants surrounding him.

''Moment we land in this burg,'' he instructed his flunkies, ''I want lots of pictures in that Army PX. You know
the kind of crap—corporate sponsor visits to thank our boys
and gals at the front.'' The FASTEN SEATBELTS sign was on,
but Jay ignored it. ''You got it? La Roche Chemicals pays
tribute to our brave boys wounded in battle. Pile it on. And

Francine—keep your fanny off the corporate gifts there.''
There was loud, raucous laughter. ''And for Chrissake cross
your legs. I don't want to see your beaver all over the *New
York Times*.'' There were more loud guffaws.

''How about in the *Investigator*, Mr. La Roche?'' It was
one of the La Roche tabloids.

''Hey! Now you're talking. Legs wide apart, Francine.''
There was another snorting, snuffling run of laughter. Francine watched him as he bent low, slightly off balance, looking out the window. If she knew anything, he was on
something—not booze, nothing you could smell. She'd seen
him like it often enough—before he'd hand her the strap for
her to play ''Mommy.''

''Maybe Lana's on duty?'' someone said. La Roche turned
around, his face thin stone. ''Hey, joker. This little soiree I
told you to fix up with our gallant boys in the sticks is costing
me change. I told the army, the navy, the fucking air force I
wanted to meet *all* the nurses. If she isn't there, joker, I'm
gonna throw someone outta the fucking plane.''

The laughter died.

After the Lear touched down on the rain-slashed runway,
droplets streaming against the Perspex, the plane taxiing toward the small, but obviously busy, terminal, Francine saw
a row of heavy khaki overcoats and navy blue uniforms. She
recognized Lana before the plane came to a stop. You could
spot her at once, Francine thought—one of those women who
looked beautiful even if you draped them in a sack. Gorgeous
figure that was flattered, not flattened, by the Navy Waves'
dark blue uniform. And the spiffy little white hat with the
snappy upturned brim made Francine sick. And Lana's dark
hair—that was the last straw. Whipped with rain and it just
sat there, full and behaving itself. Ten minutes in that weather
and Francine knew her own hair would be a wet mop.

Francine slipped on her siren-red coat, but despite the cold
she left enough of it open so there'd be no mistake about her
cleavage. Hell, she had to do something. She followed Jay

out. He shook hands with the base commander, but ignored the rest of the staff, particularly Lana, as he and his party were ushered into the waiting USO army cars. With Lana left back on the tarmac, Francine was starting to feel better already.

Colonel Rodin, the commanding officer of Dutch Harbor, loathed La Roche and his ilk, but he was a professional and he wasn't a fool. La Roche had splashed a lot of money and publicity around—and God knew the men posted in "America's Siberia" deserved a little attention. Besides, if La Roche wasn't happy and leaned hard enough on the Alaska congressman for Dutch Harbor and environs, there was a very good chance the CO could find something he loathed even more than La Roche: pushing a pen back in Washington. Even so, he afforded La Roche professional military hospitality but no more.

After the photo session, during which a bunch of reporters from Anchorage, including a photographer and reporter from *Stars and Stripes*, got their shots of the multinational financier shaking the CO's hand, Colonel Rodin excused himself. In the crowded PX he sought Lana out and told her that Washington had "requested" that they be as cooperative as possible to La Roche Chemicals, "a major military contractor."

"I'd prefer not to, Colonel," Lana said rather grimly.

"I understand, Lieutenant. I'm merely conveying Washington's wishes. Tell you—" He hesitated but said it anyway. "None of my business but I don't blame you. They don't look my sort of people either. Must be at least six guys there of draft age."

"Health exemptions," Lana said knowingly. "Four-F."

Colonel Rodin grunted. "I guess. Well, please yourself, Lieutenant. Whatever you do is okay by me. Walk out if you want."

"Thank you, Colonel. I appreciate that." But she knew she had to at least say hello or some toady back in Washington was going to get paid to complain to the Pentagon about Colonel Rodin's unhelpfulness.

As she walked over toward him through the crowd, La Roche didn't turn around but kept talking to Francine.

"She coming?" he asked.

"Yes," Francine said. "Lah-de-dah, if you ask me."

"I didn't."

"Jay."

He swung around. "Lana!"

Francine wanted to throw up but, as instructed, moved off, swiping another drink from a tray passing by, its bearer, a GI, all but losing his eyeballs to the wonders of her chest.

"How are you, sweetie?" Jay asked Lana.

"Fine. You?"

"Terrific, terrific. What you think of my little party?"

She could hardly hear herself in the buzz of the PX commotion. "Very nice."

"Yeah. Something for the boys at the front. And you gals, too, of course." He laughed easily. "Get you something to drink?"

"No, thank you."

He lowered his voice, still smiling. "Hey, loosen up, babe. Muhammad comes to the mountain, right? Isn't that enough?"

"For what?"

He reached out and took another soft drink. "See? No booze. On the wagon." He downed the pop in one go. "Want you to come back, babe. Miss you. Hey—hey—before you say anything, I want to say I'm sorry. Mea culpa. Okay?" He moved to touch her arm. She withdrew it.

"Hey, swear to God, Lana. Checked in with a shrink. The whole bit. Cost me a bundle but I'm straightened out."

"I'm glad." It was the first thing she'd said to him that she had meant.

"God, but you're beautiful."

She said nothing, unmoved.

"Lana—this stinking war—" He glimpsed Francine watching them, sipping her Diet Coke. "Changed everything, right? None of us are the same people." For a moment neither of them spoke. "Look, honey, you want the divorce, you can have it."

She looked up at him.

"Yeah. I mean it. That's what I came to tell you. But I want to do it civilly. You know—sit down, figure out a little something for your folks."

"They're all right."

"You know what I mean. Your brother Ray—all those burns—I know a few people who—"

"Ray's doing fine, Jay. He's all—"

"Okay, okay. I'm sorry. Look, I'll level with you. I wanted to see you—that's the truth. We're also opening up a new plant in Anchorage. Perfume." He laughed, that easy, gentle, good-looking laugh that had been the first thing that had attracted her to him. It seemed inconceivable now—so long ago. How she could have fallen—

"Crazy, isn't it?" he said. "Whole damn world's at war and people want to buy more perfume."

"Yes," she replied. "Well, not really I suppose—" She stopped.

"What d'you say you come into Anchorage for a day or two? We'll settle it there. I'll have the papers drawn up. Anything you don't like—hey—we're two reasonable people, right?"

"Are we?"

"Sure we are. Look, you don't have to worry. I know about Shirer." She felt the involuntary chill of a threat pass through her but said nothing. "That's fine," he went on. "I've got no problem with him. That's why I came up. I don't expect you to come back. I—" He looked thoughtfully down at his empty glass.

He's making it up, she thought. He's making it up as he goes along.

"I know I haven't been any good for you, Lana." He suddenly brightened. "On the other hand, if it wasn't for me you'd never have met this guy and—hell, don't make it hard, babe. All I'm saying is I know I gave you a rotten deal. A rotten deal. I can't go back and fix that, but I can try to make amends." He looked down at her and spoke softly. "It's partly selfish. But I need to wipe the slate clean. I need to talk, Lana. Just you and me—sit down and straighten—"

"I don't think so, Jay."

"I know. Hell, on my past performance if I were you I'd think, 'Bug off,' but you've always been fair, babe. But we can't talk here." He looked around. "In this dump—I mean—no offense but—it's a zoo, right? Look, forget Anchorage. We'll settle it here. There a hotel in this burg?"

"I'm not spending a night with you, Jay. If you think you can con me into a good-bye— Well, you know what I mean. No way."

"That's not what I meant. Hell, bring a chaperon if you like. I just want it settled." He smiled. "I'll buy you a hamburger."

She sighed. "Why don't you just send the papers through the mail, Jay?"

"You think I haven't thought of that? But my damn lawyers freaked out. I told them you'd settle easy enough. There'd be no hassle. But they want it watertight. Which means they want to charge me twenty thousand bucks. It has to do with the board, too, Lana. La Roche Chemicals. The agreement you sign has got to be—well—final. They need to see it—tell us what we can and can't change. Hell," he said. "*You* try to tell them to do it through the mail."

She recognized the relentless legality of it.

"There's a small hotel cum café—Davy Jones," she said. "It's not very fancy, but we could meet there I suppose."

He shrugged. "Fine. Eight o'clock?"

"All right." She turned to go.

"Lana?"

When she looked at him, both arms were dangling by his side in a way she'd never seen him before. He looked defeated. "I'll send a driver if you want."

"Don't bother," she said. "I'll get a base cab."

"I still love you, babe. I only wanted to see you. Is that so terrible?"

When La Roche's entourage moved out of the PX, Francine could tell something had happened to him. A young reporter, his ID press badge reading *Anchorage Spectator,* tried eagerly to get a few words from him. "My name's Johnson, Mr. La Roche. *Anchorage Spectator.* I was wondering if you'd care to say a few words about—"

"Fuck off!" La Roche told him.

"What are we doing, Mr. La Roche?" one of the flunkies asked.

"There's some rat-hole in this place called the Davy Jones. Make reservations for dinner, if they know what that is. Eight o'clock. For two. And a room for me."

"We're booked into the Excelsior, Mr. La Roche. Nice little hotel overlooking the—"

"Well go there and draw up divorce papers."

"Divorce papers?" the lawyer said. "But we didn't bring any—I mean—we didn't know you wanted anything like that on this trip, Mr. La Roche. I don't think—"

"Then give me one of the company contracts. Something that looks legal. Can you do that much?" Jay sneered.

"Yes. Right away, Mr. La Roche."

"Have them ready for me by eight o'clock so I can take 'em with me to that Davy joint. And Marvin?"

"Yes, Mr. La Roche?"

"Tell Francine to get her ass over to that hotel room. Now!"

CHAPTER FORTY-SEVEN

AUSSIE'S FAV WAS halfway down a dune when they heard the bang and felt the vehicle shuddering, Aussie steering hard into the skid. Beneath the vehicle an avalanche of slow-moving sand and stones followed, the stones as big as a man's fist.

Within seconds Aussie and David Brentwood were out, their new TOW man swiveling in his seat to make sure he could cover them for the full 360 degrees while Aussie grabbed the jack and David hit the wing nut that held down the spare.

Brentwood hoped that outflanking the ChiCom tanks would be easy, given the speed of the FAV, but he knew he couldn't be sure until the ChiCom MBTs got their first glimpse of a FAV—would they break and go after the FAVs or stay in echelon, whatever its configuration might be?

"I can hear them," the TOW operator said.

"Can you *see* 'em?" Aussie said, tightening the last bolt on the spare tire while Brentwood finished putting the emergency patch on the flat.

"No."

"Well that's no bloody use, is it? I can hear them, too. Every fucker within a mile can hear—" They intuitively ducked, the sound of ordnance passing overhead with that peculiar *chuff*ing sound like a locomotive shunting at high speed made louder by the air thick with particles of sand. They quickly put the repaired tire back on the spare rack.

"Right! We're off," Aussie said. "I'm the first one to spot a chow. Five to one on—any takers?"

David Brentwood said nothing, peering hard through goggles, the sound of sand striking them like fine hail. The TOW operator took Aussie's bet, for he could already see two blurs—too big to be motorcycle and sidecar units. "You're on," the TOW operator said. "Ten bucks."

"Done!" Aussie said.

"I see two of 'em—eleven o'clock."

"What?" Aussie said, but now Brentwood could see them, too, and flecks of tracers told him the blur, whether it was an MBT or not, was firing at them.

Aussie swung hard left into a dip between two small dunes and stopped, the engine in high rev.

"You ready, TOW?"

"Ready—go!"

"Never mind," Brentwood interjected. "Go out to the flank. It's the radar we want."

Swearing, Aussie dropped it into low gear and followed the line of the gully away from the tanks—or perhaps they had been APCs. "TOW," Aussie said. "You saw those tanks or whatever they are before you made the bet?"

"No."

"Lying bastard. Hope your prick falls off."

"Thanks, Aussie, but you owe me fifty bucks."

They followed the line of the gully for two hundred yards or so, then came up again. There was a sudden break in the dust storm—or was it the end of the storm? Then they came across a terrifying sight. From the left to right, as far as they could see, a brigade of MBTs—between 150 and 200 tanks, T-52s and T-72s—was making its way down an enormous dune in the strange half light, the tanks looking like a plague of huge, dark moles crawling down some enormous flesh-colored back. There was a streak of light and a more diffuse backblast from a TOW missile, fired from a FAV somewhere to Aussie's left, and a flash of red and yellow flame as the TOW round hit a T-59.

Brentwood was furious and on the phone network within seconds, telling the FAVs to get out to the flanks. To forget the tanks. "I say again, forget the tanks—"

His voice was all but drowned out by fire from the forward five tanks in the column, which were breaking up, going into a *jin ru you fang ti xin rong*—an echelon right—wherein each tank of the five-tank platoon broke off so that the lead tank and two others slightly behind him and to the right had their 100mm, and in some of the up-gunned tanks, their 125mm, guns pointed to the front, the two rearmost tanks having their guns pointed to the right.

Almost at the same time another one of the columns— there were fifteen tanks in it—all began moving to echelon right. It was the ChiComs' weakest point, a legacy of having been trained, like the ChiCom fighter pilots, by the Russians, who were wedded to the doctrine of central control, allowing individual commanders little flexibility unless central control released them. Of course central control was necessary to some degree in the U.S. army as well, but the release to individual decisions as in Freeman's leaving the FAV tactics up to Brentwood and the other FAV crews was not as freely given to the ChiComs. And the degree to which Cheng and Freeman would maintain central command would become crucial if it came to a night fight. Should this occur, Cheng knew, the Americans were better, with more experience in freeing individual tank commanders to exercise tactical flexibility, giving the Americans the edge when it came to tanks in an eyeball-to-eyeball confrontation.

"Fixing a flat," the FAV just chewed out by Brentwood reported. "Couldn't avoid firing a TOW . . . were taking tracers." Now Aussie swung the FAV up out of the gully to the sharp, sandy edge, and he could no longer see the tanks, the weather closing in again as they heard the clanking of the ChiCom armor far off to the left.

Brentwood requested an update on the radar vector the Kiowas were plotting. It was the same; the mobile unit hadn't moved. And Brentwood's Magellan hand-held global positioning system put them only three miles away. At thirty miles per hour, a near-reckless speed, given the fifteen-to-twenty-yard visibility, it was estimated the FAVs on both flanks skirting the Chinese armor should reach the radar site within ten minutes—unless it moved again.

The motorcycle sidecar unit came out of nowhere—from behind them. The TOW operator saw it at the last minute, swung his weapon around on the swivel mount, but the burst from the ChiCom's 7.62mm PKS hit him in the chest and face, blood pouring out of him. Aussie quickly turned left, his foot to the floor. The sidecar unit couldn't turn fast enough, and Aussie hit it full on, the FAV's double crash bar now bent back to the lights, the Chinese motorcyclist flung off his machine and Brentwood mowing him down then turning the weapon on the upturned sidecar, giving it two good bursts, the Chinese gunner inside screaming over the rattle of the ricocheting bullets.

Aussie and David Brentwood cut the TOW operator out of his harness, snapped off his dog tags, and went on.

"I'll blow that fucking radar so fucking high—"

"If we find it," Brentwood said, adding hopefully, "Should be there in ten minutes."

In those ten minutes Admiral Kuang was receiving the message from his forward AWACS—the airborne warning and control systems—that a hurricane, force five, more powerful than those that had hit southern Florida and the Hawaiian Islands in '92, with winds in excess of 190 miles an hour, born in the Marianas, was now heading for Taiwan and the hundred-mile-wide strait between it and the Chinese mainland. Reluctantly, with great sadness, he ordered the fleet to turn about and head back toward Taiwan in order to meet the hurricane head-on and hopefully ride it out. As practical a man as he was, Kuang was also deeply religious, and he saw in the hurricane's attack a clear message that the hurricane was saving him from a crushing defeat—a clear warning to wait for a more propitious time. In any case he couldn't possibly make landings in a hurricane.

"Aussie!" a cry came from somewhere in front. It was Salvini, Choir, and the news reporter who was standing up in the stilled FAV like a mummy frozen to the roll bar. Beside them were two ChiCom motorcycle/sidecar units looking the worse for their collision with the FAV. "Had a prang, I see!" Aussie said cheekily.

"Yeah," Salvini answered. "Both hit me at once."

"Ah, bullshit!" Aussie said. "You guys from Brooklyn can't drive a fucking grocery cart. Shoulda outmaneuvered 'em."

"Like we did," David added, looking at Aussie. "The one we hit."

"That was on purpose," Aussie responded. "Okay, hop in. Choir, you with the TOW. Your mate"—he meant the reporter—"in the back, too."

"What about me?" Salvini asked.

"You can fucking hoof it, Sal. Only a couple of miles."

"Fuck you!" Sal said. "I'll ride in one of your side litter trays."

"Where's your TOW, man?" Choir asked.

"Bought it a way back," Aussie said, his tone losing its jocular vulgarity as he looked ahead, the visibility up to forty yards, asking David for a GPS vector to the target.

"Steer one seven three."

"And hope they're still there," Choir said. Aussie had the FAV up to thirty miles an hour within a few seconds, then jammed on the brake, the vehicle skidding sideways, ploughing into the sand.

"What d'you see?" David asked.

"Nothing. I've got an idea." He backed up to where the two ChiCom motorcycle and sidecar units were lying. "Sal—you try the one over there. I'll try the one nearest."

"What for?"

"See if they still fucking work after you hitting 'em."

One's front wheel was bent beyond hope, while the other had its gas tank so shot up that it too was finished. The sound of armor fighting armor now drowned out Aussie's voice. Several thousand yards back in the mustard fog of dust and smoke, Freeman's first echelon had come within sight of the ChiComs. Aussie took off again in the FAV, David, his legs braced against the floor, taking a firm hold of the M-60 machine gun. For a second the FAV was engulfed with the stench of excrement. "Don't worry about it, boyo," Choir said to the La Roche newsman.

"It was Salvini," Aussie said, as Salvini lay on his side, gripping the metal lattice work of the litter for support, his head bumping on a pillow of C charges.

"What's up with you, you Australian—"

"Stop!" Choir yelled. "Target! One o'clock!"

As the FAV came to an abrupt halt in the loose, sugary sand, Choir fired his second-to-last TOW, its back-blast lighting up the FAV, the FAV in its most vulnerable position, still, giving Choir time to guide the optically tracked, wire-guided missile.

The motorcycle and sidecar unit that he'd aimed at dipped over a dune, the TOW blowing the top of the dune off like the flying spray of some enormous brown wave. Next second the sidecar unit was coming back at them out of the fold between the dunes in which it had temporarily disappeared, the ChiCom in the sidecar pointing a shaped-charge RPG at them.

"Cheeky bastard!" Aussie said, and was already into a series of S curves and dips. The RPG fired, a hot sliver of shrapnel slicing open the front left tire like butter, amputating two inches or so from the foot-long pack of C-4 plastique, ending up taking a chip out of the stock of the Winchester 1200 riot shotgun that was strapped to the cage.

Brentwood was still firing the machine gun and saw the ChiCom driver shaking as if he were some kind of machine coming apart, falling away, the long burst of machine gun fire literally chopping him to pieces. The motorcycle jack-knifed and was over on its side.

"Shit!" It was Aussie. "Two flats in one day."

"Aussie—can it." It was David, looking suddenly older than his years. "Anyone hurt?"

"No." He turned back toward the La Roche reporter, who shook his head like a child on the verge of tears, accused of something he didn't do.

"All right," David said. "Now listen up—all of you."

Salvini was already changing tires.

In the lead M1A2, General Freeman watched through his viewer while the gunner below and immediately in front of him scanned his thermal-imaging sight. Freeman was confident that with so much dust and now smoke from smoke grenades in the air it would be the Americans who would have the edge—able to see through the polluted air in the same way that Schwarzkopf had reported how the American sights had been able to better see through the hot fog of war than had the Iraqi tanks.

The concussion from the explosion of a Bradley armored personnel carrier behind him off to his left could be felt, not so much by any impact or discernible earth tremor but by the sudden surge in the M1A2's air conditioner and ventilation system, the inside pressure now rising, not to keep out poison gas, though it could do that, too, but rather the thick dust caused by the Bradley's sudden demise.

It was a shock as much to Freeman as his other three crewmen. If they couldn't see through the smoke curtain, then how could Cheng's tanks have seen the Bradley? Unless the smoke laid by the ChiCom armor was "particle infused," that is, thickened to make it harder for the thermal and night-vision viewers on the M1A2 to penetrate.

There was only one way, Freeman saw, to counter such a possibility—close the gap between him and them as fast as possible. Freeman ordered a full-speed attack in wedge formations. His two hundred tanks moved from refused right and refused left configurations to the arrowhead-shaped wedge formations wherein the lead tank pointed its 120mm gun and coaxial machine gun straight ahead, the two tanks to the left and two slightly back and to the right covering the flanks by having their main guns pointing left and right respectively. And if necessary all would be able to fire straight ahead without hitting one another.

"Must be using high-particle smoke," the gunner said, the reclined driver flexing his wrist on the handlebar control, his line-of-sight responsibility being the front, the loader on Freeman's left responsible for the left side, Freeman responsible for the right and the all-round view and with the capability of overriding his gunner.

"Well, wait till the bastards get a taste of this high-ratio gearbox," Freeman said, and with that the M1A2s moved quickly and efficiently over the sand, main gun steady, chassis undulating as if on a gimbals mounting, into the dense smoke. Ahead, the round, hunkered down domes of up-gunned T-59s and T-72s were dimly, then more clearly, discerned, the weak sun no brighter than the moon as it sank over the desert. The driver picked up the first T-59, gave its position, and the gunner readied his 120mm—the HEAT, or high explosive antitank round, streaking out of the barrel a split second later.

"One o'clock—three hundred yards!" Freeman shouted as the first T-59 exploded from the molten jet that cut through its thick steel.

"In sight!" the gunner confirmed, the loader already shoving another HEAT round into "pussy," as the breech was affectionately called, the round now en route to another T-59, the round striking its 75mm-thick glacis plate.

The fire-control computer aboard the M1A2 was already making minor adjustments for barrel drift, the gunner using the coaxial machine bursts so that his thermal imager picked up the tracer dots more easily in the smoke and dust, aligning the gun for the third shot in fourteen seconds, when a deafening bang, then a ringing noise, shook the M1A2 as if some giant had hit it with a mallet. The blow had come from a ChiCom infantry-fired RPG7, its shaped-charge round going instantly into a molten jet. But the jet of steel was prevented from penetrating the sloped armor of the M1A2 because of the tank's reactive armor pack, which blew up upon the impact of the RPG7, diffusing the molten jet. There had been much debate in the Pentagon about the pluses and minuses of reactive armor, but for the men in Freeman's tank it had worked admirably.

The moment the ChiComs' RPG hit the M1A2 another HESH round had left the Abrams and another T-59 exploded but did not stop, its buckled tracks still somehow grinding forward, keeping the tank rolling down a dune, albeit arthritically, while it continued to disintegrate as a chain reaction was set off like some massive string of firecrackers, its crew having no time to escape but one of them, the driver, visible as a charred torso dangling from the driver's exit beyond the turret. The air was pungent with diesel and gasoline fumes mixed in with the hot stench of burning skin melting into the sand, some of which was fused into glass by the molten jet of shaped charges.

"Three down!" the loader exulted, his voice a fusion of excitement and terror.

Freeman said nothing, conscious that even with a three-to-one kill ratio he might yet be unable to defeat the Chinese if they outnumbered him by more than three to one. Which they did. Freeman's driver, acutely aware that the M1A2's fuel tank was immediately to his left, started up from his nearly fully reclined position when he heard the tattoo of light machine gun fire raking the metal only inches from his ear.

"Goddamn infantry!" Freeman shouted. "Run the bastards over!"

For some inexplicable reason the driver started to laugh and couldn't stop. The loader, hearing him on the intercom, also started cackling. Freeman glowered as the loader only with difficulty thrust another round home but couldn't stop laughing. It was like a child being chased—full of fear and excitement, the vision of every M1A2 breaking formation, frantically taking off after individual Chinese, having struck the crew as insanely funny.

"What in hell's the matter with you!" Freeman said, while pressing the thumb "traverse" control and hearing the rattle of machine gun bullets hitting the cupola. The loader was laughing so hard, hunched over by the shell racks, he was afraid he might have to urinate into his helmet. It was a kind of hysterical terror that only tankers and submariners know.

Several miles southward, beyond the ChiCom tanks, the dust was thinning out as Aussie's FAV stopped just below the crest of a dune. Aussie and Brentwood, crawling on their bellies to the crest, looked down between two giant hills of sand on a sight so unexpected that it literally took their breath away—a forest so ordered and alien in its sudden appearance that they knew at once it was like the massive windbreaks of forests around Turpan—a reforestation project with menggulu or Mongolian willow forming the outer acres like a moat. There was also some shaji or seabuck thorn among them. Most of the forest, however, that looked to be about a mile wide and, through the scopes, about five miles deep, was made up of huyang—Chinese poplars, an island of green amid a sea of brown dunes.

"Well I'll be buggered," Aussie said. "So now what d'we do?"

"Over there," Brentwood said, pointing to a dune about two hundred yards off to their left. "There's one." It was a ChiCom mobile radar van whose rectangular dish, the size of a collapsible bridge table, and housing set atop a hydraulic-legged ChiCom truck resembled a U.S. TPQ-63 type so much that Aussie suspected it *was* an American unit, probably bought, despite U.S. law forbidding it, through Chinese front companies in Hong Kong.

He was right. Jay La Roche had bought ten used units supposedly on sale for Taiwan and instead delivered them to China by diverting the cargo through Hong Kong.

Not far behind and below the radar unit on a wide, stony flat nearer the closer, or northern, end of the reforested area between the dunes there was what looked like a long refrigeration truck on stout hydraulic legs beneath a webbed camouflage netting, possibly an RAM-C, a radar management center, where the radar inputs from the various mobile sites would be collated and from where the deadly AA fire network would be operated. And in a flash David Brentwood realized that if the RAM-C unit could be taken out then no matter how many mobile radars there were—Freeman's intelligence now suspected five on the move—destruction of the RAM-C would be killing the brain of the whole radar network.

The dust was clearing and the sun sinking fast. David Brentwood yearned for more smoke and dust cover, long enough for the attack. "Use the TOW!" he ordered Choir Williams.

"Yes," Aussie put in, "but for Chrissake don't miss!"

"I won't, boyo," Choir said as he aligned the weapon. He tried to fire it again—still nothing. Its circuit was dead.

"All right," David said. "Now listen. We'll have to go in with the FAV—straight for the RAM-C. Choir, you and I'll hit the RAM-C. See those two doors midway along it?" It looked like a long camper.

"Yes."

"You take the left, I'll take the right. Aussie keeps the motor running." He said nothing to the La Roche reporter who was sitting down next to Choir, his eyes glazed in a terrified stare. "Salvini, you cover us. Got it?"

"Got it!" Aussie cut in. "You have the fun while I sit on my ass!"

"You and Salvini take out any guards stupid enough to try and stop us."

"I don't see any," Aussie said.

"That's good," Brentwood said. "Come on—let's go!" The FAV mounted the crest. They heard a motorcycle/side-car unit starting up, and Aussie put the FAV into reverse. Darkness had fallen, but with their SAS-issue Litton night goggles that in the daytime converted to binoculars they could see clearly between the dunes but were still at a loss to know precisely where the noise was coming from. Choir couldn't tell, as his ears were still ringing from the thunderous sound of the titanic tank battle not far off.

"Between the dunes to the right somewhere," Aussie proffered.

David Brentwood had his 7.62mm machine gun mounted on the dash pointed in the direction of the noise. Aussie reached over for the Haskins rifle strapped to the right seat strut, Choir unclipping it for him.

"Let me have a go with the suppressor."

"Quickly then!" Brentwood said. Aussie had cut the engine and was out in a second and at the crest, looking down the dunes both ways. The dust was thinning, but it was still falling like pepper in the night-vision goggles. Soon, through this curtain, he could see a high rooster feather of dust, the motorcycle and sidecar unit now just a dot four hundred yards away and moving along the flat, skirting the RAM-C or whatever it was and climbing up toward the dune and coming in the general direction of the SAS/D group. If he didn't have to he wouldn't shoot at them and would let them pass, but if they kept coming up over the dune toward the

FAV he'd have no choice. They sure as hell were taking their time—bloody putt-putting along, as his father would have said.

Four thousand miles to the northeast in the Aleutian Islands, a bitterly cold wind howled across Dutch Harbor as Lana Brentwood, her parka hood dusted in fine white snow, made her way quickly from the motor pool's shuttle bus into the warmth of the Davy Jones Restaurant. As she entered, CNN was interrupting a pretaped senior citizens' pro golf tournament in New Orleans with news of the massive tank battle now taking place in China some three hundred miles north of Beijing and only 280 miles from the Great Wall, bad weather apparently preventing the effective use of the tank-killing American A-10 Thunderbolts.

Jay La Roche had been the only one who, complaining, "Where are we here—Hicksville?" had objected to the TV being turned on in the first place, conspicuously not watching it while most of the other patrons in the dimly lit booths had paused to hear the news flash. He sat desultorily stirring the Manhattan in front of him, having complained to the waitress that he'd ordered "on the rocks," not "a fucking iceberg!" The young, ruddy-faced reporter from the *Anchorage Spectator* came in, spotted Jay, and once again tried eagerly to get a few words from him.

"Fuck off!" La Roche told the boy, who, acutely embarrassed, started to apologize profusely, but La Roche wasn't interested. He saw Lana taking off her parka by the door and hanging it up. Immediately his expression of surly discontent vanished and he rose, smiling, moving out of the booth. She knew he was going to try to kiss her. Quickly she slid into the opposite side of the booth. "Sorry I'm late. Quite a flap on at the base. We're part of the logistical tail for Freeman's tooth. He takes quite a bite."

"No sweat," he said. "I could wait for you all day."

"Weather over there's been lousy," she said. "Some huge

dust storm or other coming out of the Gobi Desert. And the Chinese are apparently using some U.S. radar equipment against us and are trying to—''

''Hey—no shop talk. Okay?'' He sat back, spreading his arms imploringly.

She shrugged. ''All right. Where are the papers?''

''I thought we were going to have dinner first?''

''I never said that,'' she answered.

''You had dinner?''

''No.''

''Well, then—''

''I'm not hungry, Jay.''

''Sure you are. You could do with a few more pounds. They're workin' you too—''

''No thanks.'' She took her Wave hat off and put it, businesslike, beside her. ''You told me you'd have the divorce papers ready for signing.''

''Hey, Lana. I thought we'd agreed on a civil good-bye? I came all this way. Is that too much to ask?''

She paused. With a private Lear jet and all his connections, Lana knew it hadn't exactly been a chore for Jay to come ''all this way,'' as he put it. ''After what you put me through, Jay—not to mention your threatening to smear my parents in your gutter press—yes, I would say it's too much to ask. Dinner with you is too much. I agreed to meet. That's all.''

''Hey,'' he said easily, ''that's fine.''

She moved her head away from him, her hair catching the golden sheen of the candlelight. She turned back angrily and looked across the table at him. ''Jay, I have no interest in you. I don't want to see you anymore. Ever. There's no point in all the smooth talk or the smutty innuendos that your whores probably think are so cute. Have you brought divorce papers or not? We'll need a witness.''

''Yes. I've got one of my staff Xeroxing the damn set for you now.'' He looked uncomfortable, jabbing at the crushed ice with his swizzle stick. "Hey, I'm sorry, all right? I didn't want to screw this up but—I guess with you and me it's oil and water now."

"Yes," she said solemnly. "I guess it is."

"Okay—" He raised his glass, beckoning her to pick up hers. She hesitated. "Don't tell me I got that wrong, too?" he said smiling. "Give me a break. You haven't gone off martinis? Used to be your favorite poison."

She loathed him now and couldn't hide it. Her stare seemed an eternity to him.

"What's wrong?" he asked. "Now you're not gonna drink with me? Was I that bad to you?" Quickly he held up his hands. "Okay, I was. If you don't want to drink with me, fine, but it's, well—it's kind of petty isn't it? Christ—I'm going to give you a fair settlement, babe. A lot of bucks, believe me."

She was still staring at him. "I remember," she said, "in Shanghai one time you slipped me a drink. All friendly, lovey-dovey—"

"Jesus, Lana! Is that what you're on about? Paranoid. Want to switch drinks? Unless," he jibed sarcastically, "you think I got some venereal disease? Besides, I haven't touched it. Been waiting for you. For my old flame." She said nothing.

"Cheers," he said, ignoring her, raising his glass. Reluctantly she lifted her glass and let his clink against hers and took a sip. The truth was, she was thirsty and would have killed for a Manhattan after a long shift at the base and another day of worrying about Frank—where he was, wondering when next they'd see one another—if ever. She couldn't bear the possibility of him being killed.

The sound of the patrol motorcycle and sidecar was muted, its rattle absorbed by the enormous walls of sand that rose on either side of the gully between the dunes, a whirligig twisting along a crest, throwing the fine sand up like brown sugar. Then the rider turned up toward the crest, not fast and not at a steep angle but making a gradual, unhurried approach at no more than ten miles an hour.

It gave Aussie no choice. He flicked up the sand guard on the Haskins's scope, fixed the machine gunner in the sidecar in the cross hairs, inhaled, let out half his breath, held it, and squeezed. The suppressor kept the noise to a quick "bump" sound, the machine gunner's head and arms flying back like a rag doll's against the white smear of the infrared-sighted exhaust. The driver made a quick U-turn but Aussie had the cross hairs on him and squeezed again. The bike coughed once or twice like some animal and fell over on its right side, the wheel of its sidecar still spinning. Aussie made his way quickly back to the FAV, the sound of the tank battle roaring unabated in the distance. Whether Freeman was winning or losing he had no idea—every crew was fighting its own war. Handing Salvini the Haskins, Aussie buckled himself in, saying quietly, "That Haskins is the best fucking rifle in the army."

"The M-fourteen," Salvini opined.

"Balls," Aussie replied, starting the FAV up. "Ten to one you're wrong."

"Yeah—who's to judge?"

Aussie slipped the FAV into low gear and moved toward the crest. "We pick two guys each—four in all—and they fire the Haskins and the M-fourteen—winner'll be the Haskins."

"Balls," Salvini said.

"Come on—you in or out?"

"In."

"Right," Aussie whispered as they made the crest. Going down the other side they were all silent, Aussie confident that the thunderous reverberations from the tank battle would cover the approach of the FAV.

"No windows," Choir observed, looking through his night-vision binoculars at the RAM-C.

"There will be when we hit it," Aussie said.

"Remember," David cautioned, the trailer hut now only three hundred yards off, "you stay in the car, Aussie."

"Yes, mother!"

They were at the bottom of the crest where sand gave way to hard, cracked earth, when a hand clamped Aussie's shoulder in a viselike grip.

"What the—?"

"Mine!" It was the first time in the last hour or so that the La Roche reporter had said anything. No one believed him until Choir saw it, too: poorly laid but a sliver of its black circumference showing. The loose soil dug up to cover it had almost completely been blown away.

"He's right, boyo!" Choir confirmed. "Antipersonnel."

"Jesus!" Aussie said. "What now? Must be all around us. They hear one of those going off and they'll know—" He was interrupted by Brentwood, who was known to be "head fast," as they called it in the SAS/D, and now showed why.

"Back up the dune—they won't have laid them there—too much shifting sand. Come on, Aussie—back up."

Aussie did so, and when they were back over the crest Salvini reminded them that if they didn't knock out the RAM-C quickly the entire American advance would be incapable of receiving TACAIR support in time. Too much longer and the American and ChiCom tanks would be so close together, mixing it up at such close range, that not even the A-10 Thunderbolts could help.

"Aussie," Brentwood said, "you get in the sidecar. Choir, you stay here with the FAV with the dashboard machine gun. Salvini, you behind me on the pillion seat. We'll retrace their path through the mine field around the RAM-C."

"Okay," Aussie said. "Let's go." And within two minutes Aussie, taking one of the dead Chinese's helmets, was in the sidecar behind a belt-feed PKS 7.62mm gun. Salvini, with his Heckler & Koch 9mm submachine gun slung over his right shoulder, sat on the pillion seat behind Brentwood, who had taken the other Chinese helmet and who was now adjusting his night-vision goggles, lowering them and blowing grains of dust off the eyepiece before he could pick up the two-wheeled track of the motorcycle and sidecar. It ran along a fifty-yard-wide porous clay gully between the dunes for a hundred yards or so and then turned left, through a man-made gap in the dune and on to more clay around what they were certain was a RAM-C trailer a hundred and fifty yards in front of them.

The La Roche reporter was licking his lips nervously. Suddenly one of the two side-by-side doors in the long trailer opened and shut. In that moment Choir had seen the dull, bloodred glow from the interior, and through the infrared sight could see a hot, white stream coming from the man who, facing away from the FAV, was urinating. When the ChiCom turned, shaking himself, buttoning up his fly, he looked over at the motorcycle and sidecar.

Intuitively, Aussie waved. The man waved back and reentered the control center. But a second later both doors opened and David could see the orange spit of a submachine gun, its bullets chopping up the dirt around them. Aussie pulled the trigger and gave the longest burst he could remember, and bodies were toppling from the trailer.

They were only fifty yards away now, with tracers arcing over from Choir's position off to the left, ripping and thudding into the trailer until the motorcycle and sidecar were only twenty feet from it. But then the door of the mobile radar hut three hundred yards away atop a dune flung open, and several troops came out firing. Choir swung his fire across toward them. The door closed, but he could see figures moving outside in the dark, their bodies, warmer than the air, giving off an ample heat signature. He fired two bursts, saw one drop and another two scuttling under the van.

In the trailer it was chaos—men shouting, wood and aluminum splintering from Aussie's and Salvini's machine gun fire at what was virtually point-blank range. Brentwood tossed in two grenades and covered his ears. The explosions totaled the trailer, fire and smoke causing the remaining Chinese, about six of them, to come out, one firing a pistol, the other falling, another on fire, and Aussie felt himself slammed back into the sidecar seat, his left shoulder warm and wet. David could now see the motorcycle and sidecar tracks leading from the RAM-C to the radar van and within a minute was over by it, Aussie giving all the weight from his right shoulder to the machine gun's stock and spraying the hut, one man falling down the stairs, dead before he hit the ground, another coming out from beneath the hut, his hands up, frantically yelling.

Salvini kept his Heckler & Koch on him while Brentwood tossed in two more grenades. The hut boomed and issued forth a rancid electrical-fire smell, smoke pouring through the shattered door seams.

Salvini told Brentwood to take them up close to the radar van, then pulled a pin out of the grenade, stood back, counted one, two, threw it at the radar mast, and quickly dashed under the van. There was a bluish purple flash above them, and then the mast was nothing more than a forlorn and tangled web of heat-fused steel, still standing, remarkably enough, but in no shape for reuse.

"What do we do with him?" Aussie said, indicating the Chinese soldier, his hands still thrust up high in the air, standing about six yards from them. "Can't shoot the bastard. Can't take him back."

"Let him go!" Brentwood said.

"Vamoose!" Salvini said to the Chinese soldier.

"Go on!" Aussie added. "Piss off!"

The man took off in panic, glanced back briefly, and kept running.

"Oh, shit!" Aussie said, but he was too late, a mine exploding so powerfully that all Aussie could see in his night-vision goggles was a fine spray like a reddish fountain blown awry in the wind. It was the man's blood vaporized by a mine that Freeman's troops called "pink mist."

As they were tracing their way back, Choir got on the radio network, informing Freeman's HQ that "Mount Rushmore is ours. Repeat, Mount Rushmore—"

"No it isn't—goddamn it!" Freeman's loud reply came. "We're still getting radar signals from the same damn sector."

"Maybe so, General," Brentwood reported, "but they're not able to send their reports to any RAM-Center because—"

"Goddamn it!" Freeman shouted. "I called in TACAIR and we've lost three Thunderbolts already."

It was at that moment that Brentwood, looking at Aussie, experienced a sinking feeling.

"Jesus!" Aussie said. "It's in the forest. That trailer we shot up must've only been a relay. The friggin' radar management center is in the bloody forest."

"Then," Freeman shouted, "take it out!"

With that, Freeman was off the air and silence reigned over the most embarrassed SAS/D troopers in all of Second Army, until Aussie proclaimed, "Must have land lines."

"You're right," Brentwood said. "Fiber-optic probably. To stop our aircraft jamming their communication they'd have to use land lines running to a central control."

"From that trailer we shot up," Salvini put in.

"You see any?" Aussie asked. "Anyone?"

There was no answer.

"All right, let's go back," Aussie said.

"You're wounded," Brentwood said.

"Nah—just a nick in the shoulder. I'll be all right. You coming with us, CBN?" Aussie added.

"I stay here," the reporter answered.

"Can the bike and sidecar unit carry four of us back there?" asked Choir.

"Piece of cake," Aussie said. "Come on."

CHAPTER FORTY-EIGHT

"SO," JAY SAID, watching Lana looking at the crushed ice like a crystal ball, turning the glass, her mind obviously not with him. "Tell me about this Shirer guy."

"He's a pilot," she said, taking another sip. "I met him at—"

"I know when you met him. What's he like?"

"Kind, considerate." She touched the glass, tracing a line with her finger across the condensation. "He's nice."

"Well," Jay said, with an air of magnanimity, "I hope it works out."

"Thanks."

"To—" Jay hesitated. "What's his first name?"

"Franklin," she said.

"Frank!" The glasses clinked again. "Sure you don't want anything to eat?"

She was sorely tempted by the lobster cocktail. "No—I'm—" She yawned. "I'm fine."

"Fine! You're beautiful. If you'd have me back, babe, I'd—" He fell silent. She'd speared the olive with the swizzle stick and he watched her take it to her mouth, leaning forward, her breasts the more tantalizing for being hidden in the uniform, the uniform that carried with it the suggestion of regulations, conformity—the very things that excited him to violate. "God but you're beautiful. Now don't get mad. Just a compliment."

"I'm not mad," she said, taking another sip then sitting back against the plush padded wall of the booth. She looked around. It was the first time she'd been to the Davy Jones Restaurant. "It's not as bad as I thought," she said.

"Huh—oh. Thought you'd been here before?"

"No. Just heard of it. Navy lieutenants can't afford eating out. Not in restaurants anyway."

"Then have dinner. Come on, relax. I'm not trying to hit on you. You believe that?"

"I don't know anything about you," she said, her finger trailing the edge of the glass. "I thought I did once but I don't." She took another sip.

"You think I'm an animal," he said.

"Not all the time." She looked around the restaurant. "When are those papers coming?"

"Any minute."

Before she could ask him any more questions about the papers he rambled on, "Told them to take them up to my room, but I can see now there's no way you'd come up to sign them."

Lana's smile was a worldly one—a world away from the shy virgin that Jay had married and debased until she'd fought her way back to self-respect. Her look now told him, "Come on, Jay—you take me for a fool?"

"So," he said. "I'll get someone over here from the Excelsior. If you don't mind a lawyer sitting in."

"Why should I?" She took another sip, visibly more relaxed and feeling more in control of the situation.

"Okay," he said, lifting his drink. "To a civil parting of the ways. No hard feelings."

She sighed, and he saw her eyes going out of focus.

"You okay?"

"Yes." She yawned. "Why—?"

"I dunno—you don't look so good. I told you, they work you too hard at that—"

The thud of her head knocked over the glasses, and Jay was by her side in two seconds. "Hey, babe—"

The barman came over. "Is there anything wrong, Mr. La Roche?"

"No," Jay said sarcastically. "She's fine. Loves crashing on tables."

"Should I call a doctor?"

"No—she's got low blood pressure. Happens all the time. She'll be right in a few minutes."

A man appeared from one of the booths, looking concerned, coming over to see if he could help. Jay was lifting her up, putting her over his shoulder. "Better send dinner up to the room," he told the maître d'-cum-manager.

"Certainly, sir. Should I ring a doctor?"

"No, I told you it's just a bit of low blood pressure. She'll be right as rain in a little while. You could give us a hand up on the elevator."

"Of course," the maître d' said. "Marge, you clean up the table."

"Yes, sir."

Up in Jay's room the manager was still fussing.

"She'll be fine," Jay told him for the third time in as many minutes. "But listen, maybe you should hold off on the meal. I'll call down when we're ready."

"Yes, Mr. La Roche. Of course. Anything . . ."

Not long after the manager had gone, Jay heard the phone ring. It was his lawyer downstairs who had been sitting a few booths away.

"Everything okay?" Jay asked.

"No problems, Mr. La Roche. They cleaned up the booth real nice."

"You switch her glass with mine?"

"Yes, sir, Mr. La Roche. Be through the washing machine in a few minutes anyway."

"Fine. Now I don't want any interruptions for at least half

an hour. I'll call down when I want you. When I call, get your
ass up here quick. I want you here when she wakes up. Right?''

"Of course, Mr. La Roche.''

CHAPTER FORTY-NINE

WHEN THEY RETURNED to the dune overlooking the
shot-up trailer there was an eerie silence due to the wind
having dropped considerably in the last quarter hour. They
found a clump of land lines leading into the reforested area
and heard voices coming from the direction of the willows.

Aussie estimated there were about six ChiComs, and that
was the number he tapped out on Brentwood's sleeve. The
SAS/D withdrew a hundred yards back up the dune, and
Brentwood had his night-vision binoculars resting on the
crest. For five long minutes he watched as the ChiCom patrol
emerged and walked around the trailer, assessing the damage
but careful not to go too near the mine field. Even when
Chinese whispered it seemed to be at about thirty decibels.
The SAS/D group by instinct and training knew what to do—
follow the patrol back from whence it came. Brentwood took
the point.

Aussie, holding back for minute, taking the tail end position, gave himself a jab of morphine. It wouldn't last long,
but hopefully long enough.

As the Chinese returned to the forest, the SAS following
them—the infrared footprints an easy pickup with the SAS's

night-vision goggles—not a word was said. From here on in through the willow trees and if necessary deeper into the poplar, not a sound would be made, everything done by feel and by a touch code very much like that used by the SEALs when they too went "in-country."

Brentwood, following the fiber-optic line, was sure of only one thing, and that was that for ease of repair, should a break appear in the line, the ChiComs would not have mined the area either side of the land line, as it ran parallel to a line of poplars deeper into the man-planted forest, the ChiCom patrol, by Aussie's reckoning, no more than five minutes in front of them.

The four SAS/D men did not rush but used their weapons as one would use a stick to sweep either side of the fiber-optic line to make sure there were no trip wires from ankle to neck height. Had it not been for the infrared goggles that the

SAS/D were equipped with, the ChiComs would have vanished from view, but the residual body heat of the six-man ChiCom patrol was visible—at least for a while—and then, suddenly, all trace of them, infrared or otherwise, was gone.

Brentwood took out his K-bar knife and soon, joined by the other three, was probing the ground for any unnatural seam that would be formed by a trapdoor or tunnel entrance, concentrating on the area where the optic line ended and suddenly plunged underground. That the radar management center was immediately below them they had no doubt, but where the trapdoor was they still couldn't tell, until by virtue of moonlight that had penetrated the dust beyond the great tank battle, Salvini was able to spot a rather jerky infrared camera ten feet up the poplar as a squiggle in his infrared goggles, the heat caused by the friction of the camera moving so often.

The Chinese officer of the day, his red armband signifying that he was in charge of the first night watch, was watching the four SAS men on the video feed from each of the four poplar-mounted cameras. He saw the six-man patrol come in and asked them, "Were you followed?"

"No," the NCO replied confidently. "Not a sound."

With that the officer of the day nodded to the video screen, the heat lines of the four SAS commandos plainly visible on the closed circuit.

Immediately the NCO apologized and offered to take his patrol back up—take care of them right now.

"Oh yes," the OOD said, "and what will they be doing in the meantime? You go up the steps, open the double-blackout trapdoor. I don't want a firefight up there or anything else that will draw any more attention to the forest. They picked up radiant heat from down here seeping up through the trapdoor." Gently, noiselessly, the SAS/D team was quickly sliding its knives along the seam of the outer trapdoor. The NCO had lost face and begged to go.

"Very well, Comrade. Redeem yourself, but I don't want any firing up there," the OOD insisted. "We don't know how many other Americans could be in the area or if any of Freeman's Bradleys will hear a firefight on the perimeter and come to investigate. We risk revealing the whole complex. But I confess I don't want that SAS/D team up there to get back to tell Freeman where we are. Use your knives or bayonets and go through the trapdoor they haven't yet discovered. Remember it's about thirty feet away to the east so you should have ample time to come up behind them and kill them all. No firing. Understand?"

"Yes, comrade."

The OOD enjoyed the irony of it as the ChiCom patrol readied to make its way up again, the fact that the very land lines—fiber-optic cables that were far less vulnerable to EMP or other jamming from the Wild Weasels, etc.—were American made. General Cheng had purchased the best cable you could get from La Roche Industries.

Up above, Brentwood tap-signaled Aussie, Salvini, and

Choir to back off, and having been alerted to the one TV camera by Salvini, his infrared goggles picked up the other three that made a square, and the four SAS/D men went beyond this square so they were no longer visible to the monitoring eyes on the four poplars that served as markers. What the SAS/D men had no way of knowing was that the alternate entrance and exit to the underground complex was not in the more or less cleared square area bordered by the four poplars but was some twenty to thirty feet deeper in the wood, so that despite the SAS/D precaution of moving beyond the cameras, the Chinese patrol would nevertheless be coming up behind them.

But then everything went crazy. The earth began to tremble, two enormous trapdoors were thrown open from the hydraulic pressure, and up from the thirty-square-yard piece of ground bounded by four of the poplars a thing began rising from the forest floor, looking for all the world like a great bat-eared beast, four radar dishes atop a steel girder tower ascending into the night.

Below, the Chinese OOD bellowed his orders—the American general had launched another TACAIR over the battlefield a few miles off and Cheng had ordered the camouflage mast radar be put up immediately so as to throw up a radar net that could serve the deadly ChiCom triple A anti-aircraft fire, which included SAMs.

The six Chinese rushed forward toward the SAS/D team, but Aussie and Brentwood were already to ground, having heard the ChiComs the moment they'd started to run, and in a deadly burst of Heckler & Koch nine hundred rounds per minute of 9mm Parabellum, Aussie and Brentwood cut down two of the Chinese less than thirty feet from the edge of the radar mast's well. A *boomp!* erupted from Choir's Winchester 1200 riot gun, sending a cloud of perfectly aerodynamically constructed darts or fléchettes cutting through poplar and willow leaves like a scythe and taking out another two attackers.

''Aussie, take the tower—Sal, you and Choir cover him!''

Before Brentwood had finished speaking there was another *boomp!* from the shotgun and one more member of the Chinese patrol fell, propelled backward, screaming and clasping what remained of his face. Choir fired yet another fléchette round down into the retractable radar tower's well to keep Chinese heads down. He had the high ground advantage like the other three members of the SAS/D troop, and, like two men guarding a narrow bridge, they only had to stop a few who were trying to run up from the well on two narrow stone stairways.

He was reloading when he saw Brentwood using his Heckler & Koch as a staff, smacking aside a ChiCom bayonet and clubbing the man in the face with the H & K's steel butt. It was in moments like these that the SAS/D men's extraordinarily tough physical training stood them in good stead. The man went down, but to make sure Brentwood gave him a bone-crunching kick in the head.

''Come on, come on!'' Aussie hissed. He was talking to the tower, willing it up faster so that he could jump one of the girders of the triangular construction. He had to wait for the bat ears to go well beyond him before he could step aboard the tower as one would an elevator as it passed your floor. The Chinese had fired no flares so as not to pinpoint their position for TACAIR.

''Christ!'' It was Brentwood looking behind him at the tower, still rising.

''What?'' the Welshman asked.

''Aussie's arm—I forgot. Damn it!''

''He'll be all right, boyo.''

''Should've sent Sal.''

''Too late now.''

''Yes,'' Brentwood said. ''Anyway, let's keep them occupied down—'' There was a splatter of earth against Brentwood's uniform as a 7.62mm opened up from the well of the tower, the tower still going up like a Texas windmill.

"No wonder we couldn't find this bastard!" Choir said, pumping another three shots into the well. There were screams and fierce yelling but the simple fact was that so long as the three men—Choir, Brentwood, and Sal—had enough ammunition they could hold down those in the well. But sooner or later the ammo would run out, and then the Chinese could swarm up and take the troop. Salvini dropped a grenade down—more screaming and more yelling than he'd heard in a 'Frisco mah-jongg game. "Silly fuckers don't know he's on the tower!" Salvini said.

"Let's keep it that way," Brentwood said. "Look out!" A stick grenade lobbed the lip of the well. Choir calmly poked it back over with the barrel of his riot gun, then he pulled the pin on one of his own grenades, made a two-second count, and let it go. "They won't catch that bastard!"

There was a scream that gave truth to his prediction.

"I'm almost out of ammo, lads," Choir said. "Ten reloads and that's it."

"Come on, Aussie," Sal implored.

In fact, Aussie Lewis could hardly hang on. With little or no power in his left arm he could only hold himself up by locking his legs together in a scissor hold and leaning his head forward into the right angle of the girder. Then he pushed and prodded the Play-Doh–like C4 plastique into the inside angle formed by two of the girders, using the slightly banana-shaped magazine from his Heckler & Koch as a tamp for the charge to better direct the blast in toward the beam's angle. He then crushed the fuse's vial of acid, which had a ten-minute count. By then the wire holding the firing pin would dissolve.

Next he put his right arm down then under the girder he was sitting on and, his Heckler & Koch slung over his shoulder, swung down, monkeylike, his boots barely touching the next girder. He repeated this two more times, his right arm now feeling the strain as he molded the second belt of plastique into an angle of steel. As he completed packing the second charge in and tamping it, he waited for a few seconds, looking at his watch, and then crushed the five-minute vial, swung down to the next girder, and from there jumped fifteen feet down to where the other three were. Salvini lifted Aussie's good arm over his shoulder and started off down the land line back toward the FAV while Choir and Brentwood turned in a rear action, a hail of 9mm parabellum shooting forth with the darts as the ChiComs began to swarm up the steps.

"Go!" Brentwood yelled. "Go!"

Salvini wasn't even looking back, but Aussie was able to run by himself while keeping the left arm tucked in by his side.

"Withdraw, Choir," Brentwood said.

"Not without you, boyo!"

"Withdraw!"

Choir's answer was to fire another three fléchette-loaded rounds at the Chinese. Salvini was back with Choir. "C'mon, you mother!" he said, firing four three-round bursts to keep the ChiComs down in the well. Suddenly he felt something falling on him. It was a flutter of leaves, a ChiCom firing too high in his excitement. Then the earth shook a second time and went into a blur, a feral roar of fire erupting about the skeletal radar mast. The tower collapsed, telescoping in on itself in a reddish-orange column of flame, then another, after which the debris of the crashing radar tower and the fire spilled onto all of those in the well, igniting the gasoline and hydraulic fluid that exploded in a final volcanic fury, spewing bluish crimson flames hundreds of feet into the sky, scorching and setting the poplars afire like giant candles in the night.

A hundred yards to go to reach the FAV and the sidecar began rattling, taking a burst from another FAV closing in on them a hundred yards to the left, a ricochet ripping open David Brentwood's left cheek before Salvini reached forward around him, cut the throttle, and got off the pillion seat, throwing up his hands. ''Don't shoot! We're Americans.''

''Stay where you fucking are!'' a skeptical voice came.

''Mount Rushmore's ours!'' Salvini yelled.

''Stay where you fucking are, buddy!''

When they were close enough to sort it all out, there were apologies aplenty, but the apologies didn't do anything for Aussie's wounded arm or David's face, which, as Choir drove over in the other FAV to meet them, was being held together by tape until they could get him back to a field hospital.

CHAPTER FIFTY

CHENG NOW COMMITTED his reserve battalions to the battle as Freeman's line had seemed to falter. But Freeman had just given orders to slow down his advance, as he did not want to start mixing it up at close quarters with Cheng's armor and troops until TACAIR—now that the sky was clearing somewhat—had a chance to inflict maximum damage.

Cheng interpreted the slowing down of Freeman's armor, however, as a sign that his, Cheng's, advantage of four tanks to one was starting to tell. Hurriedly he ordered up more reserves as Freeman's echelons began to slow, throwing up a steady barrage of thick white smoke grenades from their launch tubes on both sides of their turrets.

With the falling off of the dust storm and darkness having already descended, the ChiComs' T-59s and T-72s could be picked up by Freeman's TACAIR—spearheaded by the A-10 Thunderbolts. With their tank-killing seven-barrel Gatling gun, its ammo drum the size of a Honda Accord, the Thunderbolts' guns poured out seventy of their 1,350 30mm armor-piercing shells per second, the planes appearing to be in a near stall as the weakest part of the Chinese tanks, their cupolas, seemed literally to soak up the fire before bursting.

Without their radar and RAM-C, taken out by Brentwood's SAS/D team, to pick up the low-flying Thunderbolts, the Chi-Com tanks were swooped upon. In eleven minutes of the most intensive infrared A-10 attacks since and including the Iraqi War, the ChiComs lost forty-two tanks, some of them reserves. But the burning Chinese tanks added to the smoke, and soon the A-10s' usefulness, impressive as it was, was nullified by the chemical-made fog of the battlefield and dark black exhaust of the ChiComs' diesel engines as opposed to that of the M-1s' clean gas turbine.

Freeman gave another order, to "Charge!"—not an order in the manual, but one that Freeman well knew would cut through static on the radio network. Soon the ChiComs and Americans were at close quarters again, mixing it up, echelon against echelon and finally tank against tank. What had been the flanks where the FAVs had been operating were now quickly being taken over by the combatants as, turrets slewing, they wheeled, skidded, and climbed the clay rise and surrounding dunes in high whine, the positions of the dozen remaining FAVs becoming more precarious in what at first sight looked like a vast crazy traffic jam.

As Choir drove, Aussie slumped in the back, holding his shoulder below the TOW mounting and next to the La Roche reporter while Brentwood insisted on manning the dash-mounted machine gun until, despite the field dressing on his face, the blood from his seeping cheek wound soaked through and caught in the slipstream. This making it impossible for him to see, he reluctantly had to give the machine gun up to Salvini while he took Salvini's place in the right-hand litter.

T-59s and T-72s were using the infrared searchlights on the Americans, and the Americans were using their own night-vision goggles. But for all the equipment it was still a confusion with blue-on-blue mistakes on both sides, and strain and cacophony of the battle added to by the almost unbelievable din of machine guns chattering, tank cannon roaring, and the sound of tanks exploding, as the deadly fireworks of magazines blew up in towering, multihued flames, some men's blood vaporizing in the heat, others' literally boiling as combinations of HESH—heat solid shot—discarding Sabot, and APFSDS—armor-piercing fin stabilized discarding Sabot—rounds exploded.

Two American commanders, frustrated by the inability of their viewers to see well enough through the smoke, took up the "Israeli" position—that is, not staying "buttoned up" but standing up in the turret for a better view—only to be killed almost instantly by the machine gun fire of Chinese armored personnel carriers.

"Two aerials! Two aerials!" Cheng's Commander Soong yelled, exhorting his men to try to pick out the command tanks. But the men of his three battalions of 180 Soviet-made T-72s, who had been hunkering down in defilade position behind the dunes' crests before the battle, knew it would be almost impossible to pick out the two-aerial tanks. It was hard enough to see anything before you yourself were seen. And at times no one knew what the huge shadow looming in the night was—enemy or friend. Soong, glued to his periscope viewer as another round was extracted from the T-72's autoloader's carousel and rammed home, did not know who was winning the massive dogfight among the tanks.

Meanwhile David Brentwood and the few remaining FAVs drove about looking for knocked-out motorcycle and sidecar units to siphon off enough gas, any hope of reaching their own refueling depots at night a slim chance at best, given the vastness of the dunes, clay flats, and a small dry salt lake bed about them where the armored battle raged in fiercely chaotic duels that would go till dawn.

The American M1A1 was more than holding its own. In fact there would be fewer American tanks remaining in the morning than Chinese because of the four-to-one ratio, but the Chinese took a terrible punishment. The victory, Freeman knew, would not go to the side who merely held its own but who could break through the other's lines of defense.

In the end it was Freeman's Bradley armored personnel carriers that turned the tide. The twenty-two-ton American IFV—infantry fighting vehicle—was markedly superior to the ChiComs' 531 with its Hongjian 8 missile launcher. The Bradley's speed of forty-one miles per hour was something to behold along with its deadly TOWs, cannon, and ball gun ports on either side. Like the M1A1, the Bradley, even over the roughest ground, could continue firing its TOWs and cannon atop an independently sprung chassis that was near perfection itself.

Through that night there was another dust storm, but this one was completely man made as over a thousand tanks and IFVs slugged it out in the darkness, the night illuminated now and then by huge white green-orange flashes, filled with the stench of cordite and the head-throbbing smell of burning diesel, tracers constantly arcing through the night, seeking the right range for the main guns. Men screamed beneath the tracks of an M-1 or T-59 bearing down on them, often their presence unknown by the tank drivers who were pressing for larger game. More sand turned to glass as molten metal jets from HEAT rounds passed through a foot of enemy armor before hitting the sand.

Gradually, by about 0314 hours, the Americans gained ground, penetrating the Chinese defenses, and at 0400 it was clear that the Chinese were withdrawing.

By 0430 there was a sudden drop-off of firing from the Chinese. By dawn they were in full retreat. Freeman kept after them, and by 0800 there were more American than Chinese tanks, the ChiCom losses being greatest in the last hour of the rout, the bodies of some of the ChiCom crews of the broken-down and burned-out hulks sitting in grotesque positions.

Freeman's victory could not have been claimed for any particular moment, but rather the turning point, like the end of weeding a garden, suddenly happened—a few stragglers captured at will. In the final hour of the battle, eye sockets dark, eyes red with fatigue, Freeman had lost twenty-seven tanks, the Chinese, 102, not counting the Chinese APCs that had fallen easy victim to the Bradleys. And none of it would have been possible but for the SAS/D FAV charge against the guns.

Numbed by the excessive battle, few thought of what would follow—all they yearned for was rest. But Freeman was exhilarated. For him it was as if the battle had injected him with a determination to press on, though he knew that in the interest of his men he would at least have to pause. And Washington was ordering him not merely to pause but to stop and not go a step further. Even this massive tank battle, the largest since Iraq, was being cheekily described by him to Washington as a "reconnaissance in force"!

Victorious in the Gobi and standing on that golden northern plain in the China dawn, the southern wind in his face, he gazed far to the southeast. "Norton. You realize how close we are?"

"General, Washington'll never go for it."

"Two days, Norton. The Second Army of the United States is only two days from the prize. Beijing, Dick—beyond that Great Wall lies the heart of China. It's within our grasp." He turned to Norton, wild with surmise. "Within striking distance, goddamn it!"

"Sir—you've been moving so fast that our supply line's

dangerously overextended, and Admiral Kuang's planned invasion hasn't materialized.''

"I know, I know. Stopped by a goddamned typhoon!''

"He's taking it as a sign, General. Maybe we should, too?''

"Balls!'' Freeman said, moving his goggles above the peak of his general's cap, looking uncannily like Rommel in the desert. "What in hell's the matter with you, Dick?'' His right hand was thrust in the direction of Beijing. "You're talking like one of those fairies in Washington. I've told you, this country isn't a country like ours. North and south China are at odds—and the controlling clique in Beijing is rotten to the core and the people know it. It's a hundred Chinas that want to be rid of those commie bastards.'' Then the general used one of Mao's axioms. " 'Let a hundred flowers bloom!' eh, Dick? 'Let a hundred schools of thought contend!' We show them the way and many'll join us.''

"How about the Chinese army, General?''

"That's why we have to strike fast, Dick. Before Cheng can recover from the beating we've given him here. Weather's cleared.''

Overhead American fighter patrols were now tangling with Chinese Shenyangs. It was no contest—"the turkey shoot of Organ Tal.'' But on the ground Cheng still had over two and a half million in arms.

"General, if you make a move on Beijing, Washington'll have you court-martialed. Already they're saying Beijing is seeking a cease-fire.''

"*Another* Yugoslav cease-fire,'' Freeman said contemptuously. "Won't last a week—if that.''

"I don't think so.''

"Alright, Norton, our supply line *is* overextended. I'll say that. And we *need* to consolidate—you're right there. But you tell me what I'm supposed to do if Admiral Kuang attacks in more clement weather—now that I'm this close?''

"We'd have to check with Washington, sir.''

"Cheng would have to defend on two fronts," Freeman said.

"I don't know, General," Norton said cautiously. "We were sent here originally to keep the peace—not start a war."

"We didn't start a war. Goddamn commies started it the moment Cheng crossed over and slaughtered that Japanese defense force. We're already in the war, Norton, or hadn't you noticed?" He saw the worry lines creasing Norton's face. "Well, have those Chinese bastards in Beijing kept their people down?" The general answered his own question before Norton could utter a word. "Hell, those jokers've been asking for it ever since Tiananmen."

Norton didn't answer. To take Beijing—it would be one of the fiercest battles in history. Even the idea of it took Norton's breath away, and he sought refuge in the logistical situation.

"But you do agree, sir, that we couldn't move yet even if we wanted to."

"Agreed, but it won't take us long to get back to full strength, Dick."

Norton had been told that July and August would be the monsoon months, and that the rain would cause Freeman further pause. It would most commanders, but that was the problem: Freeman wasn't like most commanders. He'd attacked Pyongyang at night and Ratmanov Island in a blizzard. And won.

"By God, can you imagine it, Dick? For us, the American army, to be in Tiananmen Square. To raise the Stars and Stripes. To free China." Freeman's vision was so grand it awed and terrified Norton.

CHAPTER FIFTY-ONE

AT THE MOST forward aid station outside Orgon Tal, where he sat with so many others waiting to be attended to, Aussie was already comforted by a medic telling him that his injury was a flesh wound, that he'd lost some blood and the shoulder would be badly bruised for a while but that he'd be all right once they stitched him up. A half hour later Alexsandra Malof, one of the few prisoners to survive the FAV attacks against the guns, was ushered in by a corporal. Aussie instinctively made room for her by him, patting the bench. Someone whose pain had got the better of him asked in a loud voice when they were going "to get out of this fucking dump."

"Hey!" Aussie shouted, the effort hurting his shoulder, but he got everyone's attention. "Watch the language, lads. Lady present." He offered her the rest of his coffee, and she accepted. "Must forgive the lads, miss," Aussie said. "They use a lot of foul language I'm afraid. Don't go for it myself." He extended his right hand. "Name's Aussie Lewis."

Alexsandra nodded. "I am Alexsandra Malof."

Her very breathing excited him, and he watched her breasts rise and fall in a unison that mesmerized him. Finally he told her, "They're sending us back to Khabarovsk for a bit of R and R—rest and recreation."

"Oh yes," she said.

"So how about you?"

"Khabarovsk also."

"That a fact? Look, maybe we could have dinner."

"Perhaps." She liked the soldier's easy friendliness, his openness, and he did not seem as uncouth as some of the others. Someone came in swearing about getting "fucking sand in my fucking contacts."

"Hey! Hey!" Aussie said. "Enough of that!"

David Brentwood shook his head disbelievingly, causing his cheek to bleed more. "I can't stand it," he told Choir.

"How about Olga?" somebody asked Aussie.

Lewis affected complete puzzlement, frowning. "Olga— Olga who?"

"A bird in the hand, eh, Aussie?" another of the wounded SAS/D troopers said.

Aussie shook his head as if he'd been deeply hurt, explaining softly to Alexsandra Malof, "They're very uncouth."

"Like most soldiers, I suppose," she said.

Aussie sighed. "Yes, I'm afraid you're right."

"Do you think there will be more fighting?" she asked him.

"All depends, I suppose, on whether the Chinese want to come to terms with the U.N. or not." He paused. "I heard someone say you had a pretty bad run—I mean a bad time with the Chinese."

"Yes," she said simply. "And the Siberians." But he could tell she didn't want to talk any more about it. "Oh well," he told her, "it's over now, Sandy. When we get back to Khabarovsk and have that dinner let's not talk about it."

"Yes," she said warmly. "That would be wonderful."

David Brentwood was still shaking his head. "I can't stand it."

CHAPTER FIFTY-TWO

JAY TOLD THE lawyer to get lost, and when he was off the phone Jay had disconnected the jack. Then he walked over slowly toward the bed where Lana lay on her back, legs draped over the end of the bed. Jay told himself he mustn't hurry, but by the time he'd pulled off her panty hose, rolled her over, undone her bra, and rolled her back over again, her legs lolling down further over the end of the bed, he knew he'd have trouble drawing it out. But hell, that was half the fun, and no matter what she said after coming to from the chloral hydrate of the Mickey Finn, he'd call the lawyer, who would swear blind that Mr. La Roche hadn't touched her, no matter how sore she felt or what she said.

Naked himself, standing over her, he reached down, rolled her over again onto her stomach, slipped his hands beneath her, squeezed her breasts, then took one shot with the Polaroid to make sure it was working properly. Let this fucking Shirer marry her after this little peep show had done the round of the base. Already he had the headline for his "rags," as she'd called them: WAVE OFF BASE WITH ACE. All you could see in this photo was her buttocks, but later when he flipped her again, finished doing it in her mouth—chained her up a bit—he'd take a mug shot of her. Franklin would recognize her easy enough then.

One thing he knew he could count on was that medically

she'd be clean as a cucumber. No VD pushed into her. He'd been too careful about that. And if she started squawking to anyone after, he'd remind her of what her precious daddy and mommy would look like splashed across the *National Investigator*. He spread her buttocks apart and, spitting on the soap bar, ran it up and down thirteen times. Thirteen was lucky.

There was a knock on the door. He tried to ignore it, but it wouldn't let up. Quickly he grabbed his Chinese robe with the gold brocade dragons rampant on emerald silk—the same robe he'd used when he'd had her in Shanghai. There was another knock on the door and, cursing, he went over and looked through the peephole. It wasn't the lawyer but the snot-nosed junior reporter from the *Anchorage Spectator*, intent on getting a story from La Roche. La Roche knew the type—young, persistent, dreamed of the Pulitzer, and a pain in the ass when you wanted a piece of tail. And if you told them to scram they'd write fuckin' lies about you. He opened the door. "Listen," he told the kid, "I'm busy right now."

"I'm sorry for the intrusion, Mr. La Roche, but I just wondered if I could get a few comments on the—"

The kid's fervent earnestness was all too familiar to La Roche. Everybody thought that when you were rich you knew some secret. Whenever you farted they took it to be a prediction of the market. He'd offer the kid a twenty, but he knew the kid wouldn't take it. Full of integrity and all the other loser philosophy.

"Later, kid. All right? Come around in the morning—about—"

"You remember Congressman Hailey, Mr. La Roche?"

"What?"

"A Congressman Hailey. You know, the one you said you'd show all those pictures of with other men—if he didn't try and transfer a pilot to—"

"Hey!" Jay said. "Don't you come around here—"

"I'm his son."

The bullet from the silencer passed straight through the would-be newspaper reporter's notebook into La Roche's mouth, flinging him hard against the door, coming out high up on his neck. La Roche, eyes bulging, jawbone quivering violently, staggered forward, his mouth full of blood, pouring down over his robe, turning the gold dragons red. As he slumped to the hallway carpet, James Hailey, Jr., shot La Roche again, point-blank in the face. Then he put the gun to La Roche's temple, pulled the trigger again, and, unhurriedly pocketing the firearm, walked quickly back down the fire escape stairwell, and down by Dutch Harbor.

After wiping all prints from the gun grip, he tossed it far out into the frigid black water, called a cab, and told the driver he had to catch a plane in half an hour from Dutch Harbor to Juneau and then on to the lower forty-eight.

Fifteen minutes later a shoe salesman, after checking into Davy's, found Jay La Roche lying across the hallway.

Noting the time, and after taking a blood sample from Mrs. La Roche as she lay unconscious on the bed, the police could quickly ascertain that she had been completely out of it at the time of the murder, the high concentration of chloral hydrate showing up in her blood sample. Besides which, there wasn't a weapon.

"Did Mr. La Roche have any enemies?" the Dutch Harbor police chief asked La Roche's lawyer.

The lawyer said, "Let me count the ways," and his gut began jiggling like jelly.

"What d'you mean?" the police chief asked.

"Shall we say, Sheriff, that Mr. La Roche had many competitors and, in a big business like his—a man makes enemies on the way up. People think they were badly done by."

"Then he won't be missed," the police chief proffered.

The lawyer had tears in his eyes—he couldn't hold in the laughter.

CHAPTER FIFTY-THREE

FRANK SHIRER BECAME a household word, his name splashed all over the British, European, and American press, including La Roche's tabloids, as ace extraordinaire. It wasn't that Harriers hadn't already proved themselves—they'd shot down much faster planes, Mirages, than themselves during the Falklands War—but this was the first time a Harrier had downed a Fulcrum. After the terrible losses of all nine B-52s on the successful raid over Turpan, the Harriers' victory was welcome news.

Even so, Lana was more interested in talking to Frank in her long distance call to Peshawar about when they should have the wedding. She would have preferred it to be in June, but the feeling of so many young couples was that America was locked into a war with China whether she liked it or not. It was more common than not to hear the cease-fire General Cheng had successfully gained from Washington being described cynically as another "Yugoslavian" agreement that Chairman Nie and General Cheng had cooked up merely to buy time. Support for this view was fueled by rumors that thousands of troops were being rushed from the southern provinces across the Yangtze, on anything that would float, to Beijing military district. And there was a powerful feeling within the United States itself, with its Emergency Powers Act still on the books, that Freeman, whether Washington agreed or not, would soon be in the biggest battle so far.

* * *

If Shirer got publicity for his victory over the Fulcrum, it was nothing compared to the lavish praise of Freeman and his Second Army and, in particular, the SAS/D commandos, whose praises were sung by the once-terrified CBN newsman. The press, particularly those reporters who were camp followers and too lazy to go find their own stories, were only too happy to feed off the CBN reporter's eyewitness account of the great tank battle. One of the camp followers from the press asked Aussie Lewis how the CBN reporter had fared under fire.

"He was great!" Aussie said. "He just—hung on in there."

The La Roche tabloids ran four-inch headlines—FREEMAN ROUTS REDS—and now the CBN reporter, name Frederick F. Nelson III, was booked for months ahead on every TV talk show from Larry King to Rush Limbaugh, and now, during any presidential press conferences, was sure to get his question attended to.

But of all the reports of the war—or at least the war so far—one of the most intriguing was CNN's report on the sudden appearance in Istanbul, Turkey, of what the CNN reporter called "a gunner Murphy," apparently the only survivor of the B-52 raid on Turpan. He had a lot to say about the raid, and created the distinct impression that he'd shot down half the Chinese air force before he was so unobligingly shot down himself. But what people were more interested in was his vouched-for rescue by fierce, though sympathetic, Kurdish rebels who as well as getting the American to Turkey had performed an operation on his shot-up nose that was an old procedure and well known in the region but, like acupuncture, was as yet unknown in the West.

The rebels, in an ancient surgical practice, had drugged the American, then, using a tree leaf known for its resiliency, had placed the leaf over the bridge of the remaining part of the nose, using this as a support over which skin from the man's leg had been placed and stitched down into the skin on either side of the nose. By the time the leaf had decayed, the skin had grafted—two small openings being made to serve as nostrils. It wasn't something that would enthrall the *New England Journal of Medicine*, but as Gunner Murphy had said, "It'll do till I get back to the States."

It was a story that was told again and again among the families of the lost B-52 crewmen, for it was their only tangible link, an act of mercy, that had been shown to one of their own, and from this they took what comfort they could.

When Alexsandra Malof invited Aussie Lewis to her home in the old Jewish autonomous region near Khabarovsk, she introduced him as an Australian soldier who, as Australians often did, fought next to his American friends.

"You'll be here long?" her father asked him.

"Depends, mate," Aussie said.

When he got back to camp, Choir asked him about wedding bells.

"Never know, do you?" he said, shocking them.

"Little beaver for the winter eh, Aus?" Sal joshed.

"Hey, hey!" Aussie said. "Enough of that talk, sport."

"You're not serious," Sal said. "Jeez, you couldn't go a week without cussing."

"That a bet?" Aussie said, sitting down on his bunk.

"What—yeah. Yeah," Sal said. "That's a bet."

"I'm in," Choir said.

Aussie lowered himself down gingerly on the bunk, the shoulder still hurting. "David, how about you? Ah, sorry, forgot your cheek's so puffed up you can't talk. Thumb up for ten bucks."

David put up two thumbs.

"Oh, all right," Aussie said. "Ten bucks for Bullfrog Face." He looked over at Choir and Sal. "You guys wouldn't be in on a setup here would you?"

"No," Choir said indignantly.

"Fair dinkum," Sal said. It was an Australian term Aussie had taught them and it meant "fair drinking" in the gold fields where everyone had to get drunk before playing cards—then everyone was equal.

"All right," Aussie said. "You're on."

Frank and Lana agreed on a wedding date in late May, and while they were discussing the wedding plans, Douglas Freeman was studying the street plan of Beijing.

WW III: ARCTIC FRONT

World War III is over. Or is it? Moscow has surrendered, but Siberia defies the cease-fire, and the battlefield shifts to this icy and desolate land. General Freeman must eliminate the threat of nuclear warfare and launch a bloody ground assault. However, the icy waters of Lake Baikal conceal a deadly weapon that will determine the fate of millions.

WW III: WARSHOT

The war on the Siberian front intensifies, and the Chinese brace for incursions into their buffer zone of Outer Mongolia. Extensive sabotage at home requires U.S. President Mayne to institute martial law. Provoked by a Chinese border incident, the Americans attack, launching the biggest battles ever fought on earth. General Freeman orders the greatest "cavalry charge" in history, throwing every last American resource against the massed Chinese and Siberians.

WW III: ASIAN FRONT

Led by the legendary general, Douglas Freeman, American forces seek to maintain a cease-fire between China and the new republic of Sibir (Siberia). The truce collapses, and China and the United States, the post-Cold War's two superpowers, are at war. From the Taiwan Straits to Mongolia, the battle rages, challenging and changing everyone in its path.